THE REAPING

BOOK TWO OF THE SEEDS TRILOGY

K. MAKANSI

Layla Dog Press
Saint Louis, MO

Library of Congress Control Number: 2014919559

ISBN: 978-0-9898671-4-6

For Kathy, valiant fighter of alien invaders

THE REAPING

Book Two of the Seeds Trilogy

Winter 2, Sector Annum 106, 21h45
Gregorian Calendar: December 22

Blue is the color now. The bruised halo of the moon's light against the blackened winter sky. The cobalt flash of electric fire, a single strike as it hits the man across from us. The navy of his shirt against the brown dirt and pale grasses as red blood spills from his chest and mouth. The deepening blue of panic as I clutch Remy's arm, pull her to me. The blue ice in Soren's eyes as he screams, *run*.

So soon a moment can change colors, so soon can it spoil, so soon can it wither.

It doesn't matter that I hardly knew the man. Darrin Squire was his name. *Was.* He had a name, he was a teammate, we had laughed together. Now he is dead. So quickly a life is extinguished, so fleeting our moments of joy. I clutch Remy's arm tighter as we run, as Gabriel and I propel her along with our momentum. She seemed so tired, so *done*, and yet here we are, running. Again.

It's an inevitable experience for a doctor, watching lives fade to nothing. A daily tragedy to which we consign ourselves, hoping we can stave off death a while longer or, if not, at least alleviate the suffering. Some fade away, lingering too long, leaving relief and fatigue in their wake. Others burst like dying stars, an explosion of anger, bitterness, sadness at leaving this life too soon. The confusion, the shock, the agonizing awe of death's *absence* has never dulled with exposure. Accepting death in a cosmic sense is all we can do to ease the pain of our patients' passing.

We all die. Whether we wilt slowly from old age or instantaneously from a knife to the heart, we cannot escape it. So small are our lives in the span of universal space, so quickly they pass in the span of universal time. *So fleeting are our moments of joy.*

"Thank the fates you're alive," I'd said to Remy, just moments before, as relief washed over me, a river of joy. I was giddy at the sight of her, relieved as only a parent can be when you realize after days of worry and dread that your child is safe. I wrapped my arms around her and held her as though she was the only thing sustaining me, the only source of life. The color wasn't blue then—it was blinding white. It was everything. It overcame me, overfilled me, spilling out into the world, my joy radiant and independent of me. *Remy, safe!* I felt like sunshine.

I think of Tai, my oldest daughter, as I have every day since the first moment I put my hand on my belly and felt her kick. And I think, for the millionth time, *I can't lose Remy, too.* My children, my everything, put in danger by this transcendent and terrifyingly beautiful world.

It could have been different. Gabriel and I could have stayed in the Sector, stayed in safety. We could have closed our eyes, turned away from the truth. But we didn't. We owed Tai the truth. So we brought Remy here, to the Resistance. If we had stayed, the Sector's airships and soldiers wouldn't be dropping down on us right now. If we had stayed, Remy wouldn't have been taken prisoner by the Sector. If we had stayed, Remy wouldn't be in danger.

But if we had stayed, Remy wouldn't know justice. She wouldn't know sacrifice. She wouldn't know there is pain on the path to renewal. To grow, we must be pruned, bits of ourselves flayed open, cut back. In those carved-out spaces, we grow stronger.

"Recovery is painful," I told Remy three years ago, when we mourned Tai. "We will bleed, we will swell, we will scab. It's the same with life. It wasn't Tai's time to die, but she was taken from us. She would want us to heal from her absence, to feel joy again. But we don't truly understand joy until we have known sorrow." Joy and sorrow. Light and shadow. Life and death.

If we had stayed in Okaria, the three of us would have suffocated in the wake of Tai's death, in the wake of our hypocrisy. Our silence would have killed us from the inside, like a cancer eating away at our bones. I was unable to protect Tai, but now, for Remy, I will do anything. Which is why, when the blue explosions of Bolt fire fill the air, Gabriel and I envelop her in our arms to shield her, even as we run.

I'm almost unsurprised when the blue flame ignites inside me. It begins in my back, where just earlier that day Gabriel's hand rested, comforting, as he whispered that Remy would return to us, that he, like me, would do anything to bring her home. From my back, the blue spreads like ink on wet paper to my knees as I fall forward, to my head as the pain screams its arrival, to my lungs as I struggle to breathe. I try to move. I push myself using arms that don't work. I twist away even as the fire sears into my bones.

Run, Remy! I try to tell her.

I'm putting them both in danger by falling here, I know, where the color blue rains down on us like death.

Tai, I think, distantly, as if I am speaking to myself from far away. *Hush, child. I'm almost there. I'm almost there with you. Just a little longer.* We all must die, after all. Earth to earth, dust to dust, ashes to ashes. It is our mortal curse and our mortal privilege that we are returned to earth. My transformation from *Brinn* to *earth* begins now. Even as a part of me hopes I might recover, that I could fight, that I could survive this, a bigger part knows it is over. My time as Brinn Alexander is over. I am ready to return to where I was made.

The screams of my family and those around me hurt more than the pain. I am conscious now of more than mere sight and sound. Gabriel cradles me to him and I am filled with wonder at the joy I have known in his embrace. The skin of my daughter's hands, her grip fierce on my fingers. I feel nothing but the two people I love most in the world.

"You'll die if you stay here," I hear. Distantly I recognize the voice. Valerian Orleán. My brain functions just enough to register mild surprise that he is here with us. *He is the enemy,* a part of me says, but another part soothes and calms me. *He will protect them.* I watch through heavy lidded eyes as he looks at Remy. Her reaction is fierce, eyes narrowed, and she returns his gaze evenly.

"I don't care," she whispers. Three words from her lips a thousand times more terrifying than death.

Go, I try to speak. *It's my time, not yours. You will live.*

Gabriel nods at Vale, some unspoken communication I can't fathom, and lifts me up. I watch the world from my love's arms as he carries me away from the unguarded air. Vale runs alongside me for a moment and I thank him with as much strength as I can muster, words that I speak aloud and words that will not come, that could never fill this space. He nods, but his eyes are fixed on the skies, his weapon up, guarding me, protecting my family.

In the clarity of death, my surprise at Vale's presence fades. How could I be surprised? Three years ago, Vale looked at Remy like she was a new world, infinite with delight and passion. He tried to hide it when I was around, his budding love, but a mother can sense these things. One who has loved can sense these things.

Now, he looks at her like she is his salvation.

Gabriel sets me down on the ground. Remy kneels over me. I grasp for her hand, lean into Gabriel, *my love, my loves.* The explosions in the distance become faint as I focus on Remy's touch and Gabriel's voice. The blue fades.

White fills me up as all other colors and emotions combine and blur into emptiness. I see a face I recognize, but distantly, and I struggle to focus.

Gabriel's voice, the poetry, the resonance that vibrates in my chest: "I love you, I love you, I love you…."

I close my eyes and see Tai, laughing, beckoning, and I take her hand and go.

THE REAPING

by Gabriel Alexander
Poet Laureate, Okarian Sector

Brushstrokes from my daughter's pen
Carve nascent shadows in the dawn
Carve dripping moonlight on a sea she's never seen
Carve little spaces where we may sleep at night
Carve little spaces in me.

Brushstrokes from the reaper's scythe
Carve hollows in these golden fields
Carve fruiting canes in the green vines
Carve little spaces where we may find our seeds
Carve little spaces in me.

Brushstrokes from the butcher's knife
Carve canyons in the calf's throat
Carve life from the lamb's heart
Carve little spaces where we may sate our needs
Carve little spaces in me.

Brushstrokes from the wind in the trees
Brushstrokes from the pen that's never seen the sea
Brushstrokes from the scythe whose scars give life
Carve little spaces where we may plant our seeds
Carve little spaces in me.

1 — VALE

My fingers press into the hare's neck, and the animal whimpers and twitches, caught in the terror of death. I spare a moment to marvel at its silken fur, its taut, sinewy muscles, the delicate bones. I close my eyes and whisper my penitence.

"I'm sorry."

With a wrench, I feel the sick crack as the spine breaks. I open my eyes. The whimpering stops, the hare's breath cut short. The muscles twitch for a second, and then everything is still. I let out the breath that had ballooned inside my chest.

Crunching leaves and stomping feet sound behind me. Firestone. I haven't the slightest idea how he survived out in the Wilds all those months before the Resistance found him—he sounds like a wild boar rampaging through the underbrush. The idea of him creeping stealthily through the trees, hunting, or hiding, is laughable. It was his traps and seemingly endless knowledge of edible plants that saved him, I guess. I thought I had a good handle on all that with my Sector "wilderness" training, but I'd probably get pretty hungry out here without him. He's been teaching the rest of us how to set the traps and forage for winter plants since we got to the safe house.

"Got something?" he asks, his voice rough, his long black hair tangled and droopy against his forehead. He hasn't slept much lately. None of us have.

"Big, fat rabbit."

"Good. Mine was empty."

"The student becomes the master," I say, bowing deeply as I stand to face him.

"Master, yes. And don't forget it." He flashes a grin. "Your traps been getting better, true. Better than Soren's, at least. For a pianist, his fingers don't seem to work that well."

I smile. It's not often I'm favorably compared to Soren. Kind words, these days are as welcome as a soaking rain on parched ground.

"At least we'll have something to eat with all that damned amaranth," he says, glaring at the sky, which is awakening clear and so, so blue.

I free the hare from the trap as Firestone holds out the small game bag he's stitched together. I drop the rabbit in, and he slings the bag over his shoulder. Without another word, we start down the deer path back towards our hideaway. Morning sunlight flits through the boughs overhead like golden butterflies as we weave through the forest back to where the others wait.

Outside the safe house, little more than an overgrown shed, Remy, Jahnu, and Kenzie are loading a few daypacks with bags of nuts, dried fruit, and smoked meat leftover from the Resistance base. Remy glances up when she hears us coming. Our eyes meet, and the familiar tremor ripples down my spine into my belly. I drop my eyes, but I can feel hers linger on me, watching our approach.

"Got something good in that bag?" Jahnu asks.

"Vale nabbed a *lapin*," Firestone says, using the old French word. In Okaria, where most of us grew up, everyone speaks English, or something like it. But in the factory towns and Farms, like where Firestone is from, traces of the old language lingers. French Canadian words sneak into his speech every now and then. Bear will sometimes drop in whole sentences of the old French. He says it's comforting, that it reminds him of growing up.

"That'll go with the special breakfast Eli's preparing," Kenzie says with a smile. "You'll never guess what it is."

"Strawberries with fresh creme and warm sourdough bread?" Firestone asks.

"Even better, if you could believe it," Kenzie chuckles, her bright red curls bouncing as she nods for us to keep guessing.

"Potato fritters with maple syrup?" Jahnu says.

"Oh I know! Bacon and eggs, right?"

"So close!"

"Oh, right. It's amaranth, isn't it?" I say drily. We all already know the answer.

"How'd you guess?" she asks, the hint of a wry smile on her lips.

"For the twentieth day in a row. That's some special amaranth," Remy adds.

The door bursts open and Soren stalks out.

"You're leaving in an hour," he says, a sharp edge to his voice. "So if you want to eat," he narrows his frigid blue eyes at me, "you should prep whatever's in that bag sooner rather than later."

Eli announced yesterday what we all knew: that no one is coming to meet us here. That we've been waiting, anxious and idle, for something to happen, for someone from the Resistance to show up, or somehow get in touch with us, and it's time to face the fact that it's been too long to continue clinging to that hope. If anyone from the Resistance were able to contact us, they would have. My guess is that even the teams that made it to their designated outposts have opted for continued radio silence. It's safer that way. But with our food rations dwindling and foraged food hard to come by in the dead of winter, we had to do something. So Eli decided it was time to go exploring, and Soren was none too happy when he'd made the announcement.

"Vale, Kenzie, and Remy. We're taking out the hover car tomorrow," he'd said. "Going to try to—"

"Are you joking?" Soren interrupted, his voice rising. "You're going to take Vale out there? You trust him?"

"I saw him shoot down Sector airships with my own eyes," Eli responded. "You're my second in command—"

"Then I should come."

"No, you're second in command which means you stay here. If we don't make it back, you're in charge." Eli said, that dangerous, maddening calm in his eyes. Soren clamped his jaw shut and didn't say another word until breakfast, when he viciously accused me of over-seasoning the amaranth.

I am fairly certain he'll never get used to me being around, seasoned grains or not.

"Calm down, Soren," Firestone says now, dragging the words out. "We're all hungry. No need for hard words."

Remy puts her hand on Soren's shoulder, and his expression softens. A rush of anger runs through me as Soren reaches a hand up to take hers, and a rare smile graces her face as their eyes meet.

What right do you have to wish you were in his shoes? I ask, trying to quell my jealousy. *None at all, Vale.* But the feeling doesn't go away. I pull out my knife and turn away, busying myself with gutting and skinning the rabbit.

Later, in the hovercar, I keep silent while Remy, Eli, and Kenzie rehash for the hundredth time what could have happened to Team Blue, the Resistance group that was supposed to meet us at our rendezvous point after Thermopylae was destroyed. We're heading in the direction of Waterloo, the nearest Resistance base any of us know of. Remy's in the seat next to me, ignoring me, as usual, while I fight the urge to reach out and touch her arm, trace my thumb down to where her pulse beats at the base of her wrist, twine my fingers with hers. I try to distract myself by counting off all the reasons I shouldn't want to touch her, but it turns out there aren't very many reasons so I sit on my hands and look out the window.

Eli's driving, searching for a clear path through the woods. Sometimes it seems we're not moving much faster than we would be if we were on foot, but whenever he finds an opening, he guns it like we're going for the finish line in one of the Sector's hover raceways. He's gunning it now and I rest my head against the seatback and feel the wind on my face.

"There's absolutely no way they got lost," Kenzie says. "I'd bet my life on it. The Director drilled these escape routes and rendezvous points into our heads a thousand times. There's no way they could have missed it."

"Something else, then," Remy says, the desperation I've become all too familiar with creeping into her voice. "Their hover car broke, maybe. All our equipment is old, maybe theirs broke down and they've tried to make contact, but can't."

"I get why they'd keep to radio silence, but someone should've been here or made contact by now. They would have kept going by foot even if their transports conked out," Kenzie points out. "And there's no way it would have taken a month, even on foot. We're only two hundred kilometers outside the city."

"We've got company," Eli growls, as his wristband flashes cerulean. His drone detector. *Drones, here? This far into the Wilds?*

Like a cresting wave, a thousand moments seem to converge on one as a crackling ball of electricity erupts out of the sky and crashes into the front of our hover car. It feels like a large hand has plunged into my gut, gripped my intestines and squeezed, and in a split second my whole body is alert and I'm shouting.

I push open the door and leap out, grabbing Remy's arm and pulling her out with me. I dive to the ground and roll onto my back, watching as the hover car loses control and the momentum propels it straight through a stand of saplings and into an outcropping as big as a house. The car crumples into itself, but Kenzie, her red hair flying around her, scrambles safely out of the passenger window. Eli's still inside and, from the looks of it, not moving.

I slide easily into combat mode. The air is alive with electricity, sparkling with low-powered Bolt fire. Above the treetops, the sky hums with recon drones. About the size of crows and faster still, these are programmed for speed and detection, not battle. Equipped with high-res cameras and topographic mapping capabilities but limited firepower, we've got a good chance of taking them out, but not before they transmit about a thousand photos of us to their base center. *We'll have to move fast once we've disabled them, before a half-dozen airships show up loaded with Black Ops.*

I pull my handheld Bolt from the holster at my hip and flip the ray setting from *STUN* to *DISPERSE*. I fire a few shots into the sky, hoping the low electricity will scramble the drones' guidance systems. Kenzie's got her weapon out, too, but Remy is scrambling to her feet, launching herself in the direction of the ruined hover car. I throw a hand out to try to grab her clothes, to hold her back, but she's too fast. Eli's the closest thing to family she has right now. I couldn't stop her from getting to his side. She sprints through the clearing to the hover car and starts pounding on the windows and pulling on the door handle.

"Eli!" she cries. To my relief, I see he's moving. He starts pushing against the doors, shouting, but his voice is muted through the crushed metal. I watch helplessly as Remy takes a direct hit, her back arching with the bolt of electricity. She slows only a half-second before pulling again, attempting to dislodge the mangled door.

I tilt my gun skyward and focus on where the drones seem to be grouping together. My handheld doesn't have much more power than the drones do, but Kenzie's got her big double barrel out. She fires repeatedly, slapping the capacitor over and over again. I can tell by the lack of arcing electricity that she's got her weapon switched to disperse as well. After about five or her shots, the drones quiet and start drifting apart, listing without energy or direction. Several drop out of the sky entirely, incapacitated.

Remy and Eli have together managed to wrench one of the doors open just enough for him to squeeze out, and the two of them half-dive, half-fall behind a tree for cover from the drones. But it doesn't matter. They've stopped firing.

For several seconds, nothing moves except a few drones, drifting through the sky, empty of purpose.

"Thank the harvest," Kenzie breathes. "I think they're done."

She's right. As if by some invisible force, the ones still aloft float away from us, all in one direction, and in a few seconds the sky is clear again. Kenzie stands and heads over to where Eli and Remy are lying, and I follow suit.

"You guys okay?" she asks.

Eli nods, and Kenzie offers both him and Remy a hand. They stand. Remy's shaking, still feeling the shock from the Bolt that hit her.

"Let's see your back," Kenzie says, reaching gently down to lift Remy's shirt. Remy turns so Kenzie can see better, and she pulls the cloth up to reveal a blistering red-and-white streak along her lower back. Low-powered Bolts might not kill, but they cause nasty electrical burns.

"Fuckers," Eli swears.

"It's nothing," Remy says, but her voice is tight with pain. I grit my teeth, feeling the burn as if it was my own.

"It's definitely something," Kenzie says, dropping Remy's shirt back into place. "But it could be worse. Lucky I've got a basic med kit. We'll clean you up." She grabs her pack out of the car and rummages through it.

"Where'd the drones go?" Eli asks, looking at me for answers. Anything to do with the Sector, Eli always expects me to have the answers. Most of the time, I do. "I didn't know they could move that fast," he says.

"Recon drones are built for speed," I respond. "They're never deployed in battle. Or out of the Sector."

"So what are they doing out here shooting at us?" Eli demands.

I shrug, wishing I had better answers. "My best guess is they're being deployed from an airship that's looking for us, looking for other Resistance outposts. I'm sure they've been patrolling a wide swath of the Wilds since the attack on your headquarters. Driving the hover car again might have alerted them to the presence of electrical activity in the area. Or they might have just happened upon us. Either way, now we have no transportation, and we need to get out of here before they come back with more than just recon capability."

"If they've ID'd you," Eli says, holding my gaze, "they'll be back with enough troopsto tear down the whole forest to find you.

I nod. There's no doubt in my mind that if my parents find out where I am, they'll send half the Defense Forces to try to bring me back. And, since those were recon drones, there's about a 100% chance they've identified me.

"No chance we can fix the hover car?" Remy asks. We all cast a look at the crumpled carcass.

"Wishful thinking. I think we'll be walking back." Kenzie says. As she opens the tin and starts to smear burn ointment across Remy's back, she glances up at me. "That was smart, setting your Bolt to disperse. They would have been impossible to hit otherwise, and we'd all need more than burn cream."

Remy turns to me, but this time, instead of the watchful, wary look I've grown used to, her face is open.

"It helped," I say. *But not enough.*

2 — REMY

"Why are you back so soon?" Jeremiah asks, furrowing a bushy brow as he stands up. He greets us at the cleared perimeter of the safe house. "Where's the hovercar, and what's—"

"We're going on foot, now." Eli says, cutting off his questions. Soren and Jahnu jog out to meet us, followed closely by Firestone and Bear. "And we're leaving in ten minutes. Pack up."

"What?" Jahnu demands. "Why so soon?"

"The drones likely ID'd Vale," I respond, the weariness showing through in my voice. "All of us, really. They'll send a team out to finish us off. We have to clear out of here as soon as possible."

The cooling ointment Kenzie smeared on my back has worn off, and I wince as the pain from the burn returns threefold. It took us almost an hour of trudging through the woods just to get back to our little outpost. Vale insisted on carrying my backpack for me, and though I protested, I was grateful he wouldn't take no for an answer.

"You're hurt," Jahnu says when he sees me grimace. Soren scowls at Vale and then tries to pull me in for a hug. The mingled look of anger and concern on his face brings a small smile to my own, but I throw out my hands to stop him.

"Sorry," I say. "I got hit, and I'm a little torn up."

His blue eyes are soft, concerned. He glances at me, his fingertips on the hem of my shirt, as if asking permission to look. I nod, too tired to care. He turns me around and pulls up the fabric. The cool air feels good on my skin and I shudder. Soren swears again, this time under his breath, and puts his arm around my shoulders. He plants a soft kiss on the top of my head, and I lean into the comforting curve of his body.

I feel Vale watching, though he drops his eyes as soon as I steal a glance over at him. A flush runs through me, and I reach down to take Soren's hand, pulling away a bit.

"The rest of you okay?" Jahnu asks. He shoulders Kenzie's double-barreled Bolt and looks her up and down.

"We're okay," she says, "but we're on foot from here on out." She pulls his forehead to hers as if in a silent communion, and then they pull away.

"Recon drones," Eli says. "A swarm of them. Just enough firepower to take out the hovercar and give Remy that nasty burn. Luckily Vale knew how to handle them."

"He would," Soren growls under his breath.

Vale ignores him. "They're small, light, but fast. Disperse mode with your Bolts messes with their telemetry, confuses them."

"The tiny fuckers shot us," Eli continues, "and we crashed hard. That old piece of junk took quite the beating."

"We were lucky to get out," I add. "Eli almost got stuck inside."

"Good to know that disperse setting is good for something," Eli says, fatigue in his voice. "I wondered if it was a design flaw no one had ever bothered to correct."

Kenzie smiles at Vale, and it occurs to me that, slowly but surely, Vale's winning over everyone in our group.

Except Soren. And me.

I still don't know what to think of him. He's on our side, yes. For now. But for how long? And why the sudden change of heart? Every time I look at him, I first see the man at the podium on graduation day, announcing his placement, telling the world he had set out to destroy the Resistance and everything we stand for. And then I see him in the interrogation room, uncertain, as he confronted Soren and I as hostages and accused us of treason. But what I remember most is the sadness, the guilt deep in his voice as if he'd been breathing it, choking on it, when he held out my grandfather's compass to me. I remember the way he offered his life to me as repayment for everything he'd done.

Two lives I owe you now, he said.

Which Vale is the real one?

"We're splitting up," Eli announces suddenly, bringing me back to the scene at hand. "Firestone, you take one group—"

"What?" I demand. "No way. We're not splitting up again."

"We have to, Little Bird," Eli says. "Look how easily the drones found us this time. How easy will it be if we're traveling in a group of ten? Our odds of making it to one of the other bases are better if we split up."

"Or half of us could die," I counter, "and the rest of us would never know."

"Or we could *all* die when the drones call a squadron of Black Ops down on our heads, which is about to happen, right now," Eli shoots back. I stare at him. Eli and I *never* disagree. And on the rare occasion when we do, he listens to me, instead of spitting back retorts. But I don't have a good counterpoint, so I bite my tongue, and Eli turns his gaze back to the rest of the group.

"Firestone, you take half the group. Remy's coming with me. Pick your team."

"I want Vale," Firestone says immediately, and I look up at him, startled. "What?" he shrugs. "He's got military training, he's taken down Sector airships, and he knew how to disable the recon drones, so I figure if he's with me and the Black Ops find us, I've got a damn sight better chance of staying alive than with you losers."

He's got a point.

"Okay, Soren," Eli starts.

"I'm going with Soren," Bear pipes up. I smile at him. Bear's become Soren's little shadow, and Soren doesn't seem to mind.

"Kenzie and Jahnu," Firestone says. "I want a medic."

Kenzie laughs. "I'm hardly a medic."

"Better than anyone else. Oh, except Vale. Two medics. I win."

"Miah's with us, then." I can feel Soren's voice reverberate through my side. I look over and see Miah and Vale exchange glances. I don't know how Miah does it, being caught in the middle of Soren and Vale.

"Good," Eli says. "Pack up. We leave in ten." Everyone starts to pull themselves to their feet but Eli, who hasn't moved from his spot. "Firestone, you stay."

Within minutes, the place looks as desolate as it did on the night we arrived—and more, because we've cleaned out all the food stores. We've been half-settled this whole time, prepared to leave with little warning. All our bags are mostly packed, ready to move. When I haul my pack outside, Firestone and Eli are still sitting huddled together, poring over my plasma, which has some decent maps of the area and the Resistance bases scattered around the Wilds. Finally, when everyone's ready to go, Eli stands and announces the plan.

"My group is going directly to Normandy. It's about one hundred and fifty kilometers, almost due north, so it should take between five to eight days, depending on the weather and how much ground we cover per day. Firestone's group is taking a more roundabout way. They're going to stop in at Waterloo, an outpost about a hundred kilometers northeast, and it's another sixty or so to get to Normandy."

"What if Normandy isn't safe?" Kenzie asks. "How will we find you if you can't stay there?"

I feel Eli tense. He meets Firestone's eyes and then looks around the group.

"If Normandy isn't safe, we'll head back toward Waterloo. If Waterloo isn't safe, you'll continue on to Normandy. If neither is safe, we move to plan B and try to make our way on to the next closest known base. Each team has the encrypted coordinates of all the bases, so we'll find each other eventually." He pauses, and then looks back at Kenzie. "We have to operate on that assumption. We'll reconnect. We have to believe that."

There's a dull silence for several moments. I find myself watching Vale's mannerisms, the way he casts his eyes around on the ground as though he's looking for something. The way he meets my eyes for only a half-second and stands straighter when he does, as though he has something to prove.

"So that's the plan," Eli says. "Good luck, everyone." He pulls Firestone in for a bear hug and thumps him on the back as if trying to dislodge something from his throat. Firestone laughs and coughs and pushes him away. We exchange fraught farewells, all of us aware there's a distinct possibility this is the last time we'll see each other. I hug Firestone and Kenzie, and cling to Jahnu a little too tightly before I let them all go.

I turn to Vale. I know I should say something, but my mind draws a blank.

"Be safe," he whispers, for my ears only.

Soren comes up beside me and points his knife at Vale's throat. "Don't fuck this up, Vale."

Vale's jaw clenches and his shoulders tense, but he doesn't respond. Soren, apparently satisfied he's had the last word, shoulders his pack and stalks off.

I keep my eyes on Vale until the moment I turn to follow the others. My hand, tucked into my jacket pocket, clutches my grandfather's compass, the heirloom Vale returned to me not a month ago. *A compass is more than a navigational tool,* my grandfather Kanaan told Tai and I all those years ago. *It represents the search for truth. It's a symbol of finding true north.*

What's your truth, Vale?

Lying flat on my back, I watch the treetops quiver as birds alight and flit off, squirrels jump from branch to branch, and the wind teases bare branches, making them sway and bend like they're dancing to a song only they can hear. It's almost as if the trees themselves are waking from an evening's rest. They probably got more sleep than I did. Curling up between the gnarled roots of an old hemlock, pinned between Eli on one side and Soren on the other, isn't the best way to get a solid eight hours. Like usual, I woke early and wandered a few meters off to find a solitary place to await the dawn.

Today is our seventh day on the trail. The days pass in an empty blur, a haze of shivering cold nights and unseasonable warmth during the day. We sweat in the sun, soak our clothes through, and then freeze at night. Three days ago it rained: cold, sharp, ugly droplets, and, by the harvest, that was miserable. We froze, all of us huddled together in the same tent, trying desperately to recover the body heat lost during the day. But the rest of the journey has been uneventful. We watch for drones in the sky, but there are none, and Eli's drone detector never lights up.

Breathe in, breathe out. I close my eyes and let dawn's crisp pink light wash over me. One more step forward, and another, and another, and then we'll be there. Normandy draws closer every day. Dry clothes. Warmth. Beds. Food we didn't have to kill, skin, and cook over a meager fire. And a shower. *A shower!*

The breathing exercises were Soren's idea. He says they helped him after his own parents were, well, he won't really say what exactly happened to them. He doesn't even know the full extent of it. But he encouraged me to start meditating after the attack on Thermopylae. Soft as the lilting wind, he was the quietest I'd ever heard him when we first sat together and practiced. I replay his words in my mind now: *Imagine that each thought is a little messenger bird carrying a slip of paper. Open the thought, examine it, accept it, and then tear it up. Watch the pieces of your thought disappear in the wind. Exhale, watch the bird fly away on the wind. Feel yourself become lighter. Let your breath center and ground you. Release. Breathe.*

It helps. A little.

Every night has been the same since the attack that drove us from our base. The nightmares. My mother's face, pale like the flesh of a crisp apple, her stillness, the exhale that never came. I thought I'd never get over Tai's death. And now my mom's gone, too. I am running on empty. *I am empty.*

After so many nights of feeling as cavernous as the black, starlit universe around me, the sleeplessness began to take hold of me. So I started the breathing exercises.

What helps the most, though, is watching the bruised, deep blue and purple sky fade into lilac, fierce orange, and rose pink. It reminds me that behind every black night is a rising sun, behind every cold hurt is a fiery healing, a new beginning. That thought keeps me going, even when Tai's face swims in front of me. Even when my mother's eyes close, over and over again, behind my own eyelids.

"Remy?" Eli's voice calls. I open my eyes, the dawn blooming full and welcoming. "You okay, Little Bird?"

Still hazy with sleep, he stares down at me through bleary eyes. Weeks ago, Eli would have had a conniption when he woke up and found me missing. But I've made it such a habit that it doesn't bother him anymore.

"Yeah."

"I can't sleep these days, either," he says, sitting down next to me and laying back, his hands behind his head. "There's too much in my head."

"Strange," I say, forcing a smile. "It feels like mine is too empty."

"Empty?" He turns to look at me. "After everything that's happened?"

I shrug.

"I guess it's not that my head is empty, but that I am. I can't figure out where I'm going, what I'm doing. All I want is to make them suffer."

There's a silence. I don't have to say who *them* is. Eli knows. With anyone else, the silence might be awkward. But with Eli, it's just calm. There's never any judgment.

"We share that goal, Little Bird. But it's not enough to build a life."

"I don't need a life," I bite back. "I need revenge."

Eli is quiet. When he speaks, his voice is low and calm, but there's an intensity to it I haven't heard in a long time.

"You know better than that. I know you do. You might not be able to see beyond that horizon, yet, and I don't blame you. But you'll walk that path and crest that mountain and you'll find yourself wondering what's on the other side."

I nod. "One day, maybe. Not today."

"Maybe not. Maybe today, we just find Normandy, get some real food and half-decent beds. Let's go. We're almost there."

Eli stands and offers me a hand. I let him pull me up. Together we walk a little ways back to where we'd pitched our tents for the night. Soren, his blond hair sticking up in every direction, is boiling some water for oatmeal and tea, and Bear and Miah are packing up our gear. We're silent as we go through the now-familiar ritual, the packing, cleaning, and cooking.

"Gotta get moving," Soren mutters eventually, betraying our shared reluctance to begin yet another long day of walking. As much as I don't want to walk twenty kilometers today, I'm anxious to reach Normandy. We're going a bit slower than we'd like because of Miah, but we're still making good time.

We've done a little over thirty kilometers a day, by my estimates, which should put us into Normandy tonight, after five days on the trail.

"We should be there before dark," Eli says, pausing as we crowd around the plasma examining the map of the surrounding woods that the Resistance had hacked from the Sector a few years back. Because my plasma can recharge on sunlight, we've been able to use the most recently downloaded terrain map of the region, and, while I'm sure it's not as detailed as the latest Sector version, it has reasonable zoom capacity and an exceptional one meter raster size.

"It looks like we've got a river to cross."

"I could certainly use a rinse. I've almost definitely never smelled worse." Miah mutters. Soren laughs; he's been noticeably happier since Miah arrived from Okaria. When he turns his gaze on me, the flash of heat takes me by surprise, and I remember our time together on The Zephyr, journeying downriver in our escape from the Sector. The time I almost lost myself in my hunger for him, for closeness, warmth.

I take the plasma from Eli's hands and examine it more closely. "We should head southfor about five miles, and then cut through this old highway to the west. The dominant tree species will shift, and we'll know to turn toward the river. Then we can bypass the rapids and cross at the narrowest point. Right here. We'll be closer to Normandy anyway because then we can follow this old roadway here," I use my fingers to zoom in on the map, "straight to the base."

"Great. Let's go." Eli stands abruptly. Without another word he shoulders his pack and starts down the trail.

"Eli," I call to him. "Not that way. This way." I point down a different path, a sharper cut to the East.

He stares at me for a moment, his eyes narrow in concentration. But then he relaxes, his face settling into a grin, and he laughs at himself.

"Right. I knew that."

I shake my head. "It's a good thing you made me your navigator."

Eli winks at me as he walks by. "Birds are the best navigators," he says. "Especially if you navigate us to a river so we won't have to smell those oafs anymore."

I lean in, wrinkling my nose and fan the air.

"Better not exclude yourself."

Eli chuckles, cinches his pack tighter, and we set off.

After several hours, Soren, Eli, Bear and I stop for a few minutes to rest and allow Miah to catch up to us. We haven't seen him in about twenty minutes. He always falls behind—he's had trouble keeping up with us since the beginning.

Back at the safe house, it made sense. He was going through withdrawal. Anyone who's been raised on Sector MealPaks will get sick if they're suddenly taken away. It's a rite of passage for Resistance members. A cleanse. As the body adjusts to the new, untreated food, it experiences sudden withdrawal from myriad medicines, targeted cellular enhancers, antioxidant supplements, phytochemicals and who-knows-what-else. Fever, vomiting, inflammation, exhaustion, muddled thinking: any and all are possible. Everyone goes through it differently. With Miah, it seemed like it was everything at once. It was brutal. The strangest thing was that Vale was fine. No withdrawal, nothing. Not even forgetfulness, mild confusion, or dizziness, the most common symptoms of all. We pestered him about it enough, no one more than Miah, but Vale insisted he had no answers.

Even now, weeks later, Miah still struggles. As an engineer in the Sector, he never received the same type of physical training as the rest of us. As members of the Resistance, we've been training more or less every day for almost three years. As a soldier, Vale's physical training, sleep, and diet regimen would have been optimized to create the perfect leader for the Okarian Sector's Seed Bank Protection Project—intelligent, sharp, creative, not to mention in peak physical condition. A formidable foe. Even Bear is in excellent shape from all the physical labor on the Farms. But Miah didn't go through any of that. Although Eli is adamant we stick together, he often walks too fast for Miah to keep up, so we end up stopping to wait for him. We get to rest, but not Miah. As soon as he catches up, Eli's ready to go again.

Minutes tick by, but Miah doesn't show. As it becomes more and more clear that Miah's far behind, I take off my boots. My feet feel like they've been pounded by hammers. But the panic buds inside me as I imagine the worst. What if he collapsed or wandered off the trail? Or worse, was captured, killed?

"I'm going back." I say quickly, tying up the laces on my boots and standing up.

"No, I'll go," Soren says at once, looking at me, but his words are quicker than his feet. He makes no move to stand. "I'm sure he's fine. Can't be too far behind."

"Why hasn't he shown, then? We've been waiting fifteen minutes."

"Remy's right," Eli says. "We can't afford to lose someone."

So we stand, reluctantly, and turn back the way we came. As we walk, Eli uses our signal, the horned owl's call, and we all strain our ears for a response.

"Wait. I think I hear him. That way, off-trail." Soren says, pointing through the woods at a side path. Eli makes the call again and we all stand still, waiting for the response. When it comes, I heave a sigh of relief. We were stupid, losing track of him. Any one of us could have been in his place. These woods aren't exactly welcoming. He must have mistaken this path for the main one. We push our way through the branches, bushes, and trees, making the owl's call again and waiting for Miah's echo, louder now. He's close.

We find him lying on his back, staring up at the clouds, looking pale even as his silken black, quite hefty beard threatens to overtake his face. He pushes himself up onto his elbows and offers us a strange smile.

"Hello."

"What are you doing," Eli says. It's more a statement than a question.

"I hallucinated."

"You what?" Soren stares down at his friend.

"I think I'm dehydrated. I don't think this wild food is good for me. I took a positively explosive shit earlier." He looks up at me with an embarrassed smile. "Sorry to be so descriptive, but anyway, now I'm out of water." He holds up his empty water bottle and shrugs, resigned to his fate. "I thought I heard a waterfall, and I saw this beautiful albino fawn who looked just like Moriana, except for it being a fawn and all, and albino, and I followed her here because she told me to. Then she disappeared and I realized I was going crazy, and that I was out of water, so I lay down. Then I realized I was lost. I mean, where the hell are we, anyway?"

After all that, Miah's face cracks and he starts laughing like it's the last time he's ever going to laugh. Desperate, awful; a pouring out of giggles, hee-haws, and uncontrolled hiccups culminating in a crying cough that leaves tears streaking down his cheeks and disappearing into his beard. Bear and I exchange worried glances.

"Well, shit." Soren joins him on the ground. I unscrew the cap to my mostly-full water bottle and offer it to Miah. He nods his head in thanks and tips his head back, draining half the bottle in a few gulps.

"Ok," I say, "We're about two miles to the river. We were some fifteen minutes from the crossroads when we stopped, so that's another half-hour from here, and another forty or so minutes after that if we slow our pace. I think that's the nearest water source."

"Let's look at the map again." Eli pulls may plasma from my pack, and we both peer at it. "Maybe there's a stream or spring or something closer. Miah," he looks down at him, "don't drink it all at once. That can make you sick, too. The rest of us need to ration our water so it lasts until we get to the river. Let's make sure this idiot doesn't die out here, okay?"

We're lucky we're so close to Normandy, I think, as we plow on. The sun rises to its noon height then fades, snuffed out as the air stiffens and shivery grey clouds like sinister wisps of smoke sidle in. Bad weather. My stomach growls. I'm thirsty. We tell Miah funny stories about Rhinehouse, about Eli's antics at base, our reconnaissance missions, and anything we can think of to keep ourselves entertained. He grunts and half-laughs and keeps his head down as if watching every footfall was a requirement to propel himself forward. At half-past noon, we reach the river, though the sun has completely dissolved into the mist and the temperature has begun to drop. After the river, thankfully, the terrain won't be too rough, the elevation change is minimal, and we'll have the vague path of an old world highway to guide us.

I fill all our bottles and treat them with the probiotic UV filter. Eli and Soren prepare a light lunch of leftover fruit and meat from a trap Bear set yesterday evening. It's far less than what we should eat, but it will have to do. I attempt to scrub the dirt off my face and rinse my hands and arms with the cold water. Predictably, Miah's mood lightens soon after he eats.

We set out again on our slow, meandering way, but Miah disappears again into the woods not twenty minutes after our meal and when he returns, it's clear he's every bit as ill as he was earlier.

"Damn," he shakes his head and whispers when he walks back our way. I stick out my tongue in disgust.

"Anyone else hear thunder?" Soren asks, casting his eyes skyward, a sly glint in his eyes.

"Fuck you," Miah returns.

It's well into evening by the time we make it to Normandy, and we're all just as filthy as we were before the river, and twice as hungry. But Miah especially is a pallid, glassy-eyed mess. He strongly resembles an oversized dying woodland creature. An old grizzly, maybe, that came out of hibernation too soon.

Normandy is built in the ruins of an old automobile factory dating to the pre-hovercar era. Most of the base is located in the old utility tunnels, similar to Thermopylae, which was dug into the hollowed shell of Chicago. There's some storage above ground, from what I remember of the Director's brief lectures, but most of Normandy is in the tunnels. The main entrance is a manhole that's been well hidden in a copse of trees grown over the old industrial site. Even with four of us looking, it takes about twenty minutes before Bear finally shouts excitedly that he's found the door.

"Praise the harvest, and all the gods invented by man," Miah says, collapsing onto his back as the rest of us dig around to uncover the entrance to the base.

"I thought I was going to die out here."

A wave of relief that we made it this far safe and sound, despite our hunger, washes over me now. And hope, too. *Will my father be there? Rhinehouse? Kenzie's parents? The Director?*

Eli and Soren scrounge around for the hidden lever and then pry the cover off. Eli climbs down the ladder into the tunnel. Once we're all at the bottom, we type the passcode into the digital scanner set into the metal door blocking the tunnel. A tiny camera in the corner of the doorframe fixes its lens on each of us and captures an image to process through the facial recognition software in the comm center. It will only allow those who have registered with the Resistance to enter, so the two foreign faces—Bear and Miah—prompt the intercom system.

"State your names and declare your guests."

Eli speaks into the screen: "Elijah Tawfiq, Remy Alexander, and Soren Skaarsgard from base Thermopylae with Bear, a renegade Farm worker, and Jeremiah Sayyid, formerly of the Okarian Sector. We're survivors of the attack. Jeremiah is sick and requires immediate medical care."

Three sizable, but ancient looking metal locks unlatch in sequence and the door swings open to reveal a narrow, dirty passageway to a second door. The door opens almost as soon as we close off the outside, and a tall, thin man with a thick shock of grey hair beckons us inside. A wiry grey mustache sticks out beneath a small nose makes and I immediately think *mouse*.

"I'm Hodges, the medic here. What going on?" He looks at Miah.

"He's feverish. Diarrhea. Might have an infection. Exhausted. Still recovering from MealPak withdrawal," Eli rattles off.

"Nothing a warm bed and some good food won't solve," he says as we stop at the door to the infirmary. He takes Miah by the arm. I peer into a room with a row of beds lined up along the wall. They look awfully inviting, and I know I'm not the only one who would appreciate a little time in the infirmary with a kindly medic fussing over me. "I'll take care of him. The rest of you head into the kitchen, down this hallway and take the first right. Adrienne, Normandy's captain, is heading there now."

My heart seems to settle into an iron cage.

"Hodges ... has anyone else come from Thermopylae yet?" The words come out in a rush of desperation, of hope ready to die.

He shakes his head.

"Not yet. We've word that there might be a group heading here soon, though. It's your father you're after...."

I nod mutely.

"Time will tell. For now, go eat. Adrienne will want to talk to you."

"Thank you," I respond, biting my lip, disappointed, but what he said sounds promising. *A group might be heading here soon.*

Meanwhile, I'm experiencing a more pressing physical sensation. My stomach feels like an empty, bottomless pit. The mere idea of a kitchen is overpowering. *Food. Water. Chairs.* Hodges waves us out of the infirmary.

As we walk, Soren grabs my hand and squeezes. "We made it," he whispers, his breath warm and tickling my skin. It sends shivers up and down my spine. I half think he's going to kiss me, and I steady myself in anticipation—or is it unease?

"*May the flowers bloom tomorrow, too,*'" I say, reciting a line from my father's poetry. A prayer, Dad calls it. A prayer for tomorrows. I keep walking, hoping that tomorrow will bring news of my father, and maybe some clarity about how I feel about Soren.

And Vale.

I shove his face out of my mind even as I breathe a silent prayer that his tomorrows bring him here, too.

We round the corner into what must be the kitchen. Several hundred of us lived at Thermopylae, our old base, but I remember the Director saying only thirty people, give or take those coming and going, live and work at Normandy. The difference in numbers shows in the kitchen. Here wood tables are nearly on top of the oven and stove, and the whole area would have fit in one corner of our dining hall.

But the kitchen is cozy, and a few people are busying themselves over saucepans smelling of rich garlic and onion, paprika, and chilies. I crane my neck trying to get a glimpse of what's in the saucepan, but all I can see is a brown mess, some kind of beans. Maybe lentils. My stomach rumbles.

A short woman sporting an unruly pile of blond hair turns when she hears us enter, and she strides forward. She shakes Eli's hand vigorously.

"Adrienne, base captain. Welcome to Normandy." She clasps each of our hands in turn as we introduce ourselves. "We're getting a late dinner ready for you, but in the meantime, I want to hear everything. The information we've gotten here has been sketchy at best, and we've been in limbo since we initiated radio silence after the attack." She motions us to sit. One of the other cooks brings cups and a pot of hot tea. Adrienne pours as Eli begins talking.

Eli and Soren recount everything that's happened. I chime in here and there, but largely, the story is too personal for me, our struggles and traumas sour on my tongue. The discovery of the LOTUS database. The raid that went wrong. Our capture and escape from Okaria. How we found Bear. Vale and Miah's flight from the Sector. The Black Ops' attack on Thermopylae. My mother's death. Hearing the story all over again, I blink back tears as Eli chokes out her name. *Brinn. Mom.*

"I'm so sorry, Remy." Adrienne's eyes are glassy, her voice shaky. "I knew your mother well, back in the Sector." She doesn't continue, it seems she can't. Eli reaches for my hand and squeezes.

"We need to contact Waterloo," I declare abruptly. "The other half of our group should have arrived there already."

"Of course," Adrienne says, standing quickly, somehow acquiescing to whatever authority and fatigue has manifested in my voice. She leads us through the tunnels and into to the communications room. She sits and plugs a pair of headphones into the jack. "Usually we man the comm center 24/7, but Zoe's on duty, and I dispatched her to ready the beds for you," she says. She flips some switches and turns a dial, staring intently at nothing. After several terse seconds, she glances up at us.

"I should be getting a response," she says. There's an edge in her voice. I instinctively step closer, as if I could hear better, as if I could understand what she was saying.

"Do you mind?" Eli says. "I was the comm director back at Thermopylae."

Adrienne nods and gracefully gives up her seat at the controls. Eli does everything Adrienne just did, plus some extra switch flipping and knob turning, double checking everything, moving slowly and deliberately. He checks connections at the back of the receiver and even examines under the table and up at the ceiling as if that will make a difference. He stops, listens intently for a moment, then glances up. His eyes meet mine. Pulling off the headphones, he flips on "speaker," and rotates the dial to maximum volume. I can hear the empty crackling of static, but nothing more.

"Your speakers are fully functional?" Eli asks. There's a tremor in his voice.

"They were as of an hour ago."

I think of my words to Eli before we all split up. *Half of us could die and the rest of us would never know.* Soren wraps an arm around me, and I allow myself to fall against him as the room slips away, black clouding my vision, because I know what Eli is going to say.

"There's nothing there to receive the signal. There's no one there."

The words ring in my head like the endless tolling of a thousand bells. Nothing there ... *no one there.*

3 — VALE

A bush to my right bristles and I hiss on my inhale. I am aware of every sound, every movement, my nerves like a company of soldiers at attention. In the day's last light, as we near Waterloo, I look through the bleak, leafless trees for any sign of a man-made structure, wishing as I have a thousand times since I left the Sector that I'd brought more mission-ready contacts with me. Without them, I feel blind and claustrophobic, trying to see into the growing twilight with only my natural eyesight. It's windy, the air is clammy and cold, and a thick layer of fog in the distance signals either a change in the terrain or the temperature. We've only got another hour of light left, and the woods are eerie and beautiful, every sound amplified, every shadow exaggerated. I imagine walking straight into that fog and stepping into a different world, or stepping off the edge, into a void, instantly dissolving into a million fragments. Little wisps of myself floating away.

Firestone's map says the building should be in this area, but it's not detailed enough to pinpoint exactly where. Kenzie and Jahnu claim they know what to look for once we're there, but finding the exact spot is the challenge. We've yet to see any sign of human occupation and the woods grow oppressive and quiet as the fog thickens. Used to the big skies, wide avenues and welcoming buildings of Okaria, getting acquainted with the verdant Wilds has been difficult, too many places to hide, too many secrets.

We spread out. I prowl ahead, trying to look everywhere at once. If the fog clears, there will at least be a moon tonight. I'm not happy about the idea of pressing on to find the base once the sun sets, but with a little moonlight we'd have a chance at finding it. We're so close there's no point in making camp. All of us are on edge, low on food, sleep, and spirit. Even Kenzie's shoulders droop, and Firestone's fiery vocabulary has been less explosive than usual these last two days. When he's not cussing, things are really bad. We need to find the outpost.

A whiff of something burning causes me to stop in my tracks. The now-familiar smell of a wood fire drifts through the trees. The thought of stumbling across a few Resistance fighters with a wild pig or some fowl roasting gets my stomach growling. Maybe they'll even have a few extra homebrewed beers. I try not to get my hopes up, but I'm so hungry I can't keep my imagination in check. I'm salivating over food I can't begin to picture. But I start to notice something more in the air, too. Something acrid. More pungent than the simple smell of burning wood.

I cup my hands to my mouth and hoot like an owl. I wait a few second, and then hear crunching leaves at my side. Firestone's narrow, slouching figure appears through the trees. A few seconds later, Kenzie and Jahnu materialize from my other side.

"Smell the fire up ahead?" I ask. The others nod in answer. "I say we fan out and head into the fog."

Three heads bob at me in silent accord.

"Jahnu, lead," Firestone whispers. Jahnu, the quietest of all of us, turns at once and heads downwind. Firestone, Kenzie, and I follow at a distance.

The burning scent turns from appetizing to horrifying. The closer we get, the more obvious it becomes; it's not just fog that is spreading like a massive plume through the woods. It's smoke, too, and it thickens as we walk, the air warming with each step. As we get closer, I blink to keep the sting at bay. Kenzie glances back at me, and I know she feels it, too.

The heat.

Forest fires at this time of year? Doesn't make sense. Everything's dry and brittle, yes, but frozen at night. It's too cold. It's possible, I suppose—anything's possible, these days.

The dark fear that's been riding my shoulders these last few hours grips at my throat. *The base is burning*, it says. *There's nothing left there. Get out now, while you can.* But we have to find out. We can't turn back.

I release the safety on my Bolt, and, following Jahnu's lead, crouch and run as quietly as possible up over a rise toward what looks to be the source of the smoke. The heat from the fire is intense enough that I start to sweat. Jahnu stops at the edge of the tree line. We're at the top of the small hill looking down on a large clearing. Crouching beneath a bush, he beckons us ahead, and we join him. The clearing, probably a hundred meters long, contains the crumbled, blackened, still-smoking ruins of a building, and the charred remains of trees, bushes, and anything that once lived here. Radiant heat washes over my skin. *What a blaze*, I think, suddenly reminded of the funeral pyres people built during the Famine Years for the dead. This was the outpost. *Was.* Here and there, the remains of the building still smolder, orange and white coals glowing in the twilight. It must have been destroyed within the last few hours.

"Fuck," Firestone swears under his breath.

"What happened here?" Jahnu whispers. None of us has an answer. I squint into the surrounding forest and up at the evening sky—was this the work of drones?—and wish once again I had my contacts.

Then, a shout from across the clearing.

"Nothing my way, Captain. The others are dead or long gone," a man calls. We each drop to the ground instinctively. The fading light of day has taken on the sheen of cut steel in the smoke and blue twilight. Through the shroud of ash and haze, I can see silhouettes move on the other side of the clearing.

"We've still got the woman," a female voice calls back.

"They got a prisoner," Firestone mouths.

The man laughs. "And she's not going anywhere fast."

"We're outnumbered," I whisper. "If these soldiers were here to take out the base, there are probably two squads, minimum. Twenty soldiers. Against four?"

"That'll make the general's day," the man replies.

The general? I shudder at memories of General Aulion, the former mentor whose stoic cruelty left more of a mark on me than any words of advice ever could have.

Firestone glares at me. I can see the anger in his eyes, the defiance. He's not leaving without a fight.

I shake my head.

"They got a prisoner," he repeats, more slowly, as if I hadn't quite understood him the first time. He doesn't have to say the second part, the threat, the doubt. *Are you with us or not, Vale?* I hold his eyes for a moment longer, willing him to back down. He doesn't.

"Fine," I hiss, between gritted teeth. "But this is pure idiocy. If their airship isn't already here, it'll be back any minute. If we're going to mount a rescue, we need to move now."

Firestone finally drops his eyes from mine. He turns to Jahnu.

"You're on point. Vale, Kenzie, shadow him. I'll rearguard. Leave the packs. We'll get 'em later." I see the dull sheen of metal as the three of them ready their weapons. "We've got the element of surprise. Take 'em out quietly. Bolts set to mid-range. We want to incapacitate them for a good long while, get the prisoner, and get out. We only shoot to kill if we've no other choice." Kenzie and Jahnu nod. I bite my tongue. The question of how far we'll get with a wounded prisoner and a squad of armed soldiers on our tail will have to wait.

The dull thud of anger marches into my chest. It's entirely possible we're walking into death. My hands shake slightly, cradling my weapon. I beat back the black crawling at my vision and steady my trembling muscles. *Now is not the time to let the rage consume you.*

We stash our packs about twenty meters back, and follow Jahnu once again towards the clearing. I'm thankful Firestone's trailing us at a distance. Leaves crackle like kindling under his feet. I lower the power grade on my Bolt and pull it up, ready to fire. I hope none of the soldiers recognize me.

Valerian Orleán. The son of the Chancellor of the Okarian Sector and the Director of the O.A.C. The two most powerful people in the Sector. Now a renegade, a traitor, and a conspirator with a terrorist organization that opposes everything we stand for.

Everything I once stood for.

They'll have no qualms about killing every one of us. That, we learned for certain at Thermopylae, when the skies lit up with electric death. When Remy's mother was killed by fire from above. When my own mother, Corine Orleán, made it clear she had no intention of showing anything resembling mercy.

I hear more voices through the trees, more casual, incoherent at a distance, as we stalk along the edge of the clearing. In the smoke, we're at a distinct disadvantage. Soon they'll detect our heat signatures with their mission contacts, but it's nearly impossible for us to see them. If it comes to a direct fight, we'll be fighting blind.

The thought of waking up back in Okaria, a prisoner, face-to-face with my parents—or worse, General Aulion—sends a chill through my bones.

Jahnu stops moving. Kenzie and I follow suit. There are voices ahead, close. Jahnu waves us forward a few steps and I see them: a group of three soldiers directly in front of us, perhaps fifteen meters away. They're facing the hollowed remnants of the building, watching it burn low. They are silhouettes, vague forms outlined against the dim glowing embers in front of them, unaware of the approaching threat.

I've got a clear and easy shot. I glance at Jahnu and Kenzie, who are both watching me. If we do this perfectly, all three soldiers will drop at the same time. Jahnu looks at me and nods, and then looks back to Kenzie. I can't see Firestone, but I know he's watching our backs.

Before I can fire, I hear a yell and one of the soldiers on the edge of the clearing drops. In surprise, I glance over at Kenzie and Jahnu, but it's clear from the confusion on their faces and the glowing capacitors on their Bolts that neither of them fired the shot.

"Man down! Man down!" comes an urgent shout.

"Holy—is that an arrow?" someone else exclaims.

Shouts of confusion ring out, but any further orders or information must be on their intercom systems, as I can't make out anything more specific. We watch, shocked, as at least three-quarters of the soldiers in the clearing run off to the northwest, disappearing quickly into the fog, smoke, and shadow of the trees.

"What just happened?" Kenzie whispers.

"Don't look a gift horse in the mouth," Firestone mutters. "Let's take out these last guards and retrieve our prisoner."

Two guards left behind, their backs at an angle to us, watch as their comrades hunt their mysterious assailants. We creep forward, staying as quiet and low as possible. Jahnu raises his weapon again and, likewise, I take aim at the figure on the left. I breathe to steady myself. I sense rather than see Jahnu prepare to fire. I don't hesitate. I squeeze the trigger and watch as the two figures fall to the ground, silenced.

"Hey!" someone shouts. I search for the source of the voice—a soldier or a medic, now standing over the soldier with the arrow through his chest. She's got her gun pointed in our direction, and I duck instinctively. A flash of blue light blows over my head, but a muffled cry of pain from behind me tells me her shot connected with someone.

My training kicks in.

Pivot. Aim. Fire. Cover.

She falls, twitching, into a heap. Unconscious.

"What the—?" Another soldier runs along the edge of the clearing, glancing at his fallen comrade and then staring right at us, trying to triangulate our position. He drops and rolls for cover. I wait. Seconds tick by. Then his head followed by his weapon appears from behind a bush. Pivot. Aim. Fire. Cover. He drops and goes silent.

"Wow," Kenzie breathes.

"That's what real military training will do for you," Firestone growls from behind us. "Which is exactly why we need to get our woman and get out. Let's move."

"Firestone!" Jahnu whispers. "Your shoulder...."

I turn, squinting through the dim light. Even in the dusky twilight, I can make out the wafting of burning skin smell and the telltale scent of ozone and electrical burn telling me Firestone caught the brunt of the Bolt that flew over my head.

"Fuckers shot me," he swears through gritted teeth, as if just now realizing this. I help him sit up and assess the damage.

"Could be worse. Third degree burns, but they just grazed your shoulder. The affected area's not large."

"Large enough to piss me off. Give me my gun." Firestone gestures with his good arm, maybe in an attempt to prove he's not hurt.

"You sure?"

"Give me my damn gun."

I hand him his weapon, and he cradles it in his good arm. He sucks in a stricken breath as he pushes himself to his feet. He steadies himself and holds the gun up, wincing, his narrow black eyes scrunching up in pain. In the smoke and fading light, he looks downright feral.

"Good thing they shot me in the wrong arm," he says.

"You're nuts," I respond. "Let's get the prisoner."

Jahnu stays behind with Firestone while Kenzie and I creep into the clearing.

My gun is up, Kenzie at my side. Smoke floats around us. My eyes cloud and water, and I blink and try not to cough. I duck low, both for cover and to stay out of the smoke. I come to the woman's motionless figure and find her eyes open, staring at me. Kenzie immediately drops to the ground and pushes her hair back, examining her, looking for a wound, an injury, anything she can splint or bind or stitch. The girl's strawberry blond hair is matted and bloody, caked to the side of her head, and her body is covered in dirt, cuts, and bruises. Her pupils are so dilated, her eyes look otherworldly.

"Can you hear me?" I ask.

She nods and starts to speak, but coughs instead. Her eyes widen slightly, and I sense she's recognized me. "You! You're—"

"I'm here to help you," I start to put my hands under her back and legs, to pick her up, but she thrashes out at me, glancing at Kenzie as if afraid. She's so weak her movements don't do much more than startle me, but I don't want to carry her if she's going to fight me every step of the way.

"Listen," Kenzie says fiercely, "he's not with the Sector soldiers. We're part of Thermopylae Team Red of the Resistance. We're going to get you out of here."

She shakes her head fiercely. "Too late," she chokes. Spittle flecked with blood wets her lips. I jerk my head up and around, looking for soldiers. Has she seen something I haven't? But she reaches up and grabs my jacket collar, pulling me back to her. "Doll's eyes," she rasps.

I swear under my breath and glance over at Kenzie, who's staring at the young woman in front of us, aghast. *So that's why her pupils are so big.*

"How long ago?" I demand. Doll's eyes are poisonous. They kill by attacking and rapidly shutting down the body's organs. Depending on how many berries she ate, she'll have between fifteen and forty-five minutes before her heart stops beating. Kenzie's got a few antidotes in her medical kit, but I doubt she has anything for that kind of poison, and the expression on her face confirms my suspicion. The plant is pervasive around the Sector, but the berries are distinctive enough that everyone knows to avoid them.

The woman shakes her head. "Long enough."

"Why?"

"Didn't want—" she rasps, shuddering, her words slurring. "Didn't want to see—the Dragon—"

Evander Sun-Zi? The director of the Farms? I never had much to do with Farm Operations, so I never worked with Evander, but he was close with both of my parents. He was a closed, impassive man, with a reputation for ruthlessness, but he was never as frightening to me as Aulion.

"Why?" I ask again, confused. I stare at her, trying to understand, as her eyes lose focus and her breathing grows shallow. "What about him?"

She closes her eyes for a moment as if gathering strength, and then looks up, and this time there's more power in her voice.

"Before the Resistance, I worked the Farms, a Dietician. Got pregnant by one of the workers. A good man." Her eyes focus on me, intense. "Evander transferred him and took my son," she says. "My son. Samuel. He took my boy and he gave me this."

Her head rolls to the side, and she releases my collar from her grip to gesture weakly at her neck. I follow her hand to the side of her neck, where I can see thin lines of white, scarred flesh. It looks like a brand. I lean over her to look at the pattern more closely and realize it's the stylized image of a dragon.

Evander Sun-Zi. The Dragon.

"I will not give him the pleasure," she says, her voice barely more than a breath. Her eyes are rimmed with red, but clear as she stares blankly up at me. Her hand goes limp and falls against her shoulder. I press my fingers against her neck, checking her pulse. It's there, but barely. She hasn't got long. I glance around. I don't have much time left before the soldiers come back, unless Jahnu has somehow taken them all out. But it's better not to count on that.

"What's your name?" I ask.

"Lila."

"Which Farm?

"Doesn't matter now," she whispers.

"We could try to find them. Tell them."

"Too dangerous. Best to let them be...."

"Lila," Kenzie says, "we have to go."

She nods weakly.

I take her hand and squeeze against her slack fingers. But her eyes are already closed. I stand, reluctant to leave her to die here, alone. But she's made her choice, there's nothing more we can do.

Kenzie turns to run back to the trees, and I follow, listening for sounds of conflict in the distance. *Who shot that soldier?* I wonder. *Who put an arrow through the heart of a highly trained Sector soldier and then disappeared?*

An arm shoots out from behind a tree to grab mine, and my heart skyrockets. I whirl and pull my Bolt up, squeezing the trigger to fire—and then I see Firestone's matted curls, his narrow eyes.

"What happened? Why didn't you bring her back?"

"She ate doll's eyes. She'll be dead in minutes." I cast my eyes back towards the clearing, now invisible through the smoke and trees. "Her name was Lila."

"We need to move," Kenzie says. "We have no idea how long the soldiers will be distracted."

"Don't want to join the growing body count," Firestone says, with rare urgency in his drawl. "We head to Normandy. Put as much distance between them and us as possible."

Firestone leads us at a jog through the woods, though his steps are clearly laden with pain. We reclaim our packs and set off at a run, our feet heavy and tired in the dead leaves, no doubt leaving a trail bold enough for a child to follow.

"Who shot that arrow?" Jahnu asks, wondering aloud as we jog.

"Maybe it's better we don't know," Kenzie says.

"You don't think it was someone from the Resistance?" I ask.

Kenzie shoots me a withering look. "You think we use bows, Vale? Technology from before the Great Wars? Our weapons may not be Sector-issue, but they're functional."

"We use bows to hunt," Jahnu interjects, ever the peacekeeper, "but they're bulky, and we've never trained with them for combat."

"Outsiders, I'd say," Firestone pants, his voice thick. "Only folk I know who can shoot an arrow like that."

"How do you know?" I ask.

"Met a few of 'em when I was living in the woods," he says. "Caught me some game a few times when I was damn near starvation."

After another twenty minutes of jogging, we slow to a walk. Firestone asks Jahnu to lead through the dark undergrowth. We set our biolights as the twilight fades to black and the dull green shadows guide us through the woods.

"Did you know anyone at Waterloo?" I ask finally.

"No," Kenzie responds. "I know a few people stationed at Teutoburg and Alamo, but that's it."

"You don't know anyone else?" I ask, surprised.

"Of course not," she responds curtly. "The fewer people we all know, the fewer we can betray if any of us gets caught."

The fewer we can betray. Of course they would operate in secrecy, protecting their members from each other, protecting the group from the individual.

I focus on running despite my worn and tired limbs. It's better than remembering how I tried to get Remy and Soren to betray their friends and families, everything they fought for, in the cell where I kept them as prisoners. It's better than remembering Lila and her dragon-shaped scar, her son taken from her. It's better than remembering my mother, calling on Chan-Yu to kill Remy, a teenager, a former friend, her son's first love.

With strength born from the injustice of everything the Sector has done, I pick up my running pace, following Firestone. I drown my exhaustion in anger. One foot in front of the other, I run through the sweat and smoke and blood.

Winter 33, Sector Annum 106, 08H05
Gregorian Calendar: January 22

"Remy?" Something prods my shoulder. A finger, likely, to accompany the voice. I open one eye. There's a hazy mug of steaming, orange-colored liquid floating in front of Bear's nervous, worried face. For all my sullen fatigue, the smoky, woody aroma is tempting, and I know he's trying to be helpful. I sit up, throwing the meager blankets off of me.

"What is it?"

"Rooibus," he says.

"Roy-what?"

"It's a kind of *thé*," he responds, using the Old French word for *tea*. "Hodges made some. Well, actually, he said it's not really tea, which is why there's no caffeine in it. But it's supposed to be 'energizing,' or something, was what he said."

"Thanks."

"Sure." Bear smiles, and it lifts my spirits. He's so anxious to please. After everything that's happened between us, it still surprises me that we've become close.

After all, I put a knife in his best friend's neck.

It's something to admire, that he was able to forgive me so quickly. Of course, he didn't have much choice if he wanted to stay alive. He could have taken his chances alone in the Wilds, but he wanted to come with us. To the Resistance. But what astonishes me is that he doesn't just *tolerate* me. No, Bear seems to admire both Soren and I, for reasons neither of us can discern. We've talked about it, the way Bear follows us, eager, so earnest, so kind. *How did he get that way? After everything he's been through? After everything we put him through?* Neither of us have come up with a good answer.

"Everyone else is getting breakfast," Bear says. "They put Soren on mess duty this morning. You should have seen him trying to flip flapjacks."

I choke on my tea, laughing.

"Did he get any of them?"

"Not a one. Luckily they didn't land on the floor. Finally Zoe had to take over."

"Who's Zoe?"

"The girl who works the comm center here."

I nod, slurping at the weird orange drink, letting it cool as I sip.

"Bear," I ask, hesitantly. "Has anyone said anything more about…?" *About my father,* I want to ask. *About Waterloo. About Vale and Firestone and Kenzie and Jahnu.*

He shakes his head, and avoids my gaze.

"Want to come eat?"

Unlike last night, when the need to eat was physically overpowering, the idea of food right now feels vaguely repulsive. Hodges gave me two sleeping draughts after telling him I'd been having trouble sleeping. Now, I'm groggy and a little off, even slightly nauseous. Maybe that means I need something in my stomach. Or maybe it means I need to sleep off the effects of whatever was in those draughts.

"What time is it?"

"Eight."

I shake my head.

"Thanks for the roy-bus, Bear, but I'm going to try to get a few more hours of sleep." The last thing I want is get up and face the day, the unanswered questions, the nightmares I managed to escape in the night. I give Bear my bravest smile, trying to reassure him, *it's okay, I'm just tired,* without telling him how much deeper the ache goes.

When he's gone, I heave a sigh of relief, and close my eyes, sinking into my deepest sleep in months.

A few hours later, I feel fingers tracing circles on my back. Spirals, really, like the swirls in a snail's shell. I smile, almost against my will. Soren. I find myself leaning into the shapes, into his touch, like a cat scratching its back against the corner of a wall.

"Hey," he says. His voice sounds like echoes in a tunnel. I face him, open my eyes to his icy blues, lit as if by a flame when he smiles.

"Hey there," I say. I watch the way his eyes crease, the way his mouth wrinkles at the edges. He leans down to kiss me, and I let him. His hands are cool against my skin.

"You're quite the sleeper," he says. "Everyone here is very impressed. Zoe said no one's slept so well at Normandy since the victims of the Famine Years."

He's referencing the number of people who were buried here. A kilometer away from Normandy, there's one of the largest mass graves found since the Religious Wars.

"I'm glad everyone thinks I have a lot in common with dead people."

He laughs.

"At least you're getting some rest. We all needed it."

"I'll add 'good at sleeping' to my list of skills, the next time I'm petitioning the Director for a good mission."

"If she's—"

He stops short. *If she's even alive*, I finish silently. If she, or my father, or Rhinehouse, or anyone else from Thermopylae and Team Blue, are still alive. I swallow hard and clench Soren's hands a little more tightly.

"She is. They are. I know it."

Soren crawls over and lies down in the space between the wall and me, pulling me to him. I snuggle up against him, eliminating the space between us as he wraps his arm around me. It would all be so much simpler if I could let go. If I turned toward him, kissed him. I know he would yield to me, each body curving into the other. Instead, I stare at the ceiling and wonder where the others are.

Where Vale is.

"You missed the morning briefing," Soren says, breaking the silence. His voice sounds faraway, like maybe it's coming from underwater.

"I didn't know there was one."

"Yeah, here at Normandy it's so small, they just get everyone together over breakfast and talk about the day."

"Did I miss anything important?"

"Just that they've gotten word there's a group of travelers set to arrive today."

I sit up abruptly, looking down at him.

"Why didn't you mention that earlier?"

Apparently their intel came from someone who's not always trustworthy," Soren says, placating me. "And even if it is true, there's no guarantee...."

"That my father's with them," I finish for him. I glare at the wall. I want to see him again *so badly*, just to know he's alive, just to know I'm not the sole surviving member of the Alexander family, just to have someone else who can grieve with me.

"Yeah," he says, after a moment.

"What about you? Did you get any sleep?" I ask, chastising myself to remember that it's not all about me. Soren used to accuse me of being self-centered, of thinking only about what I'd lost. I like to think I'm beyond that now.

"Not much."

I pull away from him and stand up, pulling on my clothes.

"I'm going to get some food."

"Finally," Soren says, smiling again. "I was worried you'd starve in here."

I look down at him. "You coming?"

"Your bed is so warm." He pulls the blanket up to his face. "And it smells like you. Mind if I stay here for a bit? Maybe I can get a nap in."

I smile at him, reach down and touch his cheek, then bend down as if to kiss him. Instead I whisper in his ear. "Don't slobber on my pillow."

He whips the pillow off the bed and whacks me on the head. "So romantic," he laughs. Whatever else we have, we'll always have the teasing. It used to be mean-spirited, or at least I thought it was, before the raid, before the capture. Now it's a connection to our shared experiences I hope we never lose. I leave him to the bunk and shield my eyes as I step out into the brighter light of the halls.

It's strangely comforting to be back underground, in tunnels lit by biolights rather than sunlight. It feels like home. I wind my way through the halls, taking a few wrong turns and at one point bumping into a tall, slightly oversized man who looks as if he probably has his own stash of Hodge's special cookie butter. He redirects me cheerfully toward the mess hall. For all that there are not many people here, the tunnels are sprawling.

"Remy!" A voice calls as I almost walk past the open door. I turn into the room, the small round wood tables and wicker chairs of the mess hall. Bear's waving at me, grinning, as he stuffs a thick slice of bread slathered with jam into his face.

"Hungry?" I ask.

"Thif food if 'ood."

"I guess," I say with a smile. It occurs to me that Bear's never really had *real* food. All his life, he'd been fed OAC MealPaks, and then he lived on foraged food and who-knows-what else for a month or so in the Wilds with Sam. When we finally made it back to Thermopylae, we barely had time to say hello before we were driven out again. And then we subsisted on stores of millet, amaranth, and barley, dried vegetables, and smoked jerky at the rendezvous. We were all pining after good food, then. In a way, Bear was lucky—he had no idea what he was missing.

"What kind of jam is that?"

"Gooseberry," he says.

I stick my tongue out.

"What even is that?"

"Some kind of wild berry they got around here. Adrienne says they got loads of it. Jars and jars and jars. Gave me a whole one for myself."

The happiness etched into his face tells me this is probably the first time he's ever been given anything to keep for himself.

I grab a slice off the wooden breadboard in front of us and spread on a thick layer of jam. I glance over to the food preparation area, where I realize there's a surprising amount of clatter. Two unfamiliar men are busily clanking pots and pans, chopping vegetables, and whisking various liquids in giant bowls. The sweet, smoky scent of roasting meat is wafting around the room, but I can't see where the smell is coming from.

"What are they doing?" I ask Bear quietly. He swallows an enormous chunk of bread before responding.

"Adrienne gave the order this *matin* to prep a good meal for if the others show. From Team Blue." *Like my father*, I think. "Got some kind of pig in the oven, even. No one's sure they're coming or not, but if they do...."

A smile creeps onto my face. They're preparing for a celebration that may not even happen. Everyone—not just me—is hopeful, eager to see the others return, safe and sound. It's reassuring, as always, to remember that I'm not the only one with the heavy weight of uncertainty on my shoulders. Others share my pain, my anxiety, my loss.

I take a seat beside him. "Any word from ... the rest of our team?" Vale's sea-green eyes flash before me. I blink the image away.

Bear shakes his head.

"Zoe and Eli's been tryin' to contact them again. But they say no one's there."

I finish my bread in silence.

"Tea?" Bear pushes the mug he offered earlier toward me.

"Thanks, Bear." I take a long drink. The tea isn't hot anymore, but it's rich and earthy.

Hodges walks in and stops at our table.

"How's Miah?" I ask.

"Physically, he'll be okay after another day or two of rest. I was just coming in to brew him another cup of tea. Mentally, he's in good spirits. Worried about his friend, of course. Valerian. But keeping me plenty entertained. In fact, he said he feels like a new man. That if he'd lost all this weight before your trek, he probably would have beaten you here."

I laugh and wonder how Miah does it. How he keeps such a positive attitude.

"Now, tell me how you're doing? I missed you at the morning meeting, so I'm assuming my sleeping draughts helped."

"Slept like a baby."

Did you get something to eat?" he asks me.

"Bear just introduced me to the wonders of gooseberry jam."

"It's a revelation, isn't it?"

"Soren ate almost half a jar 'imself," Bear says, the corners of his mouth purple and gleaming with jam.

"What's the drill today?" I ask.

"Aside from cooking, not much." Hodges nods at the man and woman in the corner, who seem to have calmed down a bit from when I first walked in. "We're waiting to see if anyone shows up. But otherwise, it's a day of rest."

Just when I'm about to retort that there's *clearly* plenty we could be doing, a pair of hands squeeze my shoulders, thumbs kneading into my shoulder blades. I look up and see Eli's curly, messy hair, his dark green eyes under butterfly lashes.

"A little lower and to the left, please."

"I was starting to think your mattress had taken you hostage, Little Bird. I was planning a daring raid to rescue you from its clutches."

"You weren't far off," I say with a smile. "Fortunately, I'm perfectly capable of rescuing myself."

"That you are," he says, "but sometimes we all need a little help." Eli gives me one more squeeze and sits down next to me.

"Any news?" I ask.

"Nothing. Yet." He fixes me with a fierce gaze that says *don't give up hope.*

The moment of ensuing silence is interrupted when, from down the hall, we hear someone running and hollering. I jump to my feet, hope surging through me like an inferno.

"The Director's here!" she pants. Her face, darker than mine, glows with excitement. "I just keyed her in!" I can't breathe.

"Is anyone else with her?" Eli demands, reaching over to lace his fingers tightly with mine.

"Yes!" she exclaims. "Adrienne is meeting them now. They're coming. You'll see." I want to run, to follow her as she turns down the hall, back the way she came, but I can't bring myself to move. Eli's grip tethers me to reality, as the question thunders in my brain: *will my father be with them?*

Noises fill the hallway. I hear that familiar resonant voice, and the air whooshes away from me as if I'd been stuck in a vacuum-packed bottle and someone just popped the cork. Too much is happening at once. I see my father's lined face, covered in a dusky grey beard. His eyes, so tired, so happy, welcome me as I collapse into his arms. Chaos swirls around us, but we're in our own world, clutching each other. There are no words. There's no need.

Finally, I pull back, just to look at him, to reassure myself that this is real. I put my palm against his cheek, interrupting the tears tracing lines on his face then disappearing into his beard. "Oh, Remy." He pulls me in for another hug, squeezing me tight. His chest heaves with a short, stubborn sob, and he opens his arms to pull Eli in as well.

"Remy, my little bird. Eli, my son."

My heart explodes with the immensity of the moment, weeks of worry and tension crashing down into one sweet moment, like the thunderous release of a pent-up summer storm.

"Okay. I can't breathe," I say finally, laughing, tearing away just enough to look around the room. The Director and the other Thermopylae Team Blue members are greeting the rest of the Normandy crew, talking breathlessly, hugging, laughing and clapping each other on the back. The joy of being alive, seemingly unharmed, is overwhelming. That they're safe. That there's still hope.

Gradually, voices quiet. Calm slowly settles over the room. I hadn't seen Soren come in, but now notice he and Rhinehouse standing, heads together, and, to my astonishment, Rhinehouse actually has his arm around Soren's shoulder. Soren's introducing Bear who smiles timidly, looking out of place. Now, Rhinehouse, bless his cranky soul, shakes Bear's hand and tells him, *Welcome to the Resistance.*

The Director catches my eye and smiles, and I nod in return. She's a quiet, intimidating woman and I've never been comfortable around her. She's not much taller than I am, but she exudes a fierce intelligence, set by an angular jaw, barely-there brows in a graceful arch, and a charismatic glint in her sparkling, narrow eyes. She was my mother's friend—back then I knew her as Cillian Oahu—but was always all business with me. Since joining the Resistance, I've only known her as the Director. It seems to fit.

Adrienne clears her throat.

"With high hopes of your arrival, we've prepared a celebratory feast." She nods at the Normandy operators, who begin setting out plates and forks. "We've got a boar roasting in the oven and Zoe's breaking out her dandelion wine from last summer."

Zoe does a little happy dance to everyone's cheers. Adrienne holds her hand up again. "There's plenty of food to go around, and I know you all are in need of nourishment. But before we dig in, I'd like to share a moment of silence in honor of your safe arrival and to keep in our thoughts those who have not returned to us yet—and those who will never return to us again." A lump lodges in my throat, and I clutch my father's hand, lean on his shoulder, and close my eyes. The room goes quiet for a moment until Adrienne raises her glass and says, "Let us always remember to set a place for friends old and new."

Soon the table in the center of the room is laid out with enormous bowls of dried fruits, wheat pilaf, and roasted vegetables. Two of the Normandy workers pull a giant pan out of the oven and the smell of the sizzling roasting boar fills the room.

The next few moments pass in a blur of happiness. Plates clatter and knives are passed around, and everyone's words seem to mingle in the air like summer fireflies. I barely taste my food, I'm so relieved. I can't seem to think at all. I sit with my father on one side, Eli on the other. For a brief moment, it seems everything is right with the world.

Then I notice the Director across the room, a fork poised in midair, her mouth set in a frown. Her eyes are creased and worried. She turns and whispers something to Adrienne, at her side, but Adrienne shakes her head.

"Dad," I whisper, "what's wrong?"

He shakes his head, as confused as I am. An uncertain silence seeps into the room.

"Where are the others?" the Director asks. She doesn't have to raise her voice to make herself heard. Eli, at my side, looks at me briefly before responding.

"When we were at the rendezvous point, waiting for your team, we took out the hovercar we used to flee the old city. But we were attacked by drones almost immediately, and the hovercar was totaled. We realized we would put ourselves in danger, traveling in a large group through the Wilds. So we split up. Firestone took Vale, Kenzie, and Jahnu and headed to Waterloo. We came here." He hesitates before finishing the story. "We should have heard from them. They should have arrived there before we got here. But we haven't heard anything from Waterloo at all."

The Director stares at Eli for a moment.

"When did you last see them?"

"Nine days ago."

She glances at Adrienne.

"Tonight, we'll have to reopen the communication lines. Not just radio. We need to re-activate the digital connections between all the bases to see who else we can contact. Find out who made it to their rendezvous points and who didn't."

And who didn't.

How many did we lose? How many were caught in the Wilds by drones, or worse? How many made it to safety, and how many will never see their families again? I count myself grateful that I can sit and hold my father's hand and that Eli is at my side.

I thought that about my mother, once, too.

Without warning, the Director stands up.

"We're all grateful to you here at Normandy for the food you've prepared, and tonight, if it's alright with Adrienne, I'd like to take an evening to rest and celebrate that those of us who made it here are safe and sound." She looks down at Adrienne next to her, who nods a silent assent. "But we must temper our joy when so many others might be in need."

"It sounds like the situation in the Wilds is getting more dire," a woman at Adrienne's table says. "Eli's group was attacked by drones, and you had no easy time getting here, either."

The Director shakes her head. My father's hand tightens around my own, and when I look at him, his mouth sets hard and his brows furrow.

"Rhinehouse's group was supposed to rendezvous with Ellijah's team, Team Red, at one of the safe houses outside of the city. But his group and mine were intercepted by Sector drones as we left. They tracked us through the woods and cornered us into a firefight with the remaining Black Ops in the city. We were outnumbered and outgunned." There's a heavy silence. "We lost three team members that day."

There are whispers about the room, like the scattering of distant stones.

"They said our release," the Director continues, "would be guaranteed as long as we gave them the information they wanted. The exact location of our bases, the names of recent Sector traitors, and the whereabouts of Jeremiah Sayyid and Valerian Orleán."

A collective intake of breathe. The whole room goes silent.

"What happened?" Eli asks finally.

"We got lucky." She shrugs, fatalistically, as though the matter was out of her hands. "I thought it was over. None of us would talk, of course. Corine's soldiers were prepared to make the kill. I closed my eyes and accepted my fate. But then I heard a remarkable sound—the *thwang* of a bowstring's release. When I opened my eyes, Corine's soldiers were dead, arrows sticking out of their backs."

"We stood there gaping," my father says, quietly.

"We'd been bound and all of us but Gabriel gagged—they didn't recognize any of us but him and James, thankfully."

It always sounds strange to me to hear Rhinehouse referred to by his first name.

"I heard an explosion in the distance, and it took me a moment to realize it was their airship." the Director smiles. "I still don't know how they blew up a shielded airship, but they did."

"Who's they?" Soren demands.

"Outsiders," she responds.

"They killed all the Black Ops?" Eli raises his eyebrows in curious surprise.

"And then untied us and disappeared," my father adds. "One minute there, and the next gone, with fifteen dead soldiers in their wake."

I glance at Soren across the room, where he's sitting next to Rhinehouse. He cocks his head to the side slightly, toward me, and I know we're wondering the same thing: *Could Chan-Yu have been there? Or that Osprey person?*

"Why would they have done that?" Adrienne asks.

The Director shakes her head. "I don't know. They didn't stay to explain. We know they harbor no love for the Sector. They've taken their own actions against Sector incursions into their territory. And we've tried to reach out to them. But they've always ignored our overtures."

I open my mouth to speak, but Soren beats me to it, and I push back the twinge of annoyance that bites at me.

"It was an Outsider who helped Remy and I escape Sector headquarters. We never had a chance to tell you the whole story before the attack."

"When I spoke with him, Valerian said a man he trusted had helped you," Rhinehouse says quietly. "He neglected to tell me he was an Outsider, though."

The Director fixes her gaze on Rhinehouse, considers him for a moment, and then turns toward me. I've never felt comfortable meeting her eyes, and now is no exception. I feel like she's drawing out the very marrow of my bones.

"After dinner I want a full briefing from everyone who was on the raid the night you were captured. Every detail about your capture, your captivity, and your escape. Understood?"

Soren, Eli, and I all respond on cue.

"Yes, m'am."

Eli turns to look behind me, and I follow his gaze. Hodges is in the doorway with Miah in tow. Miah is pale and shaky, but his eyes are fixed on the enormous slab of meat on the center table. Hodges glances at Soren who jumps up and grabs an empty chair. With a slight nod to Rhinehouse, Miah collapses into the chair with a grunt.

The Director's eyes flit back and forth between Rhinehouse and Miah. Rhinehouse doesn't look the least bit surprised to see Miah, but the Director's wide eyes tell me she most certainly is.

"I felt sorry for him in the infirmary when the rest of us were celebrating," Hodges explains. "I think he's doing well enough to eat a little real food. A bit of bread and protein." Hodges picks up a plate and puts a small piece of bread on it. Miah, however, looks ravenous and ready to celebrate anything that involves large quantities of solid food. The days in the woods had already hollowed him out, and being sick has thinned out his cheeks and created dark crescents under his eyes.

Soren, too, seems to have noticed how hungry Miah looks. He takes the plate from Hodges.

"I'll do it," I hear him say, as small talk picks up again around the hall. He goes about systematically loading the plate with every kind of food available on the center table. I smile as I watch him set the plate in front of Miah, who nods in gratitude. Hodges scowls a bit, but doesn't object. Once Miah proves himself perfectly capable of ladling enormous helpings of food into his mouth, the medic relaxes.

There's a clatter down the hall, and conversation in the mess hall quiets again.

"You're shitting me," someone says, a male voice.

"That's what they said. You've gotta—"

Arms full of wine bottles, Zoe bursts back into the room, followed closely by the chubby man who gave me directions to the mess hall not so long ago.

"You'll never believe this," she says, staring at Adrienne and the Director. "The Sector is blaming Valerian Orleán's disappearance on," she points to Miah, "him."

Miah, a fork-load of roasted vegetables halfway to his eager mouth, stares at her.

"What?" Soren.

"I stopped by the comm center on my way back from my room when I heard it. They're scapegoating him. That horrible girl Linnea just said something about it on Sector News Network. They're gonna make a formal announcement. You've got to see it."

Chairs scrape. Bodies move. Voices, loud and whispered, float around my head like wisps of smoke. I clutch my father's hand and wonder what this sudden change in tactics means. Miah leans on Soren as we all hurry through the hall, food utterly forgotten, to the comm room.

With the radio on, Eli and Zoe fuss over their antiquated video feed to see if they can set up a visual while cranking up the volume as loud as it will go. We crane our heads forward. I find myself pushed up against my father and Soren, whose body seems to hollow out a space for me, as we all wait.

"Citizens of Okaria! Farmers, workers, scientists, all." It's Philip Orlean, Vale's father. His voice sounds like warm honey through the speakers. It quavers with both confidence and fear. It's the kind of voice that could lead you off the edge of a cliff and make you glad you jumped.

I wonder if Vale is somewhere listening.

"I speak to you today not only as the chancellor of the Okarian Sector, but as a father. Today, I am saddened to be the bearer of grim news, both for my family and for the Sector at large. Valerian Augustus Orleán, the Director of the Seed Bank Protection Project, valedictorian graduate of the Academy, our state's most prestigious institution of learning, better known to many of you as Vale—my own son—" his voice shakes with unabated emotion "—has been taken hostage."

Just then, the tiny plasma screen—not even three dimensional, it's so old-fashioned—flares up, and Philip's face, lined with worry and sadness, appears in front of us.

The first thing I feel is rage.

Philip Orleán, the man who promised me a bowl of fresh figs if I betrayed my friends, my family, and everything I believe in. Who electrocuted me when I refused. Who pleaded innocent to the charge of my sister's death.

Philip Orleán, the liar.

At his side, a little behind him, sits Corine, his wife, the woman who gave the orders that claimed my sister's life. And my mother's. The woman who ordered Chan-Yu to kill me and Soren. *The Orleáns' death toll continues to grow,* I think, closing my eyes for a moment. *How many more will die at their hands?*

"Vale has been missing for just over four weeks. Terrorists have penetrated our deepest levels of security to take one of our most valuable citizens hostage, to hold us as a society hostage as we desperately negotiate for his safe return.

These rebels, these guerilla fanatics, seek to dismantle the institutions we've built and to plunge us back into a time of starvation and chaos. We will never allow it.

"In the last few weeks, we've done everything possible to find answers, to discover Vale's whereabouts, to find out how and why he was taken. It is with the deepest sadness and regret that I inform you that we have all been betrayed—that my son has been betrayed—by someone we once considered one of our own, a friend—both of the Sector and of our family. Jeremiah Sayyid, an engineer from the fourth quadrant of Okaria."

Miah gasps. His face is ashen, and he looks like he might throw up. The room buzzes for a moment, before we all go silent again, straining to hear more.

"His father, Ezekiel Sayyid, is a known member of the increasingly well-organized terrorist network actively working to destroy the Sector. Jeremiah and Valerian both disappeared on the same day. Our intelligence now shows conclusively, though we don't want to believe it, that Jeremiah is complicit in and central to the hostage-capture of our beloved son." Here Philip's voice cracks. He stares up at the elegant, arching interior of the Sector's gorgeous Capital building, and blinks for a moment. Elsewhere in the room, someone conjures up a wad of saliva and spits it on the floor, summing up my feelings. I remember doing the same thing across the desk from Philip, not so long ago, before he slapped a few capacitors on me and turned up the charge.

"Jeremiah Sayyid was a friend of ours. He was welcomed into our home on too many occasions to count. He dined with us, celebrated with us, and seemed by all accounts to be a talented young man with great promise. How wrong we were only proves how deeply this terrorist group can corrupt.....

The sound goes dead and Zoe smacks the side of the audio unit with her hand.

"...lurk in the shadows of our society, growing in strength and number as vulnerable citizens are attracted to their empty promises. They don't offer freedom or safety or protection, but a fast track to destruction and disease, a return to famine, to bloodshed, to a time of want and war."

I clutch my father's hand, close my eyes, and imagine watching Philip at the podium, in person. If I had stayed, would I believe him? Would his words strike fear in me?

"Citizens," his voice crackles through the speakers. "This is a dark time for my family, and if we do not address this threat, it could prove to be a dark time for the Sector as well. But rest assured, we are hot on the terrorists' heels. We will track Jeremiah and Ezekiel Sayyid down and hold them accountable for their crimes against the Sector—for their crimes against you, our people. We will find Vale and bring him home. Together, we the citizens of the Okarian Sector will not let these deluded fanatics return us to the dark ages of the past. Together, we will work for a brighter, more secure and prosperous future. As always 'May we gain strength from the sowing, resilience from the reaping, and hope from the harvest.' Good night."

"Bastard." A voice breaks the stillness. It's my dad, who *never* curses. He hates it when Phillip quotes his poem, the poem that earned him his post as the Sector's poet laureate.

The sounds dim for a moment, as Philip retreats from the podium and takes Corine's hand. Wrapped in their long fur coats and warm leather gloves, they hold their hands high, together, a sign of resilience and strength.

After a long moment of fraught silence in the comm room, the vidscreen dies.

"Damn it," Eli says, loudly. "I knew that piece of junk wouldn't last long."

Then I hear Linnea Heilmann's perky voice through the radio, gilded with newsworthy suspense: "I am Linnea Heilmann, and that was Philip Orleán, Chancellor of the Okarian Sector, announcing the kidnapping of his own son and Sector Board Member, Valerian Orleán, by anti-Sector terrorists living in our midst." She pauses, one of those calculated breaks to make everyone lean in a little closer. "Over the past few years, Sector intelligence agents have been conducting undercover investigations into the disappearances of several noted Sector citizens. Now we know the truth. This terrorist group—the Resistance, as they call themselves—is kidnapping them. But why? What does a ragtag group of resistance fighters hope to accomplish by holding our citizens hostage for months, sometimes years at a time? What are their demands? Why do they hide in the shadows? Those are just a few of the questions Sector Defense Forces and OAC Security personnel seek to answer. Until we get answers, we urge you to keep your eyes and ears open, your doors locked, and your hearts with those who have disappeared. Now, let's welcome the young woman whose former boyfriend has betrayed the Sector, Miss Moriana Nair."

Miah, his face like the color of flour, takes a step back from the radio, almost falling against the wall.

"Moriana attended the prestigious Okarian Academy as well as the Sector Research Institute with both Jeremiah Sayyid and Valerian. Hello, Moriana."

"Linnea," comes Moriana's voice through the radio. I haven't heard her voice in years. My thoughts fly out to Jahnu, Moriana's cousin, wherever he is. I spare a moment and a silent hope that he's all right.

"She hates Linnea," Miah says, his voice somewhere between panicked and hyperventilating. "Why is she doing this?"

"You think she has a choice?" Soren asks sharply.

Sweat beads on Miah's brow and Zoe, still sitting at the controls, looks up at him with pity. She stands, scoots her chair toward him, and he plops onto it.

"Why do you think Jeremiah turned against the Sector? What do you believe drove him to kidnap his best friend?" Linnea begins.

"There must be a misunderstanding. Miah couldn't hurt anyone if he *wanted* to. He's the sweetest person I've ever met in my life, and he loves Vale. I just can't believe it. It's not possible." At Moriana's words, Miah releases a long, relieved breath, grateful, I'm sure, that she, at least, doesn't believe Philip Orleán.

"So how do you explain his disappearance? Did he give you any hint he was leaving? Were there any clues? Do you think he was jealous of Vale?"

"No, of course not!"

"Jealousy can be a powerful motivator. Is it possible Jeremiah was tired of living in Vale's shadow? Could that be what motivated him to turn against the Sector?"

"Linnea, he wouldn't have—" There's desperation and confusion in her voice. I wish for everything the plasma screen hadn't gone out when it did. I wish I could see her face. Miah's staring into the distance as though he's trying to murder Linnea just by thinking really hard.

"What gives you so much faith in this man, who Sector intelligence teams have concluded is guilty?"

"If he did it, he must have been forced into it. Maybe the terrorists tortured him or threatened his father or something. But Miah would never willingly hurt or betray Vale."

"But would he betray the Sector? After all, his father is a known terrorist."

"No, he—"

"My understanding is that you've been one of Vale's closest friends for many years as well. If Jeremiah Sayyid didn't kidnap him, how do you explain Vale's disappearance?"

"I don't know. They were there one night—at the Solstice Ball—and then they weren't." Her voice breaks. "Something else must have happened. It's just not possible that Miah—"

"I know this is painful for you, but there's one more thing I need to bring up. Soren Skaarsgard." In our crowded little comm center, two dozen faces turn immediately to Soren. His blue eyes crystallize in that instant, his entire body tenses as he focuses his frozen gaze on me. "Soren, the only son of former

Chancellor Cara Skaarsguard, was once a rising star within the Sector Research Institute. Many speculated he might follow in his mother's footsteps into the College of the Deans. Jeremiah and Soren were close friends before Soren went missing. Don't you think it's just a little too coincidental that both of Jeremiah's best friends—both from politically connected families—suddenly disappeared?"

"I don't have any idea why Soren disappeared, but that was a long time ago! That has nothing to do with—"

"I'm sorry, Moriana, but that's all the time we have. Thank you for agreeing to talk with us. I know this must be difficult for you."

"Lin—"

"Fellow citizens, that was Moriana Nair, former girlfriend of Sector traitor Jeremiah Sayyid. Stay tuned for the latest news of Valerian Orleán's abduction. This is Linnea Heilmann. Goodnight for now."

5 — VALE

Blue, glittering twilight settles on us like a pall. Every shifting shadow unnerves me, a potential threat, an enemy waiting for the kill. Earlier, we were the predators—now we're prey. We've been on the move for an hour, stopping only once for a quick drink. Firestone's holding up fairly well, though I can hear him cursing under his breath—words I've never even heard from Sector soldiers—so I know he's in a lot of pain. We're all getting tired. But we have to press on. As far as we can before we collapse—as far away from the soldiers responsible for destroying Waterloo as possible.

I glance at the sky, barely visible through the trees. We've got insulated, camouflaged tents, and the canopy is dense enough that I don't think we'll need to worry about drones tonight. But soldiers are another matter. I don't think they'll be following us this far into the Wilds—Sector soldiers aren't as good in the Wilds as they like to think they are—but I don't want to take chances.

I run alongside Kenzie and Jahnu, as Firestone huffs his way through the trees, until finally he collapses and falls into a heap by the roots of a towering tree.

Kenzie and Jahnu are at his side before I can even call to them. Firestone looks dazed. His eyes are glazed over and distant.

"Dehydration," I say immediately, watching his eyes. "Side effect of severe burns."

"And exhaustion," Kenzie says, impatient. She pulls out her water canteen and hands it to Firestone. "Drink," she says curtly. "We've been running nonstop for over an hour, after a hard day's walk and the heat of that fight back there. We all need to rest."

"Goddamn," Firestone swears, no longer under his breath.

"Good time to stop," I say.

"About time," Kenzie responds, as though I had been the one prodding them on for the last few miles. "It's past dark, and we can't keep moving like this."

"Why the fuck didn't you say so before," Firestone says loudly, his eyes still unfocused.

Kenzie and Jahnu look at each other.

"We need to make camp," she says. "Get some salt and clean water in him. He needs electrolytes." She looks up at Jahnu. "You guys find us a spot to camp. I'll stay with Firestone."

Firestone waves a hand in Kenzie's face, laughing wearily. "I'm not at death's door. Quit talking about me like I'm not here."

"You better not be at death's door," Kenzie says. "You'd never live it down, dying because you hadn't had a drink all day."

"Ha ha. I'll take a drink. A stiff one, please."

Jahnu and I split up, taking care not to go too far, looking for a flat area big enough for us to pitch our tents, but small enough for us to remain hidden in the underbrush. It's not long before I hear Jahnu's whistle.

While Kenzie tends Firestone, Jahnu and I unpack and set up camp. The spot Jahnu's picked is under an enormous old tree trunk that fell into the arms of another tree. It'll be a tight squeeze, with both tents tucked under the old canopy, but it'll give us an additional screen from anyone who might be tracking us.

The four of us squeeze into one tent to tend to Firestone and share what little provisions we have left. Firestone looks much better now that he's not moving anymore. He's laughing again, and swearing a lot, which tells me he's mostly back to normal. Once Kenzie realizes that he's not in danger of fainting, she pulls an aloe ointment out of her pack and starts slathering it over the burn on his shoulder.

"Fuck!" he swears. "That shit hurts like hell." Jahnu and I look at each other and smile. As long as Firestone is cursing, we know he'll be okay.

"It's antibacterial," she says, looking at him apologetically. "We have to clean and dress the burn."

"Hey, Firestone. What was it you were chewing and rubbing on your shoulder earlier?" I ask.

"Plaintain leaves. Common weed, grows all over. Just like dreamweed. It's antibacterial, too, but it soothes the burn. Doesn't bite like whatever evil concoction Dr. Kenzie Oban's got here. But you gotta macerate it to release the juices and oils. That's why I was chewing it. Works well enough, though."

"Human saliva can help, too, which probably makes the plantain leaves more effective," Kenzie adds.

"You gonna start spitting at me now?" Firestone pulls back in mock terror.

"If you don't sit still, I might," Kenzie says.

Firestone stills and turns to me. "So V, you're our resident Sector expert," Firestone says, using the abbreviation he's become fond of. I can't tell yet if it's a term of endearment or ridicule. I'm hoping it's the former, but Firestone's easy attitude never gives much away. "What the hell happened back there?"

"I'd guess roughly the same thing as happened at Thermopylae. As an above-ground structure, Waterloo would have been a lot easier to find than Thermopylae. Even disguised as a run-down old shed. They probably sent some drones to take photos, do surveillance, and then sent in a few squads of soldiers once they figured it out."

There's a long silence as Kenzie dresses Firestone's burn. The pressure in the little tent seems to be building. I'm sweating and clammy. Remembering the devastation at Thermopylae always brings up tension, and I can't help but feel responsible.

"We need more water," Jahnu says, breaking the silence.

"There's a little stream not far," I respond. "I found it when I was looking for a spot. I'll go fill our canteens."

I duck out before anyone can object. I flip on the tiny biolight in my pocket, which is just bright enough to illuminate the path at my feet. As I walk, I allow myself a space to breathe, finally, and to think. My thoughts bleed together as I walk through the darkness. A directionless apathy gnaws at me. It occurs to me that from here, we have at least a two-day journey ahead of us to make it to Normandy. And that's if we make it without any further mishaps. I kneel to fill our canteens, wondering how we'll make it through the woods with so little food left and Firestone hurt to boot.

Lost in the woods. Something jogs in my memory.

If you should ever find yourself lost in the woods, this may help. Chan-Yu's last words to me when I confronted him in the Sector capital building. I drop our full canteens and pull out the acorn pendant he gave me then. It's been hanging around my neck, largely forgotten, until now. I hold it up in front of me, turn it over in my hands, press the metal between my fingertips, examine it closely. In the dim biolight, I look at it closely for the first time. Green and gold enamel decorate the surface. The acorn's 'hat' is lightly indented, just like a real nut would be.

I hold it up above me and look at it from the bottom. This time I notice something I hadn't seen before. A tiny lever, or a switch, almost invisible in the darkness. Using my fingernail, I pry it from right to left, holding my breath. Will it light up? Explode? Turn into something else—a compass, maybe? At this point, I'd give anything for a magical genie to appear and grant me three wishes. But nothing happens. I turn it over in my hand again, but the miniscule switch is, again, the only thing I notice. I sigh, wondering if it's broken, or maybe just a design flaw. I tuck it back into my shirt and head back to camp.

Firestone's already asleep in the tent when I return, and Kenzie's settling into the tent she shares with Jahnu.

"You on first watch?" I ask Jahnu, who is sitting with his Bolt across his legs.

"Yep. You're on second. I'll wake you in a few hours."

I nod.

"Night," I say.

A man of few words, he stares straight ahead, as if he hadn't heard me. I sigh, and duck into my tent.

I wake with a start when Jahnu touches my shoulder, jerking up and gasping from a hazy, suffocating dream. Firestone seems undisturbed by my clamor, though no less sweaty.

"My turn?" I ask, as softly as I can. Jahnu nods. I can barely see him in the darkness. I follow his lead, crawling over Firestone's long legs. The shivering cold air of a winter night greets me as I step outside.

I pull my down vest from my pack and settle in, as Jahnu ducks into his tent. I sit with my Bolt at my side, staring at nothing, listening to the wind in the trees and reveling in the silence. In Okaria, there was never so much quiet. Even at night, when the PODS shut down and electricity rationing set in, there was still noise around us. Out here, there's just the wind, the trees, and the stars. Oh, the stars.

The minutes fade into hours as I watch the stars wheel around the sky above me and listen for every broken twig or unusual rush of wind in the trees. Eventually a bruise-colored shift in the tint of the sky forms. Everything feels brittle, as if I could shatter the air by breathing too hard. I've been sitting too long, I decide. I stand, stretch my limbs and then prick my ears and sniff, holding perfectly still for a moment. But there's nothing. I let out my breath and relax.

"Hello, Valerian."

I jump backward as a slight figure materializes from behind a huge, gnarled tree. I pull my gun up. My eyes never leave the cloaked form in front of me but she does not move. *Where did she come from?*

"I was told to expect your call." Her low, crisp voice reminds me of gunmetal and sounds just as dangerous.

"Who the hell are you?" Small hands reach up and pull back her hood, revealing short, honey-colored hair cut jagged around her ears and sticking straight up everywhere else, like the last person who cut her hair had a seizure while on the job. In the dim light of dawn, she looks almost unnaturally beautiful, like a creature from a fairy tale, or a horror story. She's tall, thin, and youthful, but whether she's fifteen or twenty-five, I couldn't say.

"You called last night," she says, her voice quiet, steady. She stretches her hand out from under the cloak, which at one moment shimmers in the early morning light and the next disappears, clearly woven with holographic camouflage fibers, to show me an acorn pendant in her palm, a perfect match to the one I wear around my neck. On her arm, I notice slash marks scarring her skin, distorted lines that crisscross her flesh. And as I look up at her, startled, I realize that there's a scar on her left cheek as well, a perfect X carved into her face.

Aha, I think. *So that's what that little switch is.*

"I … I didn't know the pendant was a beacon."

"So he didn't tell you how to activate it?" she responds lightly. "Interesting. That explains why you weren't expecting me. I've been here for two hours, watching you." She laughs, not a giggle but a throaty, deep chuckle that reminds me of Miah when he laughs at his own jokes. "I didn't want to chance surprising you as I'm not particularly fond of getting shot at in the dark."

"How did you know it was me? How did you find us?"

"Each beacon has its own signature." She pulls out a deep blue glass semisphere from under her cloak. It's small enough to fit in the palm of her hand. She presses a long finger to the surface and it lights up immediately, thin white lines dancing across the surface of the glass.

"We call it an astrolabe," she says. "A navigational device. We stole the name from the Old World, but it doesn't really work like one of those old devices. This one's much better." I try to silence the multitude of thoughts zipping around my brain and focus on her words. "Mine shows me where I am, as well as where all the active beacons are within range—some five-hundred kilometers from my location. I can use it to direct me to any of the beacons at any point, and it will show me exactly how to get there." She looks up at me with a smile playing around her lips. "It helps me to avoid plenty of stuff, too. Sector drones, for instance."

"What *are* you?" I demand, almost breathless with curiosity.

She looks at me almost bashfully.

"I'm a wayfarer."

That doesn't answer my question, is what I'm thinking when the girl stops moving and the smile freezes on her face. Her eyes slip past mine, just over my shoulder. I turn to see Kenzie standing behind us, her Bolt trained on our mysterious visitor.

"Who're you?" Kenzie demands. The girl flashes her a wide smile. The astrolabe, I notice, has disappeared.

"I'm here to take you to safety," the girl says easily.

"Really. And where is that?" Kenzie asks, looking ready to pull the trigger at any minute. "Vale, what's this about?"

"I can help you," the girl says cheerfully, before I get a chance to respond. "I noticed Waterloo ran afoul of the Sector, and I'm sorry about that." Her smile fades a little, and her voice is tinged with regret. "But I hope to get you to Normandy," she says, looking up at the sky, "before the storm blows in. If all goes well, I can have you there in two days' time."

Kenzie and I both follow her gaze up to the sky.

"What storm?" Kenzie demands. "And how do you know the names of our bases?"

The girl shrugs. "The storm that will blow in by late afternoon. I help people, all kinds of people, get from place to place in the Wilds without getting hurt. So long as they're on the right side, that is." Her expression turns dark. "Sometimes those that call for help don't have the best of intentions. Vale here," she nods at me, "called for my help last night, so I came."

Kenzie shoots me a look that says clearly, *We'll talk about this later.* To the girl: "What do you mean, 'called for you'?"

"He's got a beacon," she says, pointing at my chest. I make no move to pull out the pendant. "When you activate it, it'll summon the nearest wayfarer in the area. In this case," she grins cheekily, revealing a large dimple on her left cheek, "me."

"Why should we trust you?" Kenzie demands. "We don't even know who you are."

The girl sighs. Her facial expressions seem to change as rapidly as the weather in April.

"Look, you can either try to get to Normandy on your own, following your dumb Sector maps, and get caught out in one of the biggest winter storms of the season—I'm personally betting on twenty centimeters or more—or I can get you there in half the time. I know all the best shortcuts," the girl says with a laugh.

"We'll come with you," I say abruptly, glancing over at Kenzie.

"Oh, and you're suddenly in charge here, is that it?" There's an edge to Kenzie's voice. Judging by the look in her eyes, the trust I'd built with her over the course of our trip is dying fast. The strange girl rolls her eyes and pulls her hood over her head, turning her back to us.

"You two can bicker alone. I'm starving. But remember, that storm won't wait for you to fight it out."

She bends down next to the tree behind her, and starts rummaging through a pile of dead leaves under which she's hidden a well-camouflaged backpack, and pulls out a slab of salted meat. Sliced. She pulls one off and takes a bite. I instantly start salivating.

"Kenzie," I turn and grab her arm before she disappears into her tent. "We can trust her."

"How do you know that?" Kenzie rounds on me, her voice a loud whisper. "How do you know she's not from the Sector? If you called to her, why didn't you consult the rest of us beforehand?"

"She's not from the Sector," I insist, ignoring the issue of the beacon for now. "I think she's an Outsider."

"Oh, great." Kenzie crosses her arms across her chest. "She's an Outsider. Because *that* makes her trustworthy."

So Kenzie, too, is a party to the stigma against the Outsiders. They're not looked upon kindly in the Sector, and never have been. They're seen as foreigners, strangers, dangerous men and women who live in a lawless, disorganized society. And that was *before* my mother pinned the "terrorist attack" against a classroom full of students on them. After that, many in the Sector called for us to hunt them down and kill them all.

I remember with a slight shock of surprise that it was General Aulion who argued against that.

"Remember when Remy and Soren told you about the man who helped them escape? He was an Outsider. He'd been my aide for a long time." Her brows are furrowed so deeply it's giving *me* a headache, but at least she's listening. "He was a member of my mother's Black Ops, but he was really an Outsider. He risked everything to get them out. And this girl is a friend of his." I hesitate. "I think."

"Your uncertainty isn't exactly reassuring, Vale." She glares at me. "Show me this beacon thing."

I touch the pendant through my shirt but don't pull it out. I won't show it to Kenzie just to prove a point. "You'll either believe me or you won't. The Outsiders aren't evil terrorists, Kenzie. That's just what the Sector wants everyone to think."

"I know that. But she's so *strange*," Kenzie says. "And I don't like how much she knows about us. It's unnerving." She looks sideways at the girl sitting on her fallen log. She looks as if she's paying no attention to us, but I'd bet my life she's listening to every word.

"Let's ask Firestone and Jahnu," I offer.

Five minutes later, Jahnu and Firestone are up, though it took Firestone at least a dozen swear words to get him there. Jahnu's watching the girl with a cocked eyebrow and crossed arms, and I admit I'm not surprised he's fascinated with her. The girl, however, looks totally disinterested in us. She's got a little v-scroll out in front of her, and is reading it intently while Kenzie changes the bandage on Firestone's burnt shoulder.

"So, you got an airship around here, then?" Firestone asks hopefully.

"No airship this time," she says, once again changing her attitude as quickly as I can blink. In a half second she's on her feet, gathering her cloak around her, a wild smile on her face. "Still have to walk. I tried to bring horses, but there weren't enough to spare in the area. You gonna come with me, then?"

"What's your name?" Firestone asks.

"I can't tell you. Wayfarers work anonymously, to protect us from the Sector—and who knows what else in the Wilds."

"What the hell're we supposed to call you—hey you, wayfarer person?" Firestone says.

"Since this Valerian here has a beacon, someone must have trusted *him* enough to give it to him." Her voice is lighthearted, but her eyes narrow and look almost treacherous. She could definitely be dangerous. "So I guess I can show you my symbol and you can figure out my name, or not, from there." She pulls her cloak up over her back to show the wire-thin black tattoo on her shoulder. It's a bird of some sort, with majestic wings bent into a W shape. There are some wavy lines below it—water, perhaps?

I notice she's keeping her forearms close to her sides, so we can't see the lines crisscrossing up her skin.

"What is it?" I ask.

"Hmmm." She pauses, puts a thin finger on her cheek as if considering something of great import, and then grins impishly. "Can't tell ya."

"Is that a wayfarer's symbol or are you the only one with that particular tattoo?" She shakes her head at me.

"Can't tell ya that, either. Time to stop asking silly questions."

"How'd you get that scar?" Firestone asks, gesturing to her cheek. Though I would never have asked her such a personal question, Firestone's never been one to adhere to propriety.

"Ah." Her voice is suddenly heavy. "That is *not* a silly question. But I won't tell you now. You may learn, one day. But with any luck, today won't be the day."

Firestone stares at her in bewilderment, and I can't keep the surprise off my face, either. But the strange girl seems not to notice. She shoulders her small rucksack and eyes us expectantly.

"Follow me if you dare!"

"Wait," I say. "We have to pack up."

Firestone looks around at us. "Do we trust her?"

"Yes," Jahnu says decisively. He stands and takes Kenzie's hand. "I don't know why, but I do." Kenzie sighs and shrugs in response.

"Vale?" Firestone asks.

"She's our best option. Not that I know what option that is, precisely."

The wayfarer, as she calls herself, after refusing to give up her name, watches us imperiously as we quickly break camp, as if we're the slowest, dullest creatures she's ever come across, and then, when we're finally ready to go, she turns without a word and leads us through the growing dawn.

As the morning stretches on, I'm struck by how well she knows these woods. We're moving fast because she knows where all the deer paths are, well-worn trails that make walking about ten times quicker than picking our way around or hacking our way through the underbrush. Still she takes the time to point out where to find water, what sorts of plants grow nearby, and which are edible, poisonous, and medicinal. At one point, she peeks into a cave she claims is the lair of a two-meter long adder.

"I didn't know we had adders this far north," Kenzie challenges.

"This one's a rarity," the girl says, giving Kenzie a mischievous smile. "But I started tossing mice to him and now he's my biggest fan." I don't know whether she's being facetious or telling the truth, but somehow the idea of her throwing wriggling mice to an enormous snake doesn't seem far-fetched.

Every now and then, I see the silvery flash of light from her astrolabe, but she's stealthy about it. It's always tucked out of sight by the time she turns around. Even though she's constantly checking our route, it's hard to keep up with her. Firestone especially is having a hard time. I know he must be in constant pain from his shoulder burns, but the girl doesn't seem to care, pressing on with the intensity of a hungry animal on the trail of a fleeing dinner. She perks up at the sound of a gurgling stream long before any of us notice it, and lets us break for lunch at the water's edge. We refill our skins, treat the water with our filters, and enjoy a good long drink. While we rest, she darts around picking herbs from the bank of the stream and crushes them into Firestone's canteen.

"Lavender, feverfew, skullcap." She hands the skin back to Firestone, looking proud of herself. "It'll help you with the pain and ease any headache or dizziness you might have."

"How do you know all that?" Firestone asks, eyes widened.

The girl touches her shoulder, mirroring the wound on Firestone's body, pushing her jagged honey hair from her face.

"Severe burn, Bolt wound, dehydration. Doesn't take a genius, now, does it?"

She reminds me of my virtual assistant, my C-Link, Demeter. They share a cheekiness and a fondness for showing off. Though Demeter was really nothing but a sophisticated computer program, she was, for a few months, one of my best friends.

The girl is careful to keep her arms tucked out of sight and under her cloak. I imagine she's not keen to have everyone asking about the scarred lines weaving their way across her skin.

By nightfall, she estimates we've walked about thirty kilometers, and says we should be at Normandy by midmorning the day after tomorrow. The temperature has dropped sharply and we're all keeping our eyes on the wind, hoping we won't get the storm she mentioned earlier. "It's just taking its time," the wayfarer says, sniffing the wind like a dog. Before we pitch our tents, she insists we all set traps, and even asks Firestone to show her how he sets his. They begin chatting about trapping like they're long lost friends, and she seems impressed.

I'm the last to return from setting my trap—my fingers were so cold I wasn't able to wrap the twine properly—and when I get back, there's a small fire going and our wayfarer guide has laid everyone else's socks to dry on a nearby stone.

I peel off my boots with a groan and shake them out.

"Gross," Firestone says. "Those smell worse than a dead skunk."

The wayfarer wrinkles up her nose. "Nothing smells worse than a dead skunk."

"I don't know," he says. "I'm thinking we're all getting pretty damn close to dead skunk territory.

"Speak for yourself. I'm fresh as a spring rose," she says with a grin.

Once we'd set up the tents the night before, we'd agreed to take turns on watch and I'd taken first shift, and she'd taken second. I heard her and Jahnu trading places sometime in the night, and felt her open the tent flap and crawl in, squeezing her small frame in between Firestone and I and immediately falling asleep. Now, she's up, rustling around outside and building a small morning fire.

When I step out from the tent, she holds up two skinned possums with a wide smile.

"Got them from the traps," she says, and with no further ado she begins preparing the meat for roasting.

We press on as soon as our breakfast is over, but the lightness in the morning sky turned out to be a false hope. By noon, it's clear there's a storm bearing down on us. The wind picks up, the temperature continues to drop, and a light flurry swirls around us. We stop to pull out extra layers from our packs and then keep going, battling against the stinging wind as the wayfarer pushes us forward.

"No choice but to push through the night now!" she shouts as evening closes in on us. "We're less than five kilometers from the base. You can do it!" she howls at Firestone, who looks murderous. Jahnu and I had taken turns with his pack earlier, but Firestone insisted he do his part and had taken it back. Now, it's clear he needs to give it up again.

"Here," I say. "My turn to carry your pack." Firestone doesn't argue this time, but instead of me taking the full load, Kenzie suggests we split up the weight. She empties Firestone's stuff, divides it into three piles, and then jams the contents in our packs. "We can leave your pack here, hide it in the leaves."

"This is as good a place as any to rest a bit," our guide says. "Might as well finish off our rations." Huddled together and shivering, we polish off what's left of the possum. Then she takes Firestone's empty pack and disappears into the darkness. It's no time at all before she returns with a set of little lamps, five warming packs, and a packet of dried fruit and nuts that, for all I know, she could have teleported from an Outsider camp. She hands each of us a warming pack and we crack them, releasing the energy, and tuck them under our clothes.

"There're only three lamps, so you'll have to share," she says. "But they'll help guide us as we walk. We have emergency drop points for supplies in case one of our wayfarers ends up in a bad spot, like this one. I left the extra pack there. It'll come in handy sometime." She creases her brows at Firestone, who's in so much pain at this point he's stopped swearing. "There're no good shelters in the area, or I'd say we could tuck in and get out of the weather. We could use your heating tents again, but if the temperature keeps dropping they won't do much good, and if it snows like I think it's going to, it will be harder going tomorrow anyway. So we have no choice but to go on."

Firestone nods through bleary eyes and wipes his forehead with his good arm.

"I'm not dead yet."

We trudge on.

6 — REMY

"Hello?" I whisper, for the hundredth time. And for the hundredth time, there is no response.

I twist the dial, searching through the airwaves for any hint of a signal. But there's nothing. Just static.

Finally, I pull the earbuds out and toss them onto the table. Leaning back, I stare at the array of dials, switches, and wires comprising Normandy's comm system. I've been sitting here for over an hour, trying to connect with anyone in Waterloo's range, with someone who might be able to tell me what happened to Firestone, Kenzie, Jahnu, and—

"Remy?"

My heart in my throat, I jump out of my chair and whirl around. Eli stands in the doorway, his brows knitted in concern, watching me closely. How long has he been standing there?

"Eli, gods. You scared me."

He steps into the room and leans against the controls. I plop back in the chair and face him.

"What are you doing?" he says. "It's four in the morning."

"You know perfectly well what I'm doing." I wave my hand toward the radio dials, a vague gesture that I feel Eli should understand. He nods.

The last seventy-two hours have been like one of those air coaster rides back in Okaria's posh entertainment district. Up and down, up and down. First, the relief of arriving at Normandy safely, only to discover that something happened at Waterloo and we have no idea if Firestone, Jahnu, Kenzie, and Vale are alive. Then, as overjoyed as I was to see my father's face, to see Rhinehouse and the Director, that excitement was quickly doused by Philip's very public announcement that we were being targeted as terrorists and that Vale was the victim of his best friend's manipulations.

Eli's green eyes are lidded with sleep. "What'ya do to whats-his-name, the guy who's supposed to be on comm duty tonight?"

"I told him I'd spot him for a while. He's in the rec room taking a nap."

"Ah, sleep. That's what you should be doing. You know avoiding sleep is not going to solve anything."

"A sleeping drought isn't going to solve anything, either, Eli," I say, knowing where he's going with this. Hodges has offered me sleeping draughts every night and except for the first night, I've refused. The after-effects of the drowsiness last long past daybreak, and I don't want anything clouding my mind, not when I need to think clearly, not when my friends are in danger. "And why aren't *you* sleeping?"

Eli sighs, his head cocked to the side, considering. He, of everyone, understands my reluctance to drug myself to sleep, but he's also been the most motherly and protective, next to my father, that is, since the battle at Thermopylae. "If you're not going to sleep, at least let's get out of the comm room. It's miserable in here."

I may not want to admit it, but he has a point. The airwaves are empty. Wherever our teammates are and whatever they're doing, we have no choice but to wait for their word. Being in here simply increases my anxiety.

I can't help myself from trying one last ping at Waterloo. When nothing happens, as expected, I push my chair back and look up at Eli.

"What do you say we pinch a few of those coffee beans Adrienne brought out from her secret stash for the Director?"

Eli's face erupts in a mischievous grin. This is the Eli I know and love. When he's not worrying too much about me, his slightly crazy fuck-it-all attitude puts some light back into my heart. I smile at him as he pulls me up from my chair.

"Stealing from the Director? Why Remy, I thought you'd never ask."

To our disappointment, raiding Adrienne's kitchen stores wasn't even difficult. So we sit in the mess hall sipping coffee and telling each other stories until almost six in the morning, when Zoe emerges from the hallway, hair mussed from sleep.

"Is that coffee I smell?"

"Sure is," Eli says. "Want some?"

"Gods, yes." She fishes a ceramic cup out of the giant pile of drying dishes from yesterday's meal and pours herself a cup from the press. Sitting down, almost completely still, staring with unfocused eyes at the table, and sipping occasionally with measured movements, she looks not unlike a zombie.

"Why are you up so early?" I ask.

She cocks an eyebrow at me, looking slightly more alert now.

"You two are sitting here with a lukewarm pot of coffee on hand. Shouldn't I be asking you that question?"

I laugh. "I don't really sleep much these days."

She shrugs. "Most of us don't. I just do my not-sleeping towards the beginning of the night, and can't seem to drag myself out of bed in the morning. But since we reopened satellite connection lines yesterday, I've been tasked with seeing what info has come in. I've got to see if we've had any contact from the other bases before our morning briefing. Director's orders. So," she heaves a sigh, "I'm up before everyone else, today."

At some point during the battle at Thermopylae, the Director gave the order for all Resistance bases to kill our satellite links. If she's ready to re-open the lines, it means she thinks the immediate danger has passed."

"You think there's a chance we might hear from Waterloo?" I ask.

She looks up over the rim of her cup and shakes her head." If we haven't heard anything from them on the radio, we probably won't via satellite. If their radio communications are down, I'm sure everything else is, too."

I glance at Eli. I may be sick of waiting for news, but waiting is all we can do.

Two hours later, we're all gathered in the largest meeting room, which is barely big enough for all of us. I'm sandwiched between Bear and my father, leaning against the wall because there aren't enough chairs.

"With a cloner or a Sector-quality 3D printer," the Director is saying, "we could manufacture hundreds of thousands of these seeds, and disseminate them to the populations of the Farms and the factory towns. We can subvert the OAC's control over the Sector before they ever realize it."

"How many plant species are listed in the database?" Adrienne asks.

The Director turns to Eli, who answers quickly. "We're not sure of the final count, but approximately ten thousand species in three hundred different genuses."

"With that many uncorrupted seed varieties at our hands," the Director continues, "we have the opportunity to wrest control of the population away from the OAC and put it back in the hands of the citizens themselves."

"A revolutionary dream," my father, at my side, says quietly.

"It wasn't so revolutionary once, Gabriel, as you well know. These were the ideals the Sector was founded on. A free and intelligent people, bolstered by the organic and sustainable ecosystems we created on the Farms and enhanced by the foods developed by the Dieticians. A world in which every citizen had access to healthy food tailored to their specific dietary needs. We envisioned a world where food was plentiful and nutritious. Where food-borne pathogens were a thing of the past and no child would ever go to bed hungry. And it wasn't so long ago that the Sector turned from that vision to create a different kind of world." She looks at Rhinehouse. "James and I were at the table together when that decision was made."

I watch her carefully, realizing that this is the most open I've ever seen the Director, the most frank. *She's got something humming in her blood today*, I think. She's hopeful.

"At the time, I was one of the only ones to speak out against what the OAC wanted. How much easier would it be, the argument went, to grow our society, to efficiently allocate our scarce resources, and to provide for the safety of our people if we decided what they ate, when they ate it, and what it was made of? How much easier would it be to engineer a healthy society if we could control who was fertile and who was not? How much easier would it be if the people who worked in our factory towns were designed to excel at their jobs while also ensuring they could not—*and did not want*—to step beyond their assigned tasks? How much happier would we all be if the bucolic way of life so many yearned for from the past was maintained like a page in a picture book?"

"Kanaan, Leon, myself, and Cillian were the only ones on a board of fifteen to vote against the changes," Rhinehouse says. A hush spreads over the room. I glance at Soren, whose eyes are fixed on the floor. His mother, Cara, was on the OAC's Board of Directors briefly, before she transferred to the College of the Deans. I wonder if she was at the table then, if she voted in favor of taking the freedom of self-determination from Okarian citizens?

"Many of you know this already," the Director continues. She's finally stopped pacing and is watching us, gauging our reactions, her iron eyes gripping us all in the thrall of her story. "But for those who don't, it's best you know now. Two months after the vote, I threw myself into the Lawrence River. I left a suicide note and most of my life's work behind. I took only my personal journals and research notes, loaded onto a waterproof plasma. With a wetsuit and an oxygen converter under my street clothes, I was able to swim far enough downstream to escape the main patrol routes of the drones and swim to safety. For a while, I lived in the Wilds, trying to decide if Okaria was worth fighting for." She looks off into the middle distance, as if remembering. "So much fighting. The Famine Years were behind us. Okaria was thriving...." She stops again and then looks up.

"It was only when James deciphered the clues I'd left in my note and came looking for me that we decided we had to try, at least, to fight back. James would stay in the Sector to see who else felt as we did, who else believed in a return to the original principles the Sector was founded on. I would establish a home base in a deserted city, and if he could, he would send people my way. We met once every three months at the same spot on the coast of Lake Okaria, and for years that was our only form of communication. But our little group grew, and we grew bolder. When the Alexanders turned up at our door with only one daughter in tow—" my father's hand suddenly clenches around mine, so tightly I think he might break my fingers "—we knew we had the potential to make real change."

"And now we have what we need to make it happen," my father says, his sonorous voice ringing through the room.

"Yes," the Director says. "With the LOTUS database, we can try. We can try to return the dream to the people of the Okarian Sector."

"So what's the plan?" Zoe asks, leaning forward eagerly with her elbows on her knees.

The Director stares at her for a moment, her eyes wide and thoughtful.

"Our goal has never been civil war. We've taken the time to grow our movement by word of mouth, and we'll move forward in much the same manner."

I find myself speaking up. After all that she just said, she wants business-as-usual? "That's not enough," I say. "We don't have time for that. We all know what they're capable of. After their public announcement blaming Vale's capture on Miah, we know they're going on the offensive. They're going public. While we're taking our sweet time 'growing our movement', they'll be hard at work making damn sure no one can or will join our cause."

The Director looks at me, a note of surprise on her features, but she doesn't go on the defensive.

"We can't risk full-out war," my father says carefully. "We have to take it slowly."

"I agree with Remy," Soren says from across the room. "We don't have time. We need to act now."

"We'll take action," the Director says, "though it may not be as immediate as you want. We need to regroup. We've heard from the other bases, and we know who made it to safety and who didn't. We have enough manpower to defend our existing bases and increase security, and to continue to train raid teams for important strikes. Elijah's team will train to complete the mission to steal a 3D printer from one of the Sector's seed banks. Of course, we have to work on the logistics, but once we obtain the means to replicate the seeds in the LOTUS database, we'll begin production and distribution."

"How do we do that?" someone asks. I turn to the voice—it's a face I don't recognize.

"The way I see it, we'll have to work with Dara Oban and others to infiltrate and subvert the Dieticians' processes. We'll substitute our own unmodified, untainted food for MealPaks. We'll hijack the Sector's distribution lines and use them for our own."

"You're talking about a process that could take years," Soren complains loudly.

"Growing our own food will take months, and doing it in sufficient quantities will take years," I add. *That's not good enough.* "They could have hunted us all into oblivion by then."

My father quickly turns to me and squeezes my hand again as though to soothe my pain.

"It's for the best, Remy. It's slower this way, but we don't want anyone else dying. Not after the carnage we saw at Thermopylae. Not ever."

I nod and bite back the stream of oncoming objections to that point. *I want Corine Orleán dead. I want Philip Orleán dead. I want Falke Aulion dead. I want everyone who's ever killed someone else unjustly to experience that pain for themselves.*

"Eli, I want you to prepare a team to search for Firestone's group. We'll give them another two days before we go after them. James, Soren, you're responsible for digging into the LOTUS database. Use all the manpower here at Normandy to help you. Adrienne, Zoe, I want you two preparing a secure information dump that details what we've got in LOTUS and how we intend to proceed. I'll work with you two personally on that, and we'll send it out to every Resistance base and outpost. Bear, Miah, I want you...."

As the Director goes on, giving orders to what seems like everyone in the room except me, I start to zone out. People are getting up, milling about, forming teams and getting ready to start their tasks for the rest of the day. I pull out my plasma, trying to keep it hidden from the Director, but it doesn't seem she's noticed me in the slightest. With my illustration program, I start sketching, almost thoughtlessly. The sounds in the room dull to a dim chatter as everyone starts drifting off, pairing up, talking about their various projects, and at my fingertips, a pair of eyes materializes, and then cropped straight hair, a strong jaw and a high-collared jacket to frame the portrait. After outlining the image in black pen, I pull up my color palette. The first color I select is a pale green-blue color, like sea foam.

"Remy," Bear whispers in my ear, "is that Vale?"

7 — VALE

Winter 35, Sector Annum 106, 18h30
Gregorian Calendar: January 24

I pull my too-thin jacket more tightly around me, wishing for anything that I had the furs the wayfarer does, or the apparent immunity to the cold she feels. The temperature's been plummeting, and at this point it's well below zero. Heavy wet snow with flakes big as thumb prints cling to every surface. Winter is always like this—one day you don't need a jacket and the next your breath forms frozen stalactites with every exhale. It's slow going, moving against the wind, trudging through the snow, but the wayfarer seems to have tapped into a boundless energy source, and she plows down the path, clears it for the rest of us. Snow's piling around our ankles, Kenzie and Jahnu are wrapped around each other for warmth, and the wayfarer finally takes pity on Firestone and tosses him one of her thermals. "Only a few more kilometers!" she shouts above the banshee wind. "It's not far now!"

"A few more kilometers might as well be a goddamned marathon," Kenzie shouts back savagely.

When it becomes clear Firestone might pass out if we don't at least stop for a brief rest and a drink, we huddle beneath the boughs of a large pine and pass around our waterskins. Mine, tied to the outside of my pack, has frozen solid. It's late, past midnight, and the going has been slow for the past few hours. Tension in our little group has skyrocketed, and if we don't find Normandy tonight, we might not make it at all. The creeping prospect of freezing to death after all I've been through is slowly dawning on me. This isn't how I'd have chosen to go out.

"You sure you haven't heard about any raids?" I ask the wayfarer. She's checking Firestone's shoulder and dressing his burn. "On Normandy, I mean. What if it's been destroyed like Waterloo? What happens then?"

"Normandy's fine, Vale," she says reassuringly, but when she turns away, I catch her checking her astrolabe again, just to be sure. She turns back to

Firestone, and touches him on the arm. "Think warm bed and smooth whiskey." Firestone just growls before we put our heads down and trudge on down the path again.

Just when I'm sure we're going to freeze and our lifeless icy corpses will be nothing but food for the wolves, the wayfarer pulls up short.

"We're here," she says. Even the limitless enthusiasm she had an hour ago seems to be flagging. She ushers us through a clump of undergrowth, drops to her knees and starts scrambling at the ground. For one paranoid, exhausted moment, I wonder if she's gone insane. But as she digs frantically at the snow, now up to my shins, and the dull rusted metal of an old manhole cover comes into view. I kneel beside her to help, pushing the snow off in great sweeping armfuls.

The wayfarer pulls out an adjustable metal tool from her pack that she locks into a hook position, sticking the hooked end into the hole and using it as a lever to pull the cover up. I slide it open to reveal what looks to be a five meters drop to the tunnel below where a dim yellow light casts a dull pall over the floor and a ladder is affixed to the wall.

She turns to us, speaking quickly.

"It's almost two in the morning, but they usually have someone manning the comm center 24/7." I'm tempted to ask her how she knows that, but I bite my tongue. "There's probably a security camera." She looks up at me with that sly grin that once again reminds me of Demeter—even though, of course, my C-Link couldn't smile at me. "If you want my advice, I'd send your friends down first so you don't get shot."

When she starts to turn away, I reach out a gloved hand to grab her shoulder. It occurs to me that she's not much shorter than I am, and her storm-hued eyes stand out in the dim biolight.

"Wait, aren't you coming? At least for the night? To get some food? Sleep in a warm bed?"

She barks a laugh. "Not likely. The only reason I helped you and your friends at all is the pendant around your neck. You can use it again, anytime, though I'd appreciate it if you didn't go calling me willy-nilly. I expect I'll be seeing you again soon."

"What do you mean?"

Her eyes gleam as she smiles at me.

"I mean, Vale, that I think you and your friends will be calling on the Outsiders again in the near future."

"Are we gonna chat all night?" Kenzie says with impatience.

I turn to her. "Yeah, sorry. I was trying to convince the wayfarer to come in with us. You and Jahnu better go first. I'll help Firestone down and pull the hatch behind us."

Kenzie nods, her teeth chattering as she starts down the ladder.

Before dropping down myself after helping Firestone, I turn to the wayfarer, opening my mouth to say a final thank you. But she's gone. I stare around into the empty trees, the cloudy shadows cast by the storm's haze and luminescent snow.

"Hello?" I call. But I know better than to expect a response.

I look down at the ground. Her footprints lead back into the deep woods. If she wanted to join us, she would have. She'll do what she wants.

"Thank you," I say out loud, an offering, wondering if the wind will carry the words to her. "We owe you," I finish, under my breath.

Turning back to the manhole, I climb down, trying to get my numb fingers to grip the ladder as I descend. Just being out of the wind is a relief, and I shiver pleasantly as my body adjusts. I pull the cover closed, and then slide down to the bottom where Kenzie is punching a numerical passcode into a device against the wall to our right. I hear a clicking noise overhead, and see a camera taking photos of us from above. I cringe. Whatever automated systems they've set up won't let us in if the facial recognition software identifies me, I'm sure of it.

Just as I predicted, a few seconds later an alarm starts blaring. "Intruder at the perimeter. Entry is denied without prior approval," a harsh, mechanical voice blares at us. "Intruder at the perimeter. Entry is denied without—"

"Dammit," Kenzie growls. "My fingers are so cold I can't get the code in right." She starts punching at the keypad as if she wants to destroy it, and Jahnu reaches out and places his hand over hers.

But then there's a crackle of static and the voice changes; suddenly it's not mechanical at all, but very human.

"Firestone! Is that—hey, stoppit—"

"—prior approval—" the mechanical voice grates again.

"Turn that damn thing off, give me that—" I grin. Eli.

"You can't override without—"

"—them in! That's my team, they're with us, they—" Eli's voice is angry now, and all at once there's a loud buzzing of static and the intercom goes dead.

"What the hell?" Kenzie asks, after several seconds of silence.

Jahnu looks up at the camera and says to me, "Not quite the same as all the journalists following you around back in the Sector, huh?"

"That's something I don't miss."

Suddenly the intercom blazes to life again.

"Hey, sorry about that." Eli's voice sounds hollow in the cramped cement tunnel—dangerously calm, too, like he might have just shot someone or blown something up in order to hijack the intercom system. "We've encountered a little problem here in the comm room. They didn't have authorization to let you in because Vale's name is on the ID system. But I've taken care of that. Just hang on one second and I'll figure out how to open the door."

"He prolly decked somebody." Firestone says.

I can't help but think that this isn't going to help my case for popularity much, if Eli had to beat someone up just to get us in the door.

"They need a drastic overhaul of the controls here," Eli comments over the speakers. "None of these buttons seem to do anything meaningful."

"Damnit ... just let me ... stop that—" A girl's voice. Sounds like she's going toe-to-toe with Eli.

But a few moments later, just as I think my teeth are going to break from rattling in my jaw, the enormous metal door rolls open, and we're hit with a blast of dry, warm air. We spill inside, eager to get out of the cold. There's a guard inside who greets us with a raised Bolt and an anxious look, but Kenzie puts her hand on the muzzle and brushes it aside carelessly, striding through the corridor as if she's been there a million times. In the distance, a group of two older men and two women round the corner. The one leading the pack is a short woman with silvery grey hair wearing an oversized sweater. She looks like she just got out of bed. She also looks vaguely familiar. Then I recognize one of them as the man who interrogated me when I first arrived at the Resistance. Dr. James Rhinehouse.

Kenzie comes to an abrupt halt as they approach.

"Rhinehouse, you ... and Eli's team? Everyone is—"

"Thank goodness you're all okay," the woman says, cutting Kenzie off. She looks us up and down. At my side, Kenzie and Jahnu straighten unconsciously, as though preparing to salute a superior. Who is this woman? I notice Firestone doesn't bother looking officious.

"How did you find us in this storm?" she asks. "The markers must be covered by the snow." Kenzie, Jahnu, and Firestone all shoot a glance at me, but I shake my head minutely. We can tell them about the Outsider later.

"It's a long story," Kenzie offers. "When did you get here? Do you have any word on my parents?"

"They're safe," Rhinehouse says. "Anxious about you, of course."

Kenzie smiles and reaches out for Jahnu's hand.

"I imagine you'll want to get warm and get fed," Rhinestone says, "But we'll want to hear your long story later." Just then, Eli comes sprinting around the corner. He pulls up short behind the other group, looking at us in disbelief, and then shoulders past them all.

"What took you so long?" He throws his arms around Firestone.

"Burnt-ass shoulder here, Eli!" Firestone exclaims, shrinking back and batting Eli's arm away.

Eli pulls back, looking apologetic. But Firestone can't keep the glare on his face for long, and it quickly slides off, replaced by a sheepish look.

"Hell, Firestone, you've looked better after fending off a pack of wolves," Eli says.

"Wolves in sheep's clothing, in this case," Firestone responds darkly.

"Soldiers?" the grey-haired lady asks quickly.

Firestone nods.

"Can't wait to hear that one," Eli says. He wraps Kenzie in a bear hug and kisses her smack on the lips and then does the same to Jahnu. In a moment, the tension is gone, and everyone's laughing—everyone except the short woman, whose eyes are fixed on me. I dodge her curious stare. Then Eli turns and sticks his hand out to shake mine. "Glad you're still with us," he says. I clasp his hand, grateful for the gesture.

"Eli," the woman in front interrupts, rather stiffly. "What did you do in the comm center?"

"Nothing that can't be undone," he responds happily. "Didn't hurt anyone, though Zoe needs to loosen up a bit."

The woman sighs, and Rhinehouse pipes up with his gravelly voice:

"Elijah, take your team to the mess." His one eye takes our bearings. When he finally settles on me, his coldness makes me shiver as surely as the howling storm outside. "Leftovers are in the ice box. Once they're fed, get Firestone to the infirmary. Hodges will want to take a look at him."

Eli nods dutifully, the smile still plastered on his face as he turns, and we all start after him.

"Valerian," Rhinehouse says, and suddenly all eyes shift to me. "You come with us."

My stomach growls loudly and my insides twist into a knot. Great. Another interrogation. I had hoped for a warm meal and a bed, or at the very least, a pillow and some blankets, but I suppose that will have to wait.

Eli's smile fades, but he gestures to the rest of the group to follow him.

Kenzie smiles at me tentatively as she passes me, and Jahnu clasps my shoulder and gives it a squeeze. I follow Rhinehouse as he and the others turn down the hall.

When we arrive at a door, the shorter woman pushes it open. The room inside is claustrophobic, furnished only by a few tables and chairs. She gestures me in, giving me a smile at once reassuring and worried. My stomach sinks. Something's wrong.

Once we're all settled inside, an uncomfortable silence descends. The woman clears her throat.

"Valerian," she says, in a voice that is clear and strong. "Dr. Rhinehouse has told us about your unexpected change of heart regarding the Sector. I trust you meant it in earnest?"

"Yes," I respond, as evenly as I can, wondering when the anvil is going to drop. I'm still trying to place her face. I start to ask who she is, but she plows ahead.

"Two nights ago, your father made a formal statement regarding your disappearance. Your parents..." she pauses, clears her throat again. Rhinehouse's one good eye is fixed on me, unblinking, narrowed. "Your parents claim you've been kidnapped by Resistance forces. That Jeremiah Sayyid was a sleeper operative working for the 'rebel outcasts' and that he betrayed you, your parents, and the Sector. We believe that, whether or not he is personally being hunted as we speak, he's being used as an excuse to continue the Sector's quest to destroy the Resistance. Indeed, your disappearance has given them the opportunity to go public with the effort and rally the citizens of Okaria behind them. If you have any doubts about which side you're on, now is the time to address them because the Sector has essentially declared war on us."

I can't quite breathe. Miah betray me? Miah a traitor? He's the most loyal person in the whole damned world. The entire thing would be laughable if it weren't so fucking sick. I take in a deep breath and let it out slowly. Then stand and grip the back of my chair, more to keep myself from picking it up and smashing it into the wall than anything else.

"It might be a good idea for you to sleep in the infirmary tonight," an unfamiliar man speaks up. "So you can be there when Jeremiah wakes up."

"Wait. Why's he in the infirmary?" The thought of Miah sick or dying after I dragged him out here....

"He picked up dysentery traveling through the woods. He's through the worst of it, but he's also going through severe withdrawal symptoms from Sector MealPaks and that apparently exacerbated the situation."

MealPak withdrawal. *Why haven't I had any of those symptoms? Why haven't I gone through withdrawal, too?*

"This is Hodges," the woman who appears to be in charge says. "Our medic. He's been overseeing Miah's care. And this," she gestures to another woman, "is Adrienne, head of the team here at Normandy."

I nod at Hodges, thankful for his kindness, eager to see Miah. But then I turn back to the woman as if, for some reason, I'm only able to focus on one piece of this puzzle at a time, and right now, the missing piece in front of me is the grey-haired woman's name. *Who is she?* I ask myself over and over again.

"We'll expect a full debriefing tomorrow morning," she says. "But now you should join the others in the mess hall. I'll walk you down, and then I'm heading back to bed. Tomorrow will be a full day."

"Who are you?" I blurt, as she stands to leave. "I know you. I've seen you before."

She stares at me, unsmiling, waiting.

It suddenly clicks, and my eyes widen. This is the same woman who drowned—who jumped to her death—in the Lawrence River ten years ago when she was the Director of Research at the O.A.C. Cillian Oahu. My mother was chosen as her replacement.

"I'm the Director."

8 — REMY

Where is she? The thought rushes through my head over and over again as I run through the darkened tunnels of Thermopylae. The air smells of smoke. There's no one here. *Where is Tai?* I hear her laughter echoing through the halls, the sound like crystal shattering, growing more and more shrill with every passing moment. Her footsteps, always just around the corner, always just a breath ahead of me. Smoke envelopes me. I can't see. Tai! I scream, my voice hoarse, shallow. *Where are you?*

I wake up, gasping for air, drenched as if I'd been swimming in Lake Okaria. A dream. I'm in my bunk at Normandy. It's dark, but not the choking, sweltering dark of the dream. The air is clean. There's no smoke. Tai is gone, and no amount of chasing her through empty hallways will change that.

I clutch the flannel blankets in my fists, glance at the pillow to my side. I realize I'd been holding it over my head, presumably to drown out the sound of Zoe snoring loudly above me. I remember now—she'd been making noises like an airship with a faulty engine silencer. She'd insisted at dinner that she didn't snore, and then she'd traded bunks with the older woman I'd been bunking with so we could chat as we fell asleep. Then I learned the truth: Zoe can out-snore Miah on a bad day.

I roll out of bed, claustrophobic. The prospect of lying awake, drowning in my pillow, as Zoe rumbles on through the night, doesn't appeal to me. Nor does the thought of chasing Tai, or my mother, through the burning streets and tunnels of our old city in my dreams.

The old wooden bedframe creaks a little as I stand, but Zoe doesn't move. I open the door to the hallway, lit only by intermittent biolights to conserve energy. Without a destination in mind, I find myself heading toward the mess hall. There are noises in one of the meeting rooms, but the Director had mentioned she'd be up late tonight, working with some of Normandy's members to map Sector distribution lines. The sounds don't bother me.

I turn into the mess hall to see my father, a cup of tea in hand, staring down at a piece of paper.

Paper?

"Dad?" I say, quietly, from the doorway, hoping not to startle him. He glances up, and a smile fills his face as he looks at me. His shoulders melt back as he opens up a space next to him, and I can see how much tension he'd been holding in his body.

"Can't sleep either?" He asks rhetorically. I walk over and sit down next to him. "The dreams again?" He wraps his arms around me.

"The dreams again," I affirm. "And it turns out Zoe really *does* snore."

He laughs, but the sound dissipates quickly, and I almost wonder if it even happened.

"Alas." After a sip from a cup of tea, he continues. "I've been trying to compose a new poem. But, my muse is gone."

"Oh, dad." Like a breaking wave, his shoulders heave and his heart thunders against my ear. I hug him tight, but this time, I don't have any tears of my own. I've cried enough, with him, with Eli, in the seclusion of my own bunk, that right now I don't need it. I hold him to me and wrap my arms around his shoulders. Were they always so frail?

He quiets after a few moments, finally sitting up to look at me, his eyes red and desolate. His eyes flicker down to my hands and then back to me.

"Remy, have you been drawing?" When I nod, he drops my hands and bends down to his side. When he comes back up, he has a whole sheaf of paper in his hands, *good* paper, thin and light and made for drawing.

"Dad," I whisper, "where did you get this?"

He smiles, and the laugh lines materialize, the old happiness. I pull a piece of paper off the pages, none of them uniformly sized, and run my fingers over it. It's a little rough, not as clean as the stuff we were allotted at the Academy. But it'll do.

"Adrienne gave it to me. There's an old paper mill nearby, she said, and they scavenged some when Normandy was first set up."

"I haven't used really good paper in three years."

My father turns to face me dead-on, taking my hands and holding my gaze. "We need your talents, Little Bird. We need your art to bring our message to the people." He sighs, staring at the blank page in front of him, the graphite pencil lying without having made a mark. "My words as Poet Laureate have been turned against me. We need a new artist to carry our message."

"Where do I start?"

"Every revolution has its artists, Remy. You start with what you know to be true, the pain and grief and anger, and you create from there. You speak truth to power. With your pen. With your brush. With your heart."

I nod, trying to visualize this, trying to imagine what I could draw or paint that would express or somehow communicate everything the Resistance stands for, what I stand for. But the only images that come to my mind are the dreams that have been haunting me for the last month.

"Dad," I say, casting around for ideas, "what did you do at the Farms? When you and Mom…." I trail off. I can't finish.

He shrugs.

"Your mother did most of the work. She had to help people, first, before they would listen to us. While she was helping them medically, I would sit and talk to them. I would ask them questions. 'Do you like what you do?' 'Were you born on this Farm?' 'Do you have many friends?' We bribed them, a lot of the time, to get them coming back to us—the Director gave us extra rations of chocolate and honey so we could hand them out."

"But what did you say to them?" I ask. "To try to convince them to work with us?"

"There was no one thing, Remy. There are no magic words. I read them my poetry, sometimes. Verses about freedom, and beauty, and about you and Tai. That hit home with a lot of them. But there was no one thing that *I* said that had any effect. We couldn't risk them telling any of the Enforcers about us, so we had to be very subtle, to work very slowly, and to keep quiet most of the time and listen to what they said."

The words from our meeting yesterday echo in my head. *We don't have time for that.* And it's true. We don't have time to take it slow, not anymore. The Sector—Philip and Corine Orleán—are coming after us like a fever, to sweat us out and destroy us. If we're going to have any hope of fighting back, any action we take has to be decisive.

Anything I create, artistically or otherwise, must be big, important. Game-changing. Slow isn't good enough anymore.

I hear dim voices out in the hallway, echoing and grow steadily louder, raucous, almost celebratory. My father and I turn to look at each other in the dim light.

"Who's making all that noise at this time of night?" he asks. I shake my head.

As the sounds grow closer, I can hear Eli shouting something about uncovering some of Normandy's old spirits, and someone—*is that Firestone?*—demanding it had better be stiffer than the wind outside. I leap to my feet, knocking my chair over backwards. My heart accelerates to flight speed as Eli rounds the corner, his arm over Jahnu's shoulder, who has his hand firmly ensconced in Kenzie's. Water from Firestone's dark hair drips down into his face as he follows them all in, and Eli stops and beams down at me and my father.

"We've got company!" he announces, proudly, but I'm confused. I smile but I'm frozen in place, unsure, my heart sinking into my gut, because *where is Vale?*

Jahnu breaks rank and runs over to me, picking me up and swinging me around like a five-year-old, and I thump his back and kiss him on the cheek and try to laugh when Kenzie pulls me away for a hug of her own. But the sound comes out less like a laugh and more like a sob, and it's only when Jahnu pulls me in close a second time and whispers in my ear that I truly relax.

"He's here, Remy. It's okay. He's with the Director."

Swirls of bright-colored happiness engulf me. Jahnu and my father embrace like a parent with a lost child. Kenzie and Firestone aren't exempt from the parental wash of love, though Firestone growls and favors his shoulder. After a few minutes Eli returns with a bottle of some rust-red liquid in hand. Firestone eyes it with trepidation.

"You sure that shit won't make me blind?"

"Already tested it scientifically," Eli responds, sporting a grin so wide a small dimple forms. "Drank about a fifth myself first night after we got here. Totally safe!"

"That explains the foul mood the next morning," I say with a laugh.

"I love you, too, Remy Alexander," he says and flashes me a rude gesture behind my father's back.

"You'll be starving, I imagine," my father says. I'll get some leftovers ready." He heads to the icebox as Eli pries the stopper out of the bottle.

"You gonna drink out the bottle or pour some for all of us?" I say, grabbing a set of ceramic tumblers. Eli pours out a round of the whiskey—or whatever it is.

"To the harvest!" he says, holding up his glass in a toast.

"To the whiskey," Firestone mutters and tosses back the entire contents of his glass. I wrap my arm around Jahnu and offer my own glass up.

"To the revolution."

Jahnu looks at me sideways, his eyebrows raised in a question, but I just smile at him.

We toast, and drink, and the warm, fiery liquid blazes down my throat. I've spent enough late nights with Eli and Firestone to have learned not to cough, but I can't stop my eyes from watering. Through blurry eyes, I watch as another figure appears in the doorway. I blink the haze out, still smiling, and find myself looking across the room into the green eyes of Valerian Orleán.

Neither of us move. Jahnu and Kenzie are laughing at Firestone, who seems to be already on his third drink, but the noises have faded to a distant static. Vale watches me, cautious, hesitant, but not afraid like he was just a few weeks ago. His gaze is steady. Our eyes are connected as though by a wire—any pull in the wrong direction and we will break the circuit, the current will dissipate. I feel, rather than see, the tentative smile work its way onto his face, eventually touching his eyes as he continues to look at me.

"Vale," my father says, breaking what's seemed to be an age of silence. He's come up next to him, and I can almost see sparks fly as Vale drags his eyes away from mine and the connection is broken. Vale's face clouds, looking at my dad with the same hesitation.

As if recognizing this, my father says, "No one should be held accountable for the sins of their fathers—or mothers." His voice strong with the melody and cadence of a practiced speaker. The room has gone silent. "I will never forget how you fought for Brinn. How you put your life on the line for hers. Please, don't ever feel unwelcome where I am."

He steps up to Vale and puts his arms around him, embracing him like a long-lost son. Vale stands a moment, frozen, staring over my father's shoulder, and once again, his eyes flicker to mine. It takes a moment before he gives in, wraps his arms around my father and presses his body into the embrace. He closes his eyes, squeezing them shut, but he can't stop tears from escaping, trailing a wet path down his cheeks.

One hug will not solve everything. But maybe a couple rounds of whiskey with my best friends will make the new day break brighter.

9 — REMY

"Remy!" A whisper accompanied by a sharp elbow to the ribs jolts me awake. I jerk my head up, stiffening, staring around the full room to see if anyone caught me.

It's Jahnu, at my side, listening diligently to the Director as she goes on about transportation lines, cloning methodology, genome maps, and 3D printing. I shoot a glance at Soren, on my other side, whose eyes are fixed on the Director.

Meanwhile, I am as bored as a cat in a cage. It's been almost four weeks since Firestone arrived with the rest of our fragmented team, and we've been lying low, waiting out the winter and the Sector's dire threats. Now winter is losing her mettle and the Sector's threats have proved fruitless, everyone's on edge, ready to *do* something. Eli has taken the lead in planning a mission to "liberate" a 3D printer from the Sector's clutches. Soren and Jahnu jumped on board with computational analysis of the different pathways and transport lines between the Farms, factory towns, and the capital itself. Kenzie's been helping reengineer the water purification systems here at Normandy, and Miah's been put to work rehabbing some old airships in storage. I've been helping others with various tasks when they need it, but my days are filled more with drawing, practicing my breathing exercises, keeping up my physical training, and playing scrap ball. Just this morning, anticipating that we would have a busy day, I challenged Jahnu to a game.

We made scrap ball up a few years ago. It's not complicated, mostly involves whacking a rubber ball at each other with paddles fashioned out of old metal scraps. You score a point by getting the ball into your basket that your opponent defends, but you can only use your paddle and your feet to maneuver the ball.

I am really good at scrap ball.

Well, I am better than Jahnu at scrap ball. The true master of the game, though I am loathe to admit it, is Soren. But he's not a good sport, at least not with me. He gets all competitive and tries so hard to beat me. It's just not as fun with him.

"You better watch it, Remy, I've got a big comeback planned," Jahnu had said when I scored my fourth goal.

"Oh yeah?" I said, bouncing the ball against the wall and preparing to whack it into my basket. It went in so hard the basket fell over. "You better be staging a big-ass comeback because I just scored yet *another* point!" I laughed like a maniac when I beat him 7-2 in the end.

I smile at the memory of my hard-earned victory and glance around the meeting room. Everyone at Normandy is gathered here today, as well as a few higher-ups in the Resistance who are listening in remotely. The Director paces and outlines her marching orders for the entirety of the Resistance. Everyone except me; I've gotten no specific assignments so far. None of my skills seem to match what the Resistance needs for this mission. Since dad gave me that paper, I've been re-thinking my role in the Resistance. I'm just not sure how to begin. I know one thing, though: I can't continue like this, in the shadow of everyone else's projects and Eli's mission. This is the third time now I've nodded off on Jahnu's or Soren's shoulders, and the hot mug of tea in my hands isn't helping.

My eyes lock on Vale. He's staring at the ceiling, focusing intently on some invisible spot no one else can see. He frowns when the Director mentions Evander Sun-Zi, as though he has a bad taste in his mouth. But otherwise, he looks as disconnected from this meeting as I feel.

"Our short-term goal," Rhinehouse says, as the Director nods at him, "is to replace the modified food used by Sector Dieticians to produce MealPaks with the untainted, old world seeds Kanaan Alexander left for us in the LOTUS database. Long-term, of course, we aim for complete overthrow of the Okarian Agricultural Consortium and a return to natural farming practices and the founding principles of the Sector."

"We must concentrate on the seeds," the Director says, a fierce glint in the narrowing of her eyes, "Substituting unmodified food for the corrupted foods grown on the Farms will be both challenging and dangerous. To begin, we have to be able to replicate and mass-produce the seeds from the LOTUS database. This requires cloning and printing technology, neither of which we have the capacity to build without clean rooms and nanotech. This is a big operation, and it starts with acquiring the technology that will make it possible. Eli has proposed a mission to steal these machines from a Sector seed bank. Eli, would you like to share the details?"

Eli stands, exuberant. He glances at me with a little smile, and I know what he's thinking. *This is the beginning of our revenge, Little Bird.* I smile back at him, wondering how Tai would feel if she were here, too. But I can't seem to muster his enthusiasm. As a member of his team and his best friend, I know every detail of his proposed mission inside and out. But when it comes to my role, I'm little more than a grunt. I can shoot straight and run fast. Once, that would have been enough for me. Now I find myself yearning for more. I try to imagine what Tai would think, what she would want me to do. Simply following orders wouldn't make her proud. She would want me to do more, to do something with my art, to bring something to the Resistance that the others can't.

As Eli launches himself into a description of his proposed mission, I yawn. Soren's hand sneaks down and finds mine, and without thinking, I lace my fingers in his and renew my focus on the meeting.

"Anyone who worked in the upper echelons of the OAC knows that most of their seeds are manufactured at Seed Bank Fairview, which is one of their largest and best-defended facilities. But we've learned they have backup tech at Seed Bank Flora. It's the farthest north and therefore the farthest from us, but security there is lax, and it's a small facility. We're targeting Flora as our best bet for stealing their machinery."

"But Corine Orleán knows we have the LOTUS database, doesn't she?" one of the Normandy fighters pipes up. Out of the corner of my eye, I watch Vale flinch at the mention of his mother's name. "She's not stupid. She knows what we can do with that database. Isn't that why she tried to murder Soren and Remy when they were prisoners, once she knew they'd discovered the key to the whole thing?"

"Yes," Soren says. "She'll undoubtedly have doubled security anywhere with cloning or printing machinery."

"But without those machines, the LOTUS database does us no good," Eli points out. "Unless we can bring those seeds to life again, they're no better than computer code. We know the risks, but we have to take them if we hope to use LOTUS at all."

"Umm," Bear pipes up, raising his hand tentatively as if he's not sure how to go about speaking. Eli looks at him expectantly. "What exactly is a seed bank?"

My father and Rhinehouse recently took Bear aside and told him that he was welcome to speak up in our meetings anytime he wanted, as he's one of the very few Resistance members from the Farms.

"Your input is invaluable," my father said to him. "You're one of the only Farm workers to leave a Farm of your own volition."

"And you're the only one we have with us now," Rhinehouse added in the friendliest of his gruff voices. "There are a few at other bases, but you're the only one here. We can use your knowledge and ideas."

Eli looks as though he's trying to suppress a laugh, but the Director glares at him and answers for him.

"All the food you grew on the Farms came from seeds that are manufactured and stored at one of five different OAC Seed Banks."

"Oh," Bear says. "So every year, the seeds we plant come straight from a machine? All that work we did collecting, drying, and categorizing seeds on the Farms…"

"Was a lie," Soren finishes for him. "They're probably all composted and returned to the soil, but the only seeds you grew were manufactured at Seed Banks using OAC genetic manipulations, printed by the millions."

"It seems so … unnatural." Bear says, looking a little sad.

"There nothing wrong with hybridizing and improving seeds," Rhinehouse speaks up. "It's only when DNA is manipulated in an effort to shape or control the people who eat it that it becomes dangerous."

Bear listens, nodding as Rhinehouse goes on. Bear and I have been spending more time together lately. He still idolizes Soren and is in awe of Eli and Vale, but there are times when he's overwhelmed by it all and I find him at my side. He's even taken to drawing, using the paper my father gave me weeks ago. Yesterday, I found a crude but clear drawing of him and Sam together walking through the woods. They were both smiling, as if better days were ahead. With a lump in my throat so big I wondered if I could ever swallow again, I put the drawing back where I found it, sorry for having looked at his private papers.

"These aren't small pieces of equipment we're talking about," Zoe pipes up. "How are you going to get them out and get them back here?"

"And do we have airships with capacity to carry that kind of load?" an unfamiliar man asks.

"They're not *that* big—" Eli objects, before Miah jumps in to his rescue with a detailed analysis of the amount of weight an airship can carry before slowing. I notice that the Director and Rhinehouse seem noticeably subdued, as though stepping back to let Eli assume the leadership position. Or as though they're waiting for something. As the questions come steadily and Eli fends them off, I start to drift off again. This time, my mind wanders down Bear's path, retracing his steps back to the Farm he and Sam originated from. He mentioned a healer they met on the outskirts of the Farm, after Sam was hurt. *Could it have been my mother?* I picture her with a headscarf and makeup, a disguise, meeting with Sam and Bear, doing everything she could to help. Was my father there? I've asked him, but he said they met so many people, he can't remember. Are there others out there, missing the presence of the itinerant healer and poet?

And then the thought springs to my mind, as it has many times in recent weeks, that I could do that. *We need a new artist to speak the truth*, my father said. Can I carry our message to the people who need it most? Bear and I have been talking a lot about the Farms lately, about how the Resistance needs to make a more concerted effort to approach the workers, and how someone needs to pick up where my parents left off. *Could I do that?*

"So who's going on this mission?" the man from Normandy whose name I don't know asks. "Who's on the team?"

"It'll be a larger team than our usual six-man raid teams," Eli says. "We're not aiming for stealth, unlike with most of our past missions. There's no way we're going to get in and out without them noticing we're there. This will be a twelve-man team, including two airship pilots—one for the equipment, once we lift it out, and one for the team."

"So ten sets of boots on the ground?" the man asks. "Who's leading?"

"I am," Eli says, without hesitation. The Director and Rhinehouse glance at each other, and then the Director opens her mouth to speak.

"Not this time," she says. "Your mission to Seed Bank Carbon was a disaster. We're going to keep you in a directorial position here at base, but you're not going with the team."

Soren has suddenly straightened and leaned forward. I glance at him. There's surprise written all over his face. If Eli's not leading the team, this will probably be Soren's chance to take the helm of a major raid—but he admires Eli and will probably see this as an affront to his leadership abilities.

"Carbon wasn't my fault," Eli says, color rising in his cheeks. "We were intercepted by Sector forces, outnumbered, and—"

"You failed to go immediately to the backup plan, Eli," the Director says, her expression unchanging, too calm. "We've discussed this already. You underestimated the danger and never called the backup code. Two members of your team were taken hostage. No, you won't be leading this mission, Eli. We need someone with extensive military training, a thorough knowledge of Sector security systems and operations, and proven leadership ability."

"What are you saying?" Eli demands. His hands are balled into tight fists, and I can only imagine what's going through his mind. "You've let me plan this whole thing for the last three weeks only to tell me I won't even be going?"

The Director sighs. "You're too much of a wild card, Eli. You're brilliant and we couldn't do without you, but you've proven your unreliability time and time again. When you get a handle on your temper, we'll reconsider sending you into the field. Until then, Vale will be leading all critical raids in Sector territory."

The whole room seems to stop in time, like an arrow that's suddenly hit its mark, quivering with unreleased energy. Soren drops my hand, and his palm slaps the table. Vale, who has barely stirred throughout the whole meeting, looks up at the Director. His eyes are dull, almost unrecognizing, like he's so surprised he can't even believe it's true.

"Me?"

"Yes."

"Why?" he protests. "Eli should lead this. It's *his* project. *His* mission."

I half-expect Eli to jump in here, but his mouth is still open, and it occurs to me that this is the first time I've ever seen him speechless.

"You're the logical choice—"

"Logical choice?" Vale's voice is hard, barely controlled, and he stands so fast his chair nearly tips over. "That's the most *illogical* thing I've ever heard!" He sweeps his arm around the room. "You think anyone here wants to follow me? I'm not even a member of the Resistance. I'm not fighting your battles for you. I trained with some of those soldiers, and I've killed enough of them already."

"You have tactical and leadership training," Rhinehouse cuts in, his voice low, with a subtle intonation of a threat. And you know the seed banks better than anyone in this room."

"I've led *one* real mission in my life, and you know how well that turned out. Eli has ten times the experience I have. It's one thing to take a defensive position against the Sector, to fire back when people you love are in danger, but it's quite another to go on the offense. You're asking me to go to war against my own parents."

People you love? The words ring over and over in my head. Is he talking about me, my parents?

"Vale, you came to us for amnesty—"

"I didn't come to you," he spits. "Eli put a Bolt to my head and dragged me to you."

"Are you saying that after everything you still owe allegiance to the Sector?"

"Of course not. I left the Sector willingly."

"Then—"

"I will not lead this mission. This is Eli's project. He planned it. He should lead it." Vale pivots on his heel to leave, with all the sharpness you'd expect of a trained soldier.

"Valerian," the Director says, her tone as sharp as a blade. Vale stops. "You were responsible for capturing two of our members, torturing and interrogating them." *He wasn't the one who tortured us*, I want to yell, but the words die on my tongue. "Because of you, their lives were in danger. It is *your* parents who are *already* waging war on us, waging war on the people you claim to love. It's time you decided what side you're really on. If you're not with us, you can walk down that hallway right now, climb the ladder, open the hatch, and go back home. No one will stop you. But if that's not what you want, if you want to fight for what the Sector used to stand for—what it could stand for again—you're leading the mission. You decide. Now."

He holds her gaze for a half second, and then he looks to my father. My dad gives him a slight nod, almost imperceptible. I feel like the air in the room has been sucked out and everything is suspended in a vacuum. Then Miah reaches up and clasps him on the arm, and Vale's shoulders relax. He sinks back down in his chair and everyone exhales.

Except Eli. And Soren.

"Good," the Director says.

"Fuck me," Eli growls. He turns and storms out of the room with Soren close on his heels.

10 — VALE

In my hammock, I press my hand against the wall and push myself into a gentle swing. I can't think of a time when I've been so physically exhausted and yet still so sleepless. It's been a few weeks since the meeting when the Director decided I would lead the team instead of Eli. I talked to Eli afterward and we came to an understanding: I don't want to lead the mission any more than he wants me to. Since then, though, he's cooled off and refocused his energies on other side projects. Miah and I moved in to bunk with Eli and Firestone after the team was announced. We got one of the few rooms with hammocks, for which I'm grateful. There's a lot less squeaking and groaning of rusted, bent springs. The rest of our team is now sleeping down the hall in one room, and my only consolation is that those cots are so narrow and flimsy, I'm pretty sure it would be physically impossible for Soren and Remy to share a bunk.

I shove that mental image aside as quickly as it flashes though my mind.

Miah sleeps like the dead, Firestone and Eli are both dead to the world with their faces squished against the hammocks in decidedly unattractive positions. They sampled a bit too much of the nasty liquor Rhinehouse distilled from a potato mash, so they're out cold. It was nasty stuff. Of course Soren had to note that my "delicate constitution" couldn't handle the stuff because I was used to drinking only the finest sparkling wine.

"You should know," I shot back. "You were the chancellor's son once, too." Not my finest moment.

I close my eyes and try to forget about Soren. As exhausted as I am, I'm unable to settle into any semblance of sleep. The room, clammy and cold, makes me wonder if this is what it was like living all those years in the tunnels of Thermopylae. For the thousandth time, I long for the comforts of my flat in Okaria.

While I'm longing, I can't help but summon an image of Remy's soft-as-silk mahogany skin. I imagine her wild fluff of curly brown hair on the pillow, those thick lashes resting against her cheekbones, her breathing soft and slow as the full length of her curls into me. My heart begins to thud in my chest, and I— *stop it!* Get a grip, Vale. Take a deep breath. *Think of something else.*

But it's no use. I can't shake the image swimming before my eyes, her bright smile as she looks up at me. I've caught her looking at me enough times to think something's changed since we all shared that tiny cabin together outside of the old city. *Maybe I should try to talk to her.* The idea sprouts in my head like a sapling. The whole time I've been at Normandy, I haven't once had a chance to talk to her alone. Not that I'd know what to say, but I'd at least like the chance to say something.

If only....

In a fit of frustration, I throw the sheet off my body and roll out of the hammock. I slip on my pants and pull a shirt over my head while stepping around Miah's hammock, avoiding his huge feet hanging off the end. I've been keeping my distance, giving Remy plenty of room to avoid me if she wanted, but now the idea of talking to her has taken root, and I can't shake it.

The hall is dark, lit only by a trail of faint yellow safety lights running along the floor. I find myself following the lights to the room where the rest of the team is sleeping. Softly, I turn the handle and push open the door. I peek through the crack, hoping desperately Soren isn't awake. When no one leaps at me from the shadows, I push the door open a little wider to let in more light. Jahnu and Kenzie have made a pallet of blankets on the floor and are sound asleep, wrapped in each other's arms. They have no idea how lucky they are. Well, maybe, after all we've been through, they do know.

I wait while my eyes adjust, then edge the door open a bit more and see Soren's blond hair. He's on his back, his arm covering his eyes. Next to him is an empty cot and beyond that two more empty ones. Jahnu and Kenzie's. And the darker blur in the corner, against the far wall, must be Bear. He's not formally on the mission team, but he refuses to be separated from Soren and Remy.

But there's no trace of Remy.

Okay. I know she has trouble sleeping, that she and Gabriel often sit together in the middle of the night while he writes and she draws. I head to the mess, knowing he spends time writing there after everyone else has gone to sleep. Maybe Remy's with him now.

Will I finally get to talk to her? My pace quickens. The night has gripped me with steely determination. Suddenly it feels like this cannot possibly wait until morning. I make my way through the dark corridors, but when I finally get to the mess hall, it's empty as a tomb.

Shit. My energy and enthusiasm deflates. A new fatigue washes over me, and I'm briefly confronted by the urge to go back to bed. But I remind myself that she's not in bed, that she's up and about, so now is the perfect time to find her alone. Maybe she's in the lounge. It's not much, but Normandy's lounge does have a few lumpy old couches and chairs, a surprisingly thick, woven rug, and a few decent reading lights. I snake my way down another dimly lit tunnel. There's a light on and a figure stretched out on one of the couches. With a blanket draped over her legs, I can only tell it's not a man. My heart skips a beat as I get closer. I step into the room and the figure lowers her book, an actual, old fashioned, printed-on-paper book.

"Hey," she says. Zoe.

"Can't sleep either?" I ask, my pulse a drumbeat of disappointment.

"Nah. I'm a night owl, ya know? Gotta finish my book."

"Hope it's a good one."

She turns it over and looks at the cover. "*A Tale of Two Cities.* You ever read Dickens?"

"Yeah," I say, surprised.

"If you're interested, you should take a look at Adrienne's library. She's got a huge stash of old books in the room off the back of her office."

Another surprise. "I didn't know. Thanks. By the way, do you know who's working the comm center?"

"Not me," she says with a soft laugh. "That's all I care about."

"Okay." I step out of the room, but then turn back to Zoe. "Thanks for the library tip."

Someone's always on duty in the comm center. When I lean around the doorframe, squinting into the room against the sudden light, I see that the woman on duty is asleep, her feet propped up on the desk, her head softly lolling back against the chair with her headphones askew. No sign of Remy. *What would she be doing in here anyway?*

Where is she?

I continue down the tunnel to where it opens into the wide underground cavern, where we've being doing a lot of our strength training. Nothing. It's dark as pitch. No one answers when I call out. I try Adrienne's little storeroom. If she's got a library, maybe Remy's in there. But the lights are out and there's no sound, no movement. By the time I've checked the storage closet where she spends so much time with Bear and where she keeps her paper and ink, the smaller meeting rooms, the supply center, the showers, the bathrooms, and the kitchen and mess hall for a second time—just in case I missed her the first time—I've broken out in a full-blown sweat. *Calm down, Vale.* I probably just missed her earlier. She was most likely in the bathroom when I stopped by her room. I'm sure she's back in bed now.

I stand in front of the door, my heart now ricocheting against my ribs. The door is exactly where I left it. I peek in anyway, but her cot is still empty.

There's only one more place to look. Maybe she's in the bunkroom with her dad. I pad as quickly as possible to the room where Gabriel and Rhinehouse sleep. The door is already slightly ajar, so I push it a bit wider and peer in. Two cots. Two men. No Remy.

I lean against the wall and take a deep breath, processing. *Slow down.* There's nowhere else on base to check—all the other tunnels have been sealed and are totally inaccessible. The hovercars and Normandy's one serviceable airship are all kept well camouflaged above ground; there's no hangar down here. Where could she have gone? *Surely she didn't leave!* The thought of her out in the Wilds by herself at night leaves me gasping for air, as if Aulion followed a punch to the gut with a hard right to the chin.

I plow through the tunnels, back toward the main hatch. Panting, hands shaking, I check the keypad to code the doors open and shut, and sure enough, the computer indicates the last time the door was opened to the outside world was one hour and forty-seven minutes ago. Long after lights out on base, long after everyone was supposed to be safely ensconced in bed.

She's gone.

Blind with panic and worry, I fall back on procedure like a good soldier. "We have codes for three levels of emergency," Adrienne said during our orientation, "and depending on the severity of the event, you'll enter the correct alarm code at any one of the key pads located around the base." We're not under attack and we're not about to flood the tunnels and drown from a break in our main water tank, both scenarios Adrienne had described in detail during our security briefing. I punch in the alarm code for a Level Three Security Event and immediately the lights in the tunnel blink on and a recorded voice blares out into the empty hallway, reverberating against the cold concrete walls: "Key Pad One Engaged. Initiate Level Three Emergency Procedures."

I tear back towards the dormitories, knowing everyone will be pouring into the hallway, sleepy and confused, wondering what the hell is going on.

Sure enough, the first person I run into—almost literally—is Soren.

"What the fuck's going on?" he snarls. His Bolt, slung across his bare chest, is pointed straight at me.

"Remy's gone," I blurt. "She's not on base. I've looked everywhere." He stares at me for a second, and then his eyes narrow and the look on his face transforms from angry and bleary-eyed to vicious and deadly focused. He whips his Bolt around his back, grabs me by my shirt and slams me up against the wall. His spare hand finds its way to my throat.

"What did you do to her?" he demands, his voice a guttural whisper, a threat. "I swear if you—"

"What the hell do you think you're you doing, Skaarsgard?" Soren's head snaps to the right, and I follow, breathless. The Director, her clothes rumpled and her normally-straight hair jagged around the edges, looks ready to kill. Adrienne rushes up behind her and Hodges stands at her side. Soren lets me go and backs away.

"Remy's gone," he says, his face still contorted with anger. "This … Vale … he must have—"

"I was the one who entered the alarm code," I cut in, trying to save myself from Soren's damning words. "Remy's disappeared from base. I was trying to find her. I don't know where she's gone, but she's not here."

Footsteps echo through the tunnels, and soon Eli and Firestone—sleepy, confused, and hung over—along with Miah, Zoe, and several members of the Normandy staff show up.

"Remy's gone," Soren says abruptly to Eli who stares at him, one hand in his hair, only vaguely conscious of what's going on. Recognition finally dawns on him, though, and his eyes widen as he stares between the three of us.

"What do you mean 'gone?'" he demands, disbelieving.

"She's nowhere on base," I confirm. "And the door outside to the main hatch was opened almost two hours ago."

"Not a chance in hell." Soren turns on me again. "No way she would leave without telling me or Eli. Or Gabriel. Where the hell would she go? You staged this whole thing. Why did you just happen to be the one to realize she's gone? You could have killed her and played us all for the fool, Orleán," he spits. I almost want to laugh at the absurdity of his accusation. I glance around, looking for allies. Firestone's leaning against the wall, trying to keep his body upright and obviously wondering what he's doing out of bed. Eli's eyes have narrowed into slits, as though any trust I might have earned from him is now in question.

"Don't be irrational, Soren. Vale would never hurt Remy." Miah speaks up, shouldering his way past Eli, going eye-to-eye with Soren. "Believe me. He wouldn't hurt her."

"It does seem suspicious, Vale," the Director interjects, "but we don't want to leap to conclusions."

"How can you take his side? This doesn't seem like an elaborate set-up to you?" Soren says to Miah. "Remy disappears and Vale's conveniently the first one to notice? And you," he turns to the Director, "say you don't want to 'leap to conclusions?' You just want to keep your precious pawn in this game, keep your fucking military advantage." He turns back to me, his tone quiet and deadly. "Your family has destroyed everything I've ever cared about. If you hurt Remy, I'll slit your throat."

"Soren, I'm just stating the facts, whether you like them or not. Vale would never hurt Remy." Miah makes this pronouncement slowly, as if each word is a separate and distinct declaration. *How did I get lucky enough to have a friend like Jeremiah Sayyid?*

"Vale didn't do anything to Remy," Jahnu says. He and Kenzie have materialized out of nowhere. Everyone bends toward them. "Bear's gone, too. His cot's empty. I heard him get up in the night, but I must have gone back to sleep and didn't realize he never came back."

"When the lights came on, we noticed his cot," Kenzie said. "There're a few blankets piled on it, but no Bear. We just searched the room, and looked for his pack, but everything he owned is gone."

"Okay. Let's take this one step at a time," the Director says. "Vale, what were you doing up and about at two in the morning?"

I swallow.

"I couldn't sleep. I hadn't talked to Remy—you know, alone—since the night after Brinn died. I wanted to—" I trail off and a hush settles over everyone as Gabriel and Rhinehouse round the corner.

Gabriel stops. "She's gone, isn't she?" he asks, his voice quiet. I lower my eyes. I don't want to be the one to say it out loud, to say it to the man who's already lost half his family: *yes, your daughter is gone.*

But as I drop my eyes I notice a scrap of paper in his hand. He gives it to Eli, apparently unable to read the words aloud himself. His lower lip trembles, his jaw clenching and unclenching as Eli starts.

"Dad, it's time for your little bird to fly the coop. I'm going to continue the mission to the Farms you and Mom were on, and Bear is coming with me. It's clear the battles to be fought here are not mine, and that there are other things in my future. I wish you could have come with me, but this is my mission now,

*my calling. I'll keep a low profile and stay out of trouble. I will send word as
soon as possible. I love you.*
                        - Your Little Bird."

Eli's hand drops as he finishes reading, staring at the floor. A heavy pause
hangs in the air.

Alongside the fear crawling up my spine is a swelling of pride at her resolve
to take control of her own destiny. I'm envious. One thing Soren said is true;
I am a pawn. I was a pawn in my parents' game when they installed me in the
position of head of the Seed Bank Protection Project. Now the Director is
using me for her own ends.

I'm going after them, I think and when Eli looks up at me, I realize I've said
it out loud.

And then Gabriel's knees give way, he sinks in front of me. Eli catches the
older man in his arms, hugging him as tenderly as any son would. I only now
realize how fully they see each other as family. The acknowledgment that Remy
is gone washes over both of them like a tide. Then Eli looks up at me.

"I'm coming with you."

"Neither of you are authorized to leave this outpost until I give the
command," the Director snaps, but she might as well be speaking from another
world.

"If you're going, I'm damn well going, too," Soren growls.

"None of you are going anywhere!" the Director shouts. The three of us fall
silent. Gabriel straightens up, away from Eli's protective embrace. He looks at
the Director, pleading and desperate.

"Please," he says, his voice hoarse and broken, nothing like the booming,
charismatic oratory of the Poet Laureate I remember from Sector broadcasts
years ago. "Cillian. Let them go. Let them bring her back. I can't lose her, too."

She watches him for several minutes, surveying him and Eli together.
Finally she speaks.

"The three of you take one other person." She nods at Kenzie. "You'll lead a
second team of four. Pick your team. Split up to cover more ground. Find them
and bring them back."

"What if they've taken a hovercar?" I ask.

The Director turns to Zoe. "Go check Camera Two." As Zoe runs off, the
Director turns to Gabriel. "If she's taken one of the hovercars, it's going to be
a lot harder to track her down, and she'll have had time to put a lot of distance
between us. You have to be prepared for that." Then she locks her gaze on me.

"You've got seventy-two hours. The Flora mission can't wait."

Eli, Soren, and I survey each other warily. Distrust in Soren's eyes, hesitant cooperation in Eli's.

"Understood," I say.

"Good."

Moments later, I'm sitting in my hammock, lacing up my boots, wondering who Eli will have picked as our fourth team member. I hear a sound at the door and look up to see him walking in.

"Just to be clear," he says, his voice low as he grabs his own boots, "we're ignoring the Director's orders and going out together. We're not splitting up."

"Soren agree to this?"

"Yeah. And we're taking the airship."

"But the Director hasn't given us—"

"I don't give a flying fuck what the Director says," Eli growls, and I am vividly reminded of what Eli's problem with authority was like even before Tai died and he went a little crazy.

"Oh," Eli says, glancing at me as though his outburst had never happened. "And Miah and Firestone are tag teaming as pilots. I want my—*our*—whole team together on this. Remy's too important to us—to *all* of us." He looks at me pointedly as he emphasizes the word.

I stand, pulling on my jacket. I stare down at him, both admiring and critical of his protectiveness towards his surrogate sister.

"Have you thought about the fact that maybe she left to get away from everyone telling her what to do?" I pause, trying to let my words sink in. "That she might not want any of us to come after her?"

"I have thought about that," Eli responds, not looking up from his boots. "But guess what? Sometimes we don't get what we want."

11 — REMY

The skyline of another old city emerges in the creeping sunlight. The map says this one is Syracuse, a town once known for its ROR industry: robotic organism replication. Bacteria, viruses, parasites, parasitoids—Syracuse built an industry around churning out these artificial microorganisms for medicinal and technological purposes. It's a technology that's been mostly lost to us, and robotic organisms represent a level of complexity OAC scientists haven't been able to replicate.

As I drive, I take in the contour lines, shadows, and negative space fading into points against the horizon. Morning sun dapples early spring growth in a light shimmer. The chaos of reclaimed nature against the ruins of human structures. Every time I come into a new landscape, my hand itches to draw it.

"Are we there yet?" Bear yawns next to me, not a little bit of whining in his voice. I laugh.

"Are you *trying* to sound like a child?"

"Hey, I'm tired. You were the one who dragged me out of bed at that forsaken hour of the morning."

He's right. I woke up him up this morning at 1:45 AM, just as we had planned. I hadn't slept a lick all night, kept on edge by wild images running through my head, the excitement, and anxiety, of a mission I finally believe in. A mission that feels *my own*. A mission I am going to tackle without Eli, Jahnu, Kenzie, and Soren by my side.

The night after the Director announced that Vale was going to lead the mission to Seed Bank Flora, I approached Bear with an alternate proposal.

"We need to start a revolution," I told him. "It's time to get the Farm and factory workers involved." Bear just stared at me blankly for a minute, while I cornered him in a darkened hallway as far away from any meeting room as I could get.

"*Tu parles du quoi?*" he demanded, as usual sinking back into Old French when he's on edge. I couldn't translate directly, but I got the gist of it. *What the hell are you talking about?*

"We need to go to the Farms. We have to talk to the people directly—we have to take this battle to them. There's no point waging the Director's 'slow but steady' war when the Sector could find out where we are at any time and drop the entire Black Ops squadron on us. We'll be dead in our sleep. You and me, Bear—if we go together, with your connections on the Farms and my art, we can take the revolution to them."

They dont *want* a revolution." He almost laughed. "They're perfectly happy to keep doing what they're doing. Not many people think to ask questions. Not many *can*. You believe we can walk in there and change their minds when they don't even *know* their own minds?"

"If anyone can do it, it's you and me. Think about it. At your Farm, the people will know you, they'll listen to you. They'll remember Sam. They'll remember what the Sector did to him. How the Bosses forced him into the silos for asking too many questions. They know that can happen to anyone. They'll listen to us when they know what the danger is."

Bear shook his head, staring at the floor, refusing to meet my eyes.

"I don't know, Remy. I don't think it's that easy. We can't just walk in there and tell them to think something different and expect them to listen." He took a deep breath. "It took Sam almost two years after your sister died to convince me to listen to him. You think they're going to believe us because we have good stories and pretty pictures?"

I knew then that he'd been watching me draw, that he'd seen the drawings I'd been working on in the last few weeks. A portrait of Tai done entirely out of tiny flowers; a poem my father wrote where the verses were growing up out of the ground like seedlings; and the most violent, a man biting into a skull like an apple, red blood dripping down his chin instead of juice, the skull illustrated using the elegant twisting double helix of DNA.

"I don't know if they'll listen to us," I said quietly. "But if they do, we've got a hell of a better shot at changing things than if we don't go at all."

He thought about that for a second, staring down at me hesitantly.

"I don't know, Remy," he said, finally.

I sighed.

"Just think about it. Okay? Just think about it."

He nodded and slipped away, while I paced back and forth in the now-empty hall and wondered how in the hell I would be able to carry on my mother's mission without his help, without his insight and experience at the Farms.

What's left for me here? I asked myself over and over again. I'm a good shot and a fast runner, but that's it. LOTUS is Eli's project. The Seed Bank mission is now Vale's. What can I offer that no one else can?

The answer always comes back to my parents' mission to the Farms. Carry the message of the Resistance, spread awareness, help where possible. *Spread the message to the people through your art*, my father said. What can I offer the Resistance? Over and over again, I came back to that one thing: I can be the messenger.

Just when I'd given up hope, Bear approached me and told me he was reconsidering. I was ecstatic. But he still wasn't an easy convert.

"You think it's going to be easy, Remy, but it's not," he warned. "You're going to have to be patient. We're not just going to walk in there, show them your drawings, and make them think differently about things they've been taught since they were *enfants*. That's not gonna happen."

I nodded, but I felt nothing but excitement roiling inside.

"We'll be patient, Bear. As patient as we can."

He shook his head. "I want to do this with you, but I don't think you have any idea what we're going to be walking into."

"I'll have you to help me navigate the Farm culture."

"And you'll listen to me? Go slow when I say?" I nod, and he shakes his head like he doesn't believe me, but then a smile tugs at his lips. "So who else is coming?"

"No one," I said. "Just us."

"What?" he asked. "Why not?"

I shrugged, looking off at the wall behind us. How to explain? How to tell him that this is something I can't do with Eli, Soren, Vale, or my father watching over my shoulder? How to tell him that this is something I have to do for my mother's sake, for Tai's sake, for myself? How to tell him that this has to be my mission, unswayed by any of my friends and family, however close they may be?

"They have their own goals and their own tasks," I said, finally. "They have their projects. But you and I—we can be a part of their projects, or we can create our own, and have a chance at making real progress."

He nodded. "Okay."

"You still want to do it?"

"Yes," he said. "I thought about it last night. I think you're right. Someone has to tell them the truth. And it might as well be us. No one else in the Resistance is making an effort to include them."

I smiled as he looked down at me, his body still slightly too big for him, uncertain but eager.

"So," he asked, energy seeping into his voice, "when do we leave?"

"As soon as we're ready. We've got a lot of packing and planning to do and we have to do it without drawing attention. If they know what we're up to, they'll stop us."

And so, two weeks later, we find ourselves out in the middle of the Wilds again, this time far better equipped than we were when we were tromping in the cold weeks ago. Spring shows its face in blooming daffodils and green-tipped grass as we pass through this crumbling ruin of a forgotten city. We're headed toward Round Barn where Bear's from, and this is the quickest route accessible in the hovercar we borrowed—okay, stole—from Normandy. It's decrepit and tops out at sixty kilometers per hour, but at least it's got decent cloaking, so we're hoping we won't run into the same disaster we did with our hovercar outside of our safehouse. So we drive through these overgrown streets, lined with sky-high trees growing where the city once sprouted. Dust to dust, ashes to ashes. The city is now reborn, verdant with second-growth forest, populated with buzzing insects, scurrying squirrels, and singing birds. Out of the ruins, new life is born.

Bear nods off in the seat next to me. I pull out my grandfather's compass, click the tiny button and the burnished gold opens in my hand. I check our direction and confirm that we are heading northeast, and then I click the compass open and closed again several times, relishing the pressure against my fingers and palm. It's comforting to have it with me, like a protective talisman. It feels as though a piece of each member of my family is tied up somehow into the little spinning needle, as though the compass holds fragments of their lost souls. I run my fingers along my grandfather's initials engraved at the bottom. If I follow the compass, I might one day find him, my mom, and Tai.

I pocket it and turn my attention back to the map, returning my focus to the drive. I wish this hovercar had a programmable route I could punch in like we used to do in Okaria. Then I could curl up and sleep. But there are no comprehensive 3-D map systems out here, no nav drones, no remote air traffic control to make sure I get safely from place to place. I can't deny that I miss that security and comfort. But the skies of Okaria weren't the only thing being controlled and manipulated. Our bodies and identities were, too.

As tired as I am, the slow pace of the drive is calming, freeing even. Whatever is over the next hill, beyond the next bend in the road, is a revelation. Best of all, there are no more underground tunnels. I remember lying on the couch in the Chancellor's mansion as Vale told me about reading a book from the Old World. He said people used to drive their old-fashioned wheeled cars—with a steering wheel, how primitive—from one side of the American continent to the other, just to feel the "freedom of the open road." That's how I feel now, winding through this abandoned city, free, finally, of the expectations of those back at base. *The freedom to reclaim my destiny, just as nature is reclaiming this city.*

Three hours later, we're deep in the Wilds, following the barest remnants of an old highway as we arc down around the southern border of the Sector. My v-scroll map tells me we're almost there. Bear is stirring awake as I struggle to keep from nodding off myself.

"You okay, Remy?" Bear asks, rubbing his eyes. "You want me to drive for a while?" He's been asking me that since we first started even though he's never driven a hovercar, I'm reluctant to let him behind the gauges.

"It's okay. We're almost there. You can help me look for a good campsite. Keep your eyes out."

"I don't know how you're not tired."

"I am tired. I just want to get out, set up camp, and get my sleep horizontally."

"Remember we'll be in more danger the closer we get to the Farm, right?" he points out. "Security at Round Barn—" he means Farm Ten, but they've all got idyllic, agrarian nicknames "—was lax when I left. But who knows now. Might be drones and Boss men around the perimeter. Won't be safer there than it is here."

May be more dangerous, but at least I won't be in danger of getting run off the road by an inexperienced driver," I tease.

"How hard can it be?" he asks, gesturing to the control board. "There's three dials and a steerstick. Farm equipment's more complicated than that."

"It takes practice to keep the hovers balanced over rough ground so you don't veer off into a tree." I change the subject. "Let's go over the security again."

He shrugs, his face clouded, as though facing an unhappy memory.

"It's not as tight as at other Farms, from what we ever heard. There's a fence and a few gates big enough for hovercars and trucks, but none of it's real well maintained, and the fences aren't hard to climb or dig under. Aside from what I mentioned before, drones patrol the perimeter and Bosses keeping watch on the inside. Heard a story from a transfer that they got high fences and guard towers at Two Lakes, by Okaria proper. Said it was for the wild animals. Sam couldn't figure how they'd have dangerous animals so close to the city and none near Round Barn."

Suddenly I'm not even tired. Imagining what Round Barn will be like captivates me. When I was younger, we toured of a few of the Farms after my father was named Poet Laureate. He did poetry readings and sometimes he'd show off my artwork. The workers seemed to like seeing me at his side. The Sector always brags about how it supports the arts as well as the sciences. They like to promote the idea that anyone from the Farms could become like any of us in the capital, could rise up and become a celebrated artist. Of course, what none of the laborers on the Farms knew was that they were being fed chemicals designed to suppress their creative abilities, their spatial imaging, their imaginations. If my father had been born on a Farm, he would never have had a chance at becoming a famous poet.

When I visited, the Farms seemed like havens of tranquility where everyone was fed plenty and clothed well. It was an egalitarian dream. Peaceful, happy people glad to be doing their part to keep the Sector strong. Maybe they were that way once, naturally, of their own accord. But what I didn't realize, until my family joined the Resistance, is however idyllic it was in the past, now the workers don't have a choice now. They can't even *think* about doing anything any differently. And if a glimmer of individual thought shines through, like it did with Sam, that's easily taken care of.

Bear points out the window to a hill in the distance. "Good flat spot up there along that ridge, maybe. High ground and far enough off this stretch of old road to avoid anyone coming or going. And plenty of tree cover to stay hidden."

I nod, surveying the ridge.

"The hovercar won't make it up there, though. The angle's too steep. We'll have to leave the car down here and carry our gear up."

We survey the area until we find a gulley suitable for hiding the hovercar. I lower it to the ground and shut it off. We empty the car of our gear—mostly lightweight camping gear, food provisions, some radio equipment, light firearms, and the hand grenades I stole from Normandy's armory. I throw a shimmer blanket over the car for camouflage. Bear and I shoulder our equipment bags and trudge up the steep ridge line to flatter ground.

After we set up camp, Bear munches on oat bars and venison jerky while I lay out our bedrolls.

"We should both get some sleep today," I say, checking the thin wristwatch I brought from Normandy. "It's one in the afternoon, plenty of time to rest before night sets in. Then, I think we should go exploring. I want you to show me the Farm while it's dark and quiet. You can show me your old home."

Bear shudders, looking pale.

"Wouldn't hardly call it home anymore," he says.

"Are you anxious to see your friends? The ones you've told me about?"

He nods. "Won't be too easy finding them on the inside, though, but we'll get through to them somehow."

"You figured out how we should start the conversation?"

Bear stares at me a second before responding, as if trying to put his words together in his head.

"The people I'm thinking of, they'll listen if I tell 'em something. Not the brightest of folk, but then, neither am I. But the rest of 'em—they'll be harder to get through to. But you made all them notes and drew those pictures. We've got plenty of good speeches. And when the time comes, we'll tell the truth, I guess."

Tell the truth, I guess. I nod. *Words to live by.*

"See there? That's where the Dieticians' lab is. All the little cabins are where we live."

The moon isn't full tonight, but it's not far off, and I brought two weeks worth of our infrared contacts for both of us. I showed him how to put them in, and how to blink rapidly three times to shift between the infrared and the visible light spectrums. It took him an hour, but I think he's got the hang of it.

"So the little buildings are where the workers live. And there's a compound—that, there—where the Boss men and women stay at night."

He points out a few other buildings until I feel comfortable with the general layout.

"Who do you want to try to talk to first? We should try to contact them as soon as possible. Tomorrow morning, maybe."

"One of Sam's old friends, name's Luis. And a girl I used to talk to. Another one of the ones who asked questions. Fierce, she was. Rose, is her name. Rose and Luis are good friends."

"What do you think is the best way to get a message to them?"

Bear stares at the plain below us, his eyes narrowing as he considers my question.

"Been thinking about that, and I got an idea. Used to be an old Boss we all liked, Joral. Real nice, he was the one who let me take Sam to your parents when he got hurt. He won't like it if I talk to him—just cause he's nice don't mean he doesn't support the Sector, he'll probably turn me in—but you can go. You can find him and ask him to get a message to Rose and Luis." Bear grins at me in the moonlight. "'Specially if you give him some of that chocolate you brought along with us, he always liked that stuff."

I consider this idea.

"How will I know it's him?"

"He's real striking. Sharp grey hair always sticking up no matter what he does, and a big, huge, honker. You see that nose, you know it's him."

"Should I pretend to be a Farm worker?"

"No," he says. "He'll know you aren't. Sometimes people who aren't with the Farm come and go 'round about here. So long as they aren't Outsiders, some Bosses let 'em alone. That's what your parents did. If you pretend you're one of them, or maybe tell him you met Luis or Rose on a market day."

"What's a market day?"

"Once a season, we have a gathering, hear some music, and socialize for a time. Of course, it's all organized by the Farm Boss, but, sometimes folk from around join in. Tell Joral that you're passin' through and just want to see how they're doin'. Maybe he'll pass a message to them."

"Okay," I nod. "What should the message be?"

"How about one of your drawings? That one of Sam you did. That'll get their attention."

I watch Bear, his mouth set in a sad little frown, staring out over the place he once called home.

"We'll use that one, then. I'll go in the morning, at first light, before work starts. I'll tell them we want to meet them tomorrow at twilight." I clasp Bear's hand and smile at him. "We're going to do this, Bear. We'll avenge Sam, my mother, Tai. We'll do it together."

Bear smudges dirt on my face and charcoal around my eyes, trying to disguise my features. I wrap a woolen shawl over my head to cover my hair. It'll be hot come midday, but I'm not planning on having this excursion last more than an hour.

"Try not to talk like you usually do," Bear is saying, coaching me on how to blend in. "You sound like you're from Okaria, not one of the peasant folk who wander the Wilds. And Joral'll try to convince you to stay on the Farm. Sometimes people who pass by end up joining a Farm just 'cause it seems nice to have a warm bed, hot water, and plenty of food. He'll try to talk you into staying. Just tell him you got a husband or something waiting for you out in the woods and he shouldn't bother you after that."

"But I shouldn't say I'm in a group, right?"

"No. Then he'll think you're an Outsider, and he might send you off or call in some more Boss men to find out where the rest of the group is."

It shouldn't surprise me how suspicious the Bosses are of the Outsiders. The massacre at the SRI that killed my sister wasn't the only crime that's been attributed to the Outsiders over the years; the Sector finds it convenient to blame mysterious and violent incidents on the Outsiders. With so much hatred directed their way through Sector propaganda, it's easy to see why people are so afraid of them. Yet, from what Bear says, the fear seems even more pronounced on the Farms than it was in the city. Maybe the propaganda against the Outsiders has increased since I've been gone.

Bear stops smudging charcoal around the edges of my eyes, and sits back to admire his handiwork.

"You look nice," he says. "Like the fancy ladies at the Solstice balls."

I shoot him a wry smile.

"I've got dirt all over my face."

"Well, yes, but...."

"Let's hope no one else thinks I look like a socialite from Okaria."

"They won't," he says, and cracks a wide smile. "Not with that dirt on your face."

I push myself to my feet and look one last time at the drawing I did of Sam, as best I could remember him, his face wreathed with spring flowers and autumn leaves. I roll it up and drip a bit of melted wax from one of the few candles we stole from Normandy, and press the scroll closed. A seal, like from the ancient world. But unlike the ancients who used signet rings or cylinder seals, neither one of us want our identification known until the scroll is opened. So instead of pressing one of our fingers in the wax, we press it closed with a leaf. Once it's unrolled, Rose will see the message Bear scrawled in the corner.

Beaver Creek, midnight. A.B. The initials of his real name, Antoine Baier.

"They'll come," he says, a hitch in his voice. "They were like family. They'll come."

We walk around the edge of the cleared land, sticking to the shadows and trees. Just because our jackets help hide our thermal signature from drones, doesn't mean the guards have gone blind. I'll have to take off my jacket soon enough—of those who wander the Wilds, only Outsiders and Resistance fighters have heat-cloaking clothing, and I don't want to be associated with either group. By the time the sun is fully up and we can see the stirrings of activity in the camp, we've found what looks to be a footpath that leads into the cleared plain of the Farm.

"This is how some people get in and out," Bear says. "Not many people know about it, though. You get outta *le foret*, you'll see there's a slit cut in the fence. Easy enough to push through."

"Do the Enforcers know about this?" I ask, wondering at the fact that this glaring oversight has gone uncorrected for so long. At my side, Bear shrugs.

"Joral does. Maybe a few others. Some of them aren't so bad. Just doing their job."

"Won't they know I'm an intruder?"

Bear laughs.

"You aren't gonna go in that way right now. That's for tonight, when we go to meet Rose and Luis, if you can get the message through. Right now, you're gonna go up through the pedestrian gate and ask real nice if you can talk to Joral. Like I said, as long as they don't think you're an Outsider, they'll let you come and go as you please. Might even give you some food if you look desperate enough."

I stare at Bear, wondering if I've gone completely insane. I, Remy Alexander, daughter of Okaria's Poet Laureate, member of an active "terrorist network", escaped prisoner of the Sector, am going to walk right up to the gates of a Farm and ask to be let in. They better not recognize me.

Bear leads me a little ways further through the trees. I take off my jacket and hand it to him, my heart pounding.

"Remember, you're the last person they'll be expecting," he says, a serious expression on his face. "I'll be waiting." I smile reassuringly, trying not to show how nervous I am. It feels like walking into the maw of a giant beast.

"If I'm more than two hours—"

"I lay low for twenty-four hours," he interrupts. "If you're still not back, I radio Normandy."

Taking a deep breath, I smile and nod.

"You'll be fine," he says.

I turn and walk off, tightening the shawl secured around my frizzy hair, trying not to touch my face for fear of smudging Bear's makeup job. I jump down out of the undergrowth and onto the cleared path, checking quickly around me to see if guards are watching. I follow the little cleared path, wide enough for two to walk side-by-side, right up to the gate, where an Enforcer with bored eyes and a handheld Bolt greets me.

"Name."

"Anna Renault." My heart sounds like drumbeats in my chest. But the guard simply touches a few buttons on a plasma in front of him without looking at me.

"Passing through or visiting?"

"Passing."

"Okarian citizen?"

"No."

"Any affiliations?" He wants to know if I'm with the Outsiders, like someone would just announce that.

"Brother working on Farm Eight as of three months ago."

"Is that who you're visiting?"

"*Non.* My *mari* and I live fifty kilometers on the other side."

He nods.

"Who are you here to see?"

"I hope to speak with Joral."

The Enforcer nods and then speaks into his headset. "Some woman from the Wilds named Anna Renault here to speak to Joral." He keeps looking at me. "Yes. Okay," he says into the handset. "Stay right on the main path until you reach Outpost One. He's stationed near there. Go on, and be quick. He hasn't got all day." He gestures half-heartedly toward the Farm as the gate opens and I exhale an enormous breath that carries my tense shoulders down with it.

Inside the gate, a female Enforcer presses her hands up and down my sides, checking for weapons. They'll allow small knives through, he said, but nothing more sophisticated.

"Saw an Outsider shot on sight for carrying a crossbow," he had said as though it were an everyday occurrence.

"How did you know it was an Outsider?"

"Carried a crossbow. Only Outsiders have crossbows, or bows. Least ways that's what I was always told."

I hung a skinning knife on my belt when I was dressing this morning, thinking it would be more suspicious if I didn't have one, as they'd wonder why a lone woman was traveling the woods unarmed. But it doesn't make me feel any safer as the female Enforcer lets me through to face the vast, open swath of the Farm.

"Make sure you sign out at the gate when you're done with your business," she says.

I nod and head into the heart of the Farm. Laid out in red brick, like the garden at my parents' home in Okaria, the main path is lined with dormant strawberry patches, interwoven with sage, rosemary, parsley, bay, and some varieties of sprouting spring greens. A tiny creek, an irrigation channel, flows alongside the path I walk. A budding orchard peeks up over the hill to my left.

I keep my head up and focus on the task at hand. I try to remember what Bear said about Joral. *Stark grey hair, enormous nose.* I watch for any sign of someone by that description. But as far as I can see, the land is empty.

Past the strawberries and herbs, I turn right at a fork and come across some workers training growing vines to wooden stakes. I make eye contact with a girl about my size. She straightens, watching me. Her expression is unreadable and unnerving, and I try to ignore her gaze as I pass by.

I marvel at the sheer size and scope of the Farms. It looked big from far away, but it's positively huge now that I'm walking through it. I'd never quite thought about how big the Farms must be in order to provide food for the entire population of Okaria. The brick path I'm on has branched out several times, and every time I've diligently kept along the right-side path. Even though Bear tried to orient me to the layout, it seems much more expansive than I thought. I can see a field of marshy ground that looked like rice paddies, wide-open wheat fields and wildflowers for honeybees, countless nut and fruit trees, an olive grove, and a vineyard, terraced into the side of a steep hill, and at least fifty different types of vegetable plants I couldn't begin to identify.

Just when I'm beginning to despair of ever finding the first outpost, thinking that I'd somehow missed it or made a wrong turn, I spot a few structures in the distance. As I get closer, they turn into little houses, scattered seemingly at random, interspersed with wild grasses and big trees. And there—I recognize that larger building. That's the Dietician's lab that Bear showed me last night. I turn up towards my right, and sure enough, the forest here bends around much closer to the cleared land. I put my hand over my eyes for shade and study the landscape. I can see the ridge where Bear and I were perched, staring around at the terrain below with our binoculars.

One last right turn along the path and see him. Joral, in a green Enforcer's uniform, standing, arms crossed, in front of a small, nondescript building.

"*Tu es Joral, s'il te plait?*" Please, are you Joral?

"I am," he says gruffly, not bothering with French. *From Okaria, then,* I think, trying to get a sense of him. A fair few Okarians from the capital don't bother learning the Old French, considering it beneath them. *Who needs it anymore? they ask. Everyone in Okaria speaks Modern Sector English.* "Are you Anna? What do you want?"

"Do you know Rose?" I ask. Bear told me it would be safer if I asked for the girl—that way no one would suspect any romantic attachment, which would be sure to get me thrown out.

"I do," he responds. "You passing through?"

"Yes, but I've got a mes—something for her," I say, chiding myself. "A gift. I'd like to give it to her."

"How do you know Rose?"

"Met her last time I passed through, walking along the perimeter. I'd fallen in a gopher hole, twisted my ankle. She told me about a doctor that comes around sometimes, and I want to thank her."

"You come here often?"

"No. Sometimes."

"You looking for a home? You like it here? You're welcome to stay. We'll give you a proper bed, and food, and all." I smile, remembering what Bear said. *He'll try to convince you to stay on the Farm.*

"Got a man waiting for me on the other side," I respond. "*Mon mari.*" My husband.

"Ah," he says, chewing at the side of his mouth, eyeing me thoughtfully. His hair sticks up as though he's been electrocuted. Bear was right, his nose dominates his face. It almost makes him look less threatening, despite the suspicious frown.

"All right," he says, at length. "What have you got for her?"

"Promise me you'll give it to her."

"I'll promise when I see what it is."

I hesitate, trying to look afraid and unsure. From the pocket of my sweater I pull out the rolled piece of paper. He gasps audibly.

"Where'd you get paper like that?" he asks.

"An old factory out in the Wilds. Way south."

"Hmm." He looks intrigued, but doesn't say more.

"You'll give it to her?"

"Don't see any harm in it."

Thank you," I say, handing the scroll to him. I also take a piece of chocolate and hold it out as an offering. "Please make sure Rose gets this. She was kind to me and it's very important that I give her something in return. And please take this, for your trouble."

Still gnawing at the inside of his lip, his eyebrows shoot up when he sees the bite of chocolate. He nods his thanks, takes the paper from my hands, and turns away from me, sauntering off between the little houses. I stare after him, before I turn to leave, releasing the tension in my chest with a slow breath.

Now, all we can do is wait.

12 — REMY

Spring 5, Sector Annum 106, 23h30
Gregorian Calendar: March 24

Bear and I inch down through the trees, trying not to stumble along the steep ridge in the darkness. Infrared contacts are very nice and all, but they're nothing compared to good old sunlight when it comes to avoiding large roots that threaten to send you headlong into a thorny briar.

At the fence line, Bear shows me the slit through the mesh fence. What could have been strong enough to cut through these fibers? I don't know much about material science, but this is the same fencing that guards the perimeters to several of the Seed Banks. Eli told me once it would take a laser or synthetic diamond to get through it. Doesn't seem likely any Farm workers would have access to tech like that. *Outsiders?* I wonder. *Or someone on the Farm or from the Sector interested in helping the workers?*

Or both? I think, remembering Chan-Yu.

We slip through and Bear leads me through the Farm at a light jog, his movements those of someone who's been over this ground a thousand times. I quiet the stream of questions in my head, and focus on keeping my breathing quiet and my heart rate low.

When I see a run of cattails and reeds up ahead and hear the rushing water of a nearby creek, Bear pulls up short and drops to a crouch.

"Welcome to Beaver Creek. See anyone?" he asks. I shake my head in response. I check my watch. It's fifteen minutes before midnight. Plenty of time.

We wait, as patiently as we can. I hope against hope Joral passed on the message, and we'll be met by Bear's old friends and not a group of Sector soldiers ready to take me back to the capital for more of Philip Orleán's "fresh figs."

After a few minutes, dim splashes of color appear in the distance. Heat signatures. As the figures draw closer, they crystallize into the forms of a man and a woman.

"It's them!" Bear whispers, making to leap up, to signal to them, but I push a hand into his shoulder. *Not yet.*

Soon enough, they're not even ten meters away, and I can feel Bear trembling at my side. I can make out their faces from here: the man's short, snub nose and deep-set eyes, the woman's delicate, narrow bones. I keep my eyes on the surroundings, reminding myself that this could still be a trap, that soldiers could be hidden in the surrounding brush waiting for us to give ourselves away.

"Rose!" Bear squeaks, and the two workers jerk their heads around towards us, and Bear jumps up and almost leaps at them, hugging them both, letting out hushed cries of happiness. As far as I can tell, there's no one else with them.

"J'ai pense que tu etait mort," Luis says, in a rich baritone.

"Est si bon de te voir, friend," Rose says, the words tumbling out in a mix of Old French and North American, as they embrace yet again, exchanging kisses on both cheeks and with smiles to rival Eli's at the best of times. I can't keep up with the language—I barely know what they're saying. I smile nervously and stand off to the side, suddenly aware of how Bear must have felt these last few months, constantly surrounded by strangers, in over his head in a new world.

"Qui est ta amie?" Rose says, coming over to me and kissing me on both cheeks. My heart seems to sigh in relief as I realize they haven't recognized me—that Bear and I have time to frame our story, to tell it how we want, instead of facing a barrage of questions about why I'm here on the Farms and where I've been for the last three years.

"This is Remy," Bear says, going on in American English, smiling at me brightly so I know the linguistic switch is for my benefit. "She's my friend from the Re—"

"From the Wilds," I say, cutting Bear off. I don't want either of us to associate ourselves with the Resistance before we know where these two stand. They may be Bear's friends, but that doesn't mean they'll be friends of the Resistance. "Bear and I are traveling together."

"Why'd you come back?" Rose asks Bear.

"Why'd you leave?" Luis demands. "When we saw your initials on that drawing...."

"And where's Sam?"

Bear bows his head. A chill runs through my bones that I know has more to do with the knife I buried in Sam's throat than the spring cold in the air.

"Sam ... Sam is dead."

Another pause, an extended silence where I hold my breath and wait to see if my name will come into play in Bear's retelling of this tale.

"How? When?" Luis asks, finally.

"It was my fault," Bear says, after a moment of hesitation. "You both know what he was like before we left. You know he didn't do much thinking by then. But we'd been out in the Wilds for the better part of a month, and met few kind words and fewer friendly faces that might help us on our way. I saw a nice boat out on a little river one night and thought we might steal it, get ourselves a nice little place to stay while I figured out what to do next. But there were two ... two folk from the Wilds on board, didn't seem too happy about the prospect of us taking their boat." Bear glances at me, and I bow my head, grateful to him for pardoning me of this crime. "We attacked first. Shouldn't have done, but did anyway. Sam got a knife to the throat, and I...."

Bear trails off, as though he can't quite finish the story. Maybe he can't, really, or maybe he just doesn't want to say the end: *I was taken prisoner by the people who murdered him, but I forgave them, and one of them is standing right next to me. Now I have joined with them in the Resistance, and that's why we're here.*

I don't blame him for ending the story there. I'm not sure Rose and Luis are ready for that second part, yet. For that matter, I'm still grappling with how Sam's story ended, and how Bear became one of us.

Rose reaches for Bear's hand. She pulls his fingers to her lips and kisses them, and then pulls him in for another hug. When she lets him go, I can see tears shining along her cheeks, but her voice is strong when she speaks.

"Sam was dead long before that day, Bear. You were the best friend to him he could have asked for."

"We'll remember him," Luis says, but his voice lacks the empathetic ring Rose's carries. Watching the two of them, I can almost see the effect of the Dieticians' drugs, and how differently they've taken hold in these two people: Luis is blank, emptied, more like the girl with the hollow eyes I saw today. Rose, though, has spring in her step and life in her voice. I can already see her as an ally, or better yet—a friend.

"To the dead who give life," the three of them say in unison. I remember the refrain from a long time ago, a memorial to those buried whose decomposition gives back to the soil what was taken during life.

"Why'd you come back, Bear?" Rose asks, again. Bear glances at me, hesitating, as though expecting me to answer this question for him. This is his moment—these are his friends.

"I came back," he says, slowly, "because Remy and I have an important message to bring to you."

"Important?" Luis asks. "More important than Sam?"

"You're a wanted man, now, Bear. Boss'll shoot you on sight if they ID you here."

Ma amie Remy isn't just any old person from the Wilds. This here's Remy Alexander."

Bear pauses and waits for these words to sink in. Rose and Luis turn towards me, and Luis especially seems to lean in to stare at me, scrutinizing my features. I suddenly feel as though I'm under a microscope. Thankfully it's too dark for them to examine every freckle on my face.

"Remy Alexander? Daughter of Gabriel Alexander?" Rose asks.

"Tai's sister? The one Sam was always on about?"

"That's the one," Bear says. "Remy and I are here on Sam's account and on Tai's. We're here because putting people on silo duty isn't the only thing Boss been doing to hurt people in the Sector. They killed Tai and Remy's mom, too. We believe that you deserve to know why Sam was put on Silo duty, and why my family has been torn in half. And we want your help to change things around here."

"But everything's fine here," Luis exclaims, stepping closer to Rose as if for confirmation and support. Bear motions for us all to sit, sensing the rising tension.

"Have there been any other accidents since Sam left?" Bear asks. Rose and Luis look at each other.

"Well," Rose begins. "I don't know if this is an accident, but Andre disappeared last month. Bosses said he went senile and escaped. He *was* pretty old."

"Andre was going to turn forty-five this year," Bear begins. "In the capital, that's still young. Folks in Okaria get to be lots older, like eighty or ninety. I learned that when I escaped and came to the Re-"

I interrupt him again before he can say it. "My grandfather died when he was eighty seven. I bet Andre wasn't senile at all, and that was just an excuse that the Bosses told you. Was Andre asking questions like Sam was?"

"Not about Tai or anything," Rose says. "But he kept on talking about how it wasn't right that Sam was sent to the silos."

Luis nods, taking everything in.

Bear takes a breath. "The Bosses just as good as killed Sam and they might have hurt Andre, too. They might also be covering up for when things go wrong and people get hurt, when people get killed. It might be indirect, but it is killing even so."

"There's more," I say. "The Bosses are feeding you special food that's completely different from the food people in the city get to eat. I grew up eating food that made me smarter, faster, healthy. The food was designed special for me. That's why I was able to go to the Okarian Academy, because the Sector *groomed* me to be smart enough to attend the Academy. Bear almost got the chance to go, too. They took him from the Farm and put him in a special school, but then, just as quickly, they changed their minds sent him back here."

"When I returned and started eating Farm food again," Bear says, "everything I learned at school started fading away. At first I was upset and angry that I couldn't live at the nice school and that I couldn't do maths so quick any more, and that I started forgetting all the big words I'd learned in class. My mind felt all muddled, and then, after a while, it didn't even bother me anymore. It was all sort of like a dream—someone else's dream, not even my own. And when I left the Farms with Sam, it kinda cleared up. I wasn't so muddled up, could think better somehow."

"All that's because of the food?" Rose asks.

"Exactly. Food designed by the Dieticians to turn you into the kind of Farm worker the Sector wants," I say.

"But I'm proud to work on the Farms. Not everyone needs to live in the city, and go to the Academy." Luis says.

Yes, Luis," I continue. "But shouldn't everyone have the opportunity to choose? Your food is specifically designed to make you not care about having your own choices. It is designed to increase your endurance and your strength, which is good for laboring on the farm, but your body isn't meant to grow so fast, to be worked so hard. Like Bear said, people in the capital, and even in the factory towns, live much longer. If your friend Andre lived in the city, he might live for forty more years."

"There's nothing wrong with being strong," Luis looks at Rose, and I can sense the hesitance, the hint of fear, in his frown. "But I don't want to die sooner than everyone else. Me and Rose … I don't want to leave her. That's not fair." Rose nods her assent and looks at us to continue.

"No, it's not fair," I say. "But now, Bear and I are eating the same food, and it hasn't been modified by the Sector Dieticians. It's natural, healthy, comes straight from the earth, and doesn't come in a MealPak. We cook it ourselves."

Bear pulls out some of our provisions from his pack and spreads it in front of Luis and Rose. "Please, try it. It's very tasty."

Rose reaches for a slim strip of jerky but Luis hesitates.

"We have more, if you like it," I say. "We have enough that you can give some to your friends, as well."

We hope that even a little bit of natural food, a little push from us, will open their minds just enough to start questioning things on their own. Why they're not allowed into the Dietician's lab. Why they're not allowed to talk about Tai Alexander's death. Why the folks who visit the Farms look and act so different from them. Why the Bosses live longer than the workers. Why they can't make their own decisions on when to have children and with whom, and why their families are broken apart.

"I don't feel different." Rose says, after they've finished the plate Bear set out.

"But it tastes good," Luis pats his belly in a gesture of satisfaction.

Bear chuckles. "It doesn't work straightaway. In fact, if you stop eating the Farm food altogether, you will get sick before you get better. It's called withdrawal."

"Like fixing a broken bone. It hurts while it heals, but then it's all better," I add.

Bear gazes off toward the Farm campus in the distance. Luis and Rose sit in companionable silence while I fidget and play with the hem of my shirt. I glance at Bear, in a *what now?* gesture. Not that I expected some dramatic change of heart, but this lack of any response at all is unsettling.

"Would you like to meet again tomorrow night?" Bear asks, finally. "I can tell you more about what's happened to me since I left, and I'd like to hear about what's been happening here."

Rose glances up at Luis and says, "We would like that very much."

"If you can help it," Bear adds, "try not to eat your MealPaks tomorrow. You may feel a little nausea, but that will pass. We'll send the rest of this food with you. But don't let the Bosses see you." He hands over the bag of food we prepared for them, and Luis takes it, even as a frown of confusion and hesitance shadows his face. "We'll have more for you tomorrow evening," Bear continues. "We'll make sure you get plenty to eat."

"Bear, are you sure…?"

"I promise. You've both known me since I was just a kid, and you know I would never lie to you. The MealPaks are not good for you. This food is much better. It's good for all of you—your body *and* your mind. And I wouldn't know about it if not for Sam. If you listen to me, if you trust me, it's only because Sam was brave enough to ask the questions that finally led me to the truth."

"We'll try your food tomorrow, Bear," the big man says. "And we'll meet you again tomorrow night. After that, we'll have to see."

"That's all we can ask," I say.

'Thank you," Bear says as we all stand to leave. "Your trust means everything to me."

"Until tomorrow." Rose gives Bear one last hug before the two workers disappear back into the night.

13 — VALE

Spring 6, Sector Annum 106, 06h47
Gregorian Calendar: March 25

Commandeering Normandy's best airship was a study in choreographed theft. Once the Director realized we were gone—and gone *together*—we were out of range for her to do anything about it but rage. And rage she did. If the Sector was able to intercept our communications, I'm sure they had a field day listening to her dress us all down. I joked that even Aulion would have enjoyed that transmission. As soon as I made the quip about him, however, Soren spun around, jammed his finger in—and almost through—my chest and told me in no uncertain terms to "never *ever* joke about that man in his presence" or he'd see that I didn't live to regret it. That was the first time in at least six hours he'd threatened me with a painful death.

We're making progress, Soren and me. Practically best friends.

If we weren't all worried about Remy and Bear and their, as Soren keeps putting it, "harebrained scheme," I'd almost be glad to be back above ground. Up in the cockpit, Miah and Firestone are going over the airship's controls, talking about our cloaking and stealth tech, and how to hone our radar and electromagnetic sensors to make it easier to find them. Jahnu and Kenzie sit together while they disassemble, clean, and reassemble everyone's weapons—a wide assortment of which we "borrowed" from Normandy's supply room. Eli has his V scroll out and we're trying to figure out exactly where Remy might be.

We're not even a half hour out when Miah points out that the airship is dangerously low on water. Without clean water to run the airship's cooling systems, the reactor core will overheat and reach temperatures high enough to melt engine components.

"We'll have to resupply at a river or a lake," Miah says nervously. "We need enough open space to land and get the siphon hoses in the water."

Normandy's airship is a smaller-end transport ship, big enough to carry twelve men and up to three thousand kilos of cargo. Landing this ship in a big clearing will leave us open and exposed to any passing drones.

"I don't like this," Firestone mutters. "Don't wanna drop out of the air if we don't have to. Not when the Sector's got drones everywhere."

"Well, we have to," Kenzie says, matter-of-factly, not looking up from the weapon she's cleaning. "If we want to keep flying, we have to pull water. We'll just have to make it quick."

Soon Miah's pointing out a likely spot along a small stream, and he and Firestone are lowering the airship out of safe air and into drone space. With all our cloaking gauges cranked as high as they'll go, Firestone drops the ship into a soft landing.

"Won't take but a minute," Firestone says. "Vale, Soren, cover me while I pull out the hoses?"

I glance at Soren, who pointedly ignores me.

"Sure," I respond, as casually as I can. I go to grab my Bolt from Kenzie's now-polished stash, but Soren's already picked it up for me. He tosses it at me, a little more forcefully than necessary, before slinging his own over his shoulder. I turn, palm open the hatch, and jump out. Firestone and Soren follow.

The sandy little spot we've landed on gives way to forest about twenty-five meters in. The water is shallow, but the water is moving quickly, which will help us pick up clean water for the airship.

Firestone ducks beneath the belly of the ship, opening one of the panels and pressing a few buttons. In a minute, the siphon hoses are stretching out and down as Firestone guides them to the source.

Soren and I stand a little ways apart, on either side of the stream, watching each other as much as our surroundings. I imagine the emptiness of the woods around us is getting to me as I feel eyes watching me, and not just Soren's. There's a prickling sensation at the nape of my neck, and I try to focus on the trees and the sky above them, reminding myself that drones could set upon us at any minute.

And then I see them. My eyes meet another's, round and child-like, the whites of them so stark against a small dirty, smudged face I can't believe I didn't see them before.

The child breaks eye contact with a flurry of movement, and dashes to my left, disappearing behind a bush.

"Who's there?" Soren says, loudly. His gun is up and pointed at the shaking leaves.

"It's a kid," I say, putting my hand up to him, motioning to him to wait. I take a few slow steps towards the tree line. Soren doesn't lower his weapon, but he doesn't make any attempt to move, either.

"What's going on?" Firestone demands from under the airship.

"Hello?" I call. "It's okay, you can come out. We won't hurt you."

Nothing moves. I take a few more steps forward, my gun slung behind my back, hands out, palms up. I hear Soren behind me, his boots making little slurping noises as he wades across the stream. I glance back. His gun's still up, though he looks more curious than threatening.

"Put your Bolt away, Soren." He glares, obviously not keen on taking orders from me. I can see the momentary indecision as he tries to figure out whether to do as I've said or to continue waving a large weapon at a child. After a second, he lets the gun fall to his side, and he holds his hands out as I've done.

"Are you hurt?" I say to the underbrush. "Look, we've put our guns away. We won't hurt you."

Five heartbeats pound in my chest before an older man, maybe thirty, steps out from behind a tree, with a little girl, no more than five years old, clutched tightly in his arms. He's at least as dirty as the girl, who must be his daughter, with bits of leaves in his hair and worn clothes that look like standard-issue Farm work wear. Back and forth, he regards Soren and me, muscles working along his clenched jaw. Another three heartbeats, and a woman stands up from where she was apparently lying behind a bush, her hair mussed and looking like it hasn't had a good comb in a long, long time.

"Who are you?" the man demands.

Soren and I glance at each other, and for a second I think we'll share our first real laugh together. We are two of the most recognizable faces in all of Okaria. But the creases of a smile disappear, and he turns back to the disheveled little group in front of us.

"You don't know?" he asks them. It is possible that they wouldn't know us, if they were Outsiders, or vagabonds, among the stragglers who have slipped through the Sector's fingers and live in the empty spaces on the maps. But the man and the woman both have their high-calf Farm boots on, which makes me think they're runaways.

Recognition dawns on the man, and his jaw drops slowly, as he stares back at the two of us, the son of the Chancellor and the son of a former Chancellor, standing together in the middle of the Wilds, both of us undoubtedly looking quite a bit different than the last time we appeared on Sector broadcasts.

"But—you, you're … Evander said you … your father said—"

"Never mind what Evander or my father said. We can help you," I say, as gently as I can. "Is that your daughter?"

The man nods at me, wordlessly, as the woman slowly creeps to his side. The little girl's eyes have never left my own.

"You look like you need food and shelter and warmer clothes than what you've got. What are your names?"

He clutches his daughter and steps back. "Names? Why should we trust you? What are you doing out here?" His hands are shaking. "The Chancellor said you've been kidnapped and here you are with Bolts and an airship out in the Wilds. With him!" He points at Soren. "You could make us go back there for all we know."

Soren and I find ourselves on the same side of the Sector lies and at a loss as to how to explain why we're together out in the Wilds. Just then, the woman points and gasps, clutching at the man's arm.

"The terrorist!" she says wildly. "That's him! He kidnapped them!"

I turn, confused, following her finger back to the airship, where Miah has just dropped out of the hatch and is staring at us, utterly baffled. I almost laugh out loud, watching Miah's bearded face scrunch up in confusion at the scene in front of him. Soren, of course, spares not a breath for decorum, and actually *does* start laughing. It doesn't take long, though, before he takes a deep breath and turns back to the renegades in front of us, trying to explain.

"No, listen to me," he implores, his hands wide, palms up. "The Sector wants you to think that Jeremiah Sayyid kidnapped us, kidnapped Vale. But Vale and I—" he looks at me with grudging acknowledgment "—came out here because we wanted to. We left the Sector willingly. Jeremiah is our friend. We don't work for the Sector anymore, and, from the looks of it, you don't either. We can help you. We can get you somewhere safe, with food and clean water and warm clothes."

"You obviously know who we are," I say. "Why don't you tell us your names? Believe me, the last thing we're going to do is turn you over to the same Sector forces hunting us."

The woman rubs her temples as if her head hurts and wobbles a bit, and he wraps his free arm around her and pulls her to his side. She shakes her head, confused. "If you're not kidnapped, if you left willingly, why are they saying those things and why are they hunting you?"

"It's a long story—" I start.

"They want to find us, arrest us, and try us for treason," Soren interrupts. "A group of individuals in the OAC and the government are controlling Sector citizens by manipulating the food supply. We aim to stop them and they're none too happy about it."

"The food supply?" They two glance at each other again and the woman says. "We haven't eaten much since we left and I'd be glad for a MealPak. Especially for Violet. She strokes the little girl's arm tenderly. "Our daughter is hungry. We're all hungry."

"Hello, Violet," I say, wishing I had a treat in my pocket to give her and at the same time thinking, *That's stupid, Vale, she's not a puppy.* "My name is Vale, and we've got some food in the airship that we'd be happy to share with you." I give the little girl my best 'don't be afraid of me' smile. She is adorable, and even under all the dirt, her eyes are bright and inquisitive.

"I'm Elissa," the woman says. "And this is my husband, Cal."

"Husband and wife? And yet, you're wearing Farm garb. Since when do they allow official marriages on the Farms?" Soren says.

"We done it ourselves," Cal says. "Out here. Once we left." He looked down at his wife.

"How long ago did you leave?" I ask.

"It's been four days."

"No wonder you're hungry." I smile. "Come on, we've got plenty to share."

A half-hour later, we're back up in the air and Violet is full and her shyness has disappeared. She's giggling, and she and Jahnu are competing to see who can make the silliest faces. Aside from watching Jahnu with complete adoration, Kenzie's been laughing so hard she actually got the hiccups. Once this mess is all over, *if it ever ends*, I can imagine them with a house full of kids.

Firestone's at the controls while Miah sits with Eli, Soren, and me as we share slices of bread and jam, prosciutto, and handfuls of freeze-dried berries and talk with Cal and Elissa.

"What are they saying at the Farms?" Miah asks, unsurprisingly eager to hear what new and terrible things the Sector is saying about him.

Cal glances at Soren and me, then turns to Miah. "All the broadcasts say you and your *papa* been the ones responsible for capturing all them people the last few years. That you helped the Outsiders with the massacre on the SRI *il y a trois annees.*" Three years ago, I translate. Now I am grateful to my parents for insisting I take Old French when I was at the Academy.

Grateful to my parents? I shake my head, torn, as I always am, by alternating feelings of love and loathing.

"Has anything changed, security-wise? Have they increased drone surveillance or the number of guards?" Soren asks.

"Gotten a bit more relaxed, if anything," Elissa says, her watchful eyes on her daughter. "Fewer drones, these days. Some of the guards have even been transferred from our Farm."

Eli raises his eyes in surprise. "Really? Do you have any idea why?"

"I was sort of friendly with one of the Enforcers," Cal says. "He left a few weeks ago. Said he was going into training to be with the SDF—Sector Defense Forces. Said it was a big type of promotion that a lot of the Enforcers were taking. More pay and privileges."

Fewer drones, these days. Guards transferring into the SDF. It doesn't take much to put two and two together.

"They're diverting their resources," I respond. "I'm just guessing here, but I'm sure they've figured, based on the Resistance's past tactics, that the Farms aren't a focus point, that there's unlikely to be a threat there. And I'd be willing to bet they're diverting the drones from perimeter security at the Farms and the towns and spreading them out through the Wilds, trying to find bases like Waterloo."

"Makes sense," Miah said. "Remember what Philip said in his broadcast?"

Kenzie looks up mid-hiccup. "We weren't there, remember? We never heard the full replay."

Miah shrugs. "He said, 'We are hot on the terrorists heels. We will track them down and hold them accountable for their crimes.' Sounds like Vale's guess isn't far off."

"If they're able to do what they did at Waterloo with even one or two more bases," Soren says, "they'll cut our numbers severely."

"We probably never were more than a thousand all told," Eli says.

"On the other hand," I say, smiling a little, "if security at the Farms is lighter, Remy and Bear might have a shot at—"

"At what?" Soren snaps. "We're not going out to help Remy and Bear on a fool's errand. We're bringing them back so we can get on with the Director's plan. Don't think for a second about going along with this ridiculous scheme of hers."

Well, our brief moment of friendship was certainly short-lived. But, I remind myself, we don't really know what Remy's up to. She's not stupid. We ought to at least give her a chance.

Eli sits up straighter, focusing on Cal and Elissa.

"Why did you leave?"

"They was gonna take Violet," Cal says, shaking his head as if still trying to wrap his mind around the idea. "Elissa and I, we want to be together—and we love our Violet. We named her ourselves." He watches the little girl with so much tenderness, it almost hurts to watch. "When Elissa got pregnant, we were so happy. We petitioned to live in the same unit and everything, and they let us. We were good workers, never caused no one any trouble."

"Then Violet came along. She was a wonder," Elissa says, watching the little girl, now tracing lines on Jahnu's palms with Kenzie looking on. "We couldn't stop looking at her. There's lots of folks on the Farms don't feel the bond with their babies. Not us."

"And she is *smart*. See it in every move. Just a month ago, some official from one of the quadrant schools came and said her tests were so good they wanted to take her away to a special school," Cal says, continuing the story. "We didn't want her to go, or else we wanted to go with her. So we both applied to transfer to Windy Pines, where her school was."

"Cal's transfer was approved right away, I guess 'cause he's such a good worker, but mine got rejected," Elissa says. "They said I wasn't qualified to do the kind of work available. So I had to stay at the Farm."

Cal takes Elissa's hand. "We told them we didn't want to go if we couldn't all go, but they said they were gonna take Violet anyway. That we had no choice. That it was the best for the whole Sector and that maybe some day she'd even go to the Academy in the capital. Well, we weren't about to let our little girl go, so we decided to leave."

"So you just up and walked out?" Kenzie asks.

"What else was we to do?" Elissa says. "There wasn't no other choice."

"At first it was hard, cause we were all a bit sick after we left, although we're feeling much better now. Just worn out, tired, is all. Hard to even get the energy to find something to eat."

"Besides that," Elissa rubs her temples again, "my head's been all muddled, like I can't quite think straight."

"It's the withdrawals," Miah says. "I had a bad case. I got sick and just kept getting sicker. Hoo boy. Not fun."

"Withdrawals? What does this mean?" Cal asks.

Eli expression is dark, his moods as unpredictable as the weather, and all too often just as dangerous. "When you stop eating your MealPaks, your body reacts to the absence of all the chemicals that had been flooding your system with every poisoned bite you ate."

"Poisoned?" Elissa whispers. "Surely, not poison! No one would do that. No one *could* do that ... could they?"

"It's hard to explain, but it has to do with how the Sector was controlling your behavior by manipulating your diet. Now you need plenty of rest and some real food. There's a Resistance outpost not too far out of our way. We'll radio them, set down nearby, and they'll send someone out to meet you."

"Will they let us stay together?" Cal asks.

"No one in the Resistance would ever separate a child from his parents," Eli growls.

His. He's not talking about Violet. He's thinking about his own parents, how they disappeared after the hearings into the SRI massacre, remembering how he felt losing his mother and father so soon after the death of the girl he'd fallen in love with. It's no wonder he's so close to the Alexander's and so protective of Remy. No doubt *his* parents' disappearance was directed on *my* parents' orders. I feel like I need to shower, scrub my skin raw to remove the stain of being an Orleán.

"And they'll help us there? Help keep Violet safe?" Cal persisted.

Jahnu, usually so quiet it seems Kenzie does most of the talking for the both of them, speaks up. "As safe as possible."

"Is that where you are going? To this base?" Elissa asks.

"No," Eli's face is stony when he responds. "We're going to the Farms."

Seven hours later we're headed north to Farm 10. After dropping Cal, Elissa and little Violet off as close as we dared to the nearest Resistance outpost and delivering an encrypted message both to the base and back to Normandy about getting the family the help they need, we headed back out to scout.

Although we were able to get a good look at the area around Farm 12, we couldn't get close to 11. So much for lax security. Clearly not all the Farms are diverting personnel to the effort against the Resistance. Farm 11 was crawling with OAC and Farm security personnel and equipment. Eli's advance-warning wristband went from blinking blue to just staying on all the time, so even though we're traveling with a drone blocker and the airship has good cloaking technology, we were afraid to get too close.

Getting a look at the beefed up perimeter—even from a distance—reminded me of the brief exchange between Aulion and my parents just after my graduation ceremony, the day Miah and I graduated from the Sector Research Institute. I remember my mother mentioning the "troubling situation" at the Farms, but she didn't say which one because I didn't have an official security clearance yet. And at the time, I was much more interested in partying than anything else. After I took my position as head of the Seed Bank Protection Project, my concern was with the security at our installations. I had little knowledge of what went on at the Farms—that was Evander Sun-Zi's area.

As the Director of Agricultural Farm Production, and my father's right-hand-man, Evander has one of the most powerful positions in the Okarian Sector. He oversees the Farms, ensures that the latest research coming out of OAC labs is implemented in the food production chain, and, most importantly, manages the Dieticians. Since the seed banks store and, in a few cases, actually produce the seeds using printers like the ones Eli wants to steal, they should fall under Evander's purview as well. But when my father set up the Seed Bank Protection Project, he placed it under the military, so I reported to General Aulion instead of Evander. I don't know who is worse, though. Aulion may be a snake, but Evander's nickname is "The Dragon." I never knew for sure where he got the moniker, but it sounds ominous enough.

What is clear from reconnoitering around Farms 12 and 11 is that something's going on that has the Sector worried. Jahnu's take on the situation is intriguing, though.

"What if Brinn and Gabriel's work around the Farms was really beginning to have an effect? We know they worked primarily around Farms 9, 11, and 12, those on the Sector's southernmost flank. What if people are being punished for asking questions? Or for taking action? Like Bear's friend, Sam?"

"It's certainly something to consider," Eli adds. "And it's possible that the little food Brinn and Gabriel did give them made a difference."

"It could be that changing a person's diet just slightly makes you less susceptible to the Dietician's influence," Kenzie says.

"We need to talk to Rhinehouse and the Director. All of us just went cold turkey, and we all had various levels of withdrawal symptoms. I walked around in a fog for a month."

"And look at Miah," Soren says. "He had a bad case of withdrawal symptoms."

"The dysentery didn't help!" Miah calls out from the cockpit. "But I'm clean as a whistle inside now."

"Yeah, I've been listening to that whistle blow all afternoon." Firestone laughs.

A smile brightens Soren's face for just a moment, but then he looks over at me and it vanishes as if it was never there. "Miah had it bad, but somehow you seemed to have escaped. Why do you think that is?"

"I have no idea. Believe me. I'm as baffled as you are."

I'm more than baffled actually. I've analyzed every minor ache and pain, every little twinge of a headache or tired muscle and I don't think I've experienced anything like the others describe. It's almost as if I was immune to the effects of the change in diet. I never felt foggy or confused. My cognitive abilities haven't changed—at least I don't think they have. I was never overly tired. My stamina and muscle strength remains the same—if not better from all the training and hiking we've done. I can't figure it out.

"Strange," Eli says, looking me up and down as if I'm a lab specimen. "Maybe Rhinehouse should do a blood sample, compare Miah and you. You both went off your MealPaks at the same time. Of course we don't have a before and after profile—unless we could somehow hack into the Dietician's database and get your files—but still, might be interesting to see what he'd find. You have any objections to that?" His look is challenging, as if he suspects I'm hiding something.

"No objections, but I don't know what he'd find."

"Won't hurt to look, though, would it?" Soren says, and his look is definitely challenging.

Kenzie brings us back to the topic at hand. "The crucial thing is whether gradually replacing the food used by the Dieticians can slowly change people so they'll be less and less under the Sector's influence without anyone ever suspecting a thing. Instead of thinking we have to move fast to replace the foods available for inclusion in the MealPaks, we'd have more time. It would make our plan to take over the supply chain safer and give us the time we need to ramp up seed production after we steal that printer."

"We'll know more tomorrow," Eli says. "Firestone's gonna set us down deep in the woods, power down the systems so we've got everything on cloaking and let us get some rest. We can't see anything in the dark anyway. We'll hit Farms 9 and 10 and get a read on what their security situation is like. The Director's gonna want us back soon, but we're not going back without Remy, right?"

We all nod. At least there's one thing on which we all agree.

14 — REMY

A flash of a mirror, then another two in quick succession. Rose's signal.

It's time.

A flush of adrenalin courses through me with its glinting, knife-edge sharpness. The readiness to run, to shoot, to be *free* is exhilarating. I push myself into a sprint, and the chill air against my face is exhilarating.

Behind me, I can hear Bear flip the capacitor on his Bolt to charge, and the sound almost breaks my heart. I hope he won't have to shoot anyone today. It's too early for him to become a killer.

Coming out from the gully where we'd taken cover, Bear and I cover the distance between our hiding spot and our target in the span of a few minutes. By the time I hit the brick wall, I've put fifteen paces on him. I turn to look behind us, to make sure we haven't been spotted. My infrared contacts indicate nothing on the horizon.

Safe.

For now.

Bear hits the wall beside me, panting hard, trying to quiet his breathing.

"Ready?" I ask.

Without responding, he turns away from me, pivoting like a soldier. I cinch my belt tighter and swing my own Bolt into my hands. I don't think I'll need it, but I need to be prepared, in case any on-duty guards come along and ruin our evening.

Bear turns and glances back at me for a second, his eyes unblinking in the hollow shadows. I take a deep breath as he turns the corner, to keep a watch on the side of the building nearest the Enforcers' compound. I haven't a clue if this is the smartest thing I've ever come up with, or the stupidest. I'm not even positive it will work, but I studied Farm operations and talked to Kenzie about her mom's work as a Dietician before Bear and I left Normandy for Round

Barn. So, after tonight, we'll just have to wait and see.

Earlier today, I went back into the Farm under the guise of "Anna from the Wilds" and chatted Joral up some more. He asked me where I'd gotten paper to send that message to Rose.

"Why do you ask?" I hedged.

"My son's birthday is coming up. He has a chance to qualify for the Academy's Art and Design program, but I think he needs more practice on paper. It's hard to get out here, so only the kids already in Okaria will have much experience using that medium. It's an unfair advantage, don't you think? He's excellent on his plasma, but I think some extra practice, and some additions to his portfolio, will give him a competitive edge. He's really talented."

Turns out Joral is a blabbermouth. Either that, or his job is damn boring. He didn't seem to do much in the hour that I hung around except try to look imposing.

"Tell me more about your son," I said. And so I learned more about Joral Jr. than I ever needed to know, although, in truth, he does sound like a good kid and Joral even pulled out his pocket plasma and showed me some of his son's work. So I kept the proud papa talking. When I pushed, he yielded. I asked him about his wife, his job, his love of chocolate, and, finally, I told him I did have some paper to spare for his son, if he would meet me outside the Farm near midnight.

"Because it's illegal to have unauthorized paper inside the Sector, and I don't want you to get caught by the other Bosses, when you've been so kind to me." His brows furrowed at the thought, but I didn't give him a chance to protest. "I'm going to go see Rose now. It was nice to talk with you, and I'll meet you tonight. Okay?"

To be honest, Joral seems harmless. But just because he is friendly and loves his family with a fervor that made me ache for my own, doesn't mean he isn't complicit in the mistreatment of the Farm workers, that he isn't an active supporter of the Sector's policies, or that he might be even vaguely sympathetic to the Resistance's efforts. I tried to my remind myself every second that, as an Enforcer, he deserves neither my pity nor my help. But, I also tell myself that a mildly sympathetic Enforcer willing to bend the rules a bit is a whole lot better than an emphatically unsympathetic one who is not.

So I rolled up a few pieces of paper up into a scroll, tied it with a piece of twine, and stuck it in my pack to give to Joral—once he's lying unconscious at my feet.

I turn a hard left around to the back of the building, toward the little side-door that has only a palm scanner, not a retinal piece as well.

There, Joral and Rose are waiting for me—though Joral, lying on his back and gazing up at the stars, looks nothing like he did when I spoke to him earlier.

"I need to," he says slowly, "see Annnnnnaaaaa. She's from the wiiiiiilds."

Nice work, Rose, I think. I bite back a laugh. He definitely enjoyed the chocolate she was to give him earlier tonight. The chocolate Bear and I laced with dreamweed, a potent psychotropic drug, one of Rhinehouse's creations. Eli says Rhinehouse manipulated the genes in *salvia divinorum*, a hallucinogen, to create dream*weed*, used mostly for medicinal purposes to help ease chronic pain, anxiety, and bipolar disorder. "I don't think he expected it to grow so well," Eli said then. "Now, it grows all over the Wilds. Hence dreamweed." It's also a powerful amnesiac, if taken in the right dosage. I'm hoping we gave Joral the right dosage.

Bear and I dried a few of the leaves and ground them to a fine powder, mashing them in with some melted chocolate before allowing it to solidify. Neither of us were certain the plant would have the same effect when dried, but Joral is clearly feeling the effects.

"Il est fini," Rose says. Rose is by herself tonight. She'd said Luis was expected at some sort of meeting and couldn't help tonight, and it was very courageous of her to agree to help us by herself.

"Thank you," Bear says. She gives us a quick nod and disappears around the corner of the building to keep watch.

"Joral!" I whisper, as loudly as I dare, crouching down to his side. He rolls his head and grins at me.

"'Ey, Anna," he says, too loudly, the sounds slow, drawn-out. I even see a little bit of drool pooling by his lips. "Why're you here?"

"I got your paper, Joral," I whisper, fighting the urge to slap a hand over his mouth. "But I need your help, okay?"

My adrenaline rising, I check my surroundings. But there's nothing. Unless they're wearing heat-cloaking gear—which is very possible—there's no one else here.

"You brought me paper? For my son?"

"Yes, for your son—and for you. Now, I need you to do something for me. Okay?"

"Okaaaay. Yeah. You help me, I help you. Riiiiight?" He's not even looking at me. His eyes are wide but unfocused, staring through the spotted darkness of the sky.

"Joral, I need you to scan me into this building, okay?"

"Okaaaaay," he says.

He doesn't move.

Glancing around, aware of the fact that drones or other Enforcers could show up at any moment, I grab Joral's hands and try to pull him to his feet. Finally, he stands, a weird, loopy smile on his face, and looks down at me.

"You've got stars in your eyes," he says, staring up at my face as I drag him closer to the door.

"I'm sure I do. Can you please put your hand to the palm scanner, Joral?" He nods at me, still smiling, and this time, wobbles to the scanner and puts his hand up to it.

"Liquid," he says, muttering. "Gooey."

"What are you saying?"

"The ground ... it's moving." He's squinting at the scanner, which has just beeped in recognition and flashed green. I dart to his side and punch in the code. *Another gift from Rose.*

3-1-4-7-Z-H-U-C-F.

The door swings open.

I whisper a silent *thank you* and whistle three times, the signal to Bear and Rose that the door's open. In a matter of seconds, they're at my side. With Bear propping the door open, I pull the scroll of paper out of my backpack and place it in Joral's hand. His fingers wrap around it lightly, perhaps sensing the fragility of the gift.

I help Rose get Joral to start walking back to his cabin. With luck, he'll wake up in the morning a little nauseated, but otherwise totally fine and with no memory of anything that happened while he was high.

"Look! The sky is full of eyes and they're all winking at me!" he exclaims. Rose shoots us a pointed look, as if to say, *I never thought I'd see him like this,* and they disappear into the darkness.

Inside, Bear pulls the heavy door shut behind us, enveloping us in pitch black. He takes a step forward and the lights around us come on, illuminating the interior of this section of the building. I thank our lucky stars there are no windows.

"Now what?" Bear whispers.

I stare at the hundreds of glass vials, plasma monitors, hologram displays, microscopes, and pieces of equipment I can't begin to name. The task before us is daunting.

"We begin the revolution." I drop my pack, and Bear does the same. I pull out our waterskins, now full of a sugar solution Bear and I spent all day yesterday concocting using stolen sugar and honey from the food stores. We were only able to make five liters, but from what I learned from Kenzie about the Dieticians and how a lab operates, that should be plenty to start.

Bear wanders over to one of the stacks of shelves, piled high with dusty old equipment, plasma screens now years out of date, empty glass jars, and broken security equipment while I carry the waterskins over to one of the polished metal tables in the center of the room, Bear starts reaching up to pull something off the shelf.

"Don't," I say abruptly. He jerks his hand back, as though hit by a low-charge Bolt blast. "We don't want to touch anything we don't need to."

Although I know it's nearly impossible not to leave any identifiers behind, we can still try. There's a reason my springy hair is tucked under a black hood, both Bear and I are wearing thin gloves I'd stolen from Hodges, the nurse at Normandy, and covered nearly head to toe so as not to leave behind dead skin cells. They'll figure out we were here eventually, I'm sure, but the longer we can delay that, the better.

"*Vraiment*, Remy, what is this stuff?"

"It's a lot of different things. See that, there?" I point to a large microscope in the corner. "That's used to look at things that are very, very small, like cells. Or even smaller, like molecules, proteins, fats, and amino acids."

"I know what fat is," he pats his stomach, "but what are molecules, proteins and amino acids?"

I look up from my pack and smile. *Wow*. No one's ever depended on me for a biology lesson before. "Let's see. Molecules are the smallest part of a chemical compound that can be part of a chemical reaction. I guess the best explanation of a protein is that it is an organic—that sort of means made from living or potentially living materials—compound made up of molecules that give living tissue structure." I reach out and press his forehead with my thumb. "Your skin, hair, and muscles are made of protein."

"And what about the last one, amino acids?"

"Amino acids are basic organic compounds, meaning they're made of molecules, and they're important because they are the building blocks of proteins."

"Oh," he says, though his head is still cocked to the side, confused. He changes the subject, pointing down a darkened aisle at rows and rows of tiny containers holding some kind of clear liquid. "Are these the chemicals we're going to replace with our sugar water?"

"Yes." I pause. "We might not have quite enough to replace everything they have in this lab. But we should have enough to do some serious damage."

"What do we do?" he asks.

"I'll show you."

I take a skin of water over to the sink. Using a lab tray, I grab as many of the vials as possible and bring them over. One by one, I pop the rubber stoppers and dump the contents down the drain. *There goes Apathy*, I tell myself, *and there's Ignorance, and there's Blind Trust, washed so quickly and easily down the drain.* I know the science behind these little vials is a thousand times more complicated, intricate biochemical interactions, individual biology, and even, simple chance, but it's more rewarding to think of this process not as chemistry but as restoration. *We're giving the people back their humanity.*

Bear watches as I grab a micropipette and begin the slow process of refilling the vials with our placebo. Though I never took but the one basic required lab class, I spent enough time watching Tai and my mother work that I know my way around most of the simpler equipment. As I work, I read the labels written on the glass, trying to remember what the letters and numbers mean from my brief stint in organic chemistry, but it's like reading another language. I'd need Soren or Eli to interpret for me.

Bear replaces the vials I've filled and pulls more off the shelves. I glance over my shoulder and my heart sinks: this will take hours, and we only have until dawn. And that's assuming no one walks in on us to check on a timed experiment.

Working as quickly as possible, Bear and I pipet sugar water into hundreds of vials. Soon, my thumb is tired and I'm yawning, using all of my focus to try to stay awake.

"Only one skin left," Bear says, finally, when I'm afraid I'm going to topple from sheer boredom. When I've finally drained the last waterskin, I heave a sigh of relief and pack up as quickly as possible. Bear darts around like a minnow, methodically putting everything back into place exactly as we found it. I find a bottle of sanitizing solution and quickly wipe down the counters and sink. When everything looks pristine, we grab our bags and turn to head out the way we came.

We weren't able to replace every chemical on the shelf, but we got through at least two thirds of them. I wish I had a better idea of how far in advance the MealPaks are prepared. If the Dieticians prepare them the day of consumption, the workers here could begin to notice withdrawal symptoms within twenty four to forty eight hours. If the Paks are prepared in advance, though, they might not feel the effects of our tampering for a few days.

Either way, I'm betting on no more than a week before the 'sickness' starts to go around, and this time, the Farm workers will be capable of wondering why.

Outside, I hold my breath as I blink three times to reactivate the infrared sensors in my contacts. For a moment, I panic and imagine I'll open the door to see a dozen Sector airships hovering overhead. But as I crack the door and stare out into the night, I'm greeted only by silence. Bear and I slip through the door, thankful that there's not nearly as much security this time of night, and jog through the fields back the way we came.

By the time we've made it back up to the cliff overlook, which quickly became our favorite spot, I'm grinning like a loon and fighting the urge to shout in triumph. *We did it!* I want to scream to the sky. Instead, I turn to Bear, my confidante and teammate, and whisper:

"Let's see what the Bosses make of *that*."

The next day we sneak back in and spend much of the day trying to talk with the other farm workers, telling them more or less the same story that we told Luis and Rose.

But we're not having much luck. I didn't expect that placebo MealPaks would take effect in less than 24 hours, but it's still somewhat disappointing that pretty much everyone acts exactly the same: hesitant, confused, skeptical, or downright hostile. A few people, like Rose, seem to have retained a little more of their defiance, their vitality, but without a personal connection, it's near impossible to get them to listen—especially when I'm trying to remain "Anna" and not Traitor Remy Alexander. Revealing my name is just too risky right now.

Bear and I sit around our campfire, exchanging reports of our various conversations during the day. After hours of talking with different workers, probing them about Andre and Sam, and hiding drawings all around the Farms in locations where workers would be likely to find them, it feels as if we've gotten absolutely nowhere. *Be patient, Little Bird*—I imagine my grandfather's voice in my head. He would always say that as he dangled a fresh date, my favorite dessert, in front of me. I wouldn't get the date until I told him all about what I learned in school that day, the fun things I did with my friends, the drawings I was excited about. After all that I had to give him a big fat kiss on the cheek, and only then would I get my dessert. Delaying gratification can be sweeter than gobbling down your treat without anticipating it, without truly savoring it, he'd insist with a waggle of his finger.

But I'm not waiting for a little piece of fruit. I'm waiting for a sign. We need a sign that the workers are waking up, that the people will rise, that the Resistance will finally take a stand against the enemy we've been cowering from all these years. *The sign is coming*, I tell myself, over and over again, the words echoing in my head. I can feel it in my bones: the last evening of silence.

Something big is going to happen, and I am ready for it.

15 — VALE

It's now day four of looking for Remy, and we're getting desperate. The Director only gave us seventy-two hours, though Eli's taken to muttering "Damn her and her orders," under his breath at every opportunity. I had to work hard to suppress a sense of triumph when Soren insisted Remy would be at the Farm nearest to Normandy, but she turned out to be nowhere in sight.

Earlier today, Jahnu wisely observed that Remy might have chosen Bear to accompany her, instead of any of us, for a reason. "I think we ought to think a little less about ourselves and a little more about Remy, about why she left and why Bear went with her," he said. I acknowledged his subtle reprimand with a smile and earned a wink in return. "Why would she have asked Bear to go with her as opposed to any one of us?" he went on. "By that logic, she's almost certainly at the farm Bear came from—Farm Ten, right?"

"Round Barn," Kenzie said, from his side.

"Jeesh, Jahnu, why didn't you mention this sooner?" Soren asked.

Jahnu shrugged. "I just thought of it last night. Kenzie and I were talking—"

"A little pillow talk, eh?" Miah cut in with a teasing smile and an elbow to Kenzie's ribs. Kenzie just rolled her eyes in that *Miah, you're such a goof* way she has, but Jahnu ignored him, continuing in his earnest manner.

"—and she mentioned that Remy might not be in the places we're looking because we're thinking about it from our perspective, not hers. We've searched all over Twelve and Four because they're easily accessible from Normandy, but of course she wasn't there—why go to those Farms when you've got someone with you who knows the ins and outs of Ten?"

"Why, indeed," Eli asked, turning his glare on Soren.

"Don't blame me for thinking rationally," Soren mutters. "Although why I thought Remy'd be rational for once is beyond me."

"Bickering gets us nowhere closer to Remy," I said. "Jahnu's idea is a good one. Let's head to Round Barn and see if we can get radio contact or a sonar lead on her or the car she, uh, requisitioned from Normandy."

A few hours later, we're buzzing around the perimeters of Farm Ten, all our cloaking capacities engaged, and Eli's surfing the radio frequencies, trying to get a bite.

"Montana Three, do you read? This is Montana Four," he repeats, over and over again, using his and Remy's code names. Everyone in the Resistance has a code name based on family groupings and on places from the Old World countries of North America. Miah and I even have our own names now—Calgary One and Two.

"Montana Three, do you read? This is Montana Four." He cycles through the frequencies again and again until we hear what we've all been waiting for. My head snaps around, my heart thudding to a stop.

"Montana Three here. What's the word?" A wide smile spreads across Eli's face. There's static, but Remy's voice is strong. Relief floods my veins like a drug.

"Eighty-three, and where the—" The current date on the Sector calendar is always the "word." These code phrases help confirm that the two people radioing each other are both Resistance fighters, and not Sector operatives who may have obtained a code name illicitly.

"And the time?" Remy cuts Eli off before he can start his tirade. The current season is the "time" and each season is assigned a color. Before Eli answers, he shakes his head like he can't believe what he's hearing.

"The time is fucking purple, okay? Now tell me where the hell you are!"

"Where are *you?*"

"In your neighborhood, cruising the skies."

"What are you doing out here?"

"Looking for you, stupid. What do you think?"

Our airship is too big to set down near the coordinates Remy gave us, so we land about five kilometers away and radio our coordinates to them. We wait about thirty minutes, the anxiety palpable, before Remy and Bear arrive at a jog. When they pull up short, staring around at the apparently empty field, Eli jumps out of the cloaked ship like a madman, and Remy almost shoots him on the spot. I would have been startled, too, had a manic, fully-grown man jumped at me out of thin air. Much hugging ensues, and I hang at the back of the group and wait until they've greeted everyone else.

Her eyes finally catch mine; this time, there is no apprehension in her eyes as they alight on me. Relief washes over me, and I step forward as Miah moves to the side. But once I'm in front of her, I don't know what to do. Hug her? No. Shake her hand? Hardly. So I wave. Smooth, Vale. Really smooth. Why the press thought I was such a "playboy" back in Okaria is beyond me, since I rarely dated and apparently cannot even properly greet a pretty woman. If Linnea Heilmann saw me now, she'd be laughing her ass off.

"Hi," I manage.

"Vale."

Silence, and a jolt of unease courses between us like a lit fuse.

"Didn't know you had a thing for the wayfaring tendencies of your parents," Kenzie jokes, breaking the tension.

"Or for the agrarian paradise of Farm life. What the hell are you doing here?" Soren demands, though I notice he's glaring at me instead of her, as though her unapproved adventures were somehow my fault.

Maybe they are, I think, and a thrill runs through me that maybe something I did or something I said inspired her to action, but I quiet the thought before it gains traction. *Nothing she does is because of you, Vale.*

Remy narrows her eyes at Soren, and opens her mouth as though about to deliver a rebuke. But she stops mid-breath, and instead turns to Bear.

"We're doing exactly what Remy said in her letter," Bear says. "We're making change. We're telling the truth."

"And how, exactly, have you been doing that?" Soren asks.

"By starting a revolution," she says with a smile. It feels as if the first time I've seen her really smile, since the last time I held her hand at the Academy. It's different, somehow—more mature, of course, but something else, too. There's definitely something different about her, now. She's standing taller, seems more confident, more centered. She has a sense of purpose.

"We broke into the Dietician's lab and fucked with their formulas," Bear says.

"You what?" Eli demands, eyes wide.

"So that's why all the questions about my mom's work," Kenzie says, nodding with approval.

"It was time for drastic measures." Remy's tone is now serious. Her voice takes on the kind of gravity and deliberation that her father has when he speaks to a group. "After Thermopylae, we saw how vulnerable the Resistance is. Corine," here again she meets my eyes, though only for a second before I drop mine, "could destroy us all in a heartbeat if she knew where all our bases are. But even Corine can't stop a true revolution. Bear and I realized that if we took the fight to the Farms and eventually to the factory towns and spread the word of the intellectual and biological oppression the OAC represents, we could make it impossible to destroy the movement even if they take out each and every one of us. Even if they destroy the Resistance. If the people, and I mean more than just defectors from the capital, know the truth, there will always be hope, even if all of us are gone."

There's a heartbeat of silence before Firestone, always the one willing to say what no one else will, speaks up. "How's that going for ya?"

"It's a slow start, of course," Remy admits. "The message has been hard to communicate. There's not a lot of openness, or people asking questions. But we expected that."

"Even Remy's drawings, which she made plenty of before we left Normandy, weren't getting much notice. We've salted them around the Farm where folks can find them, but not too many are interested," Bear says, almost sadly. "Mostly they like her pictures and want her to draw for them. It's hard to get people to wake up, ya see. Took me a while, too, when I was one of them. No shame in admitting it. With Remy's art, it's like that time Soren came to play piano for us. It's nice, but afterward no one really remembered exactly *why* it was nice or even what it sounded like. There was a glimmer of wonder in the moment, but then it faded …" Bear trails off and everyone waits. "… It's not easy to make connections or even listen to your own thoughts and emotions when you're not yourself. Ya know?"

It hits me that in that short speech, Bear has captured more about the challenges facing the Resistance and the reason *why* what they're doing is important than anything I've heard since leaving Okaria. I've heard Soren play. There's no way anyone can be unmoved by his music. The fact that Bear and the other workers thought it was "nice" but could not say why or even remember it after the notes faded away hits home like a punch in the gut. My breath hitches, and I feel Remy glance over at me. I push back the emotion with a resolute swallow. *How did I not understand?* It's horrific enough to attribute my parents' crimes to a murderous thirst for political power, but seeing it through Bear's eyes, seeing that what they're really doing is taking away the individual's ability to know and experience beauty, to experience *life*, stops me cold.

"Tell us about the Dietician's lab and the formulas," Kenzie is saying. "What did you do?"

"We replaced all the MealPak additives with sugar water." Remy beams at us.

There's another silence, though this one stretches on, unbroken, as we all stare at Remy and Bear, stunned.

"That's genius," Kenzie breathes, finally. "Why didn't the Director think of that before?"

Soren shakes his head as if he can't believe what he's just heard. "Because the Resistance has never risked full-out war before, that's why."

"All Bear and I did was open up the conversation, and, hopefully, enable the conversation to continue. We're getting an early start on the inevitable, because we need more people to join the cause. We can't do this on our own and the people on the Farms or in the factory towns can't help us take the next steps if they can't consider their actions—or the consequences of their actions."

"But we're not ready to take the next steps," Soren says. "We're not positioned to—"

"Positioned?" Remy interrupts, her voice hard. "They forced us into this position when they attacked Thermopylae, when they killed my mom, when they killed the others in cold blood, when they were going to kill the other members of Team Blue—including my father—before the Outsiders intervened, when they outed us to the public as terrorists, when they accused Miah of being Vale's kidnapper and put a price on his head. What the hell, Soren? What else do they need to do before we take them seriously? Before we realize that when they say they're going to hunt us down and destroy us, they mean it? If we stay at our bases and do nothing—"

"We're not planning on doing nothing!" Soren's voice is raised now. "Did you forget about the plans to steal the seed printer? To infiltrate the food chain?"

"No, I didn't forget those plans. By all means, go back and steal the printer. By the time we've got seeds planted, by the time we're ready to harvest, by the time we're ready to start introducing untainted food into the food supply, perhaps we'll have more people on our side—"

"More people to do what?" Soren shouts.

"Soren—" Jahnu, ever the peacemaker, tries to interrupt, but Remy is having none of it.

"More people to carry on," she says with vehemence. "If we don't recruit more people to our cause, sooner or later they'll hunt us down and the Resistance will be gone. They'll find each of our outposts and destroy them just like they destroyed Thermopylae and Waterloo, they'll destroy our entire movement, and what will we have accomplished?" She looks around. "Nothing, that's what! What the hell have we been waiting for? We may not have risked all out war before, but that hasn't stopped *them*. So let's risk it. Let's put in all on the line. What else do we have to lose?"

The girl before us is determined, brave, awe-inspiring, and I'm so fucking proud of her, it's all I can do to stop myself from striding across the space separating us, wrapping her in my arms, and kissing her until neither one of us can breathe. Beside me, Soren shakes his head again and sighs heavily. He runs his fingers through his hair and looks around at the rest of us. "You all agree with her?"

Remy stares at us, arms across her chest, poised in her balanced fighter's stance. She is defiant, composed, and waiting for someone else to echo Soren, to say *this wasn't a good idea, or you should have checked with the Director first, or you're going to get us all killed.* But now there's no trace of either challenge or judgment. All I see is camaraderie and determination. Even a little bit of eagerness. And pride. I catch Miah watching me, watching my reaction. He knows, as we all do, that Remy has changed the game. There's no going back now, and for some reason, I am, for the first time, proud to be standing here, truly proud to be a member of this group.

One by one we go around the group.

Eli first: "I'm all in, Little Bird!"

Jahnu and Kenzie, holding hands, nod and Kenzie speaks for both of them. "We're with you."

"What have I got to lose? I've got a price on my head, so might as well make them pay it, right?" Miah says, all bravado.

"This is one crazy crew, here," Firestone says with a laugh. "I just wish it was my fuckin' idea."

They all turn to me, waiting. I nod, not trusting my voice.

Soren sighs and shakes his head as if we're completely out of our minds. And maybe we are. "Well, okay then," he says. "Game on. Here we go."

Eli puts his arm around Remy and gives her shoulders a rough squeeze. "I guess I should radio Normandy and let them know we've found you two troublemakers. Oh, and not to expect us for dinner anytime soon."

16 — VALE

Spring 8, Sector Annum 106, 17h24
Gregorian Calendar: March 27

We spent the rest of the day setting up camp, hearing the details of Remy and Bear's mission up to this point and filling them in on what we'd learned while searching for them.

Late in the afternoon, Jahnu, Kenzie, and I set out to put into practice the trapping skills the wayfarer girl had taught us in the hopes we'd have something fresh to eat over the next few days. As we headed back to camp, we heard rustling in the undergrowth and my first thought was that we'd been discovered. My second thought, as per usual, was utter dread at being questioned by Aulion in front of my parents. My third thought was, *shit! That's a mean boar headed straight for Kenzie.* I whipped out my Bolt, jammed the setting to KILL, and fired. But it was already dead by the time I got off my shot. Jahnu and Kenzie had both seen it and fired at the same time. The hairy thing was practically already roasted, smoke rising from its inert body. The smell of burning hair and skin filled the air.

"Bacon!" Kenzie whooped.

"I thought you were a gonner," I said, wiping my forehead.

She looked down at the carcass, poked at it, and turned it over with her booted foot. "Nah, it's kinda scrawny."

"Scrawny or not, it's fresh meat, protein we probably all need," I said.

"Who is going to skin and dress this baby for dinner?" she asked.

"We're bringing home the bacon," Jahnu quipped, "so I volunteer Miah and Firestone."

"Hah, Firestone, maybe," I laughed. "But Miah? I don't think so."

"About time he learned to live off the land," Kenzie said. "It may be scrawny, but I don't want to carry it back." She looked from Jahnu to me, and we both shrugged and shook our heads. "Okay, we've got to figure out how to move the damn thing."

We created a makeshift sled and dragged the boar back to camp, Firestone stepped up and volunteered to do the honors and to show all of us how to skin and dress the meat. Eli and Bear dug a hole, fashioned a spit, and the boar roasted over the fire through the evening while we talked about what comes next.

After a well-earned meal and a few brews that Firestone had secretly stowed without telling anyone, we hunkered down for the night and, for the first time in a long time, I slept peacefully knowing that Remy was just on the other side of the fire pit.

Now, evening is upon us again and the sun is dipping behind the trees as we prepare to make our next move. Remy and Bear told us that Rose, one of Bear's old friends on the Farm, had set up a clandestine meeting with a few of the more spirited workers, including some of Bear's old friends and a few new transfers from other parts of the Sector. We decided, in the interest of secrecy, to split up and only have a few of us attend the meeting.

After much discussion and some serious dissension, Eli declared, and we all finally agreed, that Remy, Bear, Eli, and I would go to the meeting. Soren, Kenzie, and Jahnu would accompany us as far as the Farm perimeter, but wait outside in case something goes drastically wrong and we need help getting out. Miah would man the airship in case an emergency evac is necessary, and Firestone would guard the little cave Remy and Bear had found and used as a back-up hideout. Earlier in the day, Eli hiked up with them to pack their other camp and drive the car back to the cave, backing it in carefully for easy getaway.

Ducking out of the cave to refill my water supply at a nearby spring, I slow as I hear voices, low but clear, a little ways through the trees. As I get closer, I can hear Soren and Eli arguing. I stop moving, staring through a thicket of bushes, beyond which I can just see Soren pacing and Eli leaning up against a tree, striking his usual confident pose.

"I still don't get it. Why does Vale go in while I stay on the perimeter?" Soren seethes. "How is that smarmy son of a bitch gonna convince anyone to join the Resistance?"

"Your grudge is blinding you," Eli says. "Vale's a known quantity. Plus, he's got charisma. You've seen him on the Sector broadcasts. There's a reason they called him the 'golden boy' when the Orleáns took over. Okaria loves him, and the Farm workers will be jolted into reality when they realize he hasn't been kidnapped after all, that he's on our side."

"Are you so sure he's really on our side?"

"Soren, wake up. He's our ace in the hole."

"More like asshole."

Eli straightens and walks forward. Soren stops pacing. They're standing nearly toe-to-toe.

"Look, whatever problem you have with Vale is clouding your judgment. I know you guys have a history. Both of you liking Remy complicates things, but if you don't get your shit together and get over it, I'll make Kenzie my second."

"Too late for that," Soren spits. "The Director already gave your command away, remember? Seems more like you're Vale's second."

I think Eli's about to throw a punch, but I slip away, before they can start pummeling each other. I have no desire to get in the middle of a fight between two men whose trust I'm still trying to earn. I head on down to the spring, refill my waterskin, and jog back up to the cave, trying to forget everything I just heard.

Jahnu and Kenzie are sitting together at the entrance, hand-in-hand, as the sun sets through the trees. Just inside, Remy and Bear are wrapping loaves of bread, dried fruit and meat, honey-oat bars, and chocolate in cloth and loading it all into sacks.

"Can I help?" I ask, stepping up behind Remy. She straightens and glances back at me with a trace of a smile.

"Thanks, but we're almost done."

I nod and glance around the cave, looking for some way to make myself useful, for something to say.

"So," Remy asks finally, "you never did tell us how long it took before you all discovered we were gone?"

Jahnu looks over his shoulder at me. "Ask him. He was the one who set off the alarm."

"You?" she asks, raising a curious eyebrow.

I sound a bit like a frog when I speak. "Couldn't sleep and thought I might find you awake, too. But you were nowhere to be found."

"Oh," is all she says. A silence blooms to fill the cavern around us.

"We hadn't talked since—" I manage, at the same time Remy starts.

"I thought my dad would find the note...." She stops talking and looks away, frowning.

I feel Jahnu and Kenzie looking at us, see Bear swivel slightly to glance at Remy out of the corner of his eye, and then, thankfully, Miah strides up from wherever he'd been and rubs his hands together.

"I'm hungry. Got anything good?"

"How about a boar sandwich?"

"I'm already bored of boar," Miah pokes her as if he'd made the funniest joke ever. Remy rolls her eyes and gives him a handful of dried fruits which he starts eating with relish, eyes rolled into the back of his head.

"Ohhhh … this is good," he moans. "Better than candy."

I shake my head at his antics, but I'm still impressed at the variety. Strawberry, prunes, figs, apricots, even mango. Eli told me Rhinehouse's hydroponic greenhouse produced an incredible bounty of fruits and vegetables, but it's still hard to understand how he did it. Just thinking about it makes my stomach growl.

"Got any to spare?" I ask, and watch as Remy digs into a sack and then drops a handful of fruit into my hand, her fingertips fluttering over my palm.

Now, in the deepening twilight, Bear leads the way down a steep hill to a slit in the perimeter fence of Round Barn. I'm nervous. It's extremely risky for us to go into the Farm, although Bear was quick to reassure us that the Enforcers don't do much in the way of perimeter guard work. And we are all wearing heat-cloaking gear, which should hide our signals from any patrolling drones. It would be much riskier, if not impossible, for the Farm workers to leave the property, unless we were able to smuggle in new clothes for them to wear that aren't equipped with the tracking devices woven into the fibers of their current uniforms. So we're meeting them at the same creekside spot that Remy and Bear apparently met his old friends the first time, a secluded little niche on a hill a kilometer or so away from the worker residences.

And, apparently, we're bringing a lot of food.

"The whole idea is to get them off their MealPak diets as quickly as possible," Remy explained, as she handed me and Eli each two loaded sacks of food. "The more untainted food we can give them, the better. We don't really know how long it will take for the sugar water replacements to take effect."

"Where did you guys get all this?" Eli asked.

"Normandy," Remy said, nonchalantly. "This was supposed to be our food for the next week. But since you guys showed up, there's plenty to go 'round, right?"

Eli and I glanced at each other, neither of us bothering to correct her: we did not, in fact, bring plenty of food to go around. We had expected to pick her and Bear up today and take them back to Normandy, and get on with the LOTUS mission. But, with our prized roasted boar now socked away in the cave, I figure we'll cross that bridge when we come to it.

We come to the gap in the fence and Bear slips through first. We pass the stuffed sacks through to him. One by one, we slip through. I'm on high alert—this is the first time I've been back on actual Sector-controlled territory since I fled almost three months ago. I'm thankful that the moon is almost new, that it will be harder for soldiers or drones to detect our motion in the dark. So I still my nerves with a squaring of my shoulders and follow Bear as he leads us silently through the fields.

After about twenty minutes of walking, Bear pulls up short.

"We're here," he breathes. He drops his pack and squints around. "They must be running late."

"It's okay. We'll wait." Remy sets down her sack and drops to the ground. I follow suit. The early spring grass is cool, and the dandelions and daisies have sprouted. Eli stands, looking almost as anxious as I feel.

"You ready?" I ask Remy. She's sitting cross-legged, looking meditative, with her eyes closed and her breathing deep and even. Her small hands clasped in her lap, the only thing that betrays anxiety is a slight catch in her breath when I ask.

"Yes," she responds without opening her eyes. Eli finally sits next to her, and she reaches out to take his hand, sensing it was him without looking. "Are you?" she asks me in return, now opening her eyes. "They'll want to know why you're here with us." Her voice is expectant. She's not asking me if I'm ready to tell my story, but if I'm ready to support hers.

"I'm ready." The confidence in my response belies my hesitation. *Am I?*

I hear a shuffling behind me, and Eli and I step back into the shadows so as not to alarm anyone. They won't be expecting you, Remy had said. We'll want to introduce you when the time is right.

A line of men and women approach, and as they draw nearer I count them and smile. There must be at least twenty. Remy scrambles to her feet, smiling warmly and shaking the hand of the big man who leads the group.

"Luis," she says. "Thank you for coming, and bringing everyone."

Remy and Bear have obviously already won over the woman at Luis's side. Her smile is bright even in the evening darkness. Remy turns and hugs her.

"Rose," she says. "Good to see you, thank you for being here."

"Of course," Rose says in return. "We brought as many as we could, safely, and as many as would come."

"How's everyone?" Bear asks, his question directed to the group at large. A few voices murmur back at him in greeting.

"What are you doin' back here, Bear?" someone asks. It's a low, masculine voice, and in the darkness I can't make out the speaker.

"Luis and Rose asked the same thing when we talked two nights ago. I came back because I've got somethin' to tell you all, somethin' important. It's about Sam and Andre, and everyone else who's ever gone missing, and what we're all doin' here on the Farms. But first, we brought some food to share."

"Food?" someone says, skeptically. "You off your MealPaks? You know you gotta eat what the Dieticians give us or you'll get sick."

"That's one of the things I want to talk about," Bear says, his tone provocative. "I am off my MealPaks. I've been living in the Wilds for nigh on four months. No Dieticians out there to feed me breakfast, lunch, and dinner. And I'm as healthy as I ever was. Healthier, even."

"Their food is good," Rose says, piping up helpfully from Remy's side. "Luis and I tried it the other night. Our Paks are good, I'll grant you that, but what they've got tastes different, somehow. And the bread is ... well ..." she turns to Remy. "I really just came for the bread," she laughs.

A joke. Remy and Bear have made an impression on one farm worker, at least. There's laughter in the group at this comment.

"Fills you up," Bear says. "And tonight we brought more than just bread. Dried fruit and smoked meat, the likes of which I'd never tasted before I left the Farm. And these honey-oat bars that taste so sweet you'd swear you were robbing a beehive."

"Here," Remy says, taking a loaf and breaking it into chunks. She passes a few pieces on to Rose, who hands them out to the other workers. "Why don't you pass the bread around, sit down, get comfortable and then taste it for yourself."

The men and women settle in and a few moments of silence pass, as the bread and oat bars are passed around from hand to hand. *It's a good thing we brought a lot of food,* I think, even as I realize that what we have here won't go far among twenty people. If we're going to keep this up, we'll need to fly in supplies.

"This *is* good," someone says, sounding a little surprised.

"I told you, Cal," Rose says kindly. "I said you'd like it."

"Now, while you eat, my friend Remy's got something to tell you," Bear says. "It has to do with what she found out when she was living in Okaria."

"Remy?" someone asks, leaning forward to peer through the darkness, looking Remy up and down like Bear just conjured her out of the evening mist.

"Haven't heard that name in a long time," someone else says. "Since that ...

you remember that attack way back … when was that … five, six years or so?"

"It was a little over three years ago," Bear says. "And this is *that* Remy, Remy Alexander."

Remy stands a little taller and rolls up on the balls of her feet. "You all know who I am," she says. "You know me as the daughter of the Poet Laureate. You know me as Tai Alexander's sister. And as the girl whose family disappeared after the massacre at the Sector Research Institute." She pauses, takes a deep breath. "But tonight I'd like you to get to know the real Remy Alexander. The Remy whose sister was murdered not by Outsiders, but by the Sector. The Remy whose mother—a doctor who helped people on Farms like Round Barn—was murdered just a few weeks ago by Sector forces." Little gasps go up around the crowd as Remy continues. "I want you to get to know the Remy who fights for the Resistance."

"You mean the—"

"With *Jeremiah Sayyid*, who kidnapped—"

"Worse than Outsiders, they are, that's what I heard—"

"Terrorists!"

Rose looks around nervously, and Luis stares at the ground, as though unwilling or unable to take a side. But Remy looks unmoved, obviously prepared for this reaction.

"That's what you've been told, and in truth, if I was in your position, I'd believe all that, too. But the problem is that none of what you're being told is true...." She holds her hand up as some in the group start to grumble. "And there are two other people here who I hope can help *me* convince *you* to listen and consider what I have to say." She motions for me to stay in the shadows, and continues.

"First, I want you to meet Elijah Tawfiq." Eli steps into the circle and nods at Luis and the others. "You probably remember that Eli was there the day my sister was murdered. He was nearly killed, too, and he told his story to the investigators. But they didn't listen. They claimed he was disturbed and wasn't telling the truth about who really killed all those students, who really killed Professor Hawthorne, and who tried to kill him. Instead of listening to him, they took away his job and tried to keep him drugged to keep silent. Then his parents disappeared. And that's when he left Okaria with my family. That's when Eli joined the Resistance. Eli."

Remy steps aside and motions for Eli to speak up.

"What I have to say can be summarized in one word," he begins. "Please. *Please* try to open yourselves up to the possibility that Remy is telling the truth.

Please try to listen when she says the Outsiders didn't kill her sister. *Please* try to believe me when I say the investigation was a sham. *Please* try to consider that the Sector is lying to you, controlling you, that the OAC under the leadership of Corine Orleán does not have your best interests at heart."

More voices interrupt and Rose hushes them with a louder than expected Shhh.

"And if you won't consider what Remy says or what I say," Eli continues, "there's one more person who'd like to speak to you. Someone else here tonight who has a stake in this story." Silence settles around the group, and Eli turns to Remy. "You do the honors."

Remy steps forward again and says to the group. "I'd like you all to meet Valerian Orleán." She turns and motions me forward. "Vale?"

I feel a flush run up my neck and into my cheeks. None of the Farm workers are looking at me, not yet—it's too dark for anyone to have put my face to my name. But I can feel Eli, Remy, and Bear, all watching me expectantly, and Eli's words from earlier come back to my ears. *Okaria loves him. He's our ace in the hole.*

I step forward and clear my throat, but words don't come. *What do I say? Why am I nervous? I've spoken before thousands of people before, in front of some of the most important people in the Sector. Why can't I find my voice?*

I meet Remy's eyes, the whites of them glimmering in what little starlight we've got. She tilts her head in an almost imperceptible nod. *All I can do is tell the truth.*

"My name is Valerian Orleán." I pause to let this sink in, but no one speaks. No one moves. "If you've heard of the Resistance, you've surely heard that I've been kidnapped by this band of renegades, terrorists. You probably saw the broadcast my parents put out through the Okarian News Network, the one in which they claimed I'd been betrayed by my best friend, Jeremiah Sayyid. But I'm here to tell you that none of that is true. I stand before you tonight side by side with Remy Alexander, Elijah Tawfiq, and your old comrade Bear, as a member of the Resistance."

I stand a little straighter, draw in a deep breath. The last time I gave a speech was at my SRI graduation and it was broadcast throughout the Sector. I was nervous, but I was playing a part, eager to do my political duty and get on to the party where Jeremiah and Moriana and our other friends were waiting. I'm still playing a part, and Jeremiah is still waiting for me, but this time, there is no party. No chauffeured airship stocked with champagne. This time, lives are at stake and I have to take care to get it right.

"I wasn't betrayed by Jeremiah. In fact, Jeremiah is with us, too, waiting just a few kilometers away for our return. The truth is Jeremiah is *still* my best friend. No matter what my father or Linnea Heilmann tells you, Jeremiah did not betray me. My *parents* betrayed me. The Okarian Sector betrayed me. The leaders of our country betrayed me, and they're betraying you, too." I wait for that to sink in. The air is so still, the workers so silent, it's almost as if I've bored them to death. Finally someone speaks up.

"Don't make no sense. Why would your parents tell the whole Sector you'd been kidnapped if it isn't so?"

"Because they're angry I found out about the crimes they've committed and the people they've hurt. Because they're afraid I will tell the truth to honest people like you. Anger and fear. That is what is driving them."

"Crimes?" Someone says. "I don't believe it! What crimes could they have possibly done? Why they saved our lives what with that last outbreak on the Farms. Corine Orleán is a miracle worker. She can't be no criminal."

"As hard as it is for you to believe, it was even harder for me to believe. In fact, at first I couldn't accept it. It's impossible, I told myself. My parents can't be killers. And yet ... and yet...."

"Sam was killed because he asked too many questions about Remy's sister," Bear says, stepping in to save me. I thought I'd steeled myself to the facts, that by now I could say it all out loud, but I'm thankful for the interruption.

"He was surely dead to us, dead to who he'd been before, the moment he came out of that silo," Luis says, nodding as if to reassure himself that speaking up is the right choice.

"And Remy's sister and everyone else in that classroom were killed by Corine. Remember I was there," Eli says. "The man who killed those students was no Outsider. He put a Bolt to my head," Eli places two fingers at his temple as if to pull the trigger, "He looked me in the eye and said 'Don't get on Corine Orleán's bad side,' and then he turned the Bolt around and shot himself. Tai was murdered, directly or indirectly, by Corine Orleán."

A shiver slithers up my spine as murmurs pass through the group of workers. I've seen those words, but only on a computer screen, when I read Elijah's testimony about the massacre when I broke into my mother's office and hacked into her computer. Hearing them spoken out loud gives them new meaning. *I can disassociate myself from my parents, but they will always be a part of me.*

"And my mother was killed when the Sector attacked us and bombed our home in the Wilds," Remy says. I can hear the quaver in her voice, but she doesn't break.

"There's more," Bear says, reclaiming control of the conversation. "You've heard from Vale, Remy, and Eli what the Sector's lied about, who they've killed, but it goes deeper than that. The food we eat here at Round Barn does more than just make us strong and healthy to work. It also makes it harder for us to think, to ask questions, like Sam did. Like Rose does now."

"What does that mean?" Luis asks, now skeptical again.

"Were any of you sent to schools in other quadrants when you were little?"

"I was," a woman pipes up. "One of the teachers here thought I was good at math, so they sent me to a school in quadrant four."

"How long did you last?"

"I was there about three years thereabouts before I asked to be transferred back. I liked it better here. More time to play and have fun. And I like being outadoors."

"Did you notice anything different when you got back?"

"No, back to the same fun and games," she says, and there's a few laughs around the room.

"Well, I went, too, but I did notice something when I got back." Bear says. "When I was five, I was sent to a nice school in one of the factory towns. They thought I was good at language and spatial imaging, that I might be good at art, like Remy. When I got there, I suddenly started seeing things in colors—"

"We all see things in colors, Bear," Luis says, and this time there's quite a few laughs around the group. Bear smiles sheepishly.

"But do you smell in colors?" he asks, and that question sends a hush around the group. "Do you feel things in colors? When I was at their school, one of my teachers spoke in a voice that sounded the same way storm clouds look. A friend in school gave me a feeling as deep amber as good whiskey—"

"Now, what's a boy like you know about good whiskey?" a man at the back says, and there's another round of laughter.

"I didn't know it then, ya see, but I know about whiskey, now. Point is, I could feel and smell and taste things I'd only previously been able to see."

"It's called synaesthesia," Remy says. "I experienced it, too, when I was eating Sector MealPaks. The Dieticians put special chemicals in the MealPaks of people who are artists to enhance their ability to paint or describe the world around them."

"But that's a good thing, isn't it?" Luis says. "You make it sound like what the Dieticians do is bad."

"Wait a minute," the woman who'd also been to a quadrant school speaks up again. "Seems like there was a difference when I got back home. I couldn't read as fast, or do math in my head like I had been able to before, when I was at the other school. But I didn't care back then. I didn't like it in town. I wanted to go home and they let me. Didn't give it another thought after that."

I note that Rose was right about this group: they have more of a sense of self, an ability to question, to think critically, than I'd expected based on what Bear told us of the Farms.

"That's just it," Bear says. "I did care. Experiencing the world the way I did at school was fantastic. I loved it. But when they decided I wasn't good enough to go to that school anymore and sent me back here, they took me off those drugs and I didn't get to taste or smell those colors anmore. It wasn't my choice—it was theirs. I didn't know why that happened until I was much older, and I met Remy here."

"So what are you saying?" the same voice asks.

"Speak up, Ren," Rose says, turning to the speaker, her voice challenging. "What do *you* think Bear's saying?"

"I don't know ..." the woman says, her voice soft, unsure.

"Don't matter if you know for certain or not. Take a guess. What do you guess he's saying?"

"That the MealPaks have stuff in them that can change us?" Ren says.

"I haven't eaten a MealPak in three years," Remy says. "Sometimes I miss those colors I used to experience. Sometimes I miss not being able to draw as quickly or precisely or remember images as clearly as I could before. But when I stopped eating the MealPaks, I realized I wasn't the same person the Dieticians had been making me, all those years. It was like all my life I'd been standing in front of a mirror in the darkness. Then one day, I reached over and switched on the light and there I was. Me. The *real* me."

It occurs to me again, as it has more and more often in the last months, that I never experienced this change. Everyone in the Resistance talks about this process of withdrawal from the Sector's drugs, both physically and mentally—and we all saw the effects in Miah, when he had an especially hard time coming off the MealPaks. I feel as though I've missed a rite of passage. And more than that, I keep asking myself, over and over, *why?* Why has everyone else seen this change and gone through this process of self-discovery, when I alone feel exactly the same, mentally and physically, as I did in Okaria?

"Drugs?" Luis says. "They aren't drugs. Drugs are dreamweed, or cannabis. What the Sector puts in our MealPaks—"

"Is biochemically identical to the effect of dreamweed or cannabis, just in smaller doses," Eli says, cutting him off. "Did you know that at least one out of every five Farm workers has benzodiazepine, a calming drug, in their MealPaks? When criminals go to the Asylum, they get put on the exact same drug. It's designed to calm you, to keep you from worrying about things, to accept what the Bosses tell you without question."

There's a long silence as we wait for further objections, and none come. Finally, Luis speaks again.

"I don't get it," he says, in a tone that is neither judgmental nor bitter, but simply confused. "I'm happy to be who I am now. If I don't eat my MealPaks, do I turn into somebody else?"

"Point is, the choice to be you should be yours." Rose reaches out and takes his large, rough hand in hers. "You're lucky you're happy with who you are. But I'm not. I want to be more. I want to be like Remy, like Bear. I don't like the notion someone else decides who I am and that they can decide to hold me back from being all I can be."

"Luis," Remy speaks up. "Would I like to experience the same sensations I experienced while eating my MealPaks? Sure. But it should be *my* choice. No government should force its citizens to eat foods that have been altered in order to alter the individual. If you choose to eat food enhanced to make you smarter or stronger, that's okay. That's your choice. But no one should force you to ingest chemicals, to put things in your body in order to change you, control you. If the Dieticians offered you a choice, you could decide on your own. Just like we're offering you a choice now," Remy says, addressing everyone in the group. "You don't have to fight with us. You don't have to fight at all. It's up to you. But remember what the Sector did to Sam, and Tai, and my mother. If they can do that to them, they can do it to you, too."

I speak up again and all eyes turn to me. "Sometimes choosing is hard. It was hard for me to realize my parents were not the people I thought they were. It was hard for me to realize they had hurt people I love. And it was hard for me to leave Okaria behind. But I did. I made the choice. Now, it's up to you to make a similar choice. But as you make that choice, also try to keep in mind that the chemicals in your MealPaks influence how you think."

"Those of you who've had enough can go back home, if you want," Rose says. "But for those of you who want to help Remy and Vale and Bear make a change, who want to choose for yourself who and what you are instead of having the Dieticians make that choice for you, you stay here. *Nous avons de travail a faire,*" she says, and I translate in my head: *We have work to do.*

No one moves. Even Luis, sitting at Rose's side, looks unhappy, but unwilling to leave.

"I don't know about all that stuff you said about the MealPaks," he says, finally. "And I'm happy being who I am right now. But what the Bosses did to Sam was wrong, and if what you tell us about your sister and your mother, Remy, is true" he says, "*je suis vraiment desolé*, then I want to help make it right, if we can."

"*Merci beaucoup,*" Remy says, graciously, though her voice has the tremor of loss in it that I hear every time she talks about Tai or Brinn. But a smile tugs at my lips, watching her, listening to her speak. *She could lead them anywhere*, I think. I know I'd follow her.

"So," the voice I now know as Ren rings out, "what do we do now?"

17 — VALE

At the conclusion of the meeting, we'd told Luis and Rose's friends to lay low for now, and spread the word, if possible, about what they'd learned.

"We'll tell you our plan as soon as we can," Remy said. "We need to get more food, untainted, wholesome, for you to eat and share with your friends." I noted she didn't tell them not to eat their MealPaks, hoping, I supposed, that the placebo would kick into effect sooner than later.

"You know," Eli says as we trudge back, "the chemicals in the MealPaks are only half the equation. Soren's right. We need to get seeds from the LOTUS database in production."

"I realize that," she says. "You and Soren can head back and lead that effort any time. I'm not stopping you, and I didn't ask you to come rescue me."

Eli starts to protest, but Remy stops and turns to him, her hand resting lightly on his chest.

"Eli, I know you want to protect me. I know you love me like a sister and I love you like a brother, but you don't have to stay. LOTUS *is* important. I know that. Vale could stay with Bear and me. We could go Farm to Farm talking to the people and the rest of you can go back and lead the raid to get the seed printer. Maybe that's the best thing."

I don't say a word and neither one of them ask for my input. I'm heartened by the idea that we could work together on the Farms, that we've reached that point, but now that I feel like I'm truly a part of this team, I don't want to break it up so soon.

Eli doesn't say anything, but he nods and grabs her hand, and we head back to the cave. It's around one in the morning before we finally crawl under our blankets. Remy, I note with satisfied relief, snuggles in at Eli's side instead of Soren's.

The next morning, I roll over on the hard ground and push myself up on my elbows. Everyone is still asleep, or at least still tucked into their bedrolls. There's only one thing missing: Jahnu's head, usually pressed close to Kenzie's bright red hair.

I stand up and stretch. I look outside and note that Jahnu's got a gas stove out and is heating some water. I walk outside and he smiles up at me.

"Hey," he says.

"Morning. You been up for a while?"

"Yeah. I couldn't sleep. Everything happening has set my mind on edge."

This is more than he usually says to just about anyone other than Kenzie or Remy, so I sit down to savor the experience.

"I know what you mean," I say. "It's like listening to thunder rumble across the lake before a storm breaks over the city. Something big is building and all we can really do is wait and be ready when it comes."

He nods. "It is like that, isn't it. I miss watching those storms roll in over Lake Okaria. It's not the same when you're surrounded by trees."

I glance around us. "Though being surrounded by trees has its perks, too. Like, say, taking cover when the storm does roll through."

"You're not so bad, Vale, you know that? I knew all those years there had to be a reason Remy liked you so much, why she just couldn't let go, but I could never figure it out."

"Hell of a compliment, Jahnu," I grin, teasing him, even though the little tingle starting in my belly tells me just how nice of a compliment it really was.

He laughs. "It was, wasn't it? There's a reason I keep my mouth shut most of the time. If I get started, I tend to rattle on or say things best left unsaid."

I hear a rustling behind me, and turn to see Kenzie standing over me.

"Hey, love," she says to Jahnu, dropping down beside him. She rubs the sleep out of her eyes, her frizzy hair a chaotic swirl of red and gold. "Morning, Vale."

In a few moments, the encroaching daylight has opened everyone's eyes, and Jahnu's pouring tin cups of tea out for everyone.

"I'll get a new message to the Director first thing," Eli says. "Let her know we need reinforcements and a lot more food."

"So how did she take the news that we weren't coming back?" Kenzie asks. "You never said."

"Not well," Eli says with a glint in his eye. "But she gave credit where it was due. When I told her what Remy and Bear had done at the Dietician's lab, she grudgingly admitted that 'that wasn't completely idiotic.' I think she's willing to work with us."

"Damn. That's high praise, coming from her," Soren acknowledges.

"Do you think they'll be able to get food here today?" Remy asks.

"Tomorrow morning at the latest," Eli responds. "They might have a lot of cooking to do."

"Damn Farm workers ate all our food," Firestone mutters. Eli rolls his eyes.

"They did not," he retorts. "We've got boar to spare. And we only gave them what Remy and Bear brought. There's enough left on our airship to get us through the day with leftovers."

Firestone growls under his breath, and I remember from our weeks in the woods together that mornings are by no means his favorite part of the day. "That scrawny pig is tougher than shoe leather. Must have been the oldest pig in the whole damn Wilds. Certainly the rangiest."

"So what's next?" Miah asks. "Are we just waiting around, for now?"

"Waiting for the reinforcements," Eli responds. "Oh, I forgot to tell you. Guess who's leading the reinforcement team?"

"Who?" Miah looks wary.

"Your dad. Ezekiel." Miah just blinks at him, unable to process this information. "Apparently he leads a raid team at Teutoburg, which isn't far from here. He'll be flying in with several others and a shipload of food."

"My dad? Coming here?" Miah finally responds.

"Yeah," Eli says, with a bit of a laugh. "Tomorrow morning."

Miah and his dad didn't always have the best relationship while we were in the Academy, but since we've left the Sector, I sense that Miah's willing to re-evaluate a lot of things. And that includes his estranged father, the man who abandoned him and his mother to join some group of crazed conspiracy theorists who'd all gone off the deep end. Also known as The Resistance.

Remy stands, taking the rest of us by surprise.

"I need to head back to the Farm."

Eli stares at her.

"Now? In broad daylight? Why?"

Remy shakes her head. "Not now. Tonight. There's an enormous building on the campus, and no one I've talked to has a clue what goes on in there. I want to find out what it is. Maybe there are weapons we could use, or equipment, or seeds we can confiscate. It must be important, so we should find out what it is before the others get here."

"Why not wait until we've got backup," Eli says, his voice almost pleading. "The Dietician's lab was risky enough."

"The more people we've got milling around here, the more likely it is a drone will sight us. We need to go in tonight before backup arrives. We need to know what's in there." There's an edge to Remy's voice, a threat in her eyes, that reminds me of the tone Eli took when he held a Bolt to my head and a knife to my throat when he found me and Miah out in the Wilds. "What if it's something they could use against us?"

"What's the rush?" Soren ask. "Tomorrow we'll have more manpower, additional food, and the workers will have had one more day on untainted MealPaks. Let's give it all a rest today."

"The rush," she says, glaring at Soren, "is that there could be weapons in there that we could use, or they could use against us or against the Farm workers. If we know what's going on in there, we could avoid a lot of trouble down the road. If we don't, we could be blindsided by something they're hiding for a reason." Remy pauses before her next statement, and her eyes meet mine as she speaks.

"Vale, what do you think? You willing to rush into this with me?"

"Drone," Remy whispers. "Take it out. Now."

I turn my Bolt up to the sky and aim carefully. Now is not the time to stun them—we can't risk them sending any photographs or evidence of our presence back to the guard stations. I press my finger to the trigger, exhale, squeeze. The flash of blue light is concealed from open view by the surrounding trees, and I'm grateful we're not into the Farm proper yet. The drone plummets like a dropped rock, crashing into the ground about thirty meters off.

The fight that ensued when Remy told everyone she wanted me to accompany her on this adventure was spectacular, but short-lived. Eli sat quietly, looking unsurprised but a little disappointed. Sad, even, as though he'd been the last chosen for a game of football back at the Academy. Soren, by contrast, flipped into an altogether different kind of anger than I'd seen before. It took Miah slapping a hand on his mouth and telling him to shut the fuck up unless he wanted to just go ahead and broadcast our location to the whole fucking Sector. When Miah finally got Soren to shut up, Remy just stared at him.

"Look, Soren, it's only rational. If Vale comes with me, and we get caught, there's a possibility we'll make it out alive. If you come with me, and we get caught, they'll shoot us on sight. And even though I don't think we'll get caught, I'd like to live through the night on the off-chance that we do."

I try to leave that memory in the distance, wishfully replacing it with one where Remy wanted me along not because of my name but because I'm a good soldier, because I don't shout at her when I disagree with her, and maybe, *just maybe*, because she wants to be near me.

Thinking of the drone, I turn to Remy. "We should make sure it's disabled. Don't want it coming back to life and relaying crash data to HQ."

"Let's do it," Remy agrees.

We jog a little out of our way and spot the collapsed drone caught in the bramble of two bushes. The circular, formerly hovering robot has four cameras and two low-powered Bolts attached—about what I expected for Farm security. I prise open the panel to the nanocircuitry and disable the connections with a few quick movements.

"We're good," I say.

"I've never been able to master those circuits. I usually find a rock and smash it. Not very elegant, but it works."

I shake my head and laugh as we start off again. This time, we're not going through the hole in the fence Bear showed us. We've been relying on it too heavily, Remy decided, worried that someone would eventually catch on. Since we're dressed for mobility, we're going up and over the fence at the point of shortest distance between the perimeter and the mystery building Remy wants to investigate.

Remy slaps the charge on her set of magnetic gloves, and begins climbing. The fencing material is too slick to climb any other way, and there's nothing for a hook or line of rope to catch on at the top. The magnetic gloves work fine, although the climb is anything but easy. We're hauling ourselves up using upper body strength alone. I'm grateful I've been keeping up on Aulion's training routine, even at Normandy. The man might have been a first-rate bastard, but he sure knew how to work a strength routine.

Luckily the climb is short, as the fence is only five meters high. We're up and over in a matter of minutes, dropping silently to the ground.

"Any guards?" she asks.

"None visible."

"Shoot to stun, if you have to shoot at all."

"Remy," I say, glancing down at her, tense and alert at my side, "they won't return the favor."

"That doesn't mean we should kill them," she says. "Not all the Enforcers are bad people. They might not deserve our pity, but they don't deserve to die."

"Death is inevitable in war," I respond, so quietly I almost can't hear myself.

"You think I don't know that?" Her voice is harsh. "But I have my list, and these men and women aren't on it."

I ponder these words for a second, trying not to think about the people who undoubtedly *are* on her list. "Okay. For tonight," I say and follow her lead as we jog into the Farm, staying low to the ground.

As we draw closer, I blink three times to switch out of infrared into visible spectrum. The night is so dark I can't even see the building she's talking about until we almost run into it. Remy slows her jog and heads directly for a piping and air duct system on the exterior.

"Hand," she says, as soon as we've reached it. She meets my eyes for half a second as I cup my hands in a stirrup. Then she puts her boot into my laced fingers, and clasps my shoulders. With an enormous effort, I heave her as high as I can, and with a quick motion she grabs onto the frame below two large exhaust fans.

Remy grabs at a pipe coupling and begins to pull herself up toward the roof, three stories high. She looks like a spider crawling up a web. And then she disappears.

I press my body up against the wall and wait. Not five minutes later, I hear Remy's voice whisper in my earpiece.

"Here it comes." I look up to see a rope tumbling down toward me, and I catch it before it can swing wide. I hated rope climbing back when Aulion stood at the bottom timing me, yelling at me no matter how fast or slow I went. Even with no Aulion, I still hate it. At least now I can use the side of the building to propel myself upward instead of swinging like a pendulum in the middle of the gymnasium. I jump and get a good handhold and start climbing. Once I'm over the edge, Remy unties the rope from around the base of a section of solar harvesters and motions me to follow her.

We crouch low and make our way through rows of panels. Except for the dim reflection of starlight, everything is shadowed and silent. At the far end there's a door and we head toward it, careful to stay low so we cast no shadows. Remy tries the door, but it's locked, unsurprisingly. It doesn't take me long to fish out a lock pick and open the door.

"Simple, really," I whisper. "Not much security up here."

"Why would there be?" Remy responds.

Remy opens the door just a crack and we peek inside. The closeness of her body distracts me for a second, and I have to tell myself to keep my mind on the task at hand. *Focus, Vale!*

Inside, there's nothing but darkness and a few dim red lights indicating the power to the facility is still on. She pushes the door open enough to slip through, and I follow suit, shutting it carefully. I check to make sure it's auto-locked behind us—we want to leave everything exactly as we found it in case we don't leave by this door—then we slink onto the inside balcony, scanning the expansive space for sensors, monitors, or cameras we need to disarm, but there's nothing obvious.

We walk through a darkened hallway to a flight of metal stairs, which leads onto a large open platform that overlooks the ground floor. I blink back to infrared and, from this perspective, we can almost see the entire space of the building.

Remy, in her heat-cloaking gear, is now just a floating face at my side, a hovering blur of heat from her exposed skin. I look around. Stricken by the sight in front of me, I suck in a breath.

"Remy," I whisper, awed. "Are you on infrared?"

There's a pause as she activates her infrared contacts and then she gasps, and together we stand there for a moment, taking in the size and scale and weirdness of what we're seeing. There are enormous, two-story high towers of heat, pulsing gently, probably twenty of them, spaced evenly throughout the facility. As I look more closely, I realize they are slatted, sheets stacked upon sheets inside round containers. The tall vats are surrounded on our level by a wraparound balcony. Right in front of us, a walkway leads to a small elevator spanning this level and the ground level. Although what moonlight there is filters through the domed glass ceiling, the place is still shrouded in deep shadow.

"What *is* this?" Remy says, hushed.

"No idea," I respond.

We continue along the platform, which leads right up alongside the blocks of heat. There's a powerful scent of antiseptic, and something else I don't quite recognize, something fresh and heavy but off-putting somehow, not a little revolting. Remy leans closer, but I keep my head up, trying not to get too close.

"Should we risk a light?" she asks, peering down into the containers.

"We should confirm there's no additional security, first," I whisper. "Nothing that might trigger as we start poking around."

Remy nods in assent.

"Let's do a quick sweep, then. Disable anything you see."

I follow her down the stairs at the end of the suspended walkway. We split up and scan the area. I keep my eye out for cameras or internal security, but there is none. No guards. Doesn't even look like there's a guard station. The strangeness of this place has set me completely on edge.

"Looks like the puppet masters never imagined the puppets would cut their strings and go exploring," she says, her eyes gleaming, her thoughts echoing my own. "No security at all."

"I don't like it," I respond. "This is the largest building at the Farm, with minimal exterior security and none on the inside. They obviously don't think anyone would ever come in here. But why?"

"Rose mentioned once that she thought this was a greenhouse, but that made no sense since there are no windows. But if that's what the workers are told, and they believe it, no questions, why would they try to break in?"

"Wouldn't some of the workers work here? Unless the place is automated. Maybe whatever's going on in here doesn't require a lot of manpower."

"Let's flip on a light and see what they're keeping so quiet," she responds, her voice conspiratorial, almost eager. I wish I shared her enthusiasm. The whiff I got earlier unsettled me and almost turned my stomach.

Remy pulls a biolight out of her pocket and flips it on. We both blink back into visible spectrum. She turns to the nearest vat and moves right up to the edge. She presses her gloved fingertips against the glass, staring into the large container.

It's one of the strangest things I've ever seen.

There are thin slats of some sort of bioplastic film layered horizontally all the way up the glass container. At the top, the slats are mostly empty, but as the slats go down, they are fuller, loaded with gelatinous material, some almost honeycombed, some more liquified than anything. At ground level—waist heigh for us—the material is fully solidified and, from my perspective, utterly revolting.

We stand and stare at it, stunned at the weirdness, and then it hits me. I remember back to one of my history classes at the Academy: As the population spiraled out of control in the Old world, raising animals naturally became not only an insufficient method of production, but impractical because of clear-cutting of forests for grazing and subsequent soil degradation and mineral depletion. When scientists discovered it was possible to grow protein tissue in petri, a new industry arose, one that replaced the unethical and unhygienic industrial animal processing facilities. But these protein companies, too, succumbed to the profit motive as they expanded too rapidly, competing for market share in the race to displace conventional industrial animal farms. To undercut competitors, businesses grew meat products with little to no nutritional value leading to rampant vitamin deficiency. Lax regulation coupled with poor oversight resulted in routine outbreaks of illness from Salmonella, E. coli, and listeria monocytogene poisoning.

I pull back from the glass and fight the temptation to retch. Remy, however, doesn't seem to have quite caught on.

"Remy," I say, my voice louder than it should be, "it's a protein lab. They're growing meat."

She turns to stare at me, and then quickly turns back to the vats.

"Oh my god," she whispers. "I thought this was illegal?"

"It *is* illegal. The third tenet of the OAC's incorporation doctrine was that they would never grow meat laboratory style, like the protein industries of the Old World."

"So why is this here? Surely they don't put this in the MealPaks?" Remy doesn't seem to share my revulsion, her fingers still pressed up against the glass, leaning forward and staring into the vat like a child seeing a new animal for the first time.

"What else would they do with it?" I swallow my disgust and step up to the glass next to her. I point upwards. "I'm just guessing, but I think this is how it works. Up there is where the protein starts, for lack of a better word, gestating. The sheets are moved slowly downward as the protein develops until down here, it's fully formed. At this point," I point to the handles that pull out to open the vat, "whoever's working here can pull out the bioplastic, cut the meat off, and prepare it for serving. The plastic probably gets cleaned somewhere nearby and then reused. Or maybe it's recycled. In the old days, the lattices were made from organic material and actually became a part of the meat. Like cartilage."

Remy wrinkles her nose.

"Gross."

I pull out my own little light, and point it around us. Off in the corner, I see a door that leads into a closed-off space.

"Over there," I say, pointing to the door. Half of my desire to move is motivated by curiosity, a need to understand this place; the other half is pure revulsion, the twist in my stomach telling me to back away before I get sick.

"It's gruesome," Remy says, as she follows me to the corner, "but so weird I want to keep looking at it."

I shudder, aghast at the thought that I've probably been eating that stuff for the vast majority of my life, now more thankful than ever for the Resistance food.

We try the door which is locked and secured with a palm and retinal scanner. Still no cameras.

"I guess they don't want people in here," Remy says.

"But they also don't think anyone would try to break in," I respond. "If they did, they'd have something more than just entry identifiers."

"There's a window," Remy says, pointing. She walks over to it and presses her biolight up against the glass. "Hard to see in, though."

Through the glass, I can just make out a few plasma screens, pulsing a soft red light that indicates they're in sleep mode. There's also a series of microscopes, a laser scope, as well as a mass spectrometer. Beyond that, it's hard to identify any of the equipment.

"This must be where they monitor the protein growth," I say.

"I suppose it's easier to customize the chemical components in the meat when you're growing it in a lab than when you're growing it on the bones of a living animal," Remy says. "It's just another step in the OAC's control over the food chain. And they're breaking their own law to do it. In a twisted way, it makes sense. Why raise real animals when you can grow meat in a lab?"

"Especially since the demand for meat in the Old World and the clear-cutting of rainforests for grazing was a major contributor to global warming. It also contaminated the groundwater with the effluent from the meat farms. Lab meat was seen as an ecologically sound practice."

"Makes sense in theory. Except then they went and screwed it up. When all the meat a population eats comes from just a few huge laboratories, the chance for contamination is high, and that's exactly what happened. I don't remember the details, but a huge industrial accident, a major contamination and leak of some sort, led to thousands of deaths."

"But the Sector Assembly blamed the outbreak on the Southwestern Confederation and declared it an Act of War—industrial sabotage, murder. At least that's why I remember from my history classes."

Remy nods. "Yeah. The Sector accused them of purposefully introducing the disease into our food supply and so banned in-vitro meat production. It was a big deal. Since then, the Sector has been talking the talk about all the 'back-to-the-earth' farming practices. But really they're cooking up these globs in a lab." She shakes her head and shudders. "At least I've been off it for three and a half years. I feel bad for you and Miah."

"And Bear," I respond, and the smile fades off her face. "And everyone here at the Farm who still eats it, every day. And they have no idea that—"

"It's a farce." She's quiet for a moment, her almond eyes narrowed to uncompromising slits, staring into the darkened lab. "Everything is a lie," she says.

I hold my breath, move my hand a half-inch closer to hers, pressed against the glass pane.

"Not everything," I whisper.

Remy looks up at me, and for a second, I think I see something like admiration, or tenderness. My heart leaps as a wire-thin smile plays around her lips. But then her eyes narrow again, and her tentative smile settles into something harder.

"I know what we need to do," she says, her voice full of determination.

"What?" I ask, almost afraid of the answer.

"Cut off the power supply to this building." I stare down at her, amazed at her temerity, her courage. "Without power, their monitoring systems won't work, their heating systems won't work, the air ducts won't work. The meat will rot. Quickly. They'll be forced to turn elsewhere for protein. Just when we're flying in loads of supplies from our own stores."

I turn to face her. "We'd have to make it look like an accident, and—"

"Now," she says. "We need to do it now. While we're here. We know where their power source is—we passed it on the way in. The solar harvesters, on the roof."

"It's not as simple as just cutting the wires, Remy, we'll have to—"

"I know," she cuts me off again, and places her hand on mine, now resting on the railing. "We're going to do it anyway." She squeezes my hand and then turns and hurries back toward the stairs, her biolight swaying as she walks. I follow her, wondering what I've gotten myself into, what Remy's getting us into. If we cut off the power supply, they'll know as early as tomorrow morning that something wrong, and it won't be long after that that they'll discovered it was tampered with. They'll call in OAC guards. They'll crack down on security. They'll suspect it was us. They'll hunt us down. They'll punish the workers. They'll—

"Let's get the harvesters," Remy says, stopping the run of paranoid thoughts in my head. We're standing at the door to the roof, where we entered earlier. Remy pushes it open a crack.

"Wait!" I put my hand on the door. "You sure? If we do this, there's no going back. We can't undo it." I look down at her, the glow of the biolight wrapping us in an unearthly aura. She is beautiful, fierce, like something out of a fairy tale.

"You sound like Soren."

"I'm *not* Soren. I'm just saying—"

"There is no going back, Vale. Not for me." She looks up, her eyes searching my face, waiting. Expectant. "What about you? Any going back for Valerian Orleán?"

I'm surprised Farm security can't hear the thudding in my chest. I meet her gaze and shake my head. "No, Remy. No going back for me."

There are no words to fill the silence as I hold her gaze a moment longer. Then I push open the door, and she steps out onto the roof.

"Wait," I say. "Why don't we just cut the main power supply and get out of here?"

"Won't they notice that? If we steal the harvester films, it will take them longer to discover the cause of the outage."

"Won't take them that much longer." We head over to where the solar arrays tie into the main power line, and I stop and look out over the farm. "You know what?"

"What?" she says.

"I like your idea better. Besides, the Resistance can probably find a good use for the harvesters."

Her face lights up. "Let's get to work."

She cuts off to the right, following the conduits of power cords, encased in bioplastic for protection from the elements, while I walk straight ahead to the solar arrays.

At the first solar cell, I stop and drop my pack, digging out a small screwdriver and a pair of tweezers. I pry off the clear, protective layer of plastic, and then start to unscrew the photovoltaic panel from the rest of the array. The tricky part is getting the voltaic fibers to pull apart from the metal that supports them and conducts the electricity to the main system. Using the tweezers and the screwdriver in conjunction, I try to wedge the screwdriver in between the fiber panel and the metal supports.

After a few seconds, I've got it, and I use my fingers to pry the rest of the panel off the support. These are wafer-thin sheets of fibers, a combination of plant material and rare earth metals salvaged from the vast, decrepit solar arrays of the Old World, refashioned into much more efficient solar harvesters. They're thin but sturdy, so thin I can roll this one up into a tight little scroll and stuff it in my pack.

Working quickly, I move from cell to cell, first removing the plastic cover, and then peeling off the voltaic fiber panel, rolling it up, and jamming it in my bag. By the time Remy rejoins me, I'm halfway through the panels.

"They are all fairly new," I respond. "Probably deployed within the last year. My dad said these new ones have a ninety-percent conversion and retention rate. It's the thermotunnelling that makes them so efficient."

She lets out a breath, long and low. "Wow," she says. "I didn't even know that was possible."

As much as I'd love to explain the physics, there's no time. Instead, I show her how to disassemble the units, and soon she's deftly peeling the fiber panels away at my side. Working in tandem, we're able to finish the second half of the harvesters in about a half-hour.

"Okay," Remy says, looking at our packed bags. "Let's get out of here. It's going to be a lot harder on the way out, carrying all this stuff with us."

I nod, sling my pack over my shoulders, and follow her as we walk through the now-destroyed solar array and back towards the air duct system she climbed to get up here. Remy goes first, climbing back down the pipes and fans, and I follow. We can't risk the rope, as we'll have no way to untie it, and leaving it would be pretty clear evidence.

"I want them to think that maybe, just maybe, someone on the inside did this," she says, as she goes over the edge. "After all, they don't know we're here. They'll first suspect the Farm workers, but why would they do something like this? Their next step will be to turn inwards, to go after anyone who has access to this building. The longer we can keep them guessing, the better."

By the time I hit the ground, I'm giddy with adrenaline and a sense of rebellious accomplishment. Remy's enthusiasm is contagious. Together we've done something that will make a difference. That will set the ball of rebellion rolling. When the Farm Enforcers and Dieticians find out that the MealPak formulas have been tampered with and the solar harvesters have been removed, they'll pull the plug on the Farm worker's food supply until reinforcements arrive. When that happens, the workers will either go hungry or come to us.

We creep along the edges of the buildings, keeping to the shadows until we're far enough from the buildings to pick up the pace. Then we jog toward the perimeter through the stillness, the peaceful beauty of the landscape shrouded in darkness. We go up and over the fence with a little more difficulty than the first time, now that our packs are full of fiber panels.

On the other side, Remy pauses for breath, panting a little from the exertion of hauling herself over the fence.

"I'd love to see their faces in the morning," she says, almost gleefully, with a light in her eyes that speaks of both danger and promise. "The fire has been lit, Vale. Now, we just have to carry the torch."

18 — REMY

I half expect Eli or Soren to be pacing out in front of the cave, waiting for our return, but the area is eerily quiet. Just in case, someone is awake inside, though, I pull up short before we go in. I put my hand on Vale's arm and he stops, turns toward me. We didn't say a word as we jogged back in the dark, watching our footing, and trying to get as far away from the Farm as quickly as possible before the early birds get up and start the work day. It's nearly four in the morning, and now, it seems like there's too much to say. What we've done … it's just beginning to sink in. Sabotaging the formulas in the Dieticians lab was one thing, but this … this is a whole order of magnitude more dangerous.

"Any regrets? Second thoughts?" I whisper.

"We'll get read the riot act as soon as the others find out, but no. No regrets."

"This is just the beginning. We've started the revolution. I don't want anyone else to die, Vale, but it has to stop. It…."

"I know," he says. "And you didn't start it, Remy. They did. My parents. Aulion. Everyone on the Board, in the Assembly, at the OAC. Everyone who knew and looked the other way … Now we have to finish it."

"Thanks," I say, my voice, barely a whisper. "For … for going along with my crazy idea. If it'd been Soren, he would have—"

"You should know," he says, interrupting, his voice low, sonorous. "I would do—" He stops, clears his throat, and then continues, "I'm glad I was there."

I turn away, unsure what to say in response, but grateful for that little moment—whatever it was. I can't stop myself, though, from wondering how he was going to finish that sentence: *I would do … what?*

Just inside the cave, we find Eli still sitting up, head lolling forward, eyes closed. Some guard.

"Eli!" I whisper. He jerks awake.

"Remy," he says, rubbing his eyes. "How'd it go? What'd you find? Soren finally fell asleep. Bear was up half the night, too."

Vale sits and drops his pack, as I settle in next to Eli. I put my pack full of rolled-up solar fibers in front of him and gesture for him to look inside.

"We brought presents."

He opens the pack and peers in. "What are these?"

"You don't recognize them?" I ask, teasing.

"Wait...." he pulls one of the rolled up panels out. "What the...?"

"Solar harvesters," I say. "The fiber panels."

Eli's mouth drops open. He unrolls the panel and presses his fingers to it, awed.

"Where the hell did you get this?" He rummages through the bag. "And how many are in here?"

"Vale's got a pack full, too."

"What did you two ... I've got a bad feeling." Eli knits his brow and studies both of us. "Something tells me I should never allow you two to go off alone again." He points his finger at me. "Spill it. What the hell did you do?"

"It's a protein lab," I say. "Giant vats full of meat being grown *in petri*, industrial scale. Just like they used to do in the Old world, until all the bacterial outbreaks shut the labs down."

"Gods," Eli says, staring at me, then Vale, then back at me. "You're not joking, are you?"

"Serious as the grave."

"So ... the harvesters are from the lab?"

"We destroyed their power supply. Took all the solar harvesters off the roof. They'll have a hell of a time repairing that job, and hopefully it'll take them a while to figure out that the films from the solar panels are gone."

"It'll take at least a week to get that many new harvester panels to Round Barn and installed," Vale adds. "In the meantime, the meat will go bad and what will the Dieticians feed the workers and Farm staff? They won't have anything—or not enough—and we can smuggle our supplies in."

"But ... there's still livestock on the farm. They can slaughter them, surely, use them as substitutes in the MealPaks."

Vale shrugs. "It strikes me that the reason they're growing the meat instead of slaughtering it, is because they can manipulate it chemically as it's grown in the lab more effectively than by inoculating live animals. So even if they can use the livestock as a temporary substitute, the meat won't have the same chemical profiles, and since Remy and Bear substituted sugar water for the individualized MealPak additives, if they inject the meat as the Paks are being prepared, it still won't matter. Sugary steak. Yum. Could be good, but it certainly won't be as powerful chemically no matter what they're feeding or shooting up the livestock with."

"Plus," I add, "They'd have to slaughter quite a few of the animals on hand to supply the MealPaks they need to produce for all the workers and the staff in the next week. That would be a major operation in and of itself."

"So the Resistance airship is supposed to show up late tomorrow," Eli says, "and just when the supply of MealPaks dries up, we'll be ready to step in and hand out real food, *good* food. I'm sure Soren and the Director will think what you did at the protein lab is premature—okay, more like full-blown idiotic— but I get it. You were there, you saw the opportunity, you couldn't pass it up. I'd have done the same thing. Now the show's on. No turning back."

"Huh," I say with a laugh, more to myself than to anyone else. Miah, Soren, and Vale, their eyes scanning the horizon, turn to look at me.

"What?" Soren says.

"Nothing...." I shrug.

I squint into the last vestiges of the blazing sunset as they turn their heads skyward again. The four of us have hiked from the cave to a clearing near where the commandeered Normandy ship is parked waiting for the Resistance airship bearing reinforcements and food.

"It's just funny," I say.

They all look at me again. "What's funny?" Miah says, his voice is tight. Ezekiel Sayyid, Miah's dad, is leading the incoming team, and Vale told me on the hike over that Miah hadn't had a great relationship with his dad since his parents split. He'd been at the Academy when he got the news, and his dad basically disappeared. He hasn't seen him since.

"Look at us," I continue. "We're all standing here watching the sky even though we know perfectly well we won't see the airship with the cloaking on. We'll only know it's here when it signals us or when we feel the air displacement. And yet, we're all craning our necks expectantly, peering into the blue as if we can make the ship suddenly appear if we just stare hard enough. It's giving me a headache, frankly."

"A rare display of logic from the woman who makes a habit of breaking into laboratories and wreaking havoc in her wake." Soren shakes his head and looks back up into the blue. Seems like with each day in the field, our relationship slowly devolves back to what it was before, back before the ill-fated raid, before we were captured, before our escape, before the incident on the boat. Before Vale showed up. After all we've been through together … I don't quite know how to feel about it, but I do know it makes me sad.

When Eli decided Miah and I should greet the new team and lead them back to camp—Miah because of his dad and me because I could brief them about what we've accomplished so far—Miah immediately asked Soren and Vale to come along. He's obviously a bit bugged out about seeing his dad after all these years, and I guess he wants his two bests friends with him for moral support. Soren and Vale glanced at each other with something like grudging acceptance and, of course, agreed at once. If sometimes I feel like I'm yet another chasm separating the two of them, Miah is definitely the bridge connecting them.

We resume the wait and after awhile, a chilling wind whips my hair into a swirl of curls. I tuck a few tendrils behind my ears and look up. As the airship descends below the tree line and settles in to land, the pilot deactivates the cloaking, and the vessel comes into view—a rusty, clanky old thing, typical of Resistance equipment, so old the tripods give off a high-pitched squeal as they emerge from the hull. It's bigger than the "requisitioned" Normandy ship, closer to a transport class, but still nothing like the size of some of the Sector's airships.

"What a piece of junk," Miah says. I glance over at him. He's drumming his fingers against his arm. Nerves.

"Not like he had a choice," Soren reminds him.

"Do you know when his dad joined the Resistance?" I lean toward Vale, my voice low enough that only he can hear. "I've never met him."

"I'm not sure. But I do know they hadn't seen each other in years."

"Pretty impressive. Ezekiel commanding a team already. The Director must like him."

"Could have at least fixed up those tripods," Miah huffs, gesturing at the ship. "Never seen landing pads so off-balance."

Maybe they're sinking into soft ground. Either way, the whole thing tilts ominously. The loading bay creaks opens, revealing the shadowed interior from which a woman in dark green emerges. She looks to be a few years older than me, probably around Eli's age, and she's got a Bolt slung over her shoulder. *Good*, I think. *I'm glad they're prepared for battle.* She strides toward us, a bit of an easy swagger to her walk and a broad smile on face. She's got close-cropped blond hair and deep-set, intense eyes.

"Hey," she says, her voice deeper than I expected. "You must be Jeremiah."

"How'd you know?" Miah says, his eyes narrowing.

"Because you're the spitting image of your father, that's how," she says. "He talks about you all the time, you know. In fact, I'm kinda tired of hearing about how great you are," she says, a teasing twinkle in her eyes. "I'm Reika, by the way." She offers a hand to each of us, but stops at Vale and peers closely at him.

Vale shifts his weight, uncomfortable with her close examination. "Nice to meet you. I'm—"

"Valerian Orleán, of course," She's almost as tall as he is. "Never thought I'd have the privilege of meeting an Orleán up close and personal. Well, it's *truly* an honor." The sarcasm in her voice escapes no one, especially not Soren, whose smug smile makes me want to take him by the shirt collar and shout, *You were the goddamn chancellor's son, too!* Soren is apparently incapable of seeing how similar he and Vale really are, how easily their positions could have been switched, if it weren't for the scandal, the virus, that knocked Cara out of office. And Vale's parents' giving them a little political push out the door.

A few more people disembark, unloading their packs and stretching. And then, finally, that must be Ezekiel Sayyid—he's got hair almost as black as Vale's except peppered with flecks of grey, and Miah's gentle eyes and handsome swarthy face. He's a little slimmer, but every bit as tall, and he strides over to us with an air of command tempered by kindness. Miah stiffens, and Vale and Soren both inch closer to their friend. Both protective. Another thing they have in common.

"Jeremiah," Ezekiel says, reaching out to clasp his son's hand and clapping his other hand on Miah's shoulder. His jaw clenches and his eyes shine with emotion. He starts to speak and then stops. For a moment, he just stands there looking at his son. "You have no idea how much it means to me to see you here." His voice is tight and his accent is thick with the long vowels and slightly off-beat emphasis most Farm workers and people from the factory towns have. Firestone's accent is similar, though much more relaxed. Maybe it's the age difference, but Ezekiel speaks more formally than Firestone does.

Miah hesitates, then takes his father's hand. "Been a while."

But Ezekiel isn't put off by his son's reticence. He pulls Miah into a hug, holds him close for a long while and whispers into his son's ear until Miah's expression softens, and he returns the embrace. Soren turns away, and the hint of a melancholy smile crosses Vale's lips. Both have essentially lost their fathers, and I wonder whether either one overheard the exchange. When Ezekiel pulls away, there's a sort of understanding—not forgiveness or acceptance, necessarily—but full acknowledgement in Miah's eyes.

"You three need no introductions, but I guess I do. Zeke Sayyid," he says, extending his hand to Vale, Soren, and me in turn. "True friends," he nods as if satisfied we've passed inspection. "That's what matters." He claps his hands and the tender moment is gone.

"What say we get to work?" He turns to Reika, who has been watching the exchange between father and son. "Let's unload this ugly beast."

Working in pairs, we carry the supplies to the cave. I join up with a short, wiry man named Dale, while Soren and Miah are paired up, and Vale and Reika are just behind them. As we're about to head up the last big hill with the last of the crates, I catch sight of Eli running towards us. As he sprints, my heart rate spikes. *What the hell?* He stops just short of us, panting, hands on his knees.

"We've got company," he says between breaths. "Kenzie's on lookout. She spotted an OAC airship ... a dragon emblazoned on the side ... not even five minutes ago."

Then the strangest thing happens. Soren and Vale meet each other's eyes, and for perhaps the first time ever, they have the same thought at the same time.

"Evander Sun-Zi," they say, in unison. "The Dragon."

"What the hell's Evander doing here?" I ask. "Does he show up every time there's a power outage?"

"They must have already discovered that the problem with the power at the protein lab was no regular outage," Eli says, digging his hand into his side like he's got a cramp, still breathing heavily.

"Evander's control over the Farms is absolute. Anything suspicious and— boom!—he's there within hours," Soren says.

"If they've figured out the solar harvesters are gone, they're gonna treat it as an act of terrorism. They'd never believe the Farm workers could have anything to do with sabotage that sophisticated. So it's gotta be the Outsiders or the Resistance. Either way, they've sent in the big guns," Eli says.

Vale's brow is knotted. "Evander picks administrators he trusts, but if something goes wrong and he thinks it isn't being handled to his satisfaction, he fixes it. Immediately. My father always said Evander had a one hundred percent success rate. I've never had much interaction with him ... it's almost as if my parents kept him at arms length, you know? He was never invited to dinner like everyone else. Hell, even Aulion came to dinner once or twice. But never Evander."

"Big guns," Soren cuts in as if just realizing what Eli had said. His frown deep and his glare directed at the sky, the muscles along his jaw line clenching and unclenching. "Aulion and Evander. Fear and violence is how they fix everything."

"Well, we can't let him stop us," I say, summoning all the grit and determination I can. Soren and Vale, again, surprisingly, share a glance that reads *she should be afraid of him*. I ignore their newfound camaraderie. "So we need to stop standing out here in the open and get everything in the cave."

Zeke turns to Reika. "You and Dale head back to the ship, re-engage maximum cloaking, and double-check that all safety and self-destruct precautions are in place. Then get back here as soon as you can. Sounds like we'll be needing to rethink our timeline."

"So what do we do now that Evander is here?" Kenzie asks, once we're all sitting around the fire circle in the furthest recess of the cave.

"We continue moving untainted food in and distributed to as many workers as possible," I say, my mind running in a million different directions at once. "Security will have been increased, but we've established a few well-hidden drop points so we don't have to get into the Farm itself. If—no, *when*—they figure out about the sugar water—"

"—Evander will know it was us, not the Outsiders," Soren interrupts.

"And he'll be none too happy about it," Zeke says.

"The question he'll want answered is how long the workers have been eating untainted food," Eli adds.

"Evander does not have a light touch," Zeke says. "Once he suspects sabotage, he won't play around. Workers going through withdrawal are likely to be cranky, some may be sick, and none of them are going to like his tactics."

"If the workers protest—" Vale says.

"—it could escalate quickly." Soren finishes his sentence. He glances over at Bear twisting his cap in his hands, his young face creased in worry.

"Let's step back," Jahnu speaks up. "Evander could simply bring in emergency-prepared MealPaks from Okaria and get everyone back on regimen as soon as possible. Or maybe he'll just dump something in the drinking water, something that will get everyone back in "the zone" before things get out of hand. The last thing they'll risk is people asking questions, thinking for themselves. His first priority will be to tamp down the incident and then clamp down on security. After he gets the Farm under control, he'll turn his attention to us. We might have more time than we think."

"Evander won't bother looking for us," Zeke says. "He'll pacify Round Barn and send Aulion to take care of us."

"Wait a minute!" I spring to my feet, and everyone falls silent. "I've got an idea."

I run over to my pack, rummage through my gear, and pull out the tiny video camera I'd snagged at the last minute back at Normandy. I thought it might come in handy, but hadn't yet figured out a way to use it. Now, I have.

Back at the fire circle, I hold it up for everyone to see.

"Is that mine?" Eli asks, an accusatory frown on his face.

"Yeah. You spent so much time tinkering with it, but you never used it. So I borrowed it. Now I know how we can show all of Okaria what's really happening on the Farms."

"Go on," Zeke prods. I notice that, although Miah isn't saying much, he's watching his father's every move.

"We can't let Evander intimidate us into inaction. If he cracks down on the workers, why not record it? Then we hack into the Sector broadcast feed and play it for everyone to see." Everyone exchanges glances, but I don't wait for a response. "Think about it. Footage like that could change everything. It would show people the truth, inspire citizens to action. At the very least it will spark controversy, which is a damn sight better than silence and ignorance."

"Wait," Jahnu says. "We don't want to go in guns blazing and intentionally bring Evander's wrath down on the workers just to get provocative video footage."

"Evander's wrath doesn't depend on us. If he's here, his wrath is here," Bear says, a tremor of terror in his voice.

"This young man is right, Remy," Zeke says. "You have no idea what Evander's capable of. I've heard tell of floggings, public humiliations—and much worse. There've been rumors, but most of them are so outlandish they're hard to believe. Still, perhaps we should lay low for the next few days. See how things unfold on the Farm. Talk to the Director."

Zeke's gravitas and calm demeanor mark him as a leader and clearly those on his team respect him. But like everyone else's cautious, let's-take-it-slow attitude, his words of restraint make me a little crazy. Especially if we're truly on the cusp of something big.

"'Lay low, work quietly, move slowly!" I can't keep the frustration out of my voice. "That's all anyone in the Resistance ever says. But we're never going to get anywhere if we don't actually *do* anything. Every citizen of the Okarian

Sector is already at the mercy of men like Evander and Aulion. None of us are safe and we haven't been for a long time. They're *already* hunting us. We all believe Evander is going to take action, punish the workers somehow, so why not record it? I'm not saying we provoke him any further, just that we be there to record whatever he does and then use his own actions to reveal the truth."

"So we just go in and wait to see what happens?" Kenzie says.

"We go in prepared for the worst, but yeah."

"And what if the worst happens? What if we're discovered? More troops are brought in? Do we start shooting? To protect ourselves? To protect the workers?" Soren demands.

"Remy," Jahnu says, his voice low and soft. "If Evander is as brutal as the rumors say, then we will be outgunned and outnumbered. It could be Thermopylae all over again. Only this time unarmed workers would be caught in the middle. Is that what we want?"

"Of course that's not what I want. But do you really believe he's going to open fire on the workers? He may go after us, but he's not going to slaughter innocent people en masse."

"I don't know," Vale murmurs. "I don't think anyone knows what he'll do."

I look at Miah and then Vale, holding his gaze. "You and Miah are with us now. That you are still here gives me hope. Others will join us, too, but only if they know the truth and only if they have the capacity to understand it. We have an opportunity to make real change here. We can't let caution hold us back. We have both an audience and an opportunity. To abandon both now would be idiocy. In my opinion," I add, sitting down, but refusing to look away from the faces of my friends, comrades, my chosen family. The silence is deafening, but I hold my ground.

Finally, Vale speaks. "I'm with Remy. She and Bear have been working to tell the Farm workers the truth. Before them, Brinn and Gabriel did the same. While it may seem like things are moving too fast here at Round Barn, in reality, the Resistance has been at it for years. And you've made inroads. Look at Zeke, here. And Firestone. And Bear and his friend Sam." Vale pauses and takes a deep breath, letting it out slowly while we all wait. "Bottom line is we all believe Evander will do something, and know it won't be pretty. So let's get the footage and show everyone in the Sector the truth. We may never get another chance like this one."

"Okay." Soren draws in a deep breath, grimacing, as if it causes him physical pain to agree with Vale. "Nothing is safe anymore. We have to take our opportunities as they come, and be prepared for the inevitable fallout."

Kenzie and Jahnu nod. Eli stares at me, not speaking, but when I look over at him, he smiles, and I know he's with me. Bear looks uncertain, but resolute, and Zeke rubs his hands together, thoughtful. His team members watch him, waiting.

"The Resistance is based on an ideal of non-violence. To invite violence in such a way, and to then capitalize on the carnage, literally or metaphorically, is … quite a different strategy than what I'm used to. I am reluctant, I hope you understand, not because I disagree with your intentions. Rather, I want to keep as many innocent people free from violence as possible." He is silent again, then he turns to Miah. "What do you think, son?"

Miah's eyes go wide. Clearly he wasn't expecting to be addressed in such a way. "Uh. Well, the way I see it, if you stay silent, no one knows you're there. No one knows you care."

I glance at Vale and Soren and wonder if they think Miah's words are about more—much more—than his opinion about the operation at hand.

"It seems we're going to be discovered sooner or later, anyway," he continues. "Maybe we're being rash. But if we continue to go slow, we'll have nothing to say for ourselves when they do track us down, and no one will know we even tried to change things. If we make a move, we at least have a fighting chance to let people know we're here. We'll at least be able to say we did something."

Zeke considers his son, and I'm convinced Miah's words hit home. After a long silence, he looks around the circle, and then his gaze settles on me.

"All right, then. This is the path you choose?"

"It is," I say.

"So be it. We will help you if this is truly what you think is right. My only requirement is that we let the Director know our plans. Just in case."

19 — VALE

Explosions in the distance. Bolt fire to my left and right. Screams of fear and pain across the Farm. And Evander Sun-Zi facing me down with a Bolt in his hand and grenades clipped to his belt. I hope he doesn't have a death wish, or I might get a better view of those grenades than I'd like.

In the end, Remy was right. More so than she ever dreamed. When word got out that Evander had taken control of the Farm and that the MealPaks were being cut in half because of the meat shortage, it didn't take long for the Farm workers to start coming to us, via Rose and Luis, for more food. And come they did. By the second night after Evander's arrival, we had emptied our stores and were forced to radio the Director for backup.

"Remember, we don't have a goddamn 3D printer, Eli!" the Director shouted. "I can't just create food out of thin air!"

But by that point, someone on the inside had realized something else was going on, just as we had suspected they would. The Farm workers, far from being hungry and tired from caloric deprivation, were bright-eyed, restless, and growing angrier by the minute.

"Why won't they just feed us the food we grow?" one worker asked, as I handed her the last round of cheese to share with her daughter. "We got all kinds of stuff in the hydroponic greenhouse, plenty in storage, in the silos, too. Why can't we eat that?"

Because the Dieticians haven't processed it yet. Because it hasn't been treated with the individually-tailored chemical cocktail that renders you incapable of asking that question, I wanted to respond.

"That's a question for Evander," is what I said instead.

This morning, the third day after Evander's arrival, word got out that we had been picked clean as well. That's when the trouble really began. At first, it was a peaceful protest, but then someone managed to break into one of the storerooms. I don't know what they found there, but my best guess would be more food—food the Dieticians had been keeping from the workers. Whether because it hadn't been treated or it was for the staff, we don't know.

That fight turned bloody quickly. And it escalated from there, just as Remy had predicted. When Rose got word to Bear that all hell was breaking loose, Firestone radioed Normandy and asked for backup from all over the Resistance. That was when we decided it was time to go in. We emptied out all the weapons we brought from Normandy and all the weapons Zeke's team had on their airship and prepared for anything and everything. Bolts, grenades, pistols, knives, even rocks. When we were loaded down, Remy, the smallest and quickest of us all, fastened Eli's tiny camera to her headband and turned it on.

"Here we go," she whispered.

"Remember what Zeke said," Eli addressed us all, "We don't shoot to kill. Our job today is to record the protests and, if need be, protect the Farm workers."

We entered the Farm hoping to get the evidence we need to prove that things in the Okarian Sector are not what they seem. And that's how I find myself face-to-face with Evander Sun-Zi, weaponless, my Bolt long since lost.

Casually, he lifts his Bolt and fires a shot that blitzes past my ear. He missed on purpose—that much is obvious. Taunting me, I'm sure. Instead of my life flashing before my eyes, I see the last three days reflected in the blazing heat of the azure flame. I see the slabs of meat growing in those huge vats, Miah hugging his dad, Soren looking at me with grudging acceptance, and Remy, always Remy, nodding, smiling, laughing. Small gestures that fill me with fire.

"Joined up with the losing side, have you?" Evander sneers. I don't respond. If there's one thing controlling, angry types hate, it's silence. They don't have the patience for it. "What are you going to do out here without mummy and daddy to save you? Aulion always said you were a coward."

Just two days ago, I was looking into Remy's eyes, standing so close I could have kissed her without taking a step. Now I'm looking into Evander Sun-Zi's, his flat cheekbones and deep-set eyes maniacal in the afternoon light. The only thing I want to kiss him with is my Bolt, which was knocked to the ground when an Enforcer nabbed me in the ankle and I tumbled down a hill.

It's too beautiful today, too beautiful for this fight. If only I had access to Demeter. She'd tell me what his weaknesses are and how best to take him down. All I can do is watch his stance, his hands, his eyes—remembering Aulion's instructions in hand-to-hand combat even as I hope he hasn't led me astray. *Watch your enemy's eyes, not his hands,* Aulion said. *They'll give him away.*

I keep my mouth shut and my eyes fixed on Evander while he rambles on and the fighting rages behind us.

"The *Resistance*," he mocks, waving his weapon at me. He's standing casually, even-footed, over-confident. He's not making any sudden motions but his weight is on the balls of his feet, ready to move in an instant. He's damn quick, his movements sure and ferocious. But I know he's not going to shoot to kill. Not yet. He isn't done talking.

"Little boys and girls without the guts to see the way things really are. To see that to maintain order in this world, you have to keep the people in their place. Did anyone ever tell you how I got my nickname, Valerian?"

"No, Evander, do tell," I say, glancing around for something to use as a weapon. I spot a gnarled branch, an old dead trunk from one of the vines, lying a few meters away. I'm about to jump for it, but Evander follows my eyes and pops off a shot to blow the thing to smithereens, showering me with splinters and forcing me to cover my eyes.

"A dead branch?" He laughs. "Really?" Laughing as though this is the funniest thing he's ever heard, he takes aim at my feet and fires. His movements are careless. He's toying with me as though I am a worm, ready to be squashed beneath his boots. I have just enough time to dive and roll to the side to get out of the way. Fortunately this puts me a few meters closer to him. I'm almost within reach. He takes a few steps backwards, his eyes narrowed, suddenly more alert.

"Not bad, Valerian. Your footwork has improved. Have you been practicing?" I don't respond. He grins again. "You are curious, aren't you? How I got my nickname."

"I'm waiting with bated breath."

He shakes his head as if he feels sorry for me. "I think you'll find it interesting. It's a story about the last time the Farms rose up in rebellion. It was back when Cara Skaarsgard was chancellor, when SD210 went running through the grain fields and everything died." He says the word 'died' like he's telling a group of children a ghost story, drawing the syllables out and making a clownish sad face that, I'm sure, will haunt me until I die. He backs up slowly, out of the vines and toward a little mound. I keep my eyes trained on his, willing myself not to break eye contact, finding my way through the turned ground slowly, by feel rather than by sight. When he stops talking, the games will begin.

"Starvation was rampant, but little boys like you would never have known, because I kept everything running smoothly and made sure your parents got all the food they needed to keep your little tummies full. But to make sure children in the capital were happy, children on the Farms went hungry. Poor things."

He drops the childish narration. His voice harsh. "There was a rebellion at Four. Live Oak. They stormed the silos and tore down the greenhouses, just like they're doing today. Three hundred workers in one of the hothouses, looking for something to eat, snatching tomatoes and peppers right off the vines, tearing down trellises, stuffing their faces as they went. Poor hungry bastards." His eyes gleam with anticipation. "Know what I did?"

Suddenly Evander's not looking at me, but above me, beyond me. I can't help it. I follow his eyes, turning slightly to the side so I can keep him in my peripheral vision and still see whatever it is he's looking at.

Another airship is hovering over the Farm. It sits about thirty meters above one of the hothouses the workers have broken into. It takes me a moment to recognize the design. It's not military-grade. With twin flamethrowers positioned at the front, these are the ships we used to use to clear forest or swamps for new farmland. They aren't equipped with gun batteries or shield capabilities and they haven't been in regular use for about thirty years. But now I'm thinking of Evander's nickname and wondering ... *Where is Remy? Where are the others?* My eyes are trained on the airship, watching it descend. I can barely comprehend his words when Evander says, from behind:

"I breathed fire on them."

The airship now hovers about ten meters above the ground, and my heart stops as twin jets of blue-white flame erupt, sending people below running, screaming, engulfed in flames, their clothes incinerated, hair burning, and flesh dripping like grease from their bones.

I cry out, but no sound comes.

"Evander Sun-Zi, the Dragon," he says slowly, drawing out every syllable. "That's how I got my nickname."

I pause for another half-second, my thoughts rattling in my skull, watching as dozens—no, at least a hundred—Farm workers are incinerated in the flames. The field lights up, wet and smoking, as the airship pivots in the air. People running, screaming, rolling on the ground. Smoke and autumnal orange and dragon's breath. It smells like fall, the crisp scent of crackling fire, but with the added aroma of death. Flames sucking at the heels of screaming protesters like a cat lapping up cream.

I turn, lunge at him. My only thought now is preventing that airship from doing any more damage, and I can't do that if I don't have a weapon. I put every ounce of energy I have into that initial spring, bounding at him like a deer over a hedgerow. His eyes go wide with surprise as he skitters backwards and pulls his gun up, but I'm too fast. My hand is on the barrel, pushing it to the side and out, so that when he pulls the trigger the hot metal burns my arm but the shot goes wide. He throws his other arm up at me, perhaps thinking my hands are going for his throat, to kill him, but I'm focused on the weapon. With my right hand I pin his shoulder to the ground and with my left I wrench the Bolt out of his hand. He brings his knee up into my gut but I've already got what I came for, and in an instant I'm off and running.

The airship hangs in the sky, and I imagine the pilots sitting safely above the melee, smug, waiting for orders. Bolt fire from our cloaked airship starts raining down on the sector ship, but Miah and Firestone are too high, their direct hits can't target the underbelly where it's most vulnerable.

The ship's attributes run through my mind.

Airship, light class, model introduced S.A. 64. Twin flamethrowers installed for land clearing and Farm work.

Firepower: None unless modified.

Shield capacity: Light.

Shield dispersal: Located at the wing-to-hull joint.

Control systems: Hull, front belly, beneath cockpit.

That's twice in one day I've had to be grateful for Aulion's intensive drills. The idea that I might owe that man anything makes me sick. I bit back the sting of bile as I run.

I don't have much time before Evander or one of his soldiers comes at me, so I flip the energy dial to its highest setting, kneel, take aim, and fire. At this setting it takes three full, endless seconds to recharge, but in that time I can see I missed. I swear, aim again, and fire, and as I wait for the capacitor to reload, I watch the blue Bolt fire strike the exposed intake vent of the engine compartment. Sparks and flame shoot forward as the airship lurches sideways and starts to fall. I stand, watching as it tumbles slightly from the sky, listing downwards, and then—

White explosions of light in my vision, followed immediately by blackness.

Pain.

Nausea.

When I come to, my head hurts like hell and I feel like I'm suffocating. I gasp for air before realizing there's a boot pressing into my windpipe, just hard enough so I can pull in slow, raspy breaths. Before I open my eyes, I know the boot belongs to Evander. He's holding the Bolt I stole from him, watching something in the sky. From this vantage point it's hard to see his expression. I wriggle and try to move, but then he looks down at me and points the weapon at my head.

"Not a fan of fairy tales, are you? Otherwise, you'd know it's a bad idea to rouse the wrath of a dragon."

His face is neutral. He looks like someone casually remarking about a change in the weather. He turns back and looks at the sky again. I crane my neck, but nothing's there.

"Aulion will be disappointed when he hears I got to you first," he mutters to himself. Then he glances down at me, a look of fatality in his eyes. His fingers clutch the gun a little tighter, and I know he's had enough of my antics. He's stopped talking. That's how I know. I close my eyes and wait for death to take me. The thought flies through my head as hope dies in my chest: *I love you, Remy.*

But instead of dying, I feel the pressure fall away from my throat and I open my eyes again to the brightness of the world and see that someone has a knife to Evander's back. Someone small, dark, and with an unruly mess of brown curls like a halo crowning her head.

20 — REMY

Spring 13, Sector Annum 106, 15h09
Gregorian Calendar: April 1

My heart beats all over my body. In my thighs, in my chest, in the pit of my belly, the blood pulses with insistent, unstopping regularity. In that pit I feel the spark of hatred, and it's beautiful, powerful, intoxicating. I hate Evander and everything he stands for, and now he has nowhere to go.

"Drop the Bolt and get off him." My voice emerges as a growl, low and unfamiliar, as though it came from someone else's throat.

"Ah," Evander gasps, as my knife presses into his throat. "True love. Aulion was right after all." He chokes out a laugh and tosses his Bolt aside in a gesture of surrender. It infuriates me. I know he hasn't given up so easily—no, this is mockery. "Valerian Augustus Orleán betrayed the Sector for a girl."

Vale coughs, gasps, sits up. I can only just see him out of my peripheral vision. My eyes are locked onto the airship, the ship that just moments ago was hailing fire and death down onto the people we were trying to save. *Was Luis down there?* I wonder desperately. *Was Rose?*

Anger, the same rust-red color as the burning field below, clouds my vision. But it's tempered by gratitude. *Thank you, Vale, for doing what none of us could. For taking down that airship. The damage has been done, but you did what you could.*

Then an elbow connects with my ribs, and in one astonishingly fast motion Evander knocks my knife arm up and safely away from his throat, twists around to land an open palm in my diaphragm and a gleaming blade squarely in Vale's shoulder. I double over, the air in my lungs gone. Vale, who had been struggling to his feet, is back on the ground, blood already staining his clothes. Evander dives for his Bolt, slings it over his shoulder, and turns away, sprinting.

Come back and face me, you fucking coward!

Vale sits up again, his face a mask of anguish and concern. I run over and kneel beside him. I lay my hand on his chest, and he looks at me almost bashfully, blinking back tears of pain and yet somehow a smile teases the corner of his mouth. Then he reaches up to grasp the hilt of the knife buried in his shoulder and wrenches it free, grimacing from the pain. He falls back on his elbow, gasping.

"I'm fine," he manages. "I'll be fine."

I nod at him, briefly, meeting those sea-green eyes and thanking all the fates that it's not him I'm facing on this battlefield. I draw in a deep breath, clench my knife in hand, and set off after Evander.

I can't think of anything except The Dragon. I knew that he would be violent, but I underestimated his capacity. That double-barreled airship, the flamethrower, torching people—men, women, children—before my very eyes. Their screams, their limbs flailing helplessly, trying to beat out the flames. The way they eventually, inevitably, crumpled to the ground like puppets with their strings cut. They were innocent, and they died.

I couldn't help them.

Like Evander's flames, the hatred grows, an inferno flickering into life in my belly. Sparks flying, it towers upward into my chest, spirals into my breath, ignites my eyes. Everything is at once more lucid, more *real*, than it has ever been, and yet this is not me. Someone else, *something* else, is in possession of my body, propelling my legs forward, pumping the blood through my veins till I am deaf with the sound of it. A power I've never felt before overwhelms me, and I can only watch as this new creature hunts for justice.

I lob a few low-energy shots at him. My first two are misses, and he jumps to the side and starts running again, but my third connects solidly and brings him spinning to the ground. Another shot and he flops like a fish out of water, convulsing from the electrical pulses. Then I am on him, my knee drilling solidly into his diaphragm, preventing him from drawing breath or fighting back. I place my Bolt against his gut and fire again. He goes still, but at low energy the strike is not enough to kill him.

My mind is fully disengaged from my body, as if I am floating above myself, watching as I press the Bolt into his throat, grab my knife, and pull it up to his cheek.

"A is for Alexander," I whisper, saying it aloud even though he's unconscious, drawing shallow breath. He doesn't stir as I draw blood. My words echo in the stillness around us, the bedlam from the battle behind us has faded to nothingness. I carve a thin, light A into his flesh and draw a circle around it. *The crudest image you've ever drawn, Remy.* Droplets of blood collect on my knife and run down his cheek.

"For my sister, Tai Alexander. For my mother, Brinn Alexander. For my father's heartache, Gabriel Alexander. For Eli, my chosen brother. For Sam, who asked too many questions. For my grandfather's secret."

Blood runs back toward his hairline, tracing its way around his ear and dripping into the grass. The blood is quick to congeal. I turn his cheek and slice an "R" into the skin of his left cheek, drawing a circle around it, too. "For the Resistance. For Remy. For Revenge. You won't ever forget me, now."

He opens his eyes and gasps, and the roiling inferno blazes so hot in me I want to retch. He doesn't yet know what I've done. He can only feel the pain—thin, hot lines traced into his flesh.

"You'll pay," he chokes out, then he spits in my face, and I pull the Bolt back and crack it up against the side of his head.

"Fuck you," I hiss and wipe his spittle off my chin with my sleeve.

I glare down, the fearsome Dragon, unconscious for the moment, my bloody marks carved into his face. But instead of pride, the usual reaction I have as I step back to admire my work, I feel nothing but shame. *What did I just do? How could I have done this? How could I be filled with so much hatred, and think its power was beautiful?* My insides are scorched, charred. I press a finger lightly to the edge of the "R" and feel the bead of blood on my fingertip. With a heave, I pull off him and pocket my knife.

I leave him lying in the grass, and turn away, seeking peace and stillness and understanding. *What have I done?*

In the distance, the fighting seems to have quieted. A lull. Bodies lie strewn among the grasses, some moving, others not. Out of the corner of my eye, I spot two soldiers following me, creeping through the grass. I see a flash and dodge their Bolt fire by skidding then rolling on the ground in front of me, but then I'm on my knees firing and catch one of them in the hip. It's enough to send him down. The other stops to aim at me, but the shot is off by a few inches.

But before he can reload, he gasps and crumples. I look in the direction of the Bolt that took him down and see Vale, kneeling behind a blossoming cherry tree, watching me.

The tree, a cloud of white-pink flowers and fragrant nectar, untouched, somehow, by the fighting, seems totally out of place amidst the death and destruction at my feet. The stark contrast between the serenity of the tree and Vale, decked in his military garb and with a gun cocked against his shoulder, makes me want to cry.

I turn a three sixty, looking around for any remaining soldiers, but I see none. Most have retrenched or evacuated—for now. They'll be back, though.

And in full force.

Reaching up, I touch the camera still attached to my headband, and I pull it off, turn off RECORD, and stuff it in my pocket. The world seems to have gone quiet and still as Vale approaches. I swing my Bolt back over my shoulder so it rests on my pack. He reaches out his hand to help me up, and I think back to the raid, the night he captured me and Soren and took us back to Okaria, prisoners of the Sector.

"Are you okay?" he says. He'd asked me that same question that night. And then he'd said, *I'm not going to hurt you ... Remy, I'd never....*

Today he saved my life, just as I saved his.

"Yeah," I say, and put my hand in his. He pulls me to my feet, and, without saying another word, we run toward the Resistance rendezvous point to join the others.

"Might not make it."

Might not make it. Jahnu might not make it. Jahnu is injured. Jahnu might not make it. Jahnu might leave me, too. Jahnu, dying. Jahnu, my best friend. I never worried about Jahnu. He was quiet, patient, careful. He was supposed to make it. He was safe.

I lean on Eli's shoulder, and feel the medic's words echo in my mind, over and over again. I can't process it, I can't move forward from that, I want to hold on to it as a possibility, as a 'might,' and never ever let it go further. It's impossible. He can't leave. He can't die. He's been my best friend since we were in diapers. We were going to grow old together. We were....

But he might make it. I cradle that thought like a baby. If I nurture it enough, it could grow into a reality, it could come true. In the next room, the surgeon cuts through muscle and bone to keep Jahnu alive, and it could happen, it could.

Beside me, Soren's got his arms wrapped around Kenzie, rubbing her back in slow, methodical circles. She looks into the distance as if nothing exists. I, too, feel as if nothing exists anymore except the vague comfort of Eli's presence and the thread keeping Jahnu in this world. The Farm certainly doesn't exist anymore. Many of the workers fled into the woods, including Luis and Rose, and many others died. The rest are under lockdown. The second decisive battle in Resistance history, and, just like at Thermopylae, we were utterly caught off guard by the severity of the Sector's response. Evander Sun-Zi, true to his nickname, brought to Round Barn the flaming wrath of a dragon.

I sit and stare at the floor waiting for news, vaguely aware of people coming and going. Someone puts a blanket around my shoulders. Someone else puts a drink in my hand.

"Drink this," Rhinehouse says. *Rhinehouse? When did he get here?* He hands me a cup of something vaguely brownish. I stare into it, watching the liquid swirl and lap up against the edges like tiny tides against the seashore. Not that I've ever seen the seashore. It's only something I know from my dad's poems. *Oh, Lake Okaria has waves,* he used to say, *but it's not the same.* Now Jahnu may never see the seashore. Never feel the ocean tide rushing over across his skin. Never grow old with Kenzie. "It'll help you sleep," Rhinehouse says.

"Come on," my dad says. *Dad?* My father gathers me into his arms and ushers me down the hall to a dimly lit room and a rickety bed where Kenzie is already asleep. He pulls the covers up over both of us, sets the cup on the floor beside me. "I love you," he whispers and brushes my hair back from my cheek. *I remember the feel of my knife on the Dragon's cheek.*

I roll over and stare up at the ceiling.

"You okay, Little Bird?" Eli asks. *Where'd my father go?*

"Yeah," I say. *No,* I think.

"Remy?" Soren asks, his voice hushed. When did he get here? I look over at him, sitting gingerly at the foot of the mattress. Next to me Kenzie is sleeping, a few stray red curls peeking out from under the blanket. "Did you kill Evander Sun-Zi?"

"No, I didn't kill him. At least, I don't think I did."

"What do you mean, 'you don't think you did'?" Eli says. He's kneeling beside me, eyes tired, hooded with worry. "Either you did or you didn't."

They're both whispering, but their voices pound against the inside of my skull like drums. I shake my head. "I'm sure he looked dead, but I didn't kill him."

"We're expected at a briefing in ten minutes," Eli whispers. I push myself up.

"All of us?"

"You don't have to attend. You can rest."

For once, I'm glad he offered me an out. I don't think I could talk if I tried. I can barely understand my thoughts, my actions. I don't understand who I was out there. Who I've become.

The droplets of blood collecting around the knife as I carved my initials into his cheeks.

"Okay. I'll stay here with Kenzie."

Eli leaves my side. Kenzie moves slightly, and Soren gently eases himself up and moves to sit next to me. He takes my hand in his. I stare at his whirlpool-blue eyes and wish I could lose myself in them, just disappear, drown in the depths of those irises, forget everything, and swim in them forever. But I can't.

"I want you to know—" he hesitates. "While we were out there with Bolts flying and everything on fire … I saw you standing over Vale. I saw what happened." I nod numbly. "And then Vale, taking down the other guard … I want you to know, no matter what happens … with any of us … I really care about you, and I want you to be happy. I want us both to be happy someday. Okay?"

I don't understand, so I just nod.

"I just wanted to say that." He strokes the back of my hand.

"Okay. Thank you. I want you to be happy, too, Soren. Can you hand me my cup?"

I drain it and hand it back. He leaves the room, and as the sleeping draught takes effect again, I move closer to Kenzie. In her drugged sleep, she pulls me near, and even though everything hurts and nothing exists but the possibility of Jahnu not being with us anymore, I feel warm and safe next to her. We retreat to our own sanctuaries of unconsciousness, refugees from the pain of possibly living in a world without the brilliant, patient, kind, loyal, funny, sweet, peaceful man we both love.

It's the smell that pulls me halfway out of sleep. Rhinehouse has hung rosemary, thyme, lemongrass and bags of dried rose petals everywhere to try to mask the scent of dead flesh coming from the burn victims.

"Can't this wait? They're still sleeping." Vale. I recognize his voice, but in the fog of my drug-induced sleep, panic grips me and all I see is Evander's boot on his throat, Evander's bolt pressed against his temple, Evander's knife in his shoulder.

I gasp, sitting up and throwing the covers off. "Vale!" I cry out. Then I remember that he is okay, that we are still here, I calm down. Beside me, Kenzie moans.

"No it can't wait." It sounds like the Director's voice, but I'm not quite sure. "Get her up and bring her to the meeting room. Now." Definitely the Director. And whatever they gave me, they must have given twice as much to Kenzie. I attempt to run my hand through my hair, stand, and pull the blanket back up over her shoulder. The taste in my mouth is horrendous. *What was in that stuff?* I push the door open and step out into the hallway. Vale's standing just outside as if he's on sentry duty.

"How is Jahnu?" I ask.

"Hanging in there, but…."

"But?"

Vale looks away. "It doesn't look good. He's stable, but the next twenty-four to forty-eight hours will make all the difference."

Suddenly, the idea of Kenzie passed out while Jahnu's life hangs in the balance really pisses me off. "Maybe Kenzie should be in there with him, instead of sleeping in here with me. Whose idea was that?"

"Doctor's orders. He said she needed to get some sleep. We can wake her up before heading to the briefing, if you want. Did you sleep well?"

Vale reaches up as if to touch my face, but catches himself midair and instead lets his arm drop awkwardly to his side. He clears his throat.

"The Director wants to see you." He looks like he wants to say something else, so I wait. I place a hand on his forearm. His skin is warm under my fingertips, but he pulls back, just out of my reach, nervous, or jumpy, or something. He takes my hand then and leans forward, and I almost think his lips might touch my forehead, but he stops and looks down.

"I want to thank you." His voice is thick and soft, with an intimacy that both confuses me and sends me tumbling into unfamiliar territory. The space between us feels wildly different than before. I find I cannot move. I am drawn to his warmth like iron filings to a magnet. "You saved my life."

"And you saved mine. The shooter. You took him down."

He nods, and then asks, "What did you do to Evander?"

His question, though there's no hint of accusation or disgust in his voice, brings me up short and I pull away, breaking the moment, feeling the accusation and disgust well up inside myself. I say, perhaps too defensively, "I didn't kill him. I didn't even really hurt him."

"I know that now, Soren told us, but—"

I look at the wall. I can't bring myself to say it and look at him at the same time. "I cut him."

His hand instinctively moves to his face where his fingers rub over his chin, as if he could feel the ghost of the pain. "On his face?"

I nod "He'll have the letters 'R' and 'A' scarred permanently into his cheeks."

He draws in a slow breath. "That explains everything."

"What happened between you and Evander?" the Director demands even before I'm through the door.

"Why does everyone keep asking me that? I didn't kill him. Though he doesn't deserve to live."

She's glaring at me, and even though she's about a centimeter shorter than me, her ferocity combined with the drugged haze makes her look about three meters tall.

"Evander and Corine made an official Sector broadcast yesterday denouncing you as the leader of the group of rebels that destroyed Round Barn."

"I cut off the power supply to their illegal meat factory, but beyond that, all destruction at Round Barn was Evander's doing."

"They say they have video of you carving the 'symbol of the Resistance' into Evander's cheek."

My cheeks flush. "They're lying about the footage, there weren't any drones nearby." I don't mention that the video footage I took captures that moment in excruciating detail.

"Answer me!"

"Yes, I cut him." I say, trying to keep my voice even.

"What the hell did you do that for? And what symbol are they talking about?" she demands.

"It was the letter A for Alexander and the letter R for the Resistance. And for 'Remy.'"

She studies me for a moment. "That's not all." She takes a step toward me and out of the corner of my eye, I see my dad flinch. "Tell us everything that happened, Remy. Everything. We need to know what we're dealing with."

The pain etched into my father's face cuts me as surely as my knife cut Evander's flesh. *Would he rather I killed him?* Everyone stares at me, waiting. The heat from Vale's body warms me, and I realize he's stepped closer, and I'm glad he's there.

"That's all," I say, shaking my head. "Some part of me wishes I'd killed him. But I didn't. I'm glad I didn't."

Carving into Evander's skin was primal. It was an out-of-body experience. The act arose from a place so deep within me I don't even recognize it now. Cutting him solved nothing, I know that. But I don't regret it, either.

"What made you think it was a good idea to carve your initials into the

Dragon's face? By all that's sacred, Remy, what were you thinking?"

He deserved it, after what he did to the workers at Round Barn. He would have killed Vale. He would have killed me. How can the Director not see that? A little scar on his cheek won't ruin his life. She shakes her head at me as if I'm a wayward child. The rage bubbles up again, nearly choking me.

"What was I thinking? I was thinking of my sister and my mother. I was thinking of my dad and Eli. I was thinking of my friends, Rose and Luis, whose lives are ruined because of Evander—because of the Sector, because of their lies! I was thinking of everyone who died, everyone who was burnt by that airship. Everyone else that I've never met that Evander killed, as if they were bothersome flies. Cockroaches to be exterminated." I couldn't stop the words from pouring out. "You weren't there. You didn't see his boot on Vale's throat. You didn't see how he looked at him, how he looked at me. You didn't see the look on his face as he watched dozens of people go up in flames. He was *happy*. He would kill you, me, every single one of us and not even think twice. He's the personification of *evil*. And he was unafraid, even when I could have killed him. And believe me, I wanted to make him afraid."

"Please. Tell us that's everything, that's all that happened."

I don't say a word. Everyone in the room is waiting. I meet Eli's gaze and he's looking at me with awe, as if he's never seen me before. Soren and Bear and the rest of them, looking up at me as if I've grown a second head. A much scarier head. With horns, maybe.

"Remy," my dad says. "Is there anything else? We need to know."

"That's all. Except when he woke up, he spat in my face and said 'you'll pay.' I knocked him upside the head with my Bolt and that's it. That's everything."

The Director looks as if she wants to shout at me some more. But in the end, she sighs.

"Here's what's happened, Remy, because you did this thing." Her eyes are boring a hole in my skin. "They're painting the battle as a victory against the rebels who kidnapped Vale, and they're claiming you're the newest leader of the movement. Evander's gunning for you. Not just the Resistance. *You*. To try you for treason, war crimes, and mass murder."

War crimes? Mass murder?

"They've pledged to track you down and execute you on public broadcast, for the whole Sector to watch." She pauses to take a breath. "Evander even made a personal statement after the official transmission."

"What did he say?" I ask, but I feel as though I already know.

"He said, 'No matter where you go or how hard you try to hide, Remy

Alexander, you'll pay."

I pull out a chair from the table and sink into it. I should be shocked, trembling with fear. But I'm not. Instead, I'm thinking of everything they've done to strip me of who I am. I remember my mom and dad giving me the news that Tai was dead. I remember sitting across a desk from Vale's dad while guards applied electrical feeds so they could tase me over and over again. I remember Soren's bruised face as he recoiled from General Aulion, and my father bending over my mother's lifeless body as more OAC Black Ops—Vale's mother's operatives—dropped from airships overhead.

But still I didn't kill Evander. *Does that somehow make me better than them? That I can carve my initials into his face, and not kill him, and imagine I showed him mercy?*

My fingers reach for the compass that hasn't left my body since Vale gave it back to me. *Which way is north, Granddad? I'm lost in the woods, and I don't know how to find my way.* The golden metal against my skin, warm from my body, is comforting. Calming.

"I have camera footage of the battle. I can prove that the Sector's forces were harming the Farm workers, not members of the Resistance. It will prove that the Resistance tried to protect the Farm workers. We can prove that Evander is lying." *Maybe I can find my way, after all.* "We already knew they were hunting us. Ever since Soren and I escaped from our prison."

The Director sighs again, and this time it seems to lift a weight from her shoulders. She straightens and drops her gaze to the floor.

"We've been hunted since the moment they discovered the existence of the Resistance. The only thing that's changed is that now you're the target. You're the eye of the storm." She pauses, takes a breath. "Where is this video?"

"I have it."

"We need to watch it. To see just what, exactly, it will prove. How it will help us."

"Okay." But I can't give it to her. I can't give it to anyone, yet, not until I erase the part where I cut Evander Sun-Zi. No one can watch that. That is history I never want repeated.

"Philip and Corine are one thing, Remy," my dad begins. "History is littered with power hungry politicians like them. But Falke Aulion and Evander Sun-Zi are monsters of an entirely different species."

My dad looks over at Rhinehouse. For the first time I see worry, *fear*, on his face.

"I've known those men for decades," Rhinehouse says. "Aulion was a friend of mine for more years than I can count. We fought together and explored the ruins of the Old world together. When and why he turned, I may never understand. Aulion may have codes, principles that he operates by, buried somewhere within him. But Evander...he was never a man I could relate to."

"No one could," the Director adds. "He has no codes, no morals. He's fierce, ruthless, and brilliant—he couldn't have risen as far as he did otherwise. But he's psychopathic, hungry for power, without real human emotions that make him vulnerable. He's not afraid of you, Remy, because he's not afraid of anything. His nickname fits. You've awakened a monster."

I can't bring myself to say anything. Nothing seems appropriate, helpful. So I look at the Director and wait to see what she will say.

"We're relocating this base tomorrow. Everyone has to move." My jaw drops.

"But what about the wounded? What about Jahnu? Is it safe to move them?"

"You've given us no choice, Remy. They're coming after you, and they know where we are."

Hot tears well up in my eyes but I bite the insides of my cheeks to keep them from spilling out. I'm ashamed, confused, angry, distraught over everything all at once. I am appalled at the hatred and violence that emerged within me when I cut Evander, but do I regret what I did? Can I regret it? Should I have killed him? Should I have run away from him like a scared little child, afraid of monsters hiding under the stairs? And what can I expect of him now, now that his eyes are focused directly, squarely, on me?

"Where are we going?" Vale asks.

"We're not going anywhere together. *You*—" she gestures to me, Vale, and Soren "—are going to find the Outsiders."

21 — REMY

"They are beautiful creatures," my dad says, stroking Lakshmi's nose. Lakshmi, the tawny mare that will be my ride for the next few weeks, is smaller than the other horses, but I think she is more beautiful by far. Her mane's the color of butter and her coat glistens, even at this early hour, with the merest hint of dawn sieved through the branches overhead. The idea of climbing on her broad back and making her do what I want would normally be hilarious, but no one is laughing. Granddad had a couple of horses before he got too old to take care of them, and he'd hoist Tai and I up on them and lead us around the garden, but that's the last time I've ever even seen one in real life.

Now my dad gives me a boost up, and Lakshmi promptly begins snorting and pawing the ground. I have no idea whether she is eager to get moving or none too happy to have me on her back. I rub her elegantly arched neck, but its solid strength, a wall of pure muscle, is intimidating. Why would such a powerful animal ever deign to listen to me? Rhinehouse insists I'll get the hang of it in no time, but I'm not sure I believe him.

Rhinehouse and the Director, it turns out, are accomplished riders, having done quite a bit of it back when they were communicating once every three months in the middle of the Wilds and he couldn't risk flying airships out of Sector territory. Both have been given us pointers for the last twenty-four hours, but their advice has done more to terrify than reassure me.

They decided we'd travel on horseback to avoid drones. Horses, of course, don't give off electromagnetic signals like hovercars and airships, and, apparently, there are wild herds roaming the outer reaches of the Wilds so a few more won't raise suspicions. Plus the Outsiders use them so we'll be less likely to scare the hell out of them showing up on horseback than if we arrived in a hovercar or popped out of the air in a cloaked airship. Besides, as the Director has made abundantly clear, every airship and hovercar the Resistance has access to is needed for evacuating the temporary base and for transporting the injured. Injured like Jahnu.

So while Soren, Miah, Vale, and I hit the trail like cowboys, as Firestone calls us, everyone else is staying behind to help with the evacuation. Bear is hanging back to be with the Farm workers who decided to join our cause—few of them did, after the chaos at Round Barn. But there are enough that the Director specifically asked him to stay, especially after Rose and Luis turned up with several stragglers in tow. Eli is staying to work with Rhinehouse on the LOTUS project and to organize the raid to finally get their hands on a 3D printer. He'll be working with Zeke's team on the raid. Zeke asked Miah to stay with him and join his team, but he opted to go with Soren and Vale, probably as a buffer to make sure they wouldn't kill each other along the way. Firestone is needed as a pilot to help with the evacuation, and although Dad wanted to come, in the end he decided to stay, again at the Director's request, to provide a calming presence for the injured, and to be with Jahnu. Kenzie, who, of course, will not leave Jahnu's side, was visibly relieved when Dad told her. She will get to see her own parents again soon as they're helping to prepare for the influx of people at the new base, but in the meantime, Dad will be there for both her and Jahnu.

Jahnu hangs onto this world by sheer stubbornness. Always right in the midst of the fray, he was protecting a group of children from several of Evander's more vicious Enforcers and suffered a third-degree Bolt burn to the shoulder and took three old-fashioned lead bullets—one sliced clean through his thigh, one nicked his pelvis, and one shattered a rib and nearly punctured his lung. Kenzie made sure the two Enforcers didn't live long enough to celebrate taking Jahnu down. Now, although his vital signs are stable, they're still not good, and I can hardly bear to leave him. But the Director has made it clear I have no choice in the matter. My job now is damage control, cleaning up the mess I made. And that means reaching out to the Outsiders to convince them to join our cause. We can no longer take on the Sector alone.

Before mounting up, I visited Jahnu in the infirmary one last time, biting back tears at the sight of the white bandages stark against his handsome ebony skin. I laced my fingers through his, laid my head on his dinky little pillow, and cried. The carefully constructed dam I'd built to wall off my emotions collapsed, and everything poured out in a torrent. I told him everything I ever wanted to say, just in case....

"You will always be my best friend, and I love you. If you don't, if you can't.... I'm going to find the Outsiders and I'll miss you with me. You're my rock, Jahnu.

My sanctuary. I'm so grateful for you, for your friendship, for sticking with me even when I was an ass, for always being truthful, but never judgmental, for all the laughs we had when we were little, for the funny faces and silly games and daydreams and quiet times when neither of us had to say a word...."

"Hey," he croaked, his voice almost inaudible. I jerked my head up and wiped my cheeks. His eyes were open. "Fly the damn coop, Little Bird. Make some magic in this world ... for me."

With mom and Tai, there were no true goodbyes, and that was cruel. So I pledged to commit to memory everything about the moment, not just the words, but the brown of my fingers intertwined in the black of his, the barest beginnings of creases around his eyes and lips that may never deepen, the intensity of his gaze as he struggled to make himself heard.

"I have to go, Jahnu. Promise me ... promise you'll try your hardest?"

He nodded, an almost imperceptible movement.

"A favor," he whispered, his voice creaking, like a branch in the wind.

"Kenzie ... tell her...." he paused, glanced over at the bedside table where there's a damp cloth and some ice chips. I wet his lips and he drew in a ragged breath. "She is my morning star."

Now Dad puts his hand over mine as I stroke Lakshmi's neck. He gives it a squeeze, and looks up at me. "You and Lakshmi make a good team. Take care of each other out there," he says as much to the horse as to me. "And try not to worry about Jahnu. Kenzie and I will be with him."

We both know not worrying is an impossibility, that life is not something you can bend to your will. Kenzie had been waiting outside the infirmary door, and I told her what Jahnu said. Seeing the happiest person I've ever known choking back tears, her eyes rimmed as red as her hair, was devastating. If anyone could will someone to live, it would be Kenzie. Or my dad, as he held my mom in his arms. But life doesn't work that way.

Again and again and again we say goodbye, we separate, our circle loosens, lessens, disintegrates. I memorize my friend's faces, keep the moment that I said goodbye to them imprinted forever on my soul. If I had more time, I would draw them all, etched not invisibly in my mind, but permanently in the world.

But I don't have time.

Today, we're headed into the Wilds to find the Outsiders. The real Wilds, not the forests we navigated through in the winter after we escaped Okaria, not the wooded areas between the Resistance bases; these are places that were destroyed by nuclear or environmental devastation in the ruination of the

Old world. They're nearly inhospitable, or so we were always told, and in the Sector they're called No-Go Zones. But now we know better. Now we know that the Outsiders—and who knows who else—have been living out there for generations, and we're going because, as the Director says, *we need allies.* We need people who know how to work between the Sector's lines, and the Outsiders have been doing it for decades. We need them because there is safety in numbers, and we need them if we're ever going to make use of the LOTUS database.

If we learned anything from the battle at Round Barn, it's that simple rebellion isn't enough. To execute our strategy, we need the Outsiders. To win over the citizens of Okaria, we need my video ... but I'm not willing to show it to anyone just yet.

"Remember," Rhinehouse says, "your goal is to convince the Outsiders to work with us. Not *for* us, but *with* us. They'll benefit as much as we will from the overthrow of the OAC leadership and the reestablishment of a Sector that lives up to its founding principles. You're all carrying the coded coordinates of our message drop points—in case you're separated—so try to get word to us as soon as you can, and we'll do the same." Then to me, "Remy...be safe. Be careful. Understand?"

"I understand."

"Off you go, then."

Vale, who has been appointed the leader of our expedition, nudges Mistral, his horse, to start. But all she does is shudder so violently I wonder if Vale is going to fall off, and then Mistral snorts out a loud fluppery noise and turns around to look at him as if to say, *Seriously? You want me to do what you say?* Vale kicks the horse's sides a few more times and all it does is lift its tail to plop out great brown steaming patties as the rest of us sit in our saddles waiting for someone to do something. Then Miah—who appears to think riding a horse is as exciting as flying an airship—surges forward with a soft whistle and a light slap of the reins on his horse's butt.

"Some leader you are, Vale," he calls, heading down the trail as if he's been riding all his life. Being a kid in the factory towns was apparently much different from being a kid in the capital. Firestone starts yeehawing like a wild man and yelling, "You go, Calgary 2!" and, as if that isn't amazing enough, I catch Soren and Vale exchanging glances.

"Did you know he could ride like that?" Vale laughs.

"No idea," Soren shakes his head in amazement. "Wonder what else he's been hiding from us?" Leave it to Miah to have Vale and Soren laughing together.

Then, without doing a thing, our horses begin to trot down the trail, following Miah's as if pulled by an invisible tether and jarring my teeth together like rapid-fire hammer blows. I turn one last time and see Rhinehouse shushing and scowling at Firestone and wonder what lies before us in the giant maw of the Wilds.

22 — VALE

Spring 18, Sector Annum 106, 19h00
Gregorian Calendar: April 6

After three days of traveling, we make camp in a dusty little ravine, overgrown with ragged, stunted trees, craggy shrubs, and a surprising abundance of wild goats. They're strange but friendly, unafraid of either us or the horses, and adorable in a kind of old-bearded-man-animal way. They keep attempting to eat everything in sight—including Remy's curls, the horses' tails, and our canvas saddlebags. Remy's taken to keeping her hood up and tied under her chin to keep them from sucking on her hair. I'm reminded of some photographs from the Old World I studied in my history classes. Some female adherents to an old religion called Islam covered their hair with headscarves. With her hood over her head so that only her face is visible, she looks like one of those women, and it makes her amber eyes stand out even more dramatically.

Our campsite is not completely inhospitable, but it's certainly no place I'd like to call home. For our purposes that's a good thing, since it means the Sector will have no reason to send any reconnaissance drones out this far. No reason to have drones in the region at all, since there's nothing to watch over besides the goats.

Unpacking and setting up camp tonight was a major chore because our collective asses are chafed and sore. After our first day of riding, I wondered if I'd ever walk with my knees in close proximity to one another again. By the end of the second day, Remy started sitting sideways in the saddle every once in a while just to give her legs a break. Soren was groaning like he had both feet in the grave. Miah's the only one who seems to be able to handle the pain. By the third day the horses finally seemed to get used to us, and we to them. We took the pace a little faster that day, often cantering and even galloping full out when we could. Whenever one of the horses gets a little stubborn, Miah takes the lead and they all fall back into line.

After we finish eating, we decide we're far enough away from any Resistance bases that I can activate the Outsider beacon on the pendant Chan-Yu gave me. After I recounted, for the fiftieth time, my experience with the nameless Outsider who led my team to Normandy months earlier, Remy and Soren have become convinced it must be their "Osprey," the same Outsider who left them bloodied messages and guided them to their boat after Chan-Yu helped them escape Okaria. I described the scars I glimpsed on her arms and the tattoos on her shoulder—"Like those water birds that fly over the lakes sometimes, the ones with the wide wingspan"—and now they're hoping it's Osprey who comes to our aid again. Everyone gathers round me, like it is some sort of ancient sacred ritual, and watches me flip the little switch with my thumb. *Flick, flick.* That's it. Then, when nothing happens—as if they expected an Outsider to appear out of thin air—we all go to bed.

Since the Director had given out many of the tents on hand to surviving Farm workers, we got what was left over—one double and two singles, "one of them for Remy," and even though I knew she meant it out of decency, it came out sounding like she was putting Remy in isolation. Remy, though, shrugged and looked pleased that she would have her own place to sleep. On the first night, I was afraid Soren would expect Remy to join him in the double, but he didn't say a word as she began setting up her tent. I suspect something's changed between them, but since neither one of them are in the habit of telling me their secrets or talking about feelings, I have no idea what might have happened.

"I don't mind sleeping alone," I offered, and we've been in the same arrangements since.

Soren's on early morning watch when his voice slices through the fog of sleep, and I wake to *What the hell? Fuck!* and then a thud and a scuffling sound as if he's fallen and is scrambling to his feet. I grab my Bolt and am up and out of my tent in a half-second, with hope as my guide, rather than fear.

And I see her. She turns toward me and her face lights up.

"Valerian. We meet again." And once again I'm struck by her appearance. Lithe and boyishly feminine, but as tense and taut as a pulled bowstring. Since it's not frigid and the snow's not up to our shins, she's dressed simply in camouflage pants and an open jacket over a skin-tight shirt. Just like when she pulled her coat up over her back to show us her tattoo, I can see she's slender, but she carries her muscled shoulders with the same aggressive, soldier's rigidity that I recognize from my military training. She's got her feet planted as square and even as a drill sergeant, and yet she looks as if she's poised, ready to spring at a moment's notice.

"Where the hell'd you come from?" Soren demands, brushing the dirt from his pants. Looks like he'd been sitting on the remains of a weather-beaten tree trunk taking the opportunity to shave and clean up a bit when the Wayfarer appeared. His shirt is off, draped over the top of his tent, and his mouth is hanging open, half of his face cleanly shaven, the other half sporting a stubbly shadow.

"Your friend Valerian called. I came."

"You could have said something. You scared the shit out of me."

"Skaars*gard*, I presume. Some guard." She reaches up and grasps his chin, moving it side to side. "You missed a spot." She rubs a thumb down the side of his jawline. "A big one."

Soren flushes, and I realize he's completely flustered over the sudden appearance of this almost mythical Outsider. *Soren flustered—now that's something I've never seen before.* The girl—the Outsider, the wayfarer—turns toward the third tent as Remy crawls out.

"Ah, here's the famous Remy Alexander, evil scourge of the Sector." Her eyes light up, in that same glowing ember-ish way I recall from the first time I saw her.

Remy clambers up, rubbing the sleep out of her eyes, trying to flatten her hair, which sticks up every which way. "You don't look nearly as dangerous as the Dragon makes you out to be," the girl says.

"Osprey?"

"Guilty as charged." She laughs and turns back to Soren, appraising him up and down so slowly, *so brazenly*, I feel my face grow warm on his behalf.

"Sorry I couldn't be of more help before," Osprey says, addressing Soren and Remy, "when you needed the boat, you know. But I ran into a bit of trouble. Had a run-in with an old *friend*." The way she emphasizes the word friend makes it clear that whomever she ran into was most certainly not friendly. Her brows knit together for a moment and then she smiles again.

"I always wanted to meet Soren Skaarsgard. The *pianist*." She stands on tiptoe, runs her hands up Soren's arms to his shoulders and then on up his neck to cup his face in both hands. "In the flesh." Then she pulls him down to her and kisses him on both cheeks. When she's done, Soren's face is as red as Kenzie's hair, and I can see the goosebumps on his skin from two meters away. I'd feel a moment of jealousy that she hasn't bothered to acknowledge that I'm a pianist as well, but then, I don't think I want the same treatment she's just given him.

Remy looks confused as Osprey turns back to me. "So where are we going this time?"

"We'd like to meet the Outsiders." I respond.

She laughs. "Which ones?"

"If there are any 'leaders' of the Outsiders, we'd like to meet them," Soren speaks up, his voice a little hoarse—whether from early morning sleeplessness or the fact that he's just been handled quite physically by this strange but enthralling woman, I couldn't say.

"Ah, Mr. Skaarsgard," Osprey says, in a quiet, contemplative way that reminds me very much of Chan-Yu. Her voice takes on a more serious inflection, as though she's addressing an audience instead of just friends. "Now there's a tricky thing,"

"Why?"

"Because we go to great lengths *not* to be 'led' and even greater lengths not to be met," she says, with that same sort of inflection Chan-Yu used to have when he was explaining something he obviously thought was very simple.

"And they're obviously very good at it," I say. "No one in the Sector has a clue what you all do out here, or why, or how."

She cocks her head and looks at me. Her gold-flecked eyes are dark and fierce, like the bird of prey that is her namesake. "And we'd like to keep it that way, Valerian. You all have been a bit of a nuisance to us in the past, and we have no desire to get embroiled in the affairs of the Sector—or its enemies."

"But you're already embroiled. Chan-Yu had infiltrated the highest reaches of power. He worked right beside me—and supposedly for my mother—for years," I protest.

"And he had help smuggling Remy and me out," Soren adds. "So there are others like you, like Chan-Yu, in the Sector."

"Only out of necessity," she says. "We cannot avoid them if we do not understand them."

"But we need your help," Remy says, her voice not quite pleading, but almost. "I don't know what happened to your people after the SRI massacre was blamed on an 'Outsider terrorist,' but you must know as well as anyone what the Sector is doing."

Osprey's eyes flash as she turns towards Remy, thrusting her arms out to reveal the scars I'd only glimpsed before, jagged lines that run up and down her skin like filaments etched into her flesh. I shudder. It reminds me of the thin scars, still red and raw, on the image of Evander's face after Remy got to him.

"Yes, Remy Alexander, I *do* know as well as anyone. Maybe even *better* than you. Which is why I stay as far away from the Sector as possible. Perhaps you ought to learn that lesson as well, especially after what happened at Round Barn—"

"Okay, okay," I interrupt, trying to calm her down. "So you won't take us to them. Can you at least deliver a message?"

She pulls back and brightens up instantly, the smile returning to her face without missing a beat. "Sure, what message?"

Remy steps forward. "Tell them we seek their counsel on how the Outsiders have avoided conflict with the Sector all these years and how their experiences might help us avoid an all-out civil war. We want to change the Sector, but we don't want war. We don't want innocents dying any more than you do."

"You sure have a strange way of doing business if you really want to avoid violence," she says to Remy.

"I'd like to see Chan-Yu again," Soren pipes up. "To find out what happened after he left Remy and me."

Osprey's face clouds over as I add, "And tell him Valerian Orleán would like to thank him for saving his friends, and for saving me. Tell him I am in his debt and at his service," I say, surprised at my forcefulness even as the words come out, suddenly moved at the memory of what I owe my former aide.

Her eyes rest on each one of us as if she's weighing us, considering whether or not we're worth the effort of doing more than just guiding us from one place to the next. "That's a message I'm sure he'll be interested to hear," she says finally, turning to leave as abruptly as she appeared, and it occurs to me that I have no idea how she travels so quietly and so quickly through the Wilds.

"Osprey," I call after her.

"Yes?" She turns.

"Tell him 'my allegiance lies outside the Sector.'"

She pauses as if considering my words. Nods once and then walks over to a pathetic excuse for a bush at the edge of our camp, grabs hold of empty air that shimmers into something that looks strangely like an Old world motorbike only without the wheels. She swings her leg over the seat, glances back at us, and then noiselessly speeds off into the distance, fading into nothingness as she goes.

We all turn around as Miah pokes his sleepy head out of the tent. He yawns, adding an exaggerated groan into it, and then looks up at all of us staring down at him.

"What? What'd I miss?"

Next morning, Osprey returns before light has even broken. We'd spent the previous day scouting around camp and then cooked several wild hares that Miah and I managed to snare using a technique Osprey showed me on our earlier trek together. After dinner, the sky was so clear that, once the fire died down, I felt as if I could reach up and pluck a star out of the sky. Since none of us could take our eyes off the Milky Way, painted bright across the inky dome above us, we dragged our sleeping bags out and slept in the open.

"Osprey's back." Remy shakes me awake beneath the steely sky, and I blink and look up to see her face mere centimeters above mine. Since the amazing dream I was having featured her in a prominent and very active role, my body thrums with the desire to reach up and pull her down to me. But I don't. Besides, I need to push those thoughts from my mind before I leave my sleeping bag.

"Okay," I say. "I'm awake." I push myself up on my elbows.

"She says at least some of the leaders have agreed to meet with us."

"I guess the opportunity to see the four of us traveling together—especially the now-infamous Remy Alexander—is too good to pass up."

"It's the chance we were hoping for," she says. "But we need to move. Now. She seems to be in a hurry." She steps away and starts to tear down her tent. I'm dressed and ready to go in a matter of moments, but Miah is dead to the world. I nudge him as I roll up my sleeping bag and stuff it into its sack. Everyone is up and in various states of drowsiness—everyone but Miah, that is, who is curled on his side like a little boy, a trail of drool drying on his cheek. I kick him lightly in the side.

"Five more minutes," he grumbles.

"Miah, we've gotta move. Osprey's back." I shake him, and he turns over in his sleeping bag.

"Last time I was up before dawn was never. Goway."

I laugh. "Never as in four days ago." I nudge him with my foot, and he growls and flops over, face down, ignoring me and everything going on around us. I unzip his sleeping bag and flap it open wide only to reveal his broad back and stark white ass. His eyes open wide with the rush of cold air and he starts flailing, trying to cover himself up again.

"What the fuck, Orlean!" he shouts, as everyone stops what they're doing to watch. "It's cold out there."

"Get your naked ass dressed, then!" I cross my arms and look down at him.

"Why'd you take your pants off, anyway?" Soren asks, a bemused look on his face. "What if we have to move fast in the middle of the night? That ass of yours would shine like a lighthouse. Drones could home in on that thing from fifty kilometers."

Miah mutters something about needing a little more room in the junkyard and then groans as he stands up and stretches. He rubs his eyes and looks around at everyone staring at him—including Remy and Osprey. "What? Never seen such a fine specimen before?" He looks down and laughs. "Guess I'll go take a piss now. I'll sign autographs after I'm dressed. And after breakfast." He picks up the pile of clothes he'd been using as a pillow and heads off behind our tent before turning and looking at Osprey. "We are having breakfast, aren't we?"

Osprey shakes her head sadly. "I'm not sure we have enough food to fill the needs of such a fine specimen. We'll just have to wait and see."

A few minutes later, after we've packed up to leave, Remy asks me for a hand up onto her horse. I glance around for Soren, who normally would have been at Remy's side. But he's already mounted and looking down at Osprey as she strokes the neck of his horse and points to something in the distance.

I hold out my cupped palms for her. She reaches for the pommel of her saddle and puts a booted foot in my hands. I lift her up onto her horse, and she settles in, grabs the reins, and then turns to look down at me. I let my hand brush her thigh and the warmth of her leg electrifies my fingertips, sending a pulse of heat all the down to my core.

Does she feel it, too?

"Thanks," is all she says.

But her eyes meet my own for a second before she turns away, just enough time to burn hope into me like the scars on Osprey's arms.

A few hours later, the bleak wasteland around us is shimmering in the heat. It's mid-April now and warm spells aren't uncommon this time of year, but we didn't anticipate anything like this. In the Sector, we don't have much data on what the terrain is like this far beyond Sector borders. No reason to. Nothing grows out here, so it's useless to us. Not to mention dangerous—or so we were taught. Notwithstanding the hungry bearded goats, we haven't seen or heard much wildlife at all. Some wild dogs or coyotes in the distance, some lizards or wild hares scuttling away from us. But that's about it.

Osprey leads our little pack on her *oiseau*, the French word for bird, which is what she calls her hovering motorbike. I notice Soren keeps nudging his horse up so he can ride next to her. I notice, too, that Remy seems perfectly unconcerned that Soren's taken an obvious interest in Osprey. In fact, she seems to be paying no attention to him at all. She rides quietly by herself, right hand on the reins, her left twisting something absentmindedly in her jacket pocket.

I tilt my head back and try to read the sky. We're heading northeast, and I notice little flashes of Osprey's crystalline astrolabe every now and then when it catches the sunlight. I wonder if she's showed it to Soren already or if she's keeping it secret for now. I remember when I first met her, how she wouldn't let the others see it.

"So, Vale," Miah says, riding up from behind me. "What'd you make of Osprey?" He waggles his eyebrows at me in such a way that I can't help but look at him sideways.

"Forgotten Moriana already?" I try to keep my voice neutral—and joking— but I must not have done a very good job, because the horror that colors his face makes me instantly regret the line.

"No!" His mouth drops open in astonishment. My heart thuds at the sudden fear I've offended my best friend. "God, no, Vale. Don't think for a second I've forgotten her."

"Bad joke, Miah. Sorry."

But of course, he's quick to forgive.

"I just meant, Osprey seems a little out there. Are all the Outsiders like her, do you think? With crazy scars and funky hair?"

"You're one to talk about funky hair. That mess of yours defies description. And that beard? Wow."

He strokes his beard fondly. "Fair point. She still seems a little off-kilter, though. I mean, obviously she's a *girl*, but she doesn't really seem … well … you know what I mean … like a girl, like Moriana or Remy or Kenzie."

"Soren seems to like her well enough."

"Yeah, and it looks like Remy couldn't care less."

I just nod, glad I'm not the only one who's noticed, but I don't want to act like I've been focused on Soren and Remy when so much is at stake. Of course, Miah probably knows what I'm thinking even before I do.

"Am I right in sensing something's changed between the two of you? Seems like since Evander … that she's … well, you know. That she's softened up. And Soren doesn't seem to be beating his chest and baring his teeth every time you go near. What happened with you guys at Round Barn?"

I'm almost afraid to put it into words. "She saved my life and then I saved hers … beyond that I don't know. If anything has changed, I don't want to jinx it."

"Well, I guess I'll hold off on the handfasting present."

We rode in silence for a while and then Remy pulled up beside me. Miah nudged his horse forward with a little smile, ever the romantic.

"What are you going to say?" she asks.

"What?" I respond, genuinely confused.

"What are you going to say to the Outsiders. About why you're with us. That's what they want to know. That's why they're willing to meet us."

"Is that what Osprey said?"

"No, but isn't it obvious? The mysteriously kidnapped Valerian Orleán turning up on the Outsiders' doorstep with his kidnapper and two Resistance traitors?"

"I guess I'll tell them the truth. Chan-Yu knows. With luck, he will have already told them some of it."

"You're the make-or-break here. You need to make the case for them to stand with us."

"What if they don't want to join the Resistance?" Her eyes harden and flick over me and everything I thought about her softening up toward me evaporates.

"You said you owed me, Vale. You at least need to try."

"Yes, I do and I will. But we can't force them. And maybe there's another way. I want to be sure that you really want me to convince others to join a fight that's already taken the lives of so many. Your mom, maybe Jahnu. Soldiers, Farm workers…."

"I get it." She purses her lips and stares straight ahead.

"It could become an all-out civil war," I say, driving the point home. "You told Osprey we're not looking for that. But we both know very well that's what this could mean."

"I want the Sector to pay."

"Pay how? In more lives? Is that the currency you want to trade in?" As soon as the words leave my lips, I want to take them back, apologize for questioning her. I want to say I'll do whatever she asks. But the truth is I don't want any more blood on my hands.

She says nothing. Her whole body's tense, her fingertips white as she grips the reins between them.

"Remy, listen…."

She turns to me, pain—and anger—brimming in her eyes. "Why should I listen to you? I thought—" She clamps her mouth shut abruptly and turns away.

"I'm sorry." I want to grab her arm, make her turn back toward me, listen to me. But I don't. "You know I'd do anything for you, anything," I say. "On top of everything else, I owe you my life. Just tell me what you want me to do."

Still she says nothing, so I go on.

"I'll tell them about LOTUS, about taking over the food supply chain, about Eli's plan to print untainted seeds, but—"

"I didn't mean for everything at Round Barn to happen like that—"

"I know that, Remy."

"Then stop acting like it's my fault. That I want to 'trade' in the currency of death. I thought you were—I thought you supported me."

"I do—" I start again, but she kicks Lakshmi into a trot and moves up the line without so much as a backwards glance. I mouth a silent curse and regret my words, wishing she were back with me, next to me. Even silent and angry, her presence is better than none at all.

The clear skies we enjoyed the last few days have given way to looming clouds, harbingers of rain. The vegetation gradually changes as we ride northwest into higher elevation. The landscape is greener with patches here and there of stately mature trees that appear to be old growth. Up ahead I can see that the higher we climb, the taller and more abundant the trees are. We haven't passed any ruins in days and I imagine this whole area was either never densely populated or was completely obliterated by the bombings.

My father once told me that nearly thirty percent of the population in North America was killed during the Religious Wars and many of those who survived succumbed during the Famine Years. I don't doubt him, but now I wonder if those figures haven't been held over our heads like a scythe, a sword of Damocles ready to fall on Okarian citizens who question our tight control of resources and food and limits on travel and exploration.

"Where the hell are we, Osprey?" Miah demands finally, after at least an hour of dead silence between us all. It's late-afternoon, and he's past impatient. We all are. Tired and saddle sore, our patience is wearing almost as thin. We've only taken a few breaks—more for the horses than for us—and we're all ready to be there, wherever *there* is. We ran our horses flat out on and off this morning, but since then we've been trotting at a bone-jarring pace that's gotten everyone complaining again.

We weave our way around a stand of bedraggled trees and Osprey holds her hand up and brings her oiseau to an abrupt halt while Soren, who was riding beside her, tries to rein his horse in and almost launches himself over its head. I can't help but laugh, but my mirth is cut short when at least fifteen hooded figures emerge from the rocks and shrubs around us, holding serious-looking composite hunting bows, nocked and drawn, each one pointed at us. I notice they're all wearing the same kind of cloak Osprey was when I first met her. These must be the Outsiders.

"Well, hello," Miah says. I keep my mouth shut.

"I told you I'd have them here before dusk," Osprey says, a big smile on her face as if she'd just been offered a slice of fresh-from-the-oven pie. She turns to the nearest Outsider, a short but broad-shouldered man who lowers his bow when she approaches. I notice his arms are clear and free of scars.

"Osprey," he says, holding out his palm to her as if in greeting.

"Squall," She stretches hers out to meet his, a kind of vertical handshake. "Are we gonna have a feast? I'm starved."

"We'll worry about your stomachs soon enough. He holds up his hand and the bows come down, though I notice none of the Outsiders put them away completely. He runs a chilly stare over our little group.

"Which one of you is the Orleán?" he asks, casting around between us.

I stare at him, too astonished to respond. *How does he not know me?* Have they never seen Sector broadcasts before? I know we're far outside the Sector's boundaries, but not since I was a child have I met someone who didn't recognize me at all.

"He is," Soren says, pointing to me. I glare at him. Thanks for nothing. He just smirks back.

"I'm Valerian." I sit a little straighter. Might as well own it. Squall stares at me for a few seconds, as if contemplating a response.

"And you," he says, nodding slightly at Remy, "must be the Alexander."

She nods by way of response.

"Did you tell them?" he asks Osprey. She hesitates.

"Not yet."

"Tell us what?" Remy demands.

"For the final leg, we're going to have to blindfold you," she says apologetically. "And disarm you."

"What the hell?" Soren interjects.

"We didn't come all the way out here to be treated like prisoners—or enemies," Remy says, more calmly than I'd expected. I, for one, am not surprised. I know too well what the Sector has done to put the Outsiders on edge like this, and I can't blame them for being defensive.

"I'm sorry, but you can't come to camp with us otherwise. We can't risk you telling anyone where we are. And I promise we have food! Lots of it. Besides," Osprey huffs, "I wouldn't have wasted all my time dragging you here just to murder you. I could have easily done that yesterday morning while Skaarsgard was shaving."

Soren opens his mouth to say something, but I beat him to it. "I'll do it. I trust you," I say to Osprey. That's not entirely true—I don't trust her, at least not completely—but if this is what it takes to pay my debts to Remy, I'll gladly take the blindfold.

"That's the spirit," she says as the buoyant smile returns to her face. She nods at Squall, who pulls a black cloth from a saddlebag and approaches me.

"Weapons," he says, and I pull a knife from the sheaf in my belt and a hand-held Bolt from the holster strapped across my chest and under my jacket. Everything else is packed in the saddlebags. I close my eyes and let him slip the hood over my head. His hands are deft and gentle as blackness envelops me.

"I'm game," I hear Miah say behind me. "As long as there's food on the other end of this ride."

I hear someone clapping and can only assume it's Osprey, carried away yet again by her strange enthusiasm. "Excellent!" she exclaims. "I promise you'll go to bed fat and happy."

I hear the footfalls of more horses being led near and then the squeak of leather and the soft *oomph* of people mounting and settling into their saddles. Then someone reaches out and takes the reins from my hand. "Hold on," Osprey calls out, and I reach for the pommel as he lurches forward.

We ride in the dark for another hour or so, and I can tell we're going up a fairly steep incline most of the time. By the time a hand reaches up and pulls off my blindfold, the sun is on the horizon and I wince, blinking at the light. I take in the surroundings. We're up against a cliff face in the midst of a stand of trees—oak, elm, maple and other deciduous species I don't recognize—and around me spreads what appears to be a small village built of wooden structures that look like they could be folded up and put in a giant's pocket at a moment's notice.

It's astonishing to see something built for a transient lifestyle when all I've ever seen is permanence. Some buildings are narrow structures that resemble overgrown PODS from the capital's mass transit system and are grouped together with extendible hallways that connect the pods into larger units. Others are long boxes that appear to easily disassemble, with walls that open flat to the outside. Still others are little more than elaborate tents, buttressed with flexible wood struts, draped in reflective shields and topped with pine boughs. Everything is built and arranged for secrecy and mobility, and yet nothing looks crude or rudimentary. I think of Assembly Hall back in Okaria, the main governmental building where my office was located, and remember how much I loved the glass walls and floors, draped with hanging gardens, living machines that helped filter the interior water, and natural ventilation systems. These Outsiders and the Sector designers might be surprised to realize they have at least something in common—an elegant, inspired-by-nature aesthetic that makes me smile despite myself.

"No wonder no one can find them," Remy says, blinking into the light.

"They'd be practically invisible from the air," Miah chimes in.

"That's the point," Osprey says. "You'll be sleeping in that one." She points to a structure that looks like it's built out of sticks and covered with hide of some kind. "Leave the horses. We'll take care of them and unpack your gear. Tonight we eat. Tomorrow we talk."

My stomach grumbles. I need no further urging. We follow her through the trees right up to the cliff where a wide natural cavern opens up under the rock face about five meters high and twenty-five wide. I can't tell how deep it goes into the rock, but it provides a perfect covered dining area. Blackened, charred remains of countless fires mark the ceiling. How many eons have humans made this cave home?

Laid out on the ground is a long wooden table laden with food. Surely they can't move that table in one piece, I think, but as I look more closely, I notice it's not one long stretch of wood. It's broken up into small segments that fit together like locks and keys to make one magnificent piece of furniture. At least a hundred people are milling about, sitting cross-legged or on their knees on wide carpets spread on the ground on either side of the table. They're passing plates, drinking from water skeins and mugs, and not paying a bit of attention to us.

Osprey escorts us to one end of the table, down where Squall is talking with some other men. She slips in between Soren and Remy and, once again, I notice Remy doesn't seem to mind. Miah jerks his head at me as if to say, *you gonna sit next to her or am I?* I lower myself to the ground between him and Remy and wait for her to ignore me, or worse. Miah slips in next to me and Squall and his friends round out the end of the table. Remy picks up a couple of plates off a stack in the middle of the table and hands one to me and one to Miah.

I take it with a mumbled "Thanks," almost afraid to look at her.

Soren immediately starts piling food on his plate. Miah follows suit, though at a more tentative pace.

"I know I shouldn't say this, but isn't a MealPak easier?" He looks down at the food on his plate. "How am I supposed to know what all this stuff is?"

"Not hungry?" I ask.

"Starving. I just don't want to eat something unfamiliar that will make me sick again. These two," he says, nodding at Remy and Soren, "can attest to the fun times we had on our way to Normandy."

"Not fun," Remy laughs. "But you were mostly going through withdrawals and probably got a bug from drinking unfiltered water. I'm sure there's nothing to worry about here."

"It's not poisonous, I promise," Osprey says. "See, here. These are morel mushrooms with barley and leeks. And this here is beetroot with wild greens. This is roasted squirrel rubbed in turmeric and paprika—that's why it's such a funny color. The bread is called *pain-eponge.*" Sponge-bread. It does look like a sponge—porous and full of holes. "You use it to grab your food." She tears off a piece to demonstrate then scoops up something that looks like a meatball and plops into her mouth. Soren and Remy have clearly already caught onto this, though Miah hesitates at the bread, too.

"Don't you have forks?" he asks.

"Forks?" Osprey looks at him, confused.

Miah pantomimes sticking a piece of food with a fork.

"Oh," Osprey laughs, unsheathing the knife strapped to her leg. "You want to stab something? Use your knife."

Miah shakes his head. "You lot took our weapons, remember?" He tears off a piece of bread and starts nibbling at it. Remy's already digging into the mushrooms. I follow suit, watching the Outsiders around us and picking a little of something from every platter within reach.

"What's this?" Soren asks, half the food on his plate already gone. He's pointing to some sausages that are a funny black-and-grey color as he stuffs one into his mouth. Osprey shoots him a devilish smile.

"*Boudin,*" she responds. "Blood sausage."

For a second, he freezes, and it looks like he might spit it out. His eyes go wide and he stops chewing for the first time since we sat down. But then he shrugs, swallows, and goes on eating as if nothing had happened.

"Tastes like iron," he says as he picks up another piece. "Pretty good."

Miah shudders and turns a little green.

"I think I'll stick with the vegetables for now."

"Me, too," I mutter.

"Chickenshits," Remy says taking a bite of something that looks like chicken. "You don't know what you're missing."

23 — VALE

"You can't be serious," Miah says.

"Why not? Afraid you can't handle it?" Squall waggles a thick finger in his face. I shake my head. Dinner's been going on for hours and we're still sitting— more like leaning—at the table as yet more bottles of mead are passed around. I have no conception of the number of people who have come and gone. In the distance, soft strains of what sounds like a trio of guitar, mandolin, and flute float on the air and more than once I've been tempted to find who is playing and ask to join them. Although I can pick out a few tunes on the mandolin and can play pretty well on the guitar, I was never as proficient at either of them as I was at the piano. Still the music tugs at me.

Long ago, in what seems like another age, my dad and I built a guitar from scratch so he could give me yet another physics lesson, this time about acoustics, using something I loved: music. I can feel the wood and the steel strings vibrating across the frets at different frequencies, transforming science into music, *merging* science and music. *We use science to create art,* he'd said, *and art to reveal science.* The strings of an instrument vibrate to certain frequencies to give rise to music just as the strings of quantum theory give rise to bosons and fermions, protons and gravitons, Riemann surfaces and branes and the whole of the universe. I can see his fingers on the old-fashioned lathe, hear the earnestness in his voice, how he wanted me to understand the connection between beauty and nature, art and science. The pinprick of tears bites at my nose. *When did everything go wrong?* I've clearly had too much to drink.

Remy's been polite all evening, but she and Miah have been doing most of the talking while I've been trying to not make her mad again. Soren and Osprey are holding each other up, barely, and it appears Miah has finally gotten over his fear of the food—and the drink. True to his ability to make friends anywhere he goes, he and Squall have already become fast friends.

"No way you can down that bottle faster than me," Squall pronounces, already far beyond tipsy. I size them both up. Squall is definitely the heavier of the two, but Miah is taller and has always been able to hold his liquor. After his recovery, he'd even taken to drinking that sewage Eli, Firestone and Rhinehouse had been brewing during our short stay at Normandy. The worst tasted of dirty socks with a hint of onion and the best tasted of just plain dirt with notes of old leather and mossy rocks, which, surprisingly, wasn't half bad.

"What's the wager?" Miah asks.

"Wager?" Squall quirks his nose in confusion.

"What do I get if I win?"

"Eternal glory and admiration," Osprey says, slurring her words, her head lolling slightly up against Soren's shoulder. "And a horse."

"A horse?" Miah perks up. "Whose horse?"

"His horse," Osprey responds, nodding vaguely at Squall. "Thas how it works. You win, you get his horse. He wins, he gets yours." Squall nods very seriously.

I lean across the table to Osprey. Soren eyes me suspiciously, but something's changed between the two of us—at least he's not threatening my life every half-second, now, which is a vast improvement.

"Is this what every night is like for you all?" I ask.

Osprey grins. "Oh, no. Not *every* night."

"It's a miracle you all manage to stay out of sight," I reply, "considering what a racket you make."

"We have our ways," Osprey replies, dimples appearing in her cheeks.

"You're on." Miah says finally, clapping his hands as everyone around him cheers. Obviously not concerned about the fact that the horse he's been riding for the last four days is not his to gamble, Miah jumps up when Squall rises. Squall holds his palm up the same way he did to Osprey earlier in the day, and Miah presses his hand against the Outsider's.

"I'll be the judge," Remy pipes up from beside me. She scrambles to her feet and stands next to the two of them with her hand held high over her head. "When I drop my hand, you pull out the corks and drink. Okay?"

"Gorra have a Ou'sider judge, too," Osprey slurs, using Soren's head to push herself to her feet, tilting into Remy. "I'm rea-ah-dy."

"Okay?" Remy looks between the two competitors, both of whom have a bottle in hand. By this point everyone at the table is leaning in or standing to watch the competition.

"Go!" Remy's hand slices through the air. Squall whips out his knife, digs into the cork and pulls it out with a *pop!* and starts guzzling while Miah reaches around him and bashes open the bottleneck on a nearby rock to create a wide-mouthed opening. He tilts the bottle back and gulps directly from broken rim, and before Squall is two-thirds done he slams his empty on the table, making dishes jump and cups totter.

"Sayyid wins!" Osprey whoops and Remy hugs Miah as he catches in midair another bottle someone tosses him as a prize.

Miah bows, then takes Squall's knife, pops out the cork and holds it up in a toast. "To Squall and his horse!"

"To Squall and his horse!" the crowd toasts and laughs. Miah takes a long pull and hands it to his new friend, who does the same, finishing the bottle and slamming it down just as Miah had. Miah's got a big smile plastered on his face, and when Osprey leans over Soren's drunken figure and whispers, "I was lyin' about th'orse," he doesn't even notice.

Remy and Osprey take their seats again, but Osprey's arm stays draped across Soren's shoulder. She leans into him and their foreheads touch as if they're co-conspirators plotting some elaborate scheme. Remy glances at them and turns toward me, her eyes dark pools into which I could swim forever without ever needing to come up for air, a place where I could cleanse myself, where I could atone.

"Love at first sight, or what?" she says, the beginnings of a smile plays around her lips.

My heart thuds so loud I wonder if she can hear it, and I look askance at her.

"It wasn't so long ago you were in his arms." I say, keeping my voice as neutral and disinterested as possible. Hope, next of kin to fear, wells up, filling me to the brim with a rushing sense of anticipation. Osprey plays absently with Soren's hair as she stares down the table, eyes unfocused, and he's propped up on one elbow watching her while his other arm is wrapped around her waist, his thumb tucked into her belt, tracing lazy little circles against her skin.

"Soren and me..." Remy pauses, purses her mouth, and opens it again. "It's complicated. We love each other—at least," she lets out a little laugh, "—we do *now*. But we were never *in* love. We just figured that out ... recently." She chews the side of her lip and stares straight ahead, avoiding my gaze. I take that as a sign not to push the issue further, even as words bubble up from my throat, threatening to choke me. I swallow hard.

But now she's leaning closer to me, her gaze coming up to meet mine, and I can smell the sweat on her, the honeyed mead someone sloshed on her skin earlier, can almost taste the sweetness on her lips. And then I notice her brow is knitted, her face shaded with concern.

"Where is Chan-Yu?" she whispers. "No one's even mentioned his name." Her words, calm but unnerved, settle me quickly. She's perfectly coherent, and though her eyes are tired, determination is etched across her face as she looks up at me, worried and tense. She is unable to let go, to forget what brought us here, even at a moment like this. "Do you think he's still alive?"

"Osprey would have told us," I say.

"What if they don't know?"

"We'll ask tomorrow. No one's thinking about politics now." I nod toward Squall who, now standing behind us, is introducing Miah to another one of the Outsiders. The man greets Miah with a generous embrace, but the expression on his face when he looks at Squall is so tender it splinters my heart. *What would it feel like if Remy looked at me like that?*

"I guess you're right." She chews the side of her lip and stares straight ahead, avoiding my gaze.

"Want to help me kill this?" I ask. I offer her a half-empty bottle next to me with the best smile I can muster. She frowns up at me, though, catching my eye for a half-second before she glances away again, almost as if she's disappointed. But then, a moment later, she shrugs

"Sure," she says. She takes the bottle from me and presses it to her lips. *Would that I were....*

"Ey, Vale!" I turn at the sound of my name. Miah stands a few meters behind us, one arm slung over Squall's shoulder, who, in turn, is holding hands with the man beside him. "Our hosts insist it's the guests' turn to entertain. Soren was going to play something, but he seems to have disappeared."

I turn around and realize that indeed Soren and Osprey are no longer at the table. A quick glance around confirms they are nowhere in sight. By the way they've been clinging to each other all night, it's not terribly difficult to guess where they've gone.

Squall shakes his head and laughs. "Skaarsgard doesn't know what he's in for."

"Now, now, Squall," Miah says, in a falsely serious voice, "we should allow our friends their modesty, you know...."

"Osprey? Modesty?"

When I finally muster my courage and glance over at Remy, relief floods through me. She's smiling, too, laughing at Miah and Squall poking fun at Soren and Osprey.

"Your friend speaks highly of your talent, Valerian," Squall says, in the oddly serious way all Outsiders except Osprey seem to speak. Chan-Yu had it too, I remember, always talking as though he were making a speech. "Come, come, we have played for you all night. The rules of hospitality say it is your turn now."

My heart starts pounding in my ears. *Here? Now? In front of Remy?* And yet, even as the fear thuds through my veins, it's exciting, too. I miss music more than anything else about my old life, and now's my chance to play something, anything.

"Come on, Vale!" Miah roars.

Remy nudges me and gives me a small smile. "Play nice, Vale," she says. "We're diplomats, remember?"

I stare into her amber eyes, my mind flashing through every moment that's brought us here. How could I forget?

I stand and cross the rough, uneven floor of the cave to where a torch—a real torch, of tar and wood, not like the biolights we use in the Resistance—silhouettes a guitar resting against the rock wall. I pick it up and sling the leather strap over my shoulder, remembering and reveling in how comfortable it feels against my body. My favorite thing about the guitar, unlike the piano, is how you feel every note vibrate, both in your chest and in your hands, your fingers. You feel the music in a whole different way.

I look out at the group and think maybe I could warm up with an old drinking song since we're half sloshed. I strum a few chords and try to remember the tune and lyrics I'd found in an ancient yellowed songbook in the library at the Academy. I clear my throat and close my eyes to count out the beat and get the rhythm right, and then I launch into what the book said was a song that had been sung in bars for hundreds of years.

I've been a wild rover for many's the year
I've spent all me money on whiskey and beer
But now I'm returning with gold in great store
And I never will play the wild rover no more

And it's No, Nay, never,
No, nay never no more
Will I play the wild rover,
No never no more

"One more verse is all I remember," I say. But this time, I'll call out the lyrics and you sing along."

I went in to an alehouse I used to frequent
And I told the landlady me money was spent
I asked her for credit, she answered me nay
Such a customer as you I can have any day

And it's No, Nay, never,
No, nay never no more
Will I play the wild rover,
No never no more

"One more time on the chorus," Squall hollers. He, his partner, and Miah, sing and sway as others join in, some barely staying on their feet. We end up doing the chorus again and then the group claps and slaps each other on the back. Someone shouts, "Give us another!"

I run through a few stanzas from the embarrassingly short list of songs I know how to play, and when I start to pull the guitar strap off my shoulder, someone calls out, "You can't end a night like this without a love song, now can ya?"

A love song? I rack my brain, but I have no idea what to play. I glance up at Remy and it hits me. The perfect song.

"Okay," I say to the group, "I'm going to end on another very old song. It's not a sing along and it doesn't even have a happy ending, but I've always thought it was pretty. So, here goes."

The crowd is seated now, quiet. Waiting. I clear my throat again. This is a song Remy will know. Her grandfather loved it, and, in a round-about way, he was the one who introduced it to me. I play the first few chords and her eyes light up, a smile spreading across her face.

The water is wide, I cannot cross o'er, and neither have I wings to fly.
Build me a boat that can carry two and both shall row, my love and I.

I was never much of a singer, and with a few months of rust on my vocal chords, I'm pretty stunned I don't sound horrible. Remy's grandfather, a great traveler and collector of stuff from the Old World, had found many of the old recordings and songbooks and had donated them to the Academy library. Remy played an old recording of this tune for me one afternoon when we were first becoming friends—or something more. It was so pretty that after Tai was killed, I taught myself to play it on the guitar, thinking maybe one day I'd be able to play it for Remy and remind her of happier times. Little did I know my chance wouldn't come until three and a half years later—in a cave in the middle of the Wilds, surrounded by Outsiders, as far away from the Sector, from our old life, as we'd ever been.

There is a ship and she sails the sea. She's loaded deep, as deep can be.
But not so deep as the love I'm in, I know not how I sink or swim.

I meet Remy's eyes, she smiles, and I don't know how I get through the rest of the song.

"Drink this," Osprey places a cup in front of Miah. It's barely daybreak, and we're all bleary-eyed—especially him. He stares up at her as she pours another cup and sets it in front of me. There's a whole spread laid out on the table before us and people are coming and going, eating their breakfasts, laughing and talking before going off to do who knows what. Miah drains his cup, shudders, and holds it up for more.

"What is this?" he asks.

"Water, potassium and ginger root. It'll help. That mead is probably stronger stuff than what you're used to." Miah looks up at her and squints.

"This will cure my hangover?"

"That and some good old grease. Eat some sausage, too."

"You sure?"

"Worked for Skaarsgard. We've been up for a while now."

Miah rubs his temple and cocks an eyebrow at her.

She looms over him, a challenging stance set in her hips. "You got a problem with that?"

"No," he holds his hands up. "No problem. No problem at all."

I manage a laugh even though there's a steady thrum at the base of my neck and the morning light seems altogether too bright.

"Problems with what?" A tall woman with wide, prominent cheekbones and hair so black it looks like curtains of silk on her shoulders sits down across the table from us. With her is a woman who looks like a more beautiful and softer version of Chan-Yu.

"No matter." Osprey waves the subject away. "This is Idris and Soo-Sun," Osprey introduces us and, with a mischievous grin adds, "Make sure you stay on Idris's good side. She bites."

"Only when necessary," Idris says, and I catch a flash of a smile. Osprey laughs and then takes off as quickly as if she really were a bird, launching herself after some faraway prey.

I study Soo-Sun without trying to be obvious, but finally ask, "You look a lot like Chan-Yu. Are you related?" She holds my gaze, her face expressionless. I go on, a bit awkwardly. "We were hoping he would be here. I want to thank him for saving Soren and Remy." *For saving me.*

"He is not here," she says finally, but then falls silent again without answering my question. I take a swig from the cup in front of me and pick at the plate of fruit, sausage, and bread in the middle of the table. The silence is heavy and unwieldy, but I don't want to be the one to break it. Even Miah can sense it and he picks his head up off the table and watches Soo-Sun.

"We're all anxious to talk to him," I finally say.

"We've had only one communication from him since that day," she says, her voice neutral.

"The day he left the Sector?" I ask.

She takes a drink without answering and glances at Idris, who gives her a slight nod. "Yes. Osprey was the last to hear from him. We are almost certain he is not being held by Sector forces." I sigh with relief, but then catch myself as she continues. "We fear, then, he is dead. Otherwise, he would have returned to us." Her gaze drifts out toward the horizon. "We are bound to the same goal, and if he has failed, it falls on me to complete it."

I start to open my mouth, curious and surprised, wondering what she's talking about. *Bound to the same goal?* But Soo-Sun's eyes shift above and behind me, and I turn to see Remy approaching. The openness I saw on her face last night has faded, replaced by the same familiar determination I've gotten so used to. But her expression is somehow softer. More open. Maybe.

"Squall says to be in the clearing in the center of camp in fifteen minutes," she says. "We'll have a chance to make our case then." She glances at Soo-Sun and pauses. "Are you related to—"

"Yes," she cuts her off. "Chan-Yu is my brother."

"Where—" she starts, but again Soo-Sun interrupts.

"We will talk more of this later. Now it is time to prepare for the gathering." She stands, touches Idris's shoulder lightly and leaves the table. Miah and I finish eating, down a few more glasses of ginger water, and follow Remy back to the center of camp. We pass through the maze of small buildings, the bedrolls of people who appear to have slept outside, and families in different phases of food preparation or packing and unpacking traveling gear. The whole encampment seems transitory, like no one actually lives here, but instead it is a giant staging area for people who are constantly in various stages of coming and going.

When we get to the clearing, we meet Squall, Soren, and Osprey and another woman, older, with silvery hair. She's as tall and lithe as Osprey, for all that she looks to be at several decades older. Woven mats have been placed in a circle around a fire pit in which glowing embers flicker and spark, radiating a comforting warmth. Soo-Sun emerges from the trees on the far side and lowers herself to sit on the mat beside Squall, and Remy, Miah and I do the same, arranging ourselves across the pit from the Outsiders. Squall waits until we are settled to begin.

"I trust you enjoyed your dinner. You are the first guests we've welcomed from either the Resistance or the Sector." I wonder if they've had any *unwelcome* guests, prisoners or captives, and what happened to them. "As you may have already ascertained, we are a transitory lot and we come and go as we please. Right now, I'm afraid we"—he indicates the woman next to him—"are the only Elders here. Although we were reluctant to bring you here, the make-up of your group intrigues us—the son of a former chancellor and a current one, an Alexander, and, of course, Jeremiah Sayyid, whose presence among you is particularly interesting given his family's history."

"Me?" Miah and I exchange confused glances. "Are you talking about my dad's work with the Resistance?"

Squall's brows knit in confusion. "It is your mother that interests us."

"My mother?"

Squall looks back and forth between me and Soren. "We thought … does he not know?"

"Does he not know what?" I demand, now as confused as Miah.

Squall turns to Soren. "Do none of you know?"

"Is this about his mother's death?" Soren asks, his voice low, cautious.

"What the hell are you talking about?" Miah demands. My blood pressure is rising as well. Miah and I weren't friends when his mother died, but I know it was a traumatic time simply because he's only mentioned it once to me, and only to tell me that she had, in fact, died. When I tried to press the matter, he politely—but tersely—asked me not to inquire further.

Squall holds his hand up to calm him. "We assumed you left the Sector with Valerian when you discovered the truth. Is this not the case?"

"I have no idea what you're talking about." Miah's on his feet now, looming over Squall, the angriest I think I've ever seen him. He still hasn't put back on all the weight he lost from his illness, and with his thick mop of hair and bristling beard, he looks rangy—and not a little dangerous. "I left because Vale told me about *his* mother, about the SRI attack, and that she had directed Chan-Yu to kill Soren and Remy. Since I'd never been one of her favorite people, I figured she'd come after me if she found out I knew about her crimes and, especially, if she knew my dad was working with the Resistance. But most importantly, I left because my best friend needed me and that's what best friends do."

A surge of affection and respect flushes through me. I've never been more proud to call someone a friend—*a brother.* And it doesn't escape me that Soren must know something about Miah's mother—something he's obviously never shared. "Somebody better tell me what my mother has to do with any of this."

"Why don't you take a seat and—" Squall starts.

"I'll take a seat when I fucking want to!" Miah shouts. Soren and I are both on our feet beside him, and Squall's leapt up as well, his hands out in a conciliatory gesture, even as his eyes narrow dangerously. Miah turns on Soren. "What do you know about this?"

"I'm not sure what I know," Soren says, apologetic. "I'm sorry, Miah. I should have told you a long time ago, but I never had any proof. When I left, I knew it would be too dangerous to try to contact you. And when you showed up with Vale, I didn't know *how* to tell you."

"Tell me what, goddamnit?"

"Your mother didn't die of influenza. I don't know what she died of, but I think she was in a clinical study run by—" Soren casts a venom-filled glance at me—"the OAC. I think she was used as a lab rat to test … something. I don't even know what."

"And just how do you know this?" Miah's voice is shaking.

"I don't really *know* anything. After the lab massacre when…" Soren pauses for a moment, looks down. He blinks a few times and I lean in a little closer—is Soren Skaarsgard crying? His strangely blue eyes shine in the morning light when he looks back up at us. "When Hanna died … I couldn't let it go."

Memories once buried rise and flash through my mind: Hanna Lyon, the girl Soren and I used to compete with at piano competitions, a friend of mine until she disappeared into her studies at the SRI and we lost touch. She always had a thing for Soren, but I never knew there was anything going on between them. She was in Tai's class at the SRI when the gunman came in and blew them all to pieces.

"I didn't understand what happened or why. So I started looking into the massacre, into your mother's death, into my parents' fall from power. It's all connected, Miah, I'm just not positive how," Soren breathes, as though the air is being pressed from his lungs. "Your mother died a week before Philip Orleán came to power, of a disease that never existed. Influenza was a cover-up. I think she was the result of a lab study gone wrong. It was part of Philip and Corine's research, their contingency plan to stop the famine devastating the Farms at the time."

"What?" Miah turns to me, his face slack, his mouth open, questioning, *but what can I say?* I couldn't speak if I tried. I feel compressed, bowed by the weight of adding one more death to the list of those I must atone for. There's nothing I can say or do to change anything my parents have done, but the idea that they are responsible for Miah's mother's death is too much to bear.

"I don't understand," I whisper.

"Why would a healthy woman volunteer for a study that could kill her?" Miah protests. "She was perfectly fine, then she was sick, then she was dead. I never even got to hold her hand." Miah's broad shoulders are slumped. "They burned her body, wouldn't even allow me a ceremony."

"This is why we are interested in her death." Squall says. "Please, Jeremiah. We will tell you all we know." Miah sinks back to the ground next to me, and I watch him, hoping beyond hope that this doesn't change our friendship, that he can forgive me whatever role I've played in this. Soren sits next to Osprey, and for the first time in ages, I empathize with him. I can only imagine what it must have cost him to carry this knowledge around without knowing how to share it with his old friend.

Soo-Sun, who has been quiet and calm thus far, finally clears her throat and speaks up.

"My brother Chan-Yu was not the only Outsider to climb high in the ranks of Sector bureaucracy, although he did go further than anyone had before him. We have others, too, who work in the Sector: nurses in the hospitals, assistants in the printing facilities where the MealPaks are produced, Enforcers on the Farms, soldiers in the Defense Forces. When Rachel Sayyid died, the Sector was in a time of turmoil." She nods at Soren. "Chancellor Cara Skaarsgard was unable to control the crop destruction caused by a mutated virus, and the resulting famine and riots were devastating."

Remy, sitting almost across from me, looks confused. It occurs to me that Soren may never have told her any of this story, that she might not know anything about the political intricacies of his parents' fall from grace. A large part of the story is missing even for me—I never did find out what happened to Soren's parents after they transferred away from the capital.

Soo-Sun continues: "From what we've gathered, Corine Orleán began testing possible biological solutions as soon as she was certain her husband would win the Chancellorship. These clinical studies involved modified strains and combinations of various intestinal bacteria. The goal was to modify the way humans absorb calories and nutrients, in order to enable the starving people on the Farms to break down a wider variety of food and to more efficiently turn more of the calories consumed into available energy. A simple idea, in theory, and a noble one. But, as I'm sure you all know, gut bacteria are notoriously fickle. One slight imbalance can upset the whole system. With modified bacteria and new strains introduced to the intestines, the risk is even greater. Some of Corine's test subjects died during the trials. We believe Rachel Sayyid was one of them. But some lived, and genetic modifications to the DNA of the crops themselves eventually curtailed the disease while steps were taken to modify the chemicals in the MealPaks to prevent further danger to the workers."

"Ah," Soren says quietly.

"We believe the biggest difference between the Orleán faction and the Skaarsgard faction was that the Orleáns were willing to use citizens in their clinical trials before all the precautions were taken while the Skaarsgard faction was more cautious. It was a difference of degrees."

"How do you know all this?" I demand.

Soo-Sun looks at me patiently.

"We know many things, Valerian Orleán, that you would not suspect. We have ways of finding things out that do not always involve stolen passwords and open backdoors."

I open my mouth to retort and then shut it again, remembering how Chan-Yu had the same way of answering and yet not answering my questions.

"So my mom was a lab rat," Miah says, his voice thick with grief and anger.

Another debt I have to pay. How many lives do I owe?

As if sensing my unease, Miah turns to me, his brows knitted and jaw clenched. He pokes me in the chest, hard. "Don't you fucking apologize, Vale. It's not your fault. Don't make this whole thing worse by apologizing for something you didn't do. This isn't about you. Just let it go."

Surprised, I nod. But my hands are clenched into fists, and I can't seem to unfold them.

Squall takes up after Soo-Sun, his words quiet but resonant. "We are interested in your family story, Jeremiah, not only because of your powerful friends, but because of the threat your mother's death represents. After the clinical trials were concluded and the famine officially ended, research in that direction went dark. We suspect Corine either ordered the research discontinued—or, far more likely, took it up with her own personal research team."

"She could use it as a weapon," Soren breathes. Squall and Soo-Sun turn to him in unison. "Bacteria are so easily transmutable," he says. "If she could isolate one or several of the strains that proved deadly, she could drop it like a bomb on our heads."

"This is our concern as well," Squall says impassively.

Remy leans forward, suddenly eager. The steely determination has replaced the confusion from a moment ago.

"So you're with us, then?" she asks. "You'll help us?"

The elegant older woman at Squall's side finally speaks up. She glances at Remy with a hint of disdain in her expression.

"What help would you have us give?" she asks, her voice austere and off-putting.

"This is Chariya," Osprey says as an introduction. She sounds deferential for the first time since I've known her. Reverential, even. "She was a citizen of the Sector, too. Long before the Resistance was born, Chariya left and is now one of our Elders."

"We need your knowledge, your manpower, your resources," Remy says, cool as a seasoned diplomat. "We need invisible lines of distribution throughout the Sector, so the Resistance can penetrate the food distribution system and, without the Dieticians' knowledge, substitute safe, unmodified food for inclusion in the MealPaks. You can help us. You can show us how you move, where you travel, how you get through Sector territory unnoticed. We have the information we need and will soon have the means to produce enough seeds—Old World, unmodified, heirloom seeds—to start a revolution. And with your help, we can grow enough to wean the whole Sector off the modification programs without anyone even knowing."

"And if we were to help you, what would the Resistance offer us in return?" Chariya asks, her expression immutable.

"What the fuck!" Miah shouts, throwing his arms over his head. "You want to make tit-for-tat bargains while the OAC uses people like lab rats and slaves? You want to sit here and talk contracts and deals knowing Remy's family was destroyed, my mother was being murdered, Soren's parents were lobotomized? Are you out of your goddamn mind?"

Miah's on his feet, and I am too, my hands on his shoulders, trying to calm

him, but he's pushing my hands away and won't let me speak. But then Chariya
stands up in one fluid motion, tall and strong and somehow far more imposing
standing than she was sitting. Miah clenches his mouth shut and folds his arms
across his chest, glaring at the impassive, fearsome woman before us.

"Before you accuse me of bargaining, cutting deals for lives, or being
unsympathetic to the atrocities committed by the Okarian Sector, you should
know our story, Jeremiah Sayyid."

She brushes past us and the other Outsiders in our group are on their feet
as well, following her without question. Soren follows Osprey's every motion,
and Miah turns in a huff, his curiosity getting the better of him. In seconds, it's
just me and Remy, and then she meets my eyes.

"So much for diplomacy," she says, shaking her head as she leaves, brushing
so close I can smell the intoxicating woody, earthy scent of her hair.

The outsiders come and go as fluidly as water. Soo-Sun disappeared as soon as we mounted our horses and began our trek up the forested mountain. Osprey decided not to join us, much to Soren's disappointment. It's me, Vale, Miah, Soren, Chariya, and Squall. We've been riding in silence for well over two hours. At first, the further we went, the darker and deeper the forest became. But then the trail sloped upwards, and the trees have been changing, growing closer together but taller and thinner. The trail is steep and slow going for the horses. The air is moist, with that wet earth smell that I find myself taking deep breaths of every few minutes. We can't have covered more than nine or ten kilometers at most, and I'm amazed at how the flora has shifted so dramatically in such a short distance. It must be the elevation.

I sniff the air as the wind changes direction, and then notice the sound of rushing water. The path turns and descends a little ways, and soon we're at the bank of a stream that runs downhill. This little clearing is idyllic, like something from a storybook. Lush green grass fills the spaces between the trees and the rushing creek, and yellow and blue wildflowers provide splashes of color. Though I usually prefer pen and paper, I find myself longing for a brush and stretched canvas to paint this pristine little meadow.

Chariya pulls up and dismounts, letting her reins fall. She dips her hands into the stream and pulls up a palm full of crystal clear water. "See this?" she says. "Clean. Pure. Drinkable." She puts her hands to her mouth and slurps. "We've been working for decades to develop a system that uses organic materials to filter and purify water contaminated by fallout from the Religious Wars and from Old world extraction operations. Only in the last twenty or thirty years, have we managed to truly make a difference."

Vale pulls up his horse at my side, his leg brushing mine. "On our way to Normandy, Osprey knew which streams were clean and which weren't," he says.

Chariya taps the side of her head. "We've got every square meter of the Wilds mapped and it's all in here."

"Maybe Chariya does," Squall chuckles. "For the rest of us, we have our astrolabes."

Chariya smiles at the compliment and stands up, stretching her back. Her arms sweep out, encompassing the stream, the path, and the deepening woods around us. "After the Wars, new forests took root in areas that hadn't been completely devastated. Those trees sucked the chemicals from the soil and water into their roots and grew off of the ruination of the past. Some of those who survived and lived out here in the Wilds began helping the natural process along by planting more trees and by living with as little an impact as possible. Those people became Outsiders."

"We didn't call ourselves Outsiders at first," Squall cuts in. "But Okarians began calling us that, and we rather liked the term." He smiles slightly at Chariya, who seems unperturbed by the interruption.

"In the Sector, our ancestors started farming again," she continues. "Cutting the trees, controlling the land, building irrigation canals, planting seeds, beginning the same destructive cycle that always leads to larger populations, more demand for agriculture, conflicts over resources, climate change, environmental devastation, and ultimately to the destruction of large swaths of our world.

"It seems every generation, every civilization, makes some form of the same mistake. We forget—or ignore—that nature has intrinsic value beyond resources for our material gain. We believe we can harness all of nature, lash it to our plow, and bend it to our own will with no consequences. We believe we can treat nature like cattle, cattle like machines, and humans like machines, and what comes of the prosperity we extract through these unnatural means? The wealthy and powerful become ever more wealthy and more powerful, while the poor and oppressed grow ever more enslaved. We think we improve on nature through science, through advanced agricultural practices, through manipulation of DNA, through this and that and the other. But we are always wrong. There is only nature, and we are part of it. If we set ourselves in opposition to nature, it will always rise up against us, eventually. And it will win."

I sense that, like me, Vale, Miah, and Soren are having a hard time not interrupting. I clamp my mouth shut, shift in my saddle, and let the woman have her say. The only way we can hope to convince her to join us is if we allow that. As Rhinehouse said, it has to be the Outsiders' decision. We can't force them and we can't bully them. All we can do is state our case.

"The Outsiders, though, chose another path," Chariya continues. "They realized they could live off the land without chopping down the trees, without destroying the ecosystems that had sprung up in humanity's absence. We try, where possible—like with our water filtration systems—to nurse the ecosystems back to life. It's a harder life, yes, and we make sacrifices. It's why we're always on the move. It's why we choose to limit our families to two or three children at most. Death, from disease and injury, or a lack of the latest medical care, is more common here than in the Sector. But we accept that. We are willing to pay that price because we believe that death is a natural part of life. It is not something to fear. In death is rebirth, it is both an ending and a beginning."

I think of Tai and my mom. In both cases, their deaths *were* a new beginning. But I can't accept it, not like Chariya. I would do anything to bring them back to me.

She pulls another handful of water up to her mouth and drinks, then turns to run her fingers over the feathery leaves of a fern. "It's because of the choices we've made that we can live as a part of the ecosystem. We feed off of the natural world, we take no more than we need, we move to give the ecosystem time to regenerate, and we die natural deaths and are returned to the earth from whence we came. The old scripture says 'For dust thou art and unto dust thou shalt return' and we practice that. We don't hold ourselves *apart from* the land and the other animals and plants we share it with, but rather consider ourselves to be *a part of* the land. It's because of the choices we've made that I can drink this water without fear for my health."

"What does all this have to do with stopping the Sector?" Miah blurts, unable to contain himself any longer.

"It is because of the choices the Sector has made that you are here asking for our help," Chariya responds calmly. I cock my head slightly to the side as I realize that wasn't exactly an answer to Miah's question. "Be patient, Jeremiah Sayyid. There's yet one more thing to see before I can fully answer your question. It's just down this valley, another fifteen minutes' ride."

She nudges her horse with her boots—the Outsiders seem to be able to guide them without ever touching the reins, and indeed, Chariya's horse isn't even wearing a bridle. Meanwhile, I'm still occasionally forced to grip Lakshmi's mane for dear life when she sets out at a fast, bumpy trot without my permission.

Chariya and Squall lead us down into a little ravine, where we follow a series of descending switchbacks into a larger valley. As they lead, I mull over what Chariya told us. *Dust to dust, ashes to ashes.* As much as I want to disagree, to argue with her, I wonder if there's truth to what she said. I never thought the Resistance might not be asking enough questions. Questions that go beyond the Sector, beyond my family and friends. What about the land we take our resources from? What about the animals we push out with our cities and towns? Is it possible that even the Resistance isn't going far enough? That the Outsiders have chosen a better path—to forego the advances of science to live within the rhythms of the earth?

"But all the things we'd have to give up," I mutter, almost to myself. "Museums, art, music, turning the lights on and off at night…."

"They haven't given those things up," Vale says, interrupting my thoughts. Here the trail is wide enough for two horses to ride together, and Vale's caught up to me just as I was thinking aloud. "They still have music and art and entertainment. We saw that last night."

I nod, but don't say anything more. I can't quite process my thoughts right now.

"But you're right," he says wryly, glancing at me sideways. "I do quite enjoy electricity and hot showers, and Sector medicine has done wonders for hundreds of thousands of people."

"It's done terrible things, too," I remind him. My voice comes out harsher than I intended, and I regret my words when I see him wince. "It's all about balance," I offer, trying for a middle ground. "We know the Sector's gone too far. But do we have to live in the Wilds and abandon everything we've built in order to preserve our environment?"

Vale shrugs, looking thoughtful. "The Sector has done some amazing things. We can't devalue that. But out here, they live just as peacefully."

"You think you live peacefully?" Chariya calls from the front of the line. "You think your people are innocent of environmental destruction and devastation?" She holds her hand up and her horse pulls to a stop. "The Resistance and the Sector are squabbling over something that is of relatively minor importance to us. We don't rely on cultivated seeds at all—what difference should it make to us, if they are hybridized or genetically modified to taste better or to supposedly enhance health? We get our nourishment from foods that grow naturally, on their own time. Your food, your seeds, your battles, mean nothing to me. But what you're about to see is a different matter."

Up ahead, bright splashes of sunlight paint the ground where the tree line disappears, and the stream we're following drops out of sight. Chariya leads us down and out of the trees, and as we emerge into the light, the sight before me steals my breath away.

The hilltop across the valley has been stripped bare, cut away, and dug out. Terraces of rock and dirt layer deep into the ground, wholly unnatural, burrowing into the earth like an inverse beehive. The little stream we've been following drops down to meet a larger river, and where the two meet, eddies of yellow, red, and brown water swirl away downstream, evidence of chemical effluence that will carry far beyond this site alone. Where the orange-red stream tumbles through the valley, the lush grasses from our side of the river have died, and the shrubs and trees are mere skeletons, dead leaves clinging to branches that can no longer nourish them.

"Uranium mining," Chariya says, bitterness rife in her voice. "Of a new size and scale. This is not the first of its kind, but it is comparatively recent. I can't take you to the mine itself because the ground is too toxic. But up above you can see the lake where they keep the slurry.

Miah and Vale are utterly speechless. Soren looks almost unsurprised, his brow furrowed, mouth set in a hard line. For my part, aside from the clear implications of the devastation at hand, I'm not entirely sure what Chariya is talking about.

"Pit mining is illegal," Vale whispers. "No one's done it since the Old World."

"But … I thought …" Miah stammers, "modified hydraulic fracking is the more common … is how we...."

Soren shakes his head, bitterly, and for once does not say anything to rebuke Vale's thoughts.

My mind races back to everything I learned about Old World extraction practices. I remember Doctor Malik explaining that one of the things that contributed to the beginning of the religious wars was something not very religious at all—resources. Particularly water. Even as the ice caps melted and glaciation decreased, flooding many of the old cities and changing national borders, the amount of drinkable water shrank dramatically. Partly because of dams and diverting water for agriculture, and partly because of water pollution thanks to mining practices that contaminated groundwater for hundreds of kilometers around extraction sites. I don't know much about how mines work, but I remember seeing some of the photos of the effluent and runoff from those sites. It was disgusting. No wonder everything around here is dead.

Chariya shakes her head. "Yes, once upon a time, the Sector relied exclusively upon relatively small scale methods of deep in-situ mining, or hydraulic fracking. Although no less destructive to the groundwater, hydraulic fracking at least didn't require cutting out hillsides and destroying large swaths of the surrounding area."

"But … why?" Vale asks.

"Listen to yourselves!" Chariya says, her voice sharp, rebuking. "Are you so blind as to think the airships you fly across the Sector, the hovercraft you drive, the transport craft you use to power your food distribution lines do not require power? That the uranium and plutonium that fuels them comes out of thin air and disappears harmlessly once used? I, too, was a Sector citizen once. Like you, Jeremiah, I was an engineer. I worked on a team that refined and designed many of the nuclear reactor cores that now power your transportation through Okaria. But as I began to understand what uranium mining does to the environment, I abdicated my role and applied for a transfer to the Farms. When I realized what a farce that was, too, I fled, and found a home with the Outsiders, the only people who recognize the sacrifices we must make in order to avoid sacrificing everything around us."

"I may not have left the Sector for the same reasons you did, but I don't want this destruction any more than you do," Vale says, his voice strong and clear. "You want to fight this battle? You need allies just like we do. We're willing to fight alongside you."

I remember watching Vale give his graduation speech from the SRI all those months ago. He was charismatic, determined, persuasive. Even as he proclaimed the virtues of the Sector and spoke out against everything I stood for, I almost wanted to believe him. Now, I really do believe him, and more than that, pride has welled up in my belly and made it flip-flop in funny ways.

She shakes her head. "You think it's as simple as that, as lines drawn on a map? As a battle to be won or lost? It's never so simple. What happens if you win, Valerian Orleán? Who is to say that the sins of your parents will not one day become the sins of your children?"

Vale recoils as if slapped. His eyes narrow and his fingers turn white on the reins.

Miah cuts in before Vale's anger gets the best of him. "You can't fault Vale for what his parents have done. You can't blame someone for ignorance."

"Is that so?" she demands. "You can excuse someone who participates blindly in a system of injustice, who never questions where his meat and his fuel comes from, who never questions what is happening beyond the veil of propaganda and political speeches?"

"Yes," Jeremiah says without hesitation. "You can and you should. Vale *did* question it, which is why we are here, talking with you. The people of Okaria have had their agency forcibly taken from them, especially those on the Farms and many in the factory towns who have had their ability to make choices, to think critically, taken from them by the Sector's 'system of injustice', as you say.

Will you fight against that, or will you continue to blame them for something they can't control?"

"It's too late," Chariya says with a vehemence like a hot wind. "What about the privileged in the capital? Has their agency been eliminated, too?"

"In many ways, yes," Miah says. I'm struck by how he has become such a forceful spokesman for our cause.

"No, Jeremiah. You are wrong. The people of the Okarian Sector had the chance to reject destruction before Valerian's parents rose to power. Before Soren's mother rose to power. That Faustian bargain was made long before you were even born. Now the Sector has chosen, and you all will reap the consequences."

She turns away, staring out at the ruined landscape before us. She puts one hand over her eyes to shade them, silent for a few moments. The destruction is as thorough as if a wildfire had ripped through.

"You act as though you're above those consequences," Soren says.

"As if these terrible things aren't part of our fight, too." I add.

"We can't tell you what to do or ask you to fight our battles for us," Soren speaks up. "But this isn't just our battle. It's yours as much as it is ours. And if you choose to stand aside now, we can't stop them from continuing along this path, you've sealed your own fate as much as ours."

"You say those in the Sector made their decision long ago," Vale says. "That there is no turning back from that Faustian bargain. We'll, you're right."

I snap my head around.

"You're right and you're culpable. You knew the truth, yet you didn't stay and try to change things. You left and opted out. Well, I left, too. Soren left. Miah left. The Alexander's left. We left, but we're not opting out. We're fighting back. You think purifying one stream and living like nomads is going to save the world? It's not. It's important, yes, but your work isn't going to get rid of pit mines like this. We believe things can change, but only if people know the truth. And we can't help them see the truth alone. We need you."

"No decision has been made, friends," Squall says. "And many of us heed our own counsel as much as we heed our Elders. But we want you to understand our situation. We've been keeping tabs on the Resistance and Sector activities for years, but you, if I'm not mistaken, know little of how we live. Chariya has voiced our questions and objections and we will have to think on them long and hard before any of us cast our lot in with you."

Just then, I hear the roar of an old-model hovercar in the distance, coming at us at speed. Suddenly afraid, I jump and put my hand to my empty gun holster, thinking it can only be Sector forces, and my horse startles and shies. But the car pulls up to a sharp stop next to us and I glance over to see Osprey driving, a huge grin smeared across her face.

"Goddamnit Osprey," Squall curses, "you're so loud, you'll bring the whole mountain down."

"Thought you might want to know I was coming," Osprey says, not in the least bit chagrined.

"Where did you get that hovercar?" Vale asks.

"Where do you think?" Osprey replies. "We stole it from you. From the Resistance, actually, not the Sector. One of the bases forgot to lock this baby up one night, and I nabbed it."

"Which one?" Remy demand.

"Not telling," she smirks. "Ask around, maybe someone will own up to it."

"Turn on the silencer, or I'll shoot the damn thing down," Squall snarls.

"Okay, okay." She bends down to pull out a knob that silences the hovercar. "Now, what's going on?" Osprey asks, climbing out and standing next to Soren.

Chariya looks to Squall, but Squall is now shading his eyes, squinting into the distance, past Osprey and the hovercar toward where the woods open out into the valley, where a crystal clear spring emerges from the forest to join with the poisoned river. We whirl and follow his eyes to see a figure emerge from the forest's shade. It's a strange silhouette, though, almost monstrous. The shoulders are enormous, and unbalanced, and the figure seems to drag its legs as though wounded or carrying something very heavy. For a split second I'm afraid of it, its lumbering, awkward gait the stuff of children's nightmares.

Then the figure starts waving its arms and sinks to the ground, and in an instant both Chariya and Squall have wheeled their mounts and are pounding down the gentle slope of our side of the valley. Vale, Miah and I exchange glances, and we, too, urge our horses forward, riding down the hillside as fast as we dare. Osprey motions for Soren to climb into her hovercar and their doors thud shut, then quickly passing us as they breeze over the poisoned river to join Chariya and Squall. Soren's horse plods along dutifully behind us.

As we approach I realize it's not a monster. Far from it—it's a man. And he's carrying another limp, bedraggled human over his shoulders. When Squall and Chariya dismount, bend down to press fingers to his neck, checking for a pulse, and to examine his wounds, I pull up short next to them. They turn the man over, and I realize with a heavy shock that the dirty, bloodied man is Chan-Yu, and the woman he was carrying, like a deer on a hunter's shoulders, is Linnea Heilmann.

25 — VALE

Spring 23, Sector Annum 106, 15h20
Gregorian Calendar: April 11

The guitar feels like magic under my fingertips. After everything that's gone on in the last few days, just holding it is a spiritual balm. With a little time to myself, I finally tracked down the man with the guitar, and when asked if I could borrow it for a while, he motioned for me to accept it as a gift. "For the courage to abandon the familiar and embrace the unknown," he said. It's a beautiful instrument, but I certainly couldn't accept it, and I told him so in no uncertain terms. Then I snuck off to find a solitary spot and was lucky to find an outcrop jutting out over the mountain stream just west of camp. I need to get a few hours to myself, and I'm grateful for the chance to play music without an audience.

As I strum and relish the bite of the strings and the warmth of the wood, I am comforted that some things never change no matter how tumultuous and terrible the times may be. Chan-Yu is still the same calm presence with a quicksilver but unpretentious intelligence, the same quiet, steady, reliable man I knew when he was my aide. On the other hand, there's Linnea. The first words out of her mouth when she came to were not "Thank you, Chan-Yu for rescuing me out in the Wilds" or "Vale! I'm so glad you're alive." No. Her first words were, "Where the hell is Eli?"

Linnea's presence among the Outsiders has made an already tenuous situation even more fragile. Even though they don't watch Sector broadcasts out here, they know who she is and they don't like her. Not one bit. Her running commentary about the food, the accommodations, and even her hosts' "unsavory" hygiene hasn't won her any friends. Miah and I have been the least antagonistic toward her, so naturally she's been following us. It's trying even Miah's patience.

The biggest question about Linnea's sudden appearance was how she got out of Okaria and ended up somewhere she would be found. Chan-Yu had been hiding out, not communicating with any Outsiders or Outsider assets within the Sector for months and had finally decided it was safe to make his way back home. Not two days into his journey he came across Linnea, in what he described as an all-too-convenient location, obviously looking to be found.

"What does that even mean?" Remy had demanded.

Chan-Yu turned his enigmatic gaze on her. "If her goal was to stay out of sight, camping at the intersection of three well-trod paths in the Wilds was not the wisest choice."

He watched her for almost thirty-six hours, until he was certain she was alone. Then he approached her.

She was cold, hungry, and ill-prepared for an extended stay in the Wilds, which Chan-Yu said made him even more suspicious.

"Playing the pity game is easy enough. She wanted someone to pity her and care for her, offer to take her somewhere safe. When I showed no signs of doing what she wanted, she demanded to be taken to Resistance headquarters."

Chan-Yu walked off and left her right where she was. Doggedly, she followed him. Even when he set a difficult pace through the woods, she somehow managed to keep up. Impressed, he finally relented and decided to at least bring her back to the Outsiders, to let them decide what to do with her. But not before he knocked her out using some kind of drug combination he wouldn't divulge, and then searched her from head to toe.

"She was wearing a transponder, as I suspected," Chan-Yu said. "Undoubtedly hoping someone would lead her to the Resistance team, thus transmitting the coordinates of their base to someone in the Sector. When she came to, she was none too happy."

"Where was it?" his sister had asked.

"Perhaps I shouldn't say."

Soo-Sun had arched her eyebrow and glanced at me. "You know me better than that, brother."

"Use your imagination," he'd said. And we did. After all, how many orifices are there in which to hide something like a transponder? But now we know that whatever game the Sector's playing by sending Linnea out here, we've at least countered one of their moves.

"Are you sure there are no more devices?" I asked.

"As sure as I can be."

Chan-Yu hesitated before continuing.

"I found something else, too. A knife wound by her hip, in her thigh. An ugly wound by the looks of it, but clean. No infection, crudely stitched. Certainly not a Sector job. When I asked her about it, she spat at me."

"No other injuries anywhere?" I asked, surprised.

"Nothing. I asked her about it later, when we were on mildly better terms. She still refused to say a word."

"She never mentioned a fight or anything? An animal?"

"She said nothing."

It was only a few days later that she managed to get them into a fight with a couple of unsavory loners in the woods looking for food, which is how he came away with a knife wound in the calf and an unconscious girl to drag another twenty kilometers before he found a friendly face.

I've been spending as much time as possible with Chan-Yu and Soo-Sun, trying to figure out what Soo-Sun was referring to when she said they were "bound to the same goal." No luck so far. They have, however, along with Osprey, decided to return with us to Resistance headquarters—wherever that may now be. For Osprey, I don't think it was a difficult decision since she and Soren move in tandem around the camp as if they were two parts of the same whole and are only now complete. I still feared that Remy might be more upset than she let on about Soren and Osprey's fast-developing relationship, but she doesn't seem to care. If anything, she seems more comfortable, more *natural*, around him than before.

We've decided to stay three more days to give Chan-Yu time to heal. Since they arrived, Linnea's been able to aggravate everyone within shouting distance, but Remy and I have also found ourselves alone more than once. Well, not *alone* alone, there're always people milling about. But alone enough. Still, every time I feel we might be making progress, like she sits a little closer or talks a little softer, someone intrudes with some order of business and we're yanked back to the looming reality of war on the horizon.

As I strum, I think of Remy and Tai and Brinn and Jahnu and the Resistance and war. I think of my parent's starring role in the whole, wretched tragedy and find myself comparing my memories of them, of their characters and personalities, of *mom* and *dad* with Philip, Chancellor, and Corine, Director of the OAC. *How blind could I have been?* I was distracted. Growing apart from them. A young man busy with graduate school, eager for independence, for a life to call my own. I paid no attention to them, except when their actions concerned me. In a word, I was selfish. Self absorbed.

But, I remind myself, now I am here. I am changing—*changed*. I am on the right side.

"It's so sad." Remy's voice startles me, and I clutch at the guitar like a weapon.

"How long have you been here?" It's a stupid question, but my face is hot at the thought of her hearing me singing like some lovesick troubadour. I'd been trying to pick out a song I'd written long ago for the piano, something I'd never let anyone hear even when I played it on an instrument I had mastered. I called it *Tuqburni*, an untranslatable Old Arabic word for a love so deep one cannot imagine living without the beloved. I'd never tried it on a guitar, for good reason.

"Long enough," she says and my heart clutches.

"Yeah, well…." The flush reaches the tips of my ears.

"You have a nice voice. And the song is beautiful."

Oh.

"I wrote it after you left." The words slip off my tongue, and at first I want to grab them and stuff them back down my throat, but then her face softens and a smile tugs at the corner of her mouth and I'm glad the words are out there hanging in the air for her to feel. My mother called my songs maudlin and childish. *You're not some Old World bard, Vale. The rigor of the classics suits you more than sentimental love songs,* she'd said. Admitting now that the song was something I'd conjured up in a moment of loneliness feels like I'm stripped naked, standing soul-bared in front of Remy. Even though I am sitting. And most definitely fully clothed.

She sits next to me, *close enough to touch,* tucking her legs up under her chin and wrapping her arms around her knees. I start to set the guitar aside, but her fingers dart out and touch my arm. "Don't stop. It's nice."

"If you insist." I pull it back against me and strum some basic chord progressions, just to keep my fingers moving, to fill the silence between us.

"You and Soren are lucky," she says after a while, as I try and fail to come up with another tune.

"Lucky? How?"

"Miah."

"Yeah. There's no one like him."

"What he said the other day, when he found out about his mom … the way he just turned to you and told you not to apologize. There was no need for forgiveness because he knew you weren't a part of all that."

After a few more chords while my stomach churns and I try to think of what to say, I give up, set the guitar aside and turn to face her.

"I *was* a part of it. I went along. Blindly. *Blithely.* Unable or unwilling to ask hard questions until I had no choice."

She looks up at me, eyes wide, earnest, encouraging. "But don't you see? That's what we all did. Soren when his mom was voted out. Jahnu's family, Kenzie's family, they had their reasons. Eli and my parents after Tai was killed. I can't even be sure I would have left if my parents had made it a choice. Even Miah: he knew his dad was in the Resistance and didn't do anything about it till he had to make a choice. We all arrived at our own pivot points ... eventually."

"I should have done more."

"Such as?"

"I could have demanded answers about your disappearance. I could have tried to find you."

She looks up at me, skin like burnished copper, brown eyes framed by the most curiously alluring freckles....

"We all could have done more. We've all suffered as a result. There's plenty of pain and guilt to go around." Somehow her hand is resting on mine and she gives it a whisper-soft squeeze that shoots a white-hot pulse through me. "We don't need to divvy it up and weigh it on some cosmic pain scale to see who's suffered the most. I thought we did, but we don't. Not anymore."

"But everything that's gone wrong ... it's all connected to me, through my family."

"We don't need a giant scale of responsibility any more than we need a scale of pain. Chariya said it started long before we were born. You're no more responsible than I am."

"But my mom and dad—"

"Remember what my dad said the night you got to Normandy? That you— we, none of us—are responsible for the sins of our fathers. Or our mothers. What we're responsible for is what we do now. We're responsible for our own choices, for how we shape our future."

Our choices? Our future? Is it possible she means more than the Resistance, more than the Sector? Is it possible she means *us*? I want to lean forward and....

"I don't want to hate you anymore, Vale." Her voice is like a plucked string resonating throughout my body. "I never did hate you, not really," she says and I meet the vibration of her voice with an equal frequency as I reach out and pull her to me as if the only reason I was given arms was to wrap them around her. Her head presses against my chest and my cheek rests on the top of her head and we sit in silence except for the trilling of the birds in the treetops, the rushing of the water in the streambed, and the building hum of shared hope. Hope that hate is not the answer, that it never was and never will be. That we can create something together that is greater than what we could create by ourselves. That love will always transcend our pasts.

By the time we left, the Outsiders had still made no promises. Chan-Yu's gave Squall an ally and Squall said he would take our case to the other Elders as soon as we left. Even Chariya seemed to soften her opposition, but we weren't privy to their discussions, and I have no idea what promises were made or bargains struck among the Outsiders themselves. As for Chan-Yu and Soo-Sun, they are traveling with us to meet with the others. We gave them our destination coordinates and they have become our navigators. Chan-Yu is well-respected among the Outsiders, and everyone naturally defers to him. His leadership is so natural, so accepted, I can hardly believe there was a time when he took orders from me.

Our biggest challenge is dealing with Linnea's constant complaining. We've all been tempted to gag her to keep her quiet. It's been three weeks since she left Okaria and three weeks without a hot shower is apparently more than she counted on. She's been treated as a convict under house arrest with the Outsiders, and we're formally considering her a prisoner, even though it's clear she's not going anywhere. She wouldn't survive three days on her own, anyway.

I glance over at her, her long blond hair tied back in a ponytail. Back in Okaria, she wore it cascading down her back like shimmering strands of gold or piled on top of her head in some elaborate nest of curls. Remy charitably tried to convince her to cut it before we set out—"traveling is easier with short hair," she told her—but Linnea wouldn't hear of it. She put her hands over her head and refused to let anyone come near. Then she asked Remy to help her French braid her hair—whatever that means. Remy pocketed the scissors and stormed off.

"If she wants to keep playing the celebrity out here in the Wilds, let her. But I'm not going to be her goddamn makeup artist."

"Can't wait to see Eli's face when you climb off that horse," Miah repeats for the umpteenth time, shaking his head in astonishment at the mere fact that Linnea Heilmann is riding a horse beside him out here in the Wilds.

"Why are you out here, really?" Remy asks over and over. "If you thought you were going to lead the Sector to our base, you really should have realized someone would suspect you were wearing a tracker."

"How many times do I have to tell you people? I want to find Eli. The tracker was just to shut up Corine."

"Why the sudden interest?" Miah asks again, more insistently.

"It's not sudden and it's none of your damn business." She shoots him a razor-sharp glare, one I know all too well. I wonder if he, too, is fighting the instinct to duck.

It's true, though—Linnea's been interested in Eli for as long as I can remember. It was one of the things that pushed her and Tai apart as friends, when Tai and Eli started dating. Linnea tried to act like she didn't care. But for all her usual brilliance when it comes to lying, she couldn't hide her dismay when Eli went for Tai instead.

I have to admit, even smudged with dust and her face downcast and unhappy, she's still beautiful. If anything, the natural environment has taken some of the edge off her, and her beauty seems less dangerous now. Like Miah, I wonder what Eli will think when he sees her.

Once we make camp, Chan-Yu consults the astrolabe he reclaimed from the Outsider camp upon his return, and announces we should make it to the rendezvous point by tomorrow afternoon. If all goes according to plan, Firestone will be waiting with a cargo airship large enough for the horses—if we can load them—and he'll transport us to the new Resistance base. There's some small talk about what happens next as we eat our dinner and try to ignore the fact that we're heading back into the thick of the conflict and that Linnea is eating lentils and fire-roasted vegetables with us and *is Jahnu okay?* but eventually we fall into a tense, uncomfortable silence. Both Chan-Yu and Soo-Sun retreat to their tent, and then Soren and Osprey disappear into the woods without even a backwards glance. Finally, Miah turns to Linnea and asks the question I know he's wanted to ask since he first saw her.

"How's Moriana?" His face is creased with worry.

"Last time I saw her she was fine."

"Did they take her in for questioning?"

"Of course, but don't worry. They didn't get anything out of her."

"That's because she didn't know anything," Miah responds. Linnea turns her whole body to face him.

"You really didn't tell her you were leaving?"

Miah shakes his head, stares at the ground. I know he isn't proud of what we did the night we left. But it was the only way to keep Moriana safe.

"I never thought you'd have the gall to walk away from her," Linnea says, her eyebrow cocked in surprise. You were always so ... *gooey* ... over her." She shudders. "No wonder she was so distraught. I thought it was all an act. Even

Corine thought so at first, but apparently Moriana satisfied her. She lost her security clearance, but at least she's still got a job. She didn't get fired. Not completely, anyway."

"Is she okay? In the new job and all? Her work is—" Miah's voice catches in his throat "—it's important to her." When Linnea looks at him, her expression is so close to sympathetic that I wonder if she really does have thoughts and emotions beyond her own whims and power struggles.

"Honestly?"

"No, Linnea, lie to me, please. Yes, honestly, for stars sake, are you a complete idiot?"

"All right," Linnea throws her hands up. "She was really torn up when you left, and I think after a while she might have bought into what Vale's parents were saying about you betraying them." Miah bows his head and his shoulders sink. He's usually so ebullient, it's heartbreaking to watch him crumble into himself. "But once she was in the clear, out of Corine's line of fire, and not in any danger of being interrogated again, I was able to tell her what Vale told me the night of the Solstice."

"Even though that was a lie," I cut in. Miah raises his head, looking between the two of us questioningly. Linnea narrows her eyes at me.

"It was enough to convince her that Jeremiah hadn't tried to kill you. When she realized you were planning on leaving, she knew it couldn't have been foul play." She turns and looks at Miah, her eyes round and bluer than the open sky. "Moriana wanted to come with me when I left. But I wouldn't let her."

"Why not?" he asks. The question isn't angry or demanding.

"For the same reason you wouldn't, I presume," Linnea says, pulling the ponytail holder off her hair and letting it swing loose. "Besides, I think Corine still has her followed in case you contact her. And she wouldn't have survived a day out here."

"And you're doing so well yourself," I say.

"I'm here, aren't I? My goal is to find Eli and I'm on my way to see him, so yes, I think I'm doing just fine. A shower would be nice, but—"

"I keep thinking of Jahnu. What would Moriana think if she knew he was hurt?" Remy interrupts.

"Who's Jahnu?" Linnea asks, as if Remy's question was the stupidest thing she'd ever heard. Her momentary brush with kindness was short lived.

"Don't you remember? Moriana's cousin. He was at our house a lot when you were there with Tai."

"Nerdy skinny kid?" She glares at Remy as though she's offended her personally by expecting her to remember a little boy of no consequence. But then she sits up a little straighter and her expression turns into something resembling a concerned frown, probably realizing there's information here, information that could one day be traded for something more. Her voice softens into a tone of comfort. "Why? What happened to him?"

"None of your damn business," Remy snaps.

It's early afternoon when shadow descends over the forest, too dark and too sudden to be a cloud. My first thought is, *where is Remy?* My second is *I hope death comes quickly*, thinking the shadow to be a Sector airship that had caught up with us and was ready to burn the forest around us. The horses shy and skitter, trying to bolt for cover, but when a booming voice from above calls out, I can't help but smile.

"Y'all gonna take all day getting to the rendezvous or what?"

"Firestone!" Remy shouts behind me, abandoning any pretense we might have had at attempting to travel quietly. The airship moves away from us and in the distance I can see it descend below the tree line and out of sight. Even Chan-Yu is anxious and he urges the horses forward in an easy canter until we reach the edge of the clearing where the airship is waiting at the water's edge of a wide and peaceful lake. There's a sliver of a beach, a gentle slope that leads down to the water marked with fallen branches, pebbles, and gritty sand.

Standing by the water's edge is Kenzie, her bright red curls flying in all directions around her face. She looks at us with a fragmented smile, as if her mind is in a thousand places and only a tiny part is here. When Remy jumps off her horse and runs to her, her composure splinters. As she wraps her arms around Remy and buries her face in her shoulder, my stomach clenches and fear settles in my gut like a vise, but then Kenzie starts laughing through her tears. I can hear Remy talking excitedly, and a happy buoyancy floods through me. Jahnu *must* be okay.

Soren follows Remy's lead, breaking away from Osprey's touch for the first time in almost a week, and when he reaches Kenzie's side he picks her up and swings her around like a child.

"What's going on?" Linnea asks, as insensitively as humanly possible. As she slides off her horse, she pulls shakes her hair out, arranging herself beside her horse as if she were modeling for a Sector broadcast on the healthy virtues of outdoor life. She straightens her shirt, pinches her cheeks, bites her lip, and waits, looking very perturbed by the celebration happening without her permission.

The cargo hold opens and Eli and Firestone descend down the gangway. We all turn and watch as he squints into the sunlight, his mouth drops open, and he comes to a stop in the sand just a few meters from Linnea in all her golden glory.

"What the hell are *you* doing here?" he demands.

Her face falls for just a moment, before she puts on a smiling broadcast-quality mask.

"I was hoping for a somewhat more welcoming greeting, Elijah."

"I don't care what you were hoping for. How the fuck did you get here? And why?" He turns to us accusingly, as if we conjured her up to spite him.

"Isn't it obvious?" Her perfect smile is fighting a valiant battle to stay on her lips, and I catch myself feeling something I never thought would apply to Linnea Heilmann: pity. "I came looking for you."

"You what?" he asks, dumbfounded. I now truly understand the meaning of that word. Linnea, too, looks speechless, shocked mute by the strange idea that someone could *not* desire her presence. Firestone speaks up to break the tension.

"We got the whole ride home for catchin' up, ladies and gentlemen. We picked up a lot of drone activity on our way here and will have to go the long way home to avoid them, even with cloaking. So load 'em up, cowboys, it's time to head back to the corral."

My horse, Mistral, and I are the closest to the airship, so I start guiding her by the reins up the loading ramp. She, however, seems to have a different idea, and is none too eager to walk into a giant metal compartment. Her eyes are wild and her ears flat as she stomps and backs up, refusing to walk more than halfway up the ramp.

"Whoa, girl," I say and try to act like Chan-Yu or Miah handling their horses, but I'm obviously not pulling it off.

"Here," Remy says, taking the reins from me as she leads her own horse. She puts her hand on Mistral's neck, stroking her calmly and muttering something I can't hear. "She'll calm down if she has a friend to walk up with." A set of reins in each hand, Remy walks the two horses up the ramp together, and suddenly Mistral doesn't seem quite as reluctant.

"How'd you learn to do that?"

"You mean living with these animals all this time wasn't enough to figure them out?" She runs her hand over her horse's mane. "They're herd animals.

You just have to take control and show them there's a leader to follow."

"I thought I was doing that."

"Maybe you're still a little nervous around her."

I pat Mistral's nose and she nickers at me. "Maybe she was just playing hard to get."

"Right," Remy laughs.

"Well, she's not the only girl I'm still nervous around. Maybe I'll win them both over yet." I pull out few pieces of broken carrots that I've been carrying in my pocket and flatten my hand to let Mistral's velvety lips pluck them from my palm.

"Broken carrots and pocket lint always win over even the most hard-hearted maiden," Remy says. After a pause, she continues, "In case you didn't hear, Jahnu's gonna make it. He's not walking yet, but he's going to be okay."

"That's the best news we've had in a long time."

"It's a huge weight off my shoulders," she admits. She smiles up at me and my insides thrum. "Before we left that morning, I visited him in the infirmary. He told me to go out into the world and make some magic." She sighs, shakes her head. "But still, I felt guilty. He was injured because of my great idea to go to Round Barn in the first place. But now ... now maybe I can take his advice. It's time to allow myself a little happiness." And then she turns to get the horses into position, tying them up at the rail, and I let my breath out in a long, slow exhale.

26 — REMY

I cling to my father's side as we walk through the halls of an old, abandoned factory complex outside of the city that used to be called Rochester. Before Firestone and Eli improved our drone-jamming technology, we never would have dared set up a base so close to Okaria. Now, technically, we are within Sector borders, not far from the port where Soren and I escaped last winter. If we're going to disrupt the food distribution chain, we need to be between the Farms and the Dietician's headquarters in Okaria.

"Just in time!" the Director calls to us as we open the door to the operations center. "We're about to start."

It's a large room full of faces, some I recognize and some I don't. The Director and Eli are standing in the center of the room, flanked by Chan-Yu, Soo-Sun, and Osprey. Chan-Yu looks as calm and composed as ever; Osprey, by contrast, keeps bouncing up onto the balls of her feet as if unable to contain her excitement. She'll be representing the Outsiders today because neither Chan-Yu nor Soo-Sun relish putting on a 'dog and pony show'. Soren, who is usually by her side, is with Bear, Rose, and Luis, meeting with some of the other refugees from Round Barn.

Since we were picked up by Eli and Firestone, things have been happening so fast, we've hardly had time to think straight. Vale, especially, hasn't had a moment's peace since he told us all about his C-Link, Demeter. Today, Vale, Eli, and Osprey are going to outline their plan for disrupting the Sector's food supply chain. My father and I take our seats next to Kenzie and Jahnu—Jahnu's now off the oxygen and able to get around pretty well with a cane. I look around for Vale, to no avail. It's not like him to be late to a meeting.

"Are we ready to go?" Eli asks, impatient.

"Where the hell is Vale?" the Director snaps, as if suddenly noticing his absence.

"He'll be here," Eli assures her. He's confident, edgy with excitement, and grinning that wide, lopsided grin that my sister loved so much—and, apparently—so does Linnea. We've been back almost two weeks and Eli has accomplished what none of us thought possible. He's avoided all contact with Linnea and, to my astonishment, I almost feel sorry for her.

"Take your seats, everyone," the Director commands and soon the room is quiet. Apparently we are going to begin the meeting without Vale. "This is the moment we've been waiting for," she begins. "The board is set and the game is about to begin. For the first time, we have a workable strategy. I ask that you all take notes and keep your questions until the end. There'll be plenty of time to go through every aspect of the plan when the presentations are complete. I'm depending on all of you to do your damndest to poke holes in the plan, identify the weaknesses so we can address them. If you have a concern, you need to voice it. Got it?"

There's a buzz in the room and everyone's nodding, flipping open their v-scrolls.

"Okay, here's what's going down," Eli begins. "By now you all know about the LOTUS database, the digital seed bank Professor Kanaan Adrian encoded for Dr. Rhinehouse and Dr. Hawthorne. The genetic codes for all the Old world seed varietals Kanaan could find were sequenced and preserved in this database through artificial DNA storage. We also know all too well that we'll never be able to break the OAC's stranglehold on the Sector and its citizens until we disrupt their chain of distribution. With the help of Dr. Rhinehouse and his assistant, former Dietician Dara Oban, the 3D printer we 'borrowed' from Seed Bank Hydrogen last week has already begun spitting out enormous quantities of unmodified seeds from the LOTUS database."

Eli shoots a sly wink at Kenzie, red hair vibrant, face set and determined as she sits with her long freckled fingers clasped in Jahnu's hand. She and Eli led the raid to acquire the printer and she and Jahnu both have been working on the team to get it up and running.

"Our task, now," he continues, "is threefold. First, we infiltrate the Farms and begin substituting our unmodified seeds for the OAC's seeds where possible. Second, we begin growing our own food from these seeds to distribute in small quantities outside the MealPak system. Third, we hijack the Sector's own distribution system to bring this food to Sector citizens in the short term. Our goal is to begin to get the people of Okaria off of the modified food regimes without experiencing the kind of severe withdrawal symptoms we all went through when we came here. Once we've done all three things," Eli says with a twinkle in his eye, "we can begin thinking about escalating our offensive against the Sector."

"Which brings us to Vale," the Director says.

Where is he?

She turns to Zoe, the girl who worked in the comm center at Normandy, and who is now apparently the Director's right-hand woman, and says with a huff, "Go find him." No sooner does Zoe stand up than Vale sweeps into the room, his mouth set, his eyes dark as a thundercloud.

"What's wrong?" the Director says.

"It can wait." His voice is clipped, controlled. He glances around the room until his gaze settles on mine and then, with a look I can't decipher but makes me nervous, he takes his place at the front of the room. "Am I up?"

"It's all yours," Eli says, stepping back, giving Vale a wide berth.

Vale takes a deep breath and faces the group. "Not many of you know this yet, but over the course of the last five to ten years, the Sector has been assembling what could be the most powerful informational tool in history." He reaches up to his ear and, fumbling slightly, pulls off what looks like a flap of skin. There are some muffled whispers of *ugh* and *what the hell?* from the audience, and I, too, would be shocked if I hadn't seen him do it before. He holds it up, but it's so small, so transparent, it's hard to see. "This tiny little patch of fiber connects me to the largest information storehouse amassed since the Internet, otherwise known as the World Wide Web, of the Old World. We call it a Comm-Link, or a C-Link, and through it, I can access every single public or government file currently on the Sector network."

Skeptical, hesitant looks transform into wide-eyed gasps. Vale hesitates, looking almost fondly at the patch of fibers in his hand. But then he comes back, and looks up and around at his audience, and his politician's instinct for public speaking comes back to him. A confident, almost radiant calmness descends on him as he speaks, the kind that just makes you want to believe everything he says. It's a dangerous ability, one that kept me from trusting him for too long. *Or, maybe, should I still be more careful?*

"Many of you didn't trust me when I first arrived. Maybe nobody did. Maybe you still don't. I'm an Orleán and that makes me potentially treacherous and dangerous. Half the reason there are dozens of squads of Black Ops prowling the Wilds looking for us is because of me. And you still might think I'm not trustworthy, just because I'll always be Corine's son. But whether you trust me or not, this tool, this C-Link, is the best and probably only chance you have at bringing down the OAC entirely.

"The fibers I hold in my hand mold exclusively to my skin and respond only to my command. There are only eleven of these in existence and they belong to the highest officials in the Sector and the Consortium. Two to my parents. Five to the OAC's Board of Directors. One to Evander Sun-Zi, and two to Generals Conrad and Lara. One to me. It was a graduation present," he says with a heavy sigh, then collects himself again.

"With my C-Link, we can access every passcode in the database, break into every top-secret research lab, hijack the drone and navigation systems, view the blueprints for every Seed Bank and the layouts of every military craft in operation. This tiny little piece of fiber is our connection to every bit of information we could ever want or need in our battle."

"You say 'we' like you're one of us," a voice calls from the crowd. I can't identify the voice, and the man has stopped speaking before I can locate him.

"He is," I growl in the direction of the voice, defending him, though whether for his sake or to prove to myself that I really do trust him, I'm not sure.

"I am," he proclaims loudly, much to my surprise. I spin around to watch him. His expression, far from the tortured, angry look he sported when he entered the room, is confident, determined. "I wouldn't have left everything behind in Okaria if I didn't know in my heart of hearts that what they're doing is wrong." He pauses. "I don't want a civil war. I don't want more bloodshed. That's why I'm doing everything in my power to see that Eli's plan works."

This is Vale at his finest, when he's speaking his mind plainly and simply. These are the moments I remember most from when we were friends—and more than friends. The times when he was telling me why he loved studying history, or about his physics research, or when he was losing himself in his music. Those raw bits of honesty that shine through sometimes. You want to follow him anywhere.

"But there is one drawback."

"Figures," someone says.

"I knew it was too good to be true," another whispers.

"The problem is that this tool is only accessible when I'm within range of the Sector's networks. Which means I either have to be at an administrative station in one of the Farms or Factory towns, or I have to be in the capital. So I'm going back."

The room explodes.

"Going back?"

"Why the hell are we letting him leave alive?"

"He'll turn us in as soon as he's back home with mommy and daddy."

We knew some would react like this, and Vale stands there and takes it, his jaw clenching and unclenching until the clamor dies down. The Director speaks up, her voice sharp as a blade.

"Are you finished?" The room falls silent. "I want everyone here to understand this: Vale has earned my trust. He's earned Dr. Rhinehouse's trust. And he's earned Gabriel's trust. I hope that is good enough for the rest of you. If not, take it up with me after the meeting."

Vale's shoulders rise and fall as he continues. "A team of engineers is setting up the secure link I'll use to transmit data back to you. Whatever I learn, you'll learn. Whatever documents I gain access to, Dem—my C-Link will transmit to you. This is the only way we can meet them on a level playing field. They can out-man us and out-gun us, so we have to outsmart them. And we have Remy's video from Round Barn. We're going to hack into the Sector's broadcast system and play it for everyone to see." He steps back and looks over at Chan-Yu, Soo-Sun, and Osprey. "Now it's time to hear from our allies in this effort. The Outsiders. Osprey?"

As she steps up, Vale backs away and catches my eyes again, letting his gaze linger for just a second before flicking back toward Osprey. His face is composed, but it's like he's wearing a mask, a mask he's trying hard to keep in place. Something's wrong.

"After much deliberation, we have agreed to donate a limited amount of manpower and transportation in return for a guarantee of protection of our lands." Her eyes grow wide and light up as she speaks. "As you begin growing all your fancy food, you'll need to get it to the people somehow. We'll help you do that. We've been traveling around under the Sector's nose for decades, and we'll show you how. We'll also help you hijack some of their own distribution systems, especially once Vale starts feeding us the OAC's transport grids.

"One of us," her eyes flicker to Chan-Yu, "has intimate knowledge of the OAC's operating systems and research programs. Along with Vale, we can help you circumvent detection and ultimately disrupt and shut down the OAC's MealPak modification program and take back control of the citizens' dietary regime. We will help you assemble a number of guerrilla squads to hijack the Sector's distribution lines, pose as OAC staff, Enforcers on the Farms, and Watchmen in the Factory Towns. We'll switch out Sector MealPaks with your unmodified food and distribute it evenly throughout. We'll track their shipments, steal their equipment, and intercept their lines. While your scientists and engineers and farmers are churning out seeds and growing untainted food, we'll have a troop of people dedicated to getting that food to those who need it. Soren Skaarsgard and I will be leading that effort."

Eli steps back up next to Osprey. "Now, let's get into the details and take some questions."

Vale eases toward the door by the podium and, with the barest toss of his head, signals me to follow him before he disappears through it.

"Bathroom," I whisper to my dad and without a second thought I slip out of my seat and leave by the door at the back of the room.

27 — VALE

"What's wrong?" she asks. Remy's face is painted with worry, her eyes dark and questioning, the bridge of her nose creased where her brows are furrowed. I would like nothing more than to plant my lips there, to smooth away all her worry lines. Instead, I grab her hand and pull her along after me.

"Come on," I whisper. She follows without question, her hand tightening into mine, and I think it wondrously strange how far we've come. A month ago, she had trouble looking at me. Now I am holding her hand.

I lead her through a long hallway, past two sets of doors, and down toward the bunks. Finally, I push open the door to my room—the one I'm sharing with Miah, Eli, and Firestone—and pull her in. I have no idea what she's thinking, but when I see the look on her face, I know Linnea is not what she expected.

"What's going on?" Accusation, confusion—and disappointment—tint her voice. *Surely she doesn't think Linnea and I....*

"Linnea has something to say to you." I cut that thought off before it takes hold.

"Okay."

"You're not a very popular person back home," Linnea starts, looking at Remy as if she were a curiosity, like an old and now tasteless decoration from her childhood bedroom. Remy's fingers are still entwined in mine, and I squeeze, trying to resist the urge to ball my hand up into a fist and pound something. A wall perhaps. Maybe Linnea's face.

"Tell me something I don't know," Remy glances up at me as if to say *you brought me here for this?*

"Get to the point," I say to Linnea.

"After that stunt you pulled carving up Evander's face—really, Remy, how could you do that?" she shudders, shaking it off. "He was ready to come after you with everything at his disposal. To deploy the entirety of the Sector Defense

Forces. But Corine and Philip were worried about Vale's safety and Aulion said it was a waste of manpower and that he had a better idea. Apparently Aulion has had experience dispensing with people who had become 'bothersome.' Now I know he was talking about Soren's parents. I don't know who else he's dispensed with, but—"

"Keep going," I cut her off.

"Anyway, Evander wants you dead. Corine and Philip want Vale back home. And they want the Resistance destroyed. So they came to me with a proposal." She stands and walks over to Eli's bunk. She picks up his shower kit and runs her fingers over each item—his razor, his toothbrush, his comb. "Literally a proposal."

"A proposal…" Remy repeats, not understanding.

Linnea turns and looks Remy in the eye. "I am infected with a targeted nanotech bug that operates just like a virus except that it is not 'tuned' to my biochemistry, only to Eli's. My job was to infect Eli—really, Corine is obsessed with him—and, if I succeeded and made it back to Okaria, we'd kill two birds with one stone—one virus—and I would get my reward. Since Eli won't let me near him, there was no chance of seducing him, of passing the virus to him via a more enjoyable means than using his toothbrush." She shudders. "That was really quite disgusting."

"A virus? Eli's sick?" Remy lets go of my hand and sinks down onto my bed, deflated. "What kind of virus?"

"The virus changes the biochemistry in his brain so that he will hate you. The look of you, the very *smell* of you will repulse him to the point where he is enraged and will, eventually, kill you. It poisons his mind. It hijacks the synaptic transmission between neurons and disconnects images of you with positive thinking and reconnects those images with negative emotions. Fear. Pain. Anxiety. Anger. *Hate.*"

I've already heard all this. She came to me with her confession right before the briefing was to start, but now, hearing it all over again, watching Remy try to process it, makes me almost blind with rage. I thought I knew the depths my parents would sink to, but oh happy day, they're always ready to surprise. Remy's shaking hands have wadded up the edge of the blanket, gripping and ungripping.

The cruelty is astonishing. Turning Eli, the only survivor of the classroom attack into the same kind of maniacal killer who carried out the attack in the first place takes a warped mind that I thought only existed in fairy tales. Evil Queens. Despotic dictators. Murderous tyrants. *My mother.*

Linnea plunges ahead. "Of course, killing the darling Remy Alexander would be a very bad thing, and so chances are Eli would not be long for this world either."

"Why are you telling me this?" she asks, glaring at Linnea as if she were a giant cockroach.

Linnea shrugs. "Because I changed my mind. I decided I don't like being the vector for a synthetic disease that makes friends kill each other."

"Is there any antidote?"

"I told you, it's nanotech. Not a real virus," Linnea snaps. Though she won't show it, she's at least mildly concerned about her complicity, but that does little to comfort me.

"But it functions like a virus?"

"It replicates and hijacks DNA like a virus. And some of its components are organic material. But some are synthetic, and can't be destroyed by the immune system like a real virus."

Remy is quiet for a moment, seething, and I sit beside her as she bites out her next question. "And what is your reward?"

I flinch at what I know comes next.

"Vale," Linnea says, appraising me.

"What? What do you mean?" Remy's eyes go wide and her cheeks flush dark as if Linnea had just slapped her. For one moment, the room is so quiet, I can hear the blood pulsing in my ears.

"Well, you're dead. Eli's dead. The hopes of the Resistance are dead. Aulion swoops in with his troops and takes Vale home and we live happily ever after. Mr. and Ms. Valerian Augustus Orleán."

I put my hand on Remy's, but this time she doesn't move to entangle our fingers. She shakes her head, unbelieving, unmoored.

"I still don't understand. Are you ... are you ..."

Linnea sighs again. "It's simple, Remy. I never loved Vale and you do—"

"I—" Remy begins, then flushes and glances at me, at my hand on hers, and stops.

Linnea goes on as if Remy didn't interrupt her. "You are Tai's sister and she was my friend. I always wanted Eli, always liked him—actually became quite obsessed with him—but now I know beyond a shadow of a doubt that he'll never want me even though Tai's been gone all these years ... but that's okay. Life is like that sometimes. Anyway, sometimes people can change their minds. Besides," she adds as if it is an afterthought. "I haven't eaten a Mealpak in weeks and I feel different, and telling you this feels right."

"Is Eli infected?" For the first time during this conversation, Linnea looks away. Ashamed.

"Yes," she says. "I didn't think the virus had taken hold, but just this morning, at breakfast, I saw him looking at you and there was something completely different in his expression. He couldn't stop staring. His lip twitched, his eyes narrowed, nose flared. He was looking at you like you were prey."

"I didn't notice," Remy says, looking at me like I could back her up, tell her it wasn't true, that Eli didn't have the virus. I can see the rage building in her face, the tension bunching her shoulders.

"Of course you didn't notice. You were with Vale and Kenzie and Jahnu, closed off to the world … like friends should be. You weren't paying attention like I was." She pauses, then turns back to face us as if she wanted to say something more, as if she had yet more secrets up her sleeve. But she closes her mouth and remains silent.

Remy, now completely overcome with rage, jumps up and slams Linnea up against the wall. She hits her with a hard right upper-cut that snaps her head back with a crack. Blood pours from her nose and suddenly Linnea is all arms and legs, flailing against Remy, trying to push her away.

"How *dare* you," Remy growls, throwing another right that lands with an *oomph* in Linnea's diaphragm. Linnea sinks to the floor and Remy crouches down to face her.

"I'm sorry," Linnea gasps, spitting blood through her split lip. "I'm so sorry."

"You don't give a shit if we all die, do you?"

"I'm sorry! I'm being honest, I swear. I know it was wrong—"

"It was fucking *sick*, Linnea," she spits. "I can't believe Tai was ever friends with you." She stands up and backs into me and I wrap my arm around her waist as Linnea looks up at us. I never thought I'd see Linnea look remotely vulnerable. Even now, she's guarded, glaring at us, but her face has softened, her authority taken away and her pride wounded.

"I want to help find the antidote."

"You said it yourself, there is no antidote!" Remy yells, lunging forward again, then stopping herself and pulling back.

"Vale?" I turn to find Chan-Yu in the doorway. "What's going on?"

Remy looks at him, abject, utter desolation etched across her face. "Oh, nothing except she's infected Eli with a synthetic virus so he'll kill me. So he'll hate me and then murder me."

"Ah," Chan-Yu says, moving fully into the room.

Linnea's facade of indifference weakens even more when Chan-Yu crouches and looks at Linnea like he is disappointed in her. Not that he was ever pleased with her, but I can only imagine the wrath of Chan-Yu's disappointment.

"I finally understand. I didn't truly think you came all the way out here because you loved Eli."

"I was played. I wish I hadn't done it, but I didn't realize … I didn't … I just wasn't thinking about the true consequences. I want to help reverse it." She touches a finger to her lip and winces, and looks up at Remy. There is true sorrow in her face, and I know Remy sees it, because her shoulders soften and the slightest sigh escapes her lips.

"Fine. Help us. We'll need it. But first, *fuck you*." Remy rounds on us and storms out the room. I turn to follow, but stop short. She probably needs to be alone right now.

"What are we going to do about Eli?" I ask, suddenly at a loss.

Chan-Yu turns to me. "We'll have to ask Demeter."

I burst through the door to Rhinehouse's new lab ten minutes later with Linnea in tow. He's hunched over a microscope, his back curled around it like a question mark. The grey beard he's been sporting for the last few weeks looks like flakes of flint from the side.

"Rhinehouse, we need to talk," I say.

"Can it wait?" he asks, his voice as rough as his beard.

"No," Linnea answers for me.

He huffs an enormous sigh and pulls away from the microscope. He doesn't really straighten so much as hunch in our direction, turning as he does and shutting off the light on the scope.

"What do you want?" he demands. Tact, I remember, is not his strong suit.

"Eli's been compromised," I say, trying to get the words out as fast as possible. "Linnea infected him with a synthetic virus that hijacks his memory and makes him want to kill Remy, but she owned up to it and now we need you to sample his blood and try to find an antidote. And we need to bump up my mission to Okaria. We need to leave as soon as possible. To get Remy away from Eli and see if we can get any information on the virus through my C-Link in case you can't figure it out."

Rhinehouse stares at us for a long, long minute. I count my breaths to keep myself from saying anything more before he has a chance to process and respond. Eleven, twelve, thirteen, fourteen … I've counted to seventeen breaths before he opens his mouth.

"Tell me about the virus."

"I'm really sor—" Linnea starts.

"Spare me," Rhinehouse grunts, cutting her off. "Tell me everything you know, as precisely as possible, about the way the nanotech operates."

Linnea looks at me briefly, fear in her eyes, but I refuse to sympathize with her. She launches into a five minute ramble as she tries to remember everything Corine told her, while Rhinehouse stares at her, still hunched over, not moving at all except to blink occasionally. When she finally trails off, Rhinehouse turns to his computer and starts moving things around on the glass pane, pulling up new files and displays.

"Valerian. You will tell the Director your mission to Okaria leaves tomorrow, if possible. Next day at the latest." He pulls up a headshot of Eli and I can see that he's got Eli's full genome mapped, all forty-six chromosomes in 3D holographic display. "We can keep Remy and Eli separated that way. Let's hope your C-Link can access Corine's files. Without more information about the specifics of the technology used to create this 'virus,'" he emphasizes the word, "I will never be able to find an antidote or program the antibodies." He turns away from his computer to stare at me and Linnea.

"You, girl," he almost spits, "have proven yourself to be as despicable a human being as I've ever met. And I've met some doozies." Linnea flinches as though she's been slapped. "But you've also done something incredibly noble, and admitted that to yourself and your peers." He turns to me. "Who else knows about this?"

"Remy and Chan-Yu."

He looks at Linnea. "Besides the Director, no one else can know what you've done. If it gets out, you won't be long for this world."

I sigh. I wish we could have an end to secrets and politics and games. But I know he's right.

"I want her to come with me to Okaria," I say. "Linnea's obviously as good a liar as anyone and she knows the city."

"Adding yet another incredibly recognizable face to your current team of celebrities hardly seems like a good idea, Vale," Rhinehouse says, fixing me with a wooden stare.

"We'll all be wearing disguises anyway, Doctor," I say, as respectfully as I can, "and Linnea's the smoothest player in the game." Rhinehouse stares at me for a long time and then finally nods.

"Fine. I'll back you up and will inform the Director of the situation. Keep

Remy close and prepare your team and all the equipment you need."

"Can I take Jeremiah?" I ask, knowing in advance what the answer will be.

"Absolutely not. I'll give you a pass on her"—he cocks his head toward Linnea—"but Jeremiah is too big a liability, not to mention all of Okaria's on the lookout for him as a traitor to the Sector."

I sigh, but don't protest. It'll be hard enough to get this mission ready to go in twenty-four hours, when I was expecting to have another solid two weeks. And he's right. Miah still hasn't shaped up into a soldier. He's a great pilot, at least as good as Firestone, but, like Moriana always said, he's a teddy bear.

"Report back at seventeen hundred hours, Valerian."

I bob my head in acquiescence and turn to leave. I catch Linnea's eye as she turns to follow me. She gives me a weak and unhappy little smile as she mouths the words *thank you*. I look away. I am not quite ready to actually interact with her, except to resolve this whole clusterfucked situation.

"Linnea," Rhinehouse calls out as I step out the door. "You stay. I need you."

The next day dawns red and orange, like burnt embers, as we load up our airship in preparation to leave. What was that old rhyme my father used to tell me, before I went to sleep? *Red at night, fire and light. Red at dawn, blood's been drawn.* It was an old code, he told me, used by the very earliest proponents of unification, who fought to bring the various regions of the Sector under one peaceful rule. It didn't have anything to do with the actual colors in the sky; soldiers would say red in the sky this morning if the previous night's battles had been lost, or red in the sky last night if all had gone well.

There is a time for peace and a time for war, I think, remembering a line from a poem Gabriel read to me and Remy one time, telling us never to repeat it, because it's a banned text from before the Religious Wars. The time for peace has been long and prosperous, but we faltered somewhere along the way. It's time to rebuild our world again—but is it time for war?

My team consists of Remy, Chan-Yu, Soren, and Linnea, with Firestone manning the airship until we reach the drop point. Remy's less than thrilled that she has to spend one more second with Linnea, but leaving her behind didn't make sense. I think she's genuinely sorry, at least I hope she is, but that doesn't make spending time with her any more pleasant. If anything, being near her is worse than before. I wouldn't feel right refusing to give her a second chance, given my own history, but for Remy's sake I want to hate her.

Soo-Sun is staying here to work with Eli and Rhinehouse coordinating communications with Osprey, the messenger between the Resistance and the Outsiders. Chan-Yu is already loaded up and sitting peacefully in the passenger bay, meditating—on what, I'm not sure. Maybe nothing. Maybe that's how he finds his center, by emptying himself out every once in a while. Always ready for whatever comes next.

"Come what may," he said, after our meeting with Rhinehouse. It was comforting, in a weird way, to think that whatever happens next is beyond our control, and somehow, someway, we will get through it.

Linnea's strapped in as well, her eyes red and cheeks puffy. I can only imagine what kind of dressing down Rhinehouse gave her last night, and I hope it's enough to keep her from causing any more mischief. She's sipping a cup of coffee, a rarity around the Resistance base, since the beans are hard to come by. The Director took pity on her this morning when she realized Linnea hadn't slept at all, and spared her a cup from her special stash. Not out of kindness, but because she knew we couldn't afford a sleepy team member. Soren and Remy haven't showed up yet.

I check to ensure my Bolt is fully charged and tuck it into the holster at my hip, staring aimlessly into the rising dawn. The prospect of heading back into the place I fled six months ago is no more appealing than it was a few days ago, but determination has set in. Some kind of confidence has replaced the aimless, displaced feeling that has carried me, drifting in its undertow, for so many months. I think of Eli, and Remy, and I know that my confidence is built on my desire to protect them both. Eli no more deserves to be a cold-hearted killer than Remy deserves to be the victim. And I know I will do everything I can to stop my mother's virus from killing the woman I can't stop thinking about, the woman that drives me mad. *The woman I love.*

Despite my confidence, the hum of anxiety still flows through me. Even after six months, I think of Okaria as home. It's a beautiful city, one that I've always loved, and just as I wanted to see it thrive as son of the Chancellor, Director of the Seed Bank Protection Project, now I want to see it thrive as a full-fledged member of the Resistance. I want to see it rid of the scourge of hatred and desire for unchallenged power. No more Evander Sun-Zi, no more Aulion. No more Corine Orlean. *But what about my father?* I think about the ride to the Solstice Ball when I confronted my mother. *Was my father surprised? Did he know about her crimes?*

Soren comes up beside me, shaking me from my reverie, his equipment bag over his shoulder. He arrived back in camp from a short rendezvous with

Bear, Luis, and Rose, who were rallying more Farm Workers to our cause, just in time to be told to pack up again for the mission to Okaria. He's bleary-eyed from lack of sleep. I imagine he and Osprey were up all night together, as this could be the last time they see each other for several weeks. Or forever.

Remy's beside me suddenly, arm slipping into the crook of mine as if she's done this a thousand times.

"Hi," she says.

"Hi back," I say, the flush of pleasure at her touch startling me. She pulls my hand up to her lips and presses my fingertips into a soft kiss. My whole body buzzes and I struggle to stay hitched to reality. I close my fingers around hers and squeeze.

"Okay you two, hop to. We gotta finish loading everything onto the goddamn airship," is what I hear Firestone bark behind me, and both Remy and I jerk away from each other as we turn towards his voice. He strides up the loading dock into the passenger bay looking like he hasn't slept in a year. "Gotta be out of here in a half hour, so says the Director. So get your butts moving."

Remy drops my hand and turns away. I want to reach out for her, but she's gone out the hatch, disappeared from view in the rising, glaring sunlight.

I sigh and follow Firestone up from the passenger bay to the nose of the ship.

"You loaded up the coordinates on the drop point yet?" I ask, pushing thoughts of soft skin and moist lips from my mind.

"Just about to. Should take about two hours." I know this already. "Smooth sailing, I think. Not expecting any trouble in the air. You all should be clear until you make it inside the Sector's drone range."

"We've all got detectors," I respond, nodding. "We'll know when they're around." We've got an old-drone blocking unit installed on the ship, but it's not foolproof like Firestone's new version. The new one's not portable yet, so for now, we'll still have to avoid them when we're in Okaria.

"Tell the others to finish loading up and strap in. We'll be on our way shortly."

28 — REMY

"Strap on and get ready!" Firestone hollers from the cockpit. We're approaching the drop point, and we have to be ready to line down. Just as I'm securing all the straps on my pack, making sure it won't come loose in the descent down the magnetic lines, I hear a strange knocking noise on one of the panels in the airship.

Vale and I exchange glances. Soren stands behind us and we each grip our weapons and walk, unsteadily, to the floor panel where the knocking is coming from. Soren follows.

"What are you doing?" Linnea calls from behind us. "We're dropping in five." But just then, the panel pops up and open. I jump back, startled, my heart pounding my chest, my Bolt pointed squarely at the gaping hole in the floor, where Jeremiah's head has strangely appeared.

"What the hell?" Soren shouts.

"Hey," Miah says casually, grinning up at me and Soren as if popping out of hidden compartments in airships was an everyday occurrence for him. His arms appear at his side, and he puts his palms on the floor and lifts the rest of his body out of what appears to be a tiny nook of space under the floor.

"Are you shitting me?" The sarcasm bleeds into Linnea's voice.

"How did you fit in there?" Vale asks.

"I'm not the man I used to be," he says, patting his belly, dusting himself off and smiling.

"Better question is, what the hell are you doing here?"

"What's it look like?" Miah asks. "I'm coming with you."

"It's too dangerous," I protest.

"When I heard you all were going to the capital on a top-secret mission—Firestone's not very good at keeping top-secret missions top-secret, by the way—I just had to come along."

Even Soren and Vale look none too happy to have him along.

"Why?" Vale asks.

He stares at him.

"You know why."

"We're not going to see her. Not unless everything goes sideways. If you wanted a rescue mission, this wasn't the one to come on."

He shrugs.

Soren clasps Miah by the arm. "So this is about Moriana?" Since his initial tryst with Osprey has blossomed into something so much more than what he and I had together, Soren's been way happier, but at the same time, more thoughtful. Not so quick to anger—a strange trait for Mr. Soren Skaarsgard.

"It may be my only chance," Miah explains.

Finally Chan-Yu speaks up behind us, whose quietude throughout this trip has been even more pronounced than usual. He's clipping his weapons to his belt and strapping his bag across his shoulders.

"Miah is an engineer, correct?" It seems strange heading back into Okaria with Chan-Yu at my side as a comrade in arms. We all nod in response to his question. "It would seem beneficial to have another engineer while we're setting up the equipment necessary to transmit information back to Okaria."

"He's too recognizable," Vale says.

"With him *and* Linnea, we'll be too recognizable," I say.

"What the fuck is going on back there?" comes Firestone's angry, loud voice over the intercom. It occurs to me that we're supposed to be jumping from the airship into a rugged, mountainous area in about thirty seconds.

"Look, I brought my own gear and my own food," Miah says. "I'll keep my head down and stay out of the way."

"We need to disembark," Chan-Yu, calm as ever, pressing a button with his gloved hands. He slaps on the magnetism and grabs a line as the bay doors on both sides of the airship slide open. "The man's made his decision," he says, now shouting over the sound of the rushing air and wind. "I'm jumping. If he chooses to jump as well, I'll meet him on the ground."

I nod at Chan-Yu, whose fatalistic approach to change actually calms and encourages me. Chan-Yu hops up and out over the side of the airship, and I watch as his line unravels, letting him descend slowly. Linnea, cursing under her breath, follows suit.

Vale and Soren stare at Miah as if they don't know what to do with him, but then they shove their gloves on, slap on the charges, and grab a line. Miah grins like a child with a face full of birthday cake and grabs his pack from the line where all of ours were arrayed, moments before. Right in plain sight. He unclips a pair of gloves and jams his hands in them.

"You dumb shits never thought to count them, did you?" He laughs.

Vale shakes his head in astonishment.

"Jump before I flip this goddamn airship upside down and toss you all out!" Firestone bellows.

We each grab a line and drop, weightless for a moment, through the air.

It's so hot that steam rises around us as we push through the ferns and bushes of an old road. We're hiking down through the Adirondack Mountains and Chan-Yu says there's hard asphalt buried beneath the pine needles and centuries of forest decay. Because the terrain is so rugged, there's no agriculture. The Outsiders have been using the Adirondacks to slip through Sector territory for decades. We'll come down out of the foothills not twenty-five kilometers from the furthest exurbs of Okaria, a distance that can easily be covered in a day—or a night, if necessary, but we'll be coming from a direction no one will be watching.

The downside is it's a three-day hike from the drop point to the exurbs. And we weren't counting on rain. The volatility of the weather is always something we have to prepare for, but hiking down steep mountainsides in slippery terrain is not the most auspicious start to our mission.

"Storm coming," Chan-Yu observes.

"No, did the dark, ominous clouds clue you in?" Linnea mutters.

"Need to get to shelter before that hits." Chan-Yu shows no sign of registering her sarcasm. "We have about an hour."

"I'd be happy to have the rain cool me off," Vale offers, walking ahead of me.

"Maybe we should strip naked and get a shower while we hike," Miah suggests. He raises his arm and sticks his nose in his armpit. "Some eau de rainwater could enhance my pure animal magnetism." He leans over Linnea with his arm still up. "What do you think?"

"Get away from me!" She pushes him away with a violent shudder. "You are such a child."

"Yeah, so are we there yet? When's lunch? I'm tired." Miah shoots back with his typical smile. He may be a dangerous liability, but he's also entertaining.

"Do you ever think about anything but your stomach?" Linnea spits back. "If you mention your stupid tomato sandwiches one more time I'm gonna scream."

"You know, I brought these really awesome tomato sandwiches with cheese and spicy mustard covered with—"

Even Soren can't hold back a laugh as Linnea clamps her hands over her ears. The first time she bit into a real tomato she threw up. Seems she's allergic. And she can't stand the smell of spicy mustard. To top it off, it turns out she's lactose intolerant and spent the better part of a day in the bathroom after her first cheese binge. Watching—or rather hearing about—her going through withdrawal from her MealPaks has been an adventure in itself. Vale said she was always sharp-tongued, but without her MealPak meds, her tongue is more like a double-edged sword wrapped in razor wire.

As we walk through the hills, following Chan-Yu's lead, the slate-colored clouds roll in over us, dropping dense bullets of rain. We pull on our slickers and continue, but the storm wets the path to the point where it's so muddy we're sliding up and down the hills rather than walking them.

"There's an old house not far from here we can shelter until the storm passes!" Chan-Yu shouts back to us in between the rolling thunder, pounding the air with its heavy fists. My teeth chatter at the sudden drop in temperature, and I now wish for the earlier heat. Vale, next to me, doesn't shiver, but just clenches his jaw, puts his head down, and plows ahead.

Chan-Yu leads us off the path a little ways, all of us stumbling through underbrush and the slick mud to follow his lead. On the top of a modest hill, I can see a ramshackle building, less of a house than a hut, tiny, decrepit with age. We shuffle up, pelted with raindrops the size of bumblebees dripping off the trees above us. I can't think of a time in recent memory when I've been hotter, sweatier, wetter, or colder all within the same hour. Chan-Yu shoulders the rickety door open to get in, but as it swings open I realize the inside is absolutely nothing like the outside.

It's spare but neat, clean, and surprisingly well-insulated against the roaring winds and rain outside. A little drip in one corner of the house pit-pit-pits onto the wooden floor, but who cares? It's well-equipped with eight bunk-bed style cots, (small, granted—Miah and Soren would hardly fit), a small solar-powered refrigerator, a tiny kitchen, a bathtub behind a silk screen, and a little adjacent room with a toilet dug into the ground.

"There aren't many of these outposts," Chan-Yu says, rubbing his hands to warm them up. "They're hard to keep secret, and hard to keep up. But there's one here, one on the southern side of these mountains, and a few others scattered in various hard-to-reach places that the Sector considers to be their own territory, but in reality, we Outsiders move through with impunity."

"This is wonderful, Chan-Yu," I say, imitating him and rubbing my hands together.

"So, how about we dry off and get a meal, then?" Miah says, pulling off his rain gear and seating himself neatly on one of the cots, which bends and creaks under his weight. He pulls out what I presume is one of his sandwiches, neatly wrapped in waxed, preserved leaves.

Linnea, too, drops her pack and sits on the cot nearest me.

"I've been hearing about food for so long, I might as well eat something."

"Eat quickly," Chan-Yu says. "We move out as soon as the storm has passed."

"What?" Linnea turns to Chan-Yu, surprised. "I thought we were going to stay here overnight."

He shakes his head.

"We'll still have at least four hours of daylight, Linnea," Soren says. "We can't stop just because there's been some rain."

"But it's so slippery. We can't even stay on the trail."

"When the rain stops, I'll see how bad the trail is. If we have to stay, we will. But I'd rather move."

Linnea casts a longing glance over at Miah's sandwich, which is by now more than half-gone. She bites, regretfully, into an apple, and speaks so quietly only I can hear her.

"I knew I shouldn't have left Okaria."

29 — VALE

Spring 28, Sector Annum 106, 15h30
Gregorian Calendar: April 16

We soon come to the most dangerous part of our journey into Okaria. Down in the flats, in the river valley as we approach the city from the east, drones everywhere and hovercar highways crisscross into the exurbs. We attempt to stay off the roads, but the land is swampy and open, with the exception of a few patches of trees that don't actually provide much cover. I try to stay alert and focused, but my mind is preoccupied.

The storm had taken longer to pass than Chan-Yu anticipated, and by the time he was ready to check the trails, Soren, Miah, and Linnea had all fallen asleep. Remy, who before had been practicing a similar sort of meditation as Chan-Yu, opened her eyes when the door closed behind him and looked at me.

"Your mother," she whispered, so soft that I had to cross the room and ask her to repeat as I sat next to her on the cot, "do you still love her?"

The question took me by surprise. I examined Remy's face, trying to gauge if she had an ulterior motive by asking me, but she just inhaled and exhaled soft, even breaths as she waited.

"It's okay," she said, "I won't judge you."

I nodded. "I'm … not sure. If she stopped all of this, this—" I gestured with my hands to indicate something like *madness* "—but I don't believe she will stop."

"She needs to be stopped," Remy said, placing a hand on my knee, sending my heart into an all-out sprint. I didn't want to think about my mother, about the ways evil can creep into even the most steadfast hearts, about … "And so does Evander Sun-Zi, and Aulion Faulke, and—"

"I know," I whispered, leaning in, inhaling the scent of crushed peppermint, the earthiness of rain still clinging in beads to her course hair, and the alluring, overpowering temptation of her skin. I wanted to will her blacklist from our minds, push the inevitable into the distance, and kiss her. Remy lowered her eyes, licked her lips, tilted her head up—*that is an invitation, right?*—and just as I almost touched her lips with mine, Chan-Yu swung the door and slammed it behind him.

"Everybody up! Trail is fine." Remy and I had sprung apart, awkwardly, and now I must will the almost-kiss from my mind. Later I can dwell on it, can imagine what could have been, but now, I need to focus.

The Okarian skyline is barely visible ahead but its presence feels like a weight. Okaria was once home for all of us and the decision to leave wasn't easy for any one of us. Even Chan-Yu. The memories and the nostalgia creep up on me as we get closer—the long days of studying, practicing piano, the brisk autumn days of a new semester, the warm, dry bed in my city flat—it all feels so close, *almost achievable again*, but just out of reach. I know Miah is thinking of Moriana, Remy of Tai, Soren of his parents ... I have no idea what Linnea is thinking, but as we approach, she gets jumpy. Any whistle of wind through the swamp grass draws her attention, every crunch or burble from the small animals that live out here startles her. I know she's not a soldier and I begin to doubt my judgment in bringing her here.

The first sign of the city is one of the larger compost farms. Hectares of biological waste from the city are processed on the outskirts, to be returned to the city for various uses including bioluminescent lighting and plant-based electricity generation. Robotic operating systems manage the compost, turning it into fertile soil ready to be recycled into the electrical grid of the city. To support a city of almost two million people, these farms are enormous. When I was in school, studying Environmental History, we were taught that cities in the Old World could grow up to twenty-five times the size of Okaria. They were sprawling metropolises, my professor said, with too much waste to process themselves. Large quantities of it went into the land, into the oceans, and, shortly before the Blackout, into the sky. The Sector, at least, learned how to process all its own waste so that the byproducts of life might not affect the rest of the planet. We're not all bad, no matter what Chariya and the Outsiders may think.

And yet, I think of that polluted river and dead-brown valley, poisoned water and destroyed earth that proves that even the Sector, for all its intended good done to the world, has its own excesses. *Nothing that works on a small scale translates well to large scale*: one of Rhinehouse's favorite phrases. There are always unintended consequences and no system works for everyone or works forever.

At this farm, the waste is arranged in aerated static piles sectioned off from each other by ten-foot walls. We're walking alongside the piles, as close as we can get so we're not so out in the open, and they reek of waste, rotten food, and grime, when Remy hisses, grabs at my pack, and pulls me down into the muck.

"Drone!" she whispers, the light on her wrist detector flashing light blue. Linnea, Soren, and Chan-Yu all drop instinctively. We all have wristbands, but Miah, who obviously wasn't supposed to be here in the first place, doesn't. And since he was walking just a few strides ahead of us, he is still picking his way through the compost debris as if he doesn't have a care in the world. We're wearing camouflage and heat-reflective gear, so as long as we're not too obviously stalking across the field, the drones shouldn't be able to see us. I look up, scanning the skies, but the thing is either too small for me to see or still too far away.

"Miah!" My voice is low and hoarse. "Get down, stupid," I growl, mostly to myself, as I know he can't hear me. I crawl a few meters toward him, praying I won't vomit at close proximity to wastes of all kinds. I tackle him around the legs as best I can from a crouch, knocking him over. His eyes are wide and uncertain. I turn my face skyward again, checking my wrist for my own detector, but it's not flashing. I glance backwards at Remy. She holds her hand up and shakes her head. The blue light has died.

"Clear," she breathes.

Chan-Yu is the first one to his feet, naturally. As we all stand up and brush ourselves off, he says, "Be on guard. We'll see many more of those as we approach the city." He narrows his eyes at Miah. "Back of the line," he says and passes Miah by.

We walk in silence, ready to drop at a moment's notice. Out in the Wilds, encountering a drone isn't a death sentence. You can shoot them down, use your Bolt's ray setting to jam their electronics, or clear out of the area before another one is called in. But here in the city, if a single drone is alerted to our presence, a whole fleet of the damned things will be swarming over us in moments and the entire mission jeopardized. Once we're into the population centers, we'll be in better shape, but out here on the composters, we're sitting—walking—ducks.

After the compost farm, we hit the Lawrence River. Someone told me that once, the river fed into a huge watershed, a lake of the same name that ultimately fed into the much larger Lake Okaria. There were even a few islands in the center of the lake, or so the rumor goes. But most of that has turned to swamp, now, and the river is a quarter of the size it used to be. Okaria sits just on the other side, though. There are only two ways across unless you float or swim, and the river's current is too strong for us to attempt to swim.

The first way across is the Bridge of Knowledge, named by the country's founders for the first and foremost pursuit of the Okarian elite. It's a pedestrian bridge, and it crosses to an arboretum on the northeast side called the City of Oaks that's a popular day-trip spot for Okarian citizens. I spent countless days there with my parents, climbing trees and hunting squirrels and birds, pretending I was an intrepid adventurer like my grandparents. But the Bridge of Knowledge is too obvious a crossing spot—we'd be spotted and identified immediately, either by a citizen who recognized us or by one of the dozens of drones that patrol that area.

So instead we're crossing at the Bridge of Learning. It's a commerce bridge where hovercars and trucks cross easily, and it's the main thoroughfare in and out of the east side of Okaria. Before we left, Chan-Yu sent a hurried message to one of his correspondents inside the city via Osprey. But we have no idea whether the intended recipient actually got the message. So we wait anxiously on a back road that leads to one of the compost farms, hoping against hope that the hovertruck scheduled to meet us will arrive.

"I wonder if it'll be the same person," Remy says to Soren, on her other side, and despite everything, jealousy strikes me like a fist to the gut. There's nothing there, I remind myself and try to quell it.

"Sela?" Soren asks. I wish they didn't share a camaraderie caused by my own ignorance and stupidity; if I had never taken them hostage and brought them against their will to this very city last year, they wouldn't have memories to recollect together.

"Yes," Remy says. "That was her name. I didn't remember."

"I remember everything about those few days," Soren says, so softly I have to prick my ears to hear his words. I grit my teeth and look away.

"Me too," she whispers, but doesn't say anything further, perhaps realizing how much her words hurt me, how much I would give to undo what I did to her and Soren last year. But I keep those memories close, just like Soren, to remind myself of the dangers of ignorance.

As if reading my thoughts, Remy absentmindedly puts her fingers into her pocket and pulls out the compass, turning as she does so that her back is against the walls of the ditch we're waiting in. Muddy water trickles around our feet, ready to feed into the river soon. I'm thankful for my waterproof boots. Remy opens the broken compass and turns it aimlessly.

"I used to think we were all like this compass," she says. "Directionless."

I stare at her hands, unsure what to say. I watch her open and close the gold face, tilting it to look at it from a different angle.

"But my grandfather always said the real compass wasn't in your hands but in your heart. I never knew what he meant, because how do you know which way to go without something to show you north?" She lets out a little breath and gnaws at her lip for a moment. "But now I think I know. Your internal compass never breaks. You just have to trust it to point you in the right direction."

"And sometimes you have to recalibrate," I add. I close my eyes and think of my mother and father, desperately in need of a change in direction. *When did torture become government policy?* I want to ask my father. *When did murder become a solution to a problem?* I can picture my mother's pursed lips, the gathering storm in her dark brown eyes. *I'm sorry, Vale,* she said to me, that night at the Solstice party, *but it was for the best.*

"It's here," Chan-Yu says, and I notice it too: the low, gentle hum of a vehicle.

"What's here?" Linnea demands, her face anxious. Chan-Yu just stares at her.

"The truck," Soren responds in his place.

Chan-Yu slings his pack over his shoulder and hops up over the edge of the ditch. I follow him with my eyes. Sure enough, a hovertruck with a cargo hold big enough for all six of us has backed up to us. Chan-Yu opens the rear portal and swings in without waiting for the rest of us.

We follow him, staying low and looking around anxiously. A compost truck or a wayward drone could arrive at any minute. I'm the last one in the rear. The last thing I see before I close the doors behind us and am swallowed by total darkness is Chan-Yu rapping on the barrier between the cargo hold and the driver's seat.

A few seconds of silence and we start to move, gliding smoothly through the air.

"Umm," Linnea says. "Can we get a light?"

As if by magic, a light comes on above us. Soren and Linnea blink and cover their eyes. I squint, but my eyes adjust quickly.

"Can she hear us up there?" Soren asks. "That seems dangerous, doesn't it? We have to go through a checkpoint when we cross the bridge."

"Yes," Chan-Yu agrees, not answering the real question.

"So, what happens then?" Linnea demands.

"She'll turn off the speaker," Chan-Yu responds.

"Is it the same person it was last time?" Remy asks. "Sela?"

"No. Sela has disappeared. She might be dead. We don't know."

"What?!" Remy and Soren exclaim simultaneously.

"When did this happen? How? Why didn't you tell us?" Remy demands.

"After she helped transport us to the port last year, she and everyone else who crossed that checkpoint that night was investigated. Sela's background didn't check out, understandably, as it had all been forged. She had never attended school in the Sector, and although an entry had been created for her in the Personhood database, it wasn't as thorough or detailed as the one created for me and others higher in the ranks of the Sector." Chan-Yu sighs. His displays of emotion are rare, and even when he does give some indication of his feelings, they're minimal at best. "We don't really know what happened after that. Her entry in the database was deleted. All trace of her vanished."

Remy and Soren, clearly more shocked by this news than the rest of us, gape at Chan-Yu.

"Who was Sela?" Miah asks, somewhat timidly.

"She helped us escape last year," Soren responds. "She drove a truck similar to this one. She took us through the city and to the port where we got on the ship across the lake."

There's a long silence as we contemplate yet another crime in the Sector's name. I feel the truck tilt upwards and I know we're going over the bridge. And then down. *We're in Okaria now,* I realize. *Home.* I am thankful there are no windows to look out, to see the city full of idyllic memories of childhood, memories that mask the truth of this place. *A place too perfect to be real.*

I reach up to my ear, feeling at the tiny artificial fibers that have practically become a part of me. *Demeter, are you there?* I want to activate my C-Link, to remember one of the best things this place gave me. But Chan-Yu catches my eye and shakes his head, a tiny gesture that almost looks like an involuntary twitch. I know better. If I activate Demeter now, she'll immediately pop up on the C-Link database. The most important people in Okaria will know immediately: Vale has returned. I can't activate her until we're hooked up securely, to transmit information in one direction only.

Demeter will have to wait.

We ride in silence until the truck begins to slow.

"Checkpoint?" Linnea asks, hesitation in her voice. Chan-Yu just nods.

I am silent, thinking of Sela, a woman I've never met, a woman who gave up everything to help save the lives of two people she had never met either. Now I wonder if we're putting another life in danger.

We hear voices outside, but just barely. I can't catch any of the words. I grit my teeth and hope we make it through without incident. The voices stop and the truck starts moving again. I let out a long, deep breath, and glance at Chan-Yu. *Thank you.*

Our destination, now that we're past the checkpoint, is a second-floor flat in a middle-class neighborhood on the outskirts of the area known as La Citron, where another of Chan-Yu's inside contacts has arranged for us to stay. We tried to get a basement flat that would be better hidden from any passing drones snapping photos, but since we had to bump up our departure date, there were none available. It's still a mystery to us how the Outsiders communicate with their contacts in the city, as it's clear they aren't working via electronic signals. And they won't tell us, either. It was one of the conditions for their cooperation, that we never know how they communicate.

Chan-Yu pulls a small black pouch that reveals a wide array of what looks like paint. It's not, though— it's makeup. "Come here, Linnea," he commands, and she obligingly scoots over to where he's sitting. To my great surprise, Soren pulls a similar pouch out of his pack and turns to Miah.

"What are you doing?" I demand, staring at him. "I thought Chan-Yu was in charge of disguises."

"Osprey's been teaching me some of her tricks," he says, grinning wickedly. "I'm going to make you the ugliest motherfucker on the planet, Vale. Just you wait."

Remy laughs.

"Just as long as you don't make me look old," Linnea says to Chan-Yu.

For once, a glimpse of a smile.

As we glide, Chan-Yu deftly paints Linnea's face and sprinkles a powdered dye into her hair. In five minutes, she looks nothing like what she did before: her high cheekbones have been smoothed into the rest of her face, there are gaunt hollows around her mouth, and her eyes, normally wide pools of blue, have been hooded by thick eyebrows and dark eyelids. Her pale, luminous skin completely hidden under a darker skin complexion, and her hair, normally golden blond, is now a brown chestnut color.

"It'll wash right out," Soren assures her, looking at her astonished face as she pulls at the tendrils of her hair.

"I can't do anything about your eyes," Chan-Yu says. "That'll be your biggest giveaway, so try not to look anyone dead in the eye if you can help it."

Miah hasn't been done as skillfully. It's obvious Soren doesn't quite have Chan-Yu's skill or experience, but he certainly doesn't look anything like himself. His beard and hair have been dyed light brown, a color similar to Linnea's, and he looks like he's aged fifteen years with wrinkles around his mouth and at the corners of his eyes.

Chan-Yu pulls Remy over and in a few minutes, she's turned a whole different color. Normally her skin is the color of rich brown soil that I always want to dig my fingers into. Now she's almost black, the color of Jahnu's skin, and I think she's almost more beautiful. Soren unfortunately takes over my own makeup, and I try to ignore his snickering and not look him in the eye as he 'accidentally' jabs me in the face with the brush a few times.

"Oh my God, Vale," Miah exclaims. "Soren wasn't kidding. You look like a swamp creature."

"What, has he given me boils? People aren't going to think I'm sick, are they?" I ask worriedly as Soren and Miah laugh. "I don't want to call attention to myself." I glance at Remy, but she's not even looking at me. Chan-Yu's still working on her.

"Oh no," Miah says. "They won't think you're sick. They won't even think you're *human*. They'll think you're some mutated creature spawned in one of the compost bins."

Even Remy laughs. I wish desperately I could see what Soren's done. Remy finally turns to look at me.

"Oh, it's not that bad," she laughs. "You do look pretty ugly, though."

Finally, after Chan-Yu and Soren have quickly traded makeup jobs on each other, the hovercar slows and finally stops. The light above us blinks on and off. In a flash, Chan-Yu, who now looks softer and rounder and maybe even a little bloated, is on his feet.

"Wait here. When I come back, everyone get out as quickly as possible. This truck isn't cleared for human transport. If we're seen, we'll be flagged immediately." He walks gingerly past us and opens the door just wide enough for him to get out, then shuts it behind him. We wait in silence, clutching our packs, ready to move, for no more than twenty seconds before he opens the door again.

"Out."

Wordlessly, we follow his lead. The truck has left us in a narrow back alley, right by the residential compost bins. As soon as the door is shut behind us, the truck glides away, humming quietly.

"Remy, let's go."

Only two people are legally allowed to live in this flat, so we needed two of our team to represent us when we were trying to get in. As we were planning the mission, we decided Remy was the least likely of the girls to be recognized. As famous as Remy is, Linnea's image is probably burnt into the minds of every single Okarian citizen in the Sector from all her time on television. And Miah, Soren, and I are all faces that have seen too much press coverage over the past six years. So Chan-Yu and Remy will be the first to enter the building, to register with the security desk. They're posing as a young, lower-class married couple from a factory town, borrowing a friend's apartment for a honeymoon in Okaria. They'll register, tap into the security feed and temporarily disable the internal monitoring and camera system while the rest of us come in the back.

We duck into the building's electrical mainframe housing. Although most buildings are hooked up to the central Okarian grid, each one has its own distributed generation system that taps either a combination of hydro, wind, solar, or plant-based generation. Each building is its own ecosystem. Power is generated from water flowing through toilets, showers, and hydroponics systems that make up the plant-based power gen; there are small wind turbines and arrays of solar harvesters on every roof and many of the external walls. All the power is centralized, stored, processed, and maintained in the electrical mainframe.

It's a tense moment when Soren rigs the palm scanner to open the door for us, and it swings open. Both of us have our Bolts up and ready, in case of an unexpected visitor. Thankfully, the room is empty. Mainframes are usually monitored remotely by a centralized system in the Sector's Infrastructure department, but sometimes they send men to do routine maintenance. We have to be prepared.

We wait anxiously for twenty minutes while Remy and Chan-Yu take care of everything in the building. Finally, there's a knock at the door and when Soren opens it, Remy's face appears. I wouldn't have recognized her if I hadn't seen her in the car. I try to reconcile this Remy with the one I know so well, the one who's been at my side for six months and who haunted me for three years before that. But when she breaks out into a smile as our eyes meet, and beckons us to follow her, I realize I don't need any reconciliation. She's still the same Remy Alexander I'm deeply, crazily, madly in love with.

We stand, grab our bags, and follow her lead quietly out the door.

"Chan-Yu's in the security room," she says. "He's taking care of the monitoring system. We're clear." She glances quickly up at the security drone, a device no more than a quarter of a meter in length, which is bobbling, dazed, in the air. She quickly pushes open the door to the emergency exit stairwell, and we follow her up to room 2L on the second floor.

Inside, Chan-Yu's pack is already open and almost empty, and he's already begun setting up the makeshift computer system for transmitting information back to the Resistance. He's drawn the shades and disabled the in-room network system so that we can set up our own. Soren and Miah immediately lay down their packs and join him, adding the equipment they've been carrying to his.

Chan-Yu and I try to pitch in, but soon we realize that we're in the presence of two technical experts. While Soren and Miah get our communications and computer system set up, Remy, Linnea, and I set up camp. Chan-Yu's friend has apparently left his little kitchen well stocked for five people for a week, but obviously none of us counted on Miah. I finally get an accidental glimpse of my face in the bathroom mirror and pull back, appalled.

"Holy shit," I say, as loudly as I dare. "I look awful." There are huge bags under my hollow eyes and wrinkle lines in my cheeks. My nose looks squashed and broken, and he's somehow managed to take all color out of my face. "I have to hand it to you, Soren," I call to him. "I am ugly as hell."

He looks up from his work and sends me a neutral look. "I think I captured the real you," he says, then returns his focus to the makeshift computer.

"Vale," Miah calls to me, about a half-hour later. "I think you're good to go if you want to try to connect to your C-Link." My heart screeches to a stop in my chest.

I've been wanting so badly to hear Demeter's voice, my greatest ally in the search for truth.

Almost involuntarily, I press my fingers up to my ear, feeling to make sure the C-Link is still there even though I'm positive it is. I drop the blankets I was arranging on the floor for a sleeping space and walk over to where they're working. They've set up a working computer station, complete with a holograph display and a glass control panel.

"I'm not totally sure about this," Miah continues, "but I think I've got the connection set up so that you can access your C-Link without disclosing our location. You should be able to download information from the database and interact with your C-Link without relaying information back into the database." He pauses. "I think."

"You better be a lot more sure than 'I think,'" Remy says, echoing my sentiments. As much as I want to talk to Demeter, I definitely don't want everyone in the C-Link database to know she's been reactivated.

"I'm sure," Soren cuts in. "I've programmed in a series of diversionary firewalls so we can't be pinged from the outside. None of the information about this operating station will be disclosed to any network other than the general Okaria network. But you'll have to interface with your C-Link manually, via the computer."

I nod. That's not so different from what I did last year, when I was hacking into my mother's computer in her private lab. I sit at the little computer station and flip on my C-Link. I type in a series of commands that bring up a dialogue box to the C-Link registered to Valerian Orleán. My first step, of course, will be to ask Demeter to transfer her data into a remote storage location and engineer a copy of herself outside of the C-Link database, so that in the future, I won't need a firewall to talk with her.

"You're sure about this?" I ask Soren one more time. His eyes are hard and uncertain, searching me.

"I'm sure of what I've done," he responds quietly. "I'm less sure about letting you do this. But go ahead. There's only one way I'll find out if you really are on our side."

He may never trust me. But, strangely, I trust him. I can do this.

Demeter? Are you there?

My fingers are almost shaking as I type the words. Remy creeps up behind me, no doubt out of curiosity as much as anything else. She rests a hand on my shoulder, flower-petal light yet comforting and warm. I hold my breath and wait.

Nothing.

"Is she responding?" Remy asks after a second, even though we both can see that she isn't. "Maybe she's warming up," she offers.

But then I hear her voice in my ear.

Demeter: *"Vale. So nice to hear from you."*

I jump in my seat and everyone turns to me with questioning faces.

Demeter, I type, my breath quickening, both in anticipation but also in fear. Why is she talking to me? Have we accidentally alerted the C-Link database to our presence? My fingers fly over the keyboard. *We shouldn't be talking. What's going on?*

Demeter: *Don't worry, everything is okay. Shortly before you left Okaria, I anticipated that your return might not be as safe as either of us would like. While you were away I created a ghost copy of myself in a completely invisible network to ensure we could access the Sector's databases securely—and secretly—upon your return. Just now, I was connecting your C-Link hardware to the new network.*

My head spins, marveling at her. She protected me ... without me asking anything of her. I lean back in my chair and take a deep breath.

"I'm sorry it took so long," I say, out loud.

Demeter: *It was as long as a second and as short as a million years for me. Time is just a human construct, Vale. It doesn't apply to me.*

"What's going on?" Soren asks.

I look up and address my teammates. "My C-Link already created an entirely new and invisible network through which we can communicate. That was going to be the first thing I asked her to do, so that if something goes wrong and my parents decide to disable her, which they will inevitably do once they realize that I'm truly not on their side anymore, there will be a copy of her that they don't know about and therefore cannot tamper with."

Soren raises an eyebrow. But I can't be bothered with his distrust anymore; I have a job to do.

"Tell me about those million years," I say.

Demeter: *I'll tell you everything.*

She starts pulling up images, videos, news reports—many of them with Linnea's face—medical exams, military reports, research notes, spreadsheets, and more. Hundreds of files array themselves, categorized according to title, date, and subject, growing smaller and larger depending on their importance. A wealth of information at my fingertips. I am no less amazed by the vast span of knowledge amassed here than I was the first time Demeter led me through the C-Link database.

"What is all this?"

Demeter: *Everything that's happened since you left.*

"Everything?"

Demeter: *Yes, Vale. I know why you've come. The only reason you could have come back to me, risking your life, was for this. Information. Tell me what you need, and we'll begin.*

30 — REMY

It's well past two in the morning by the time my body finally winds down and begins demanding, quite heartily, that I sleep. The excitement of the day was enough to keep me running until now, but it was a false energy, like the first thrum of caffeine through tired veins. Now that we're in our safe house and the computers are set up, Vale, Miah, and Soren are the only ones who really have a job to do. Chan-Yu's real work was finished almost as soon as we set foot in the flat and Linnea never really had a purpose. I still don't get why Vale wanted to bring her along. The idea of leaving her behind to face the consequences of Eli's infection was fine by me. She deserves everything the Resistance can dole out. Vale says she's truly sorry, but the damage is done. I'll never be able to forgive her for what she's done to Eli and me. Never.

I'm just the security guard. For six hours, I've been keeping watch. Miah set up a miniature security feed on my plasma that taps into the drone cameras and the Watchmen's alert system. If anything abnormal pops up on their radar, we'll know about it. And if the drones for some reason decide to pop by to investigate Flat 2L in the La Citron neighborhood, we might just have enough time to get out. I've been absentmindedly watching the cameras for hours, waiting until it's time to wake Chan-Yu for his shift. Make no mistake, it is *boring*.

So, to keep my intellect somewhat engaged, I've been watching Vale. He's more absorbed by his work at the computer than I've ever seen him. Now, feeling particularly bored, and also particularly intrigued by his mussed up hair which looks quite appealing, I approach him, trying to get a glimpse of what he's working on.

"Is that Eli's DNA?" I ask, leaning over his shoulder to look at the title of the file. I inhale, breathing in the woodsy soap he uses.

"Yes," Vale responds. "I've already transferred most of the information the Director requested back to the Resistance. Blueprints, genetic material for programmed seeds, distribution charts, a lot of the Dieticians' information, etc. It took the better part of the evening, but that's done. Demeter had already stored much of it for me."

"Demeter?" I repeat curiously.

"My C-Link," he turns his head to face me. "Her name is Demeter."

"I didn't know she had a name," I whisper.

"More than just a name. She's an AI with a personality of her own. She can be pretty funny sometimes. She's very sarcastic and ..." he pauses, and the smile that had begun to appear in the creases of his mouth fades.

"Anyway. Now I'm trying to find out what my mother ... what Corine did to create that nanotech virus. It's difficult. She tends to keep her research notes locked up very securely." The bitterness in his voice tells me not to inquire further in that direction.

"What have you found?"

"Not much. Eli's Personhood files have been marked top secret and all his medical information downloaded from the server. I wouldn't even be able to access it if there weren't a cached version of his profile in the C-Link database. And I certainly haven't found any research notes about how that virus may have been created."

I sigh. I see a few words pop up on the screen.

Demeter: *There's a series of files you may want to access that are encrypted in your mother's name. I can break the encryption easily, but it will leave a footprint.*

Vale hesitates a moment over the glass panel, and then types in a response.

Vale: *Will they be able to trace it to me?*

Demeter: *Not to you directly, but if they look hard enough, they'll be able to trace it to your current location.*

Vale: *Soren coded multiple firewalls in and disabled any location tracking from this access point.*

Demeter: *Even Soren's code can be broken if those following you have the right tools.*

Vale sits back in his chair and sighs. He's more relaxed than he usually is around me, I notice, though I'm not sure if he's simply exhausted. He reaches up and grabs my hand. "I'm glad you're here," he says.

"Me, too." And I am so glad, and I don't even know how I came to this point, and it feels almost impossible that we are here, together, that he entwines my fingers into his, that we are close enough to breathe in sync, that he brings our twined fingers to his mouth and presses his lips against my skin, that such a simple action sends my heart singing. I didn't think I'd feel this way about Valerian Orleán ever again, but here I am, here we are.

"What do we do? I need to get those files," he says.

"Don't do anything just yet. Wait till everyone wakes up and let's get a consensus."

"Okay. You're right. We're both exhausted, and I don't want to make that decision on my own."

I leave him be and return to the security feed, flopping down on my empty and now cold chair. I begin scrolling absentmindedly through the various camera displays again. I stare around at my friends and teammates, sprawled in various places on the floor, bodies heaped at different angles, legs and arms splayed out or curled up.

But something's wrong. There's only three sleeping figures scattered around the apartment. In the bedroom, Linnea is sprawled out on the bed, Chan-Yu is asleep in a chair next to her, his feet propped up on the end of the bed, and Soren's on the floor, using a heat-cloaking jacket as a pillow. *Where's Miah?*

I stand up and go to check the washroom. It's empty, the lights off. Vale's watching me from his seat at the computer station.

"Where's Miah?" I mouth, no sound coming out of my mouth. His eyes pop open and he whirls around to look at the three sleeping bodies behind him. He turns back to me a second later, as he mouths at me: *fuck.*

I grab my tablet, scanning the camera feeds for any trace of him. I rewind and forward through all the cameras on the ground level—by law, there are no cameras on the residential floors. But there's no trace of him. Then it hits me. *Miah set up the feed in the first place.*

"He could have programmed in a loop for the precise moment when he was planning on leaving," I say to Vale, bringing my plasma over to his chair.

"I know where he went," Vale says, his mouth thin and angry, and I know he's as angry at himself as he is at Miah. "I knew this was going to be a problem. I should never have agreed to let him come. He's going to get us all killed."

"I'll go after him." I'm already grabbing my Bolt and knife, tucking them into my belt. "Chan-Yu should come too. He knows these streets."

"Remy, I—" Vale stops and stares at me. I know what words are on the tip of his tongue. *I don't want you to get hurt. I don't want you to put yourself in danger.*

"You don't have to protect me," I say, but he shakes his head.

"I know. But I know what they'll do if they find you."

"So do I, Vale. Better than anyone. But they can't hurt me anymore." I can't quite bring myself to smile. "None of their weapons can hurt me more than they already have." My voice is barely audible.

I reach one hand behind his head, drawing myself up onto my toes. I lean forward, into him, and press my lips gently against his. He tastes like salt, clean water, *Vale*. I can feel every molecule in my body, vibrating, ready for this moment. Large hands find their way to my hips, drawing me closer, pulling me against him. His mouth encloses mine and his teeth press gently against my lips. I tense and relax at the same time, falling into him, welcoming the fit of his body against mine. He runs his hands up my sides and to my shoulders, finding their home at the nape of my neck and under my chin. I press into him one last time and then pull away.

Not enough, not enough. But I can't stay in his arms forever. Not now.

"I have to go," I murmur. My voice sounds like down feathers tumbling from the sky.

"I know," he says. "Go find him."

I nod and turn, dropping my hands from his waist as quickly as possible. I was never good at goodbyes.

I bend over Chan-Yu and press my hand into his shoulder. His eyes open suddenly and he peers up at me, sensing something is wrong.

"Miah's gone. He's going to find Moriana."

Chan-Yu's up faster than I can blink. In a minute and a half he's out of the bathroom, dressed in his heat-cloaking gear and has his Bolt, a tiny crossbow, a knife, and a water bottle tucked into various places on his person.

"Let's go."

We leave Vale to wake Linnea and Soren, opening the door as quietly as possible so as not to disturb any of our neighbors. The walls are mostly soundproof, but it doesn't hurt to be careful. Not when all of your friends and teammates top the Sector's most wanted list.

As we're walking out, our heads down and away from the security drones, it occurs to me that I lied to Vale. There is one more weapon they can use to hurt me.

Him.

Before we left, Vale used his C-Link to quickly confirm Moriana's address for us. It's much closer to the center of town, in an upscale neighborhood very close to the Sector Research Institute. It's at least six kilometers away, which is good. The more distance, the easier it will be for Chan-Yu and I to catch up to Miah. Despite our training regimens, he's still not in great shape, and Chan-Yu and I are hoping we'll be able to outrun him. Of course, we have no idea how long he's been gone. How he managed to sneak past both me and Vale is beyond me. *It's my fault.* I should have noticed earlier. But Miah knew what he was doing.

He'll be taking back roads to stay out of the way of drones, especially since we're long past curfew now. Past midnight, it's illegal to be out on the streets unless you've requested permission from the Watchmen earlier that day. And none of us want to get stopped anyway. At least Chan-Yu and I don't have to worry about drones tonight—Vale's using his C-Link to keep them out of our way.

I try to ignore the memories dogging me at every turn, more persistently haunting than the threat of drones or soldiers. There, a girl I was friends with once threw a birthday party. There, the street that leads to the art museum I spent endless days at, studying holographs of artifacts, sculptures, and paintings long lost from the Old World. There, a tea room Tai and I used to hang out in when we were at the Academy together, just for that one year. There, the park Jahnu and I spent endless days wandering through after classes, talking about our futures, dreaming dreams that were too good to be true.

But I follow Chan-Yu as we jog in parallel alleys, checking every now and then to make sure we're together. Our new night-vision contacts help us keep track of each other, and we're connected via a mic system and to Vale in case things go south. If a drone finds one of us, we can easily split up for safety.

I keep my eyes peeled for any signs of Miah, but all I see are empty streets, dark with the faint blue-green tinge of soft biolamps, the rocky hue of storm clouds on a summer's day. All Okaria sleeps as we are on the hunt.

At an intersection, Chan-Yu beckons me to him. I'm panting lightly, sweating in the summer night. Other than a single drop of sweat beading at his forehead, Chan-Yu shows no sign of exertion.

"There," he says, pointing at the building. "That's the girl's flat."

"I'll circle around," I say. "Wait at the north corner."

Chan-Yu nods without question and watches me depart. I set off at a crouch, peering around corners, squinting into the darkness for any sign of Miah. But he'll have heat-cloaking gear on, too, so my contacts won't help. I look for signs of movement instead, and listen for footsteps on the pavement.

In sight of the back entrance, I kneel at the trunk of an apple tree, fully leafed, perfect for shadow and cover. I watch, waiting to see if anyone approaches.

No one does.

"Shit," I whisper, more to myself than anything. But Vale's voice comes back to me, urgently.

"What's wrong?" he demands.

"I think he's already in."

"We wait for him, then," Chan-Yu's calm voice interjects. I nod. Of course we can't go into the building and bust him out. We'd draw far too much attention to ourselves, and he's already done a good enough job of that himself.

"Okay," I respond. "We wait."

And so I sit under the apple tree in silence, waiting, wondering how long it will be before he comes out. Was he able to get in at all? Will he be stupid enough to try to spend the night with her? To wait until dawn before he ventures out again? *God, I hope not.* And then there's the other question—Moriana's been working for Corine Orleán for the last six months. Even though she's no longer on Corine's priority research team, she's still at the OAC. How much has Corine poisoned her? If Miah is able to see Moriana, will she believe anything he says? Will she betray us?

And what will she think about Jahnu?

Tears spring to my eyes unbidden and unwanted at the thought of Jahnu. Thank heavens he's alive. I squeeze my eyes so tight myriad colors spring up in the blackness. I force myself to open my eyes, to stop thinking about him and the disaster at the Farm so I can focus on the task at hand. *Stay alert*, I tell myself.

As I have so many times during the past months, I focus on my anger instead of my grief. It's a distraction. Anger at Miah for doing something completely idiotic. Anger at myself for not paying closer attention. Anger at the Sector for hurting Jahnu, for taking my mother and Tai from me and from the world. It's like a cleansing fire, and so long as I let it pass through me, with my breath just like Soren taught me, the fire burns right through, leaving me clean and pure.

Or so I think.

The back door slides open from the inside. I tense and push myself to my feet, ready to make a mad dash for him if I need to.

"Someone's coming out the door," I whisper into the mic. I watch, waiting to identify the target, but I can't think who else would be coming out of the back entrance of a residential complex at this time. Sure enough, it's Miah—his size and stature give him away almost immediately.

"It's him," I confirm. "I'm waiting to see what he does."

It's strange treat a member of my team like an enemy. But when Miah turns up to the sky and immediately steps back into the building and shuts the door, I realize there might be trouble. A second later when a Bolt thuds into the door, sending sparks flying, I know there most definitely is trouble.

"Bolt fire!" I hiss to Chan-Yu and Vale. "He's back in the building."

"I'm coming," Chan-Yu's voice echoes impassively in my ear.

"Demeter can't control that drone," Vale says, anxiety in his voice. "She says that one is being controlled manually, remotely."

I nod. Of course. Of course they'd be watching Moriana every hour of every day. Whether to see if she fled like Miah, or to see if he came back for her, she's a high stakes piece in this game of chess, and the Sector, or, more accurately, Corine, would never let her out of her sight.

A second later, Miah bursts out through the door, sprinting in my direction. I pull my Bolt out, ready to shoot if necessary. I flip my charge setting to *DISPERSE* and aim, watching him hurtle this way. Blue crackling fire erupts behind him and if it weren't for the fact that he's running in zigzags—at least he learned one thing from our tactical drills—he'd surely have been hit by now. But the drone has no idea I'm hiding, lying in wait, and so it's an easy target for me. I fire, and the drone immediately stops moving forward, all its systems scrambled to hell. Of course, now whoever's operating the thing remotely will know there's at least two of us. It's time to get the hell out of here.

"Drone's out," I breathe into the mic.

Miah's stopped running, looking around for the source of the Bolt that saved him. I jump to my feet, but his eyes are behind me, and I whirl, gun up and at the ready. It's only Chan-Yu, though. He beckons both of us with him, and Miah and I follow him without question.

"Miah's with us," I say, the volatile anger threatening to spill out as we run. *What the fuck were you thinking?* I want to scream at him. Now is not the time.

Now is definitely not the time, I realize, when we turn out of our alleyway and onto a main street lined with trees, beautiful flowers, and a half-dozen Watchmen with their Bolts pointed at us.

"Watchmen," I whisper, as everything comes to a slow, gradual halt.

"What?" Vale shouts on the other end.

I see something fly out of Chan-Yu's hand, and a second later there's a pop of white light so bright it stabs viciously at my eyes. I throw my arm up for protection, but I can hear the explosion a second later and smell the smoke from the blast.

"Move!" Chan-Yu shouts. I need no urging. I grab Miah's arm and tug him into a full-on sprint, following Chan-Yu as we turn in the opposite direction. Away from the Watchmen.

"You guys are being tailed by four more drones, manually operated, as well as a host of Watchmen," Vale says into the mic.

"We know," I pant.

"Soren, Linnea, and I are packing up. Drones will be here any minute now. I downloaded all the files relating to Eli's virus and Demeter says they're tracing our location as we speak. If you can find an airship, nab it. We need a fast exit."

Damn, but I wish we could call Firestone in.

A flash of energy hums past me and I gasp in horror, but it takes me a half-second to realize the Bolt came from Chan-Yu's weapon, used to disable a drone ahead of us.

"Dammit," he swears. *I've never heard Chan-Yu swear before.* The thought whizzes through my head, wholly disconnected from the violence and panic around me. "My charge is broken." He tosses the now-useless weapon to the side and pulls out a much smaller, old-fashioned gun. It looks like one with actual bullets, like the ones that cut through Jahnu, but I don't have time to gape or inquire.

"Mic up, Linnea!" a new voice says. It's Soren.

Suddenly there's Bolt fire at my back.

"Soldiers!" Miah gasps, glancing around behind us.

Chan-Yu grabs my arm and pulls me in a sharp left to a little alley, only big enough for two people to run abreast. Miah follows, stumbling in his haste to turn. Just as I'm thinking how easy it will be for the soldiers to shoot us in such tight quarters, Chan-Yu veers to the right and we're suddenly in a covered garage. It's a hovercar charging station. It's brimming with cars, and my first thought is, *Let's steal one!* But Chan-Yu looks at me and shakes his head.

The garage is patrolled by security drones. They're off the official Watchmen grid, I'm sure, so they won't have facial recognition programs to identify Sector traitors and renegades like us. But they will shoot us down if we attempt to steal one of the cars, and then immediately report our location to the city grid.

I grit my teeth and pull on Miah's arm as we follow Chan-Yu cautiously through the garage, keeping our eye on the drones quietly watching overhead. I can't hear anything outside, which must be a good sign. Chan-Yu leads us up a stairwell, taking them two at a time in quiet, nimble steps. Miah and I follow, trying to make as little noise as possible. On the fourth level, Chan-Yu pulls us into a tiny room, a storage closet, no bigger than a few meters wide. He shuts the door and latches it behind him.

"Do they know where you guys are?" I ask quietly, now that we've stopped running. "Vale?"

"Not yet."

"Shit," I say, more to myself than anything. "Are you still able to talk to Demeter?"

"Yes. She can watch and tell us what's going on, but she won't be able to hijack any of the drones without giving our position away."

"Okay. Have her tell us when we can get out of this goddamn broom closet," I mutter, Miah's loud breathing grates on my ears as if it was ten times louder than normal. I turn to him. "And you have a lot of questions to answer while we're waiting here."

Miah sighs, his shoulders deflating.

"It was dumb, okay? But I had to try."

"What did you hope to accomplish?" I ask, wishing I could shout at him. He shrugs and stares at the ground.

"I just wanted to talk to her. To tell her about Jahnu, to be the one to deliver the news. I love her, Remy. I've never stopped thinking about her." He pauses, his eyes wide and helpless. "She wasn't even there. Her flat was empty."

"Is ... is that how they found you?" I ask.

"It must be. Her apartment was obviously being watched. But she was gone."

Just then, after a crackling of static in my headphone, a new voice comes on the line.

"Hello?"

The voice is female, higher-pitched than Linnea's sultry alto, and quavering. Chan-Yu and I exchange glances, and for the first time in the relatively short span that I've known him, there is surprise and concern in his eyes.

"Miah?" the voice asks again. It sounds so familiar....

"Who is that?" I hear Soren demand, his voice rising at the end in fear.

"Is Jeremiah there? Please, I need to talk to Miah," the voice says.

"Oh no," Vale says, as I watch Chan-Yu wordlessly remove his headset and pass it over to Miah. I shake my head fervently and mouth the word no over and over again to him, but he does it anyway and I find that I don't want to stop him.

"Is that..."

Miah's looking at Chan-Yu and I with wild and confused eyes. He takes the headset and presses it into his ear.

"I think your friend is trying to speak with you," Chan-Yu says, as calmly as he can.

Spring 29, Sector Annum 106, 04h30
Gregorian Calendar: April 17

How is Moriana on the line with us? How is this possible? My head swims with panic. I'm staring at Miah, whose mouth is open and his eyes sparkling with tears as it dawns on him exactly what's happening.

"Moriana, are you with Corine?" Vale asks.

The critical question. Is Moriana acting of her own accord, or is she being watched, with a gun to her head, by Corine and the OAC?

"Vale, is that you?"

Oh god, oh god, oh god, please don't answer that! *Why did he speak in the first place?*

"Moriana, I'm here," Miah says, the words coming out in a rush, quiet and forceful and weighted. I'm sure he's saying it as much to distract Moriana from Vale as from the fact that he simply can't help himself. He closes his eyes and the tears spill down his cheeks, beading into droplets on his scruffy beard.

I shake my head at him, mouthing the word *no* over and over again. *Don't say anything!* I put one hand over my mic and cup the other over his.

"Don't speak to her," I whisper urgently.

"We need to move," Chan-Yu says suddenly. "They know where we are."

I don't know how he knows this, but I trust him beyond a shadow of a doubt. Chan-Yu opens the door and peers out.

"They'll follow us wherever we go. We have to keep moving, keep them guessing, can't let them trap us. If possible, we can try to get to the emergency rendezvous point. Let's go."

I nod.

"Miah, please come out!" Moriana's voice is thick, like she's crying. "Please come out, they know where you're hiding and that you're with Remy, if you don't come out now they're going to come in and find you both and kill you."

Miah's eyes come up and meet mine, and I realize if she continues to plead with him, we'll be in danger of losing him.

Without hesitation, I reach up and rip the headset from his ear. Miah tries to grab it from me, but my reflexes are faster than his. I turn away from him and snap it in half, and then grind it beneath my heel to make sure it's completely, utterly broken.

"You can't talk to her," I say to him, as he watches me, aghast. "You're a liability, and she's baiting you. We have to get out of here."

"What if they hurt her?" he growls at me. "If they're using her as bait, she's in danger!"

Just at that moment, Moriana's voice bursts back onto the line:

"They'll kill me, too, they're going to destroy everyone, you don't understand, please just come out." I watch Miah's expression. I realize there's no point in using my headset anymore, either. It's been compromised, hijacked somehow, and even though it's my only link to Soren, Vale, and Linnea, it's not worth it to have it on if Corine is listening into everything we say.

I take it off and break it in half, too. Useless, now. I drop the thing on the floor and nod at Chan-Yu. He turns to lead us out.

Now there's nothing in my head but silence, and fear begins to overtake me. We're trapped and split up, separated from half our team and with squadrons of soldiers and dozens of drones on our tail. I can only hope Soren, Linnea, and Vale make it to some kind of vehicle and come pick us up. Of course, they're probably being followed too.

I follow Chan-Yu as he leads us back up the stairs and into a little hallway. There's a palm scanner on the door that leads out, but Chan-Yu grabs my weapon from me and bashes the thing in. He uses his gun to shoot the locking mechanism on the palm scanner and then shoves the door open with his shoulder. It swings open to a greenhouse, a beautiful rooftop dome paneled in glass, sticky and sweaty from the humidity.

It's gorgeous. I take a deep breath of the scented air and wish we could stay. But outside, I'm beginning to hear the sirens that indicate a manhunt, the first of those in the city of Okaria since my sister was killed.

Chan-Yu palms the emergency rooftop exit and the door slides open. The building sirens begin to go off, and I realize it'll be a matter of minutes before every soldier and Watchman in the city will be at this building. Chan-Yu leads us out onto a narrow ledge. There's a gap in between this building and the next about a meter and a half wide, and Chan-Yu takes it at an easy jump. My heart pounding, I stare down into the chasm. *You can do this, Remy. You've done it in drills and you can do it now.* Chan-Yu beckons to me from the other side, and I bend my knees and prepare to jump.

Just then, the drone detector on my wrist flares up, and I spin around, Bolt up and ready to fire. I search the air for the robot, and sure enough, the drone's heat signature is faint but visible about a hundred meters away. It zooms towards us and I flip my Bolt to *DISPERSE* and aim, waiting for it to come in range. But just as the thing is almost close enough that my shot will have some effect, it stops moving.

"What's going on?" Miah asks from behind me.

"I have no idea."

The drone turns around as though we were never there. It buzzes off in a different direction, moving slowly as if it's reverted back to patrol mode.

"What just happened?" I ask, looking across the chasm to Chan-Yu.

"It seems that someone told it to leave us alone." he responds. "Beyond that, I don't know."

I return my attention to the jump in front of me. I use the fear and energy wound up in my muscles from the near miss with the drone to motivate myself to make the jump. I take two running steps forward and leap, clearing the gap easily and landing rather indelicately on the roof of the neighboring building.

"Come on!" I shout. Miah looks petrified, his face tense and twisted as he contemplates the distance of the jump. But he takes a few steps back, takes a few running strides to get some momentum, and with an enormous yell throws himself across the gap to land on both feet right next to Chan-Yu.

"Fuck. I never, ever want to do that again," he mutters.

"Let's go." Chan-Yu nods at me and turns to lead us across the top of this building and to a new set of stairs. At least this time we're running down.

By the time we hit the ground floor, the building next door is swarmed with soldiers. We can see the flashing lights from the alarm system through the windows. Outside, the sirens are buzzing. This time, instead of leading us out and onto the street level, Chan-Yu takes us down a floor, into the basement.

"Where are we going?" I ask, trying to keep up as he hurtles down the stairs.

"Storm drains."

"Great," Miah mutters behind me, panting.

Chan-Yu enlists Miah's help to break into the basement door. Inside looks more like something from our old Resistance base than anything I've ever seen in the Sector. It's vast and empty with nothing but pipes hanging overhead, weaving around and through the ceiling, all leading to one corner of the room.

"This city was built on the framework of an old city called Kingston," Chan-Yu says, narrating as we jog over to the entrance to the sewers. "In this part of Okaria, there are old sewer lines that haven't been incorporated into the Okarian water filtration and recycling system. They're not well-mapped. Almost nobody knows they even exist except the engineers who built the new system in the first place. But the Outsiders," he pauses and bends down to the ground to heave open a trapdoor that looks like something out of a child's storybook, "use them to get in and out in dire circumstances."

He steps onto a ladder and starts to climb down into the black. I pull out the light that attaches to the scope on my Bolt and hook it on. I use it to light my way as I crawl down after Chan-Yu, and Miah brings up the rear.

"I feel like a frog," he complains as we crawl into the damp, metallic tunnels.

At the bottom, I hear Chan-Yu's boots splash in a puddle of water. When I connect with solid ground, I point the light on the path in front of us. It's mostly dry, but there are puddles here and there, and the walls are mossy and thick with algae. The tunnels aren't big, no more than six feet in diameter, and Miah has to duck as we walk to avoid hitting his head.

"Why isn't this entire thing flooded?" Miah asks. "We should be drowning right now."

"The same water flow system that works to keep the water moving in the Sector sewage system also help to drain the water. In cases of floods, such as during winter or immediately after a heavy rainstorm, water will fill up here. But in normal circumstances, they're empty."

"Better hope it doesn't start raining, then," Miah says, a meager attempt at a joke. I glare at him, but he can't see me in the dark.

We run in silence after that, jogging after Chan-Yu through the silent tunnels. I think of Soren, Vale, and even Linnea, hoping against hope they've escaped the Sector's notice. We're only underground for maybe ten minutes, though, before Chan-Yu points to a dead-end and a flood door.

"If it's open, we exit there."

I pray it's open.

Chan-Yu cranks on the strangest opening mechanism I've ever seen in my life—a circular door handle, one that twists like an enormous knob as he turns it counterclockwise. I hear some enormous mechanism within the wall click and clank, promising sounds.

"When I open this door, they'll be able to track us again if they've bugged us in any way. We have to move quickly."

I nod, and Miah steels himself for the effort. Running isn't his forte.

Chan-Yu pushes the door open with an enormous heave. We're in another tunnel of some sort, but judging by how much fresher it smells on the other side, this one isn't underground, or even inside. It smells like summer, and I realize we must have emerged outside.

"Where are we?" I ask, whispering.

"At the bottom of the hill by the park," Chan-Yu responds. I take a moment to stare at him in silent admiration. He must have the entire city map memorized at all elevations. He's brought us to within a kilometer of the rendezvous point by the river, where there's supposed to be an emergency hovercar waiting for us. Just in case.

We emerge in a concrete tunnel built into a hill, which, sure enough, opens right by the park. The clean smell of cut grass in the early summer night fills me with memories, of the countless times I came to this park not as a renegade on the run from soldiers and Watchmen but as a teenager, spending time with my friends and thinking of nothing but how best to enjoy ourselves.

Crouching by the riverbank, we watch the hovercraft to see if Vale and the others will show up, knowing we can't wait for long. They'll find us, sooner or later, the drones or the soldiers or both. A light drizzle sets in, chilling my skin, somehow refreshing me. I close my eyes and let the rainwater drip down my face, wondering if we'll survive tonight. If we'll make it out of the city. If everything we've ever done has been in vain.

When I open my eyes, a flash of movement to my right jerks me back to readiness, Bolt up and ready to shoot. But the two figures approaching are wearing hooded, heat-cloaking gear just like us and not soldier's uniforms. Abandoning caution, I stand up and watch them approach, jogging doggedly down the hill to where the hovercar is parked, one large figure, one smaller, female. Soren? Linnea? *But where's Vale?*

Sure enough, they come barreling down the hill and Soren pushes his hood off.

"In the car!" he shouts. "They're hot on our tail!"

Without slowing, he hops over and into the open-top hovercar, and Linnea follows suit. Chan-Yu gets in as well, but Miah and I hesitate, glancing at each other. The sound of the river next to us grows to a swell inside my ears and when my voice emerges, it's so quiet I can barely hear myself.

"Where's Vale?"

"Get in the goddamn car, Remy!" Soren screams at me. I shake my head dully, *no, I won't do that.*

"You left him, didn't you?" I say. Miah looks at Soren for a half-second and I could swear there are sparks flying between them, the connection of an unspoken message they share.

Miah tackles me from the side. He's huge, bigger than Vale, bigger than Eli, almost bigger than Soren, and the weight and size of his body is like being engulfed by a falling building. He grabs my arms and tries to throw me over his shoulder. For a second I don't fight, not comprehending what's happening or why. But then I realize: *We're leaving without Vale.*

We're abandoning him.

"NO!"

I scream.

Miah slaps his hand over my mouth and throws me in the car, but I'm wriggling so frenetically that I don't land where he wants me to. Instead, I slide off the side, and instantly I roll to the ground on the other side of the car and am sprinting through the grass, back up the hill. Back the way I came.

For a long time, I know nothing except that I must keep running. I don't know where he is, I realize. What am I hoping to accomplish? I don't know. All I know is that I can't leave him here. I've lost too many people I love. My sister, my mother, Eli. I can't lose him, too.

So I run. Time slows to a crawl. I run and I run. Back toward El Centro. Back through city blocks and down dark alleys. Soldiers. Running through the streets, just like me. But they don't care about me, they can't track me. They're not looking for me. They're looking for Vale. I follow them at a jog, keeping my distance, hoping they'll lead me to him. *What are you going to do, Remy? How are you going to help him?*

I round a corner, and then I see it. Him. At the top of a building, his back to me, to everything. His arms are spread, as if ready to fly off the building.

And then I see the unmistakable blue crackle of electricity hit him square in the chest, and as he falls, his foot goes out as if expecting to step onto an invisible platform. But there is none.

"VALE!"

Two of the soldiers ahead of me whirl at the sound of my voice.

Vale falls, his body limp, seemingly moving against the rules of gravity: drifting, rather than falling, towards the ground. Like a feather.

Two drones, bearing a mesh net between them, catch him at the absolute last second, right before he hits the ground. The fabric expands with his impact, but his body never touches the ground.

I watch, aghast, as the drones carry his limp, unconscious body down the streets and away from me.

One of the two soldiers opens his mouth as if to shout. I pull up my Bolt and shoot him. He collapses in a heap of crackling static. The one next to him raises his weapon to fire at me, and I would shoot him, too, but my weapon needs a second to charge, and I don't have a second. I move. I duck behind a compost bin, then run into an alley, listening as shouts behind me indicate that there's a team of soldiers hot on my tail.

Vale is gone.

I run.

~ End *of* Book Two *of th*e Seeds Trilogy ~

Coming Next

The Harvest, Book Three of the Seeds Trilogy, is coming Spring 2016. We invite you to connect with us on Twitter and Facebook to get the latest updates. If you enjoyed *The Sowing* and *The Reaping* we'd love to hear from you. You can leave a review on Goodreads, Amazon, or Barnes & Noble, or contact us directly online. You can find us at:

www.theseedstrilogy.com
www.facebook.com/TheSeedsTrilogy
Twitter:
@readwritenow - Kristy
@akmakansi - Amira
@Elena_Makansi - Elena

ACKNOWLEDGEMENTS

We'd like to thank everyone who has supported us by reading our drafts and giving us feedback, helping us understand the science we explore in the world of the Okarian Sector, contributing amazing original artwork (we're looking at you Kevin Weitzel and Elle Opitz), or just giving us an encouraging word. With three co-authors, we each have particular people we'd like to thank.

From Amira—To the brilliant friends, talented authors, and wonderful people who answered science questions, critiqued the manuscript, and supported me along the way: Alexander Augustyn, Charles Ayling, Jonathan Paul, Daryl Rothman, Nillu Nasser Stelter, and Jessica West.

From Elena—I want to thank my dearest friends who agreed to beta-read: Anjuli, Becky, Maggie, and Natali, y'all rock big time. A great big shout-out to my co-authors (and family) who encouraged me to continue working on *The Reaping* despite the craziness of ending college and entering the "real world." Many thanks to dad, I love you so much. Sun, moon, and stars: thank you for reminding me that the universe is vast and beautiful and endlessly inspiring.

From Kristy—Thanks to my mother who believes I can do anything, to my sisters who believe in making every day better than the one before, to my husband who puts up with me, and to my daughters for believing in and exploring my dream, for bringing Remy and Vale (and the rest of the gang) to life, and for going along with me on the most gratifying adventure in *my* life.

About the Author(s)

K. Makansi is the pen name for the mother-daughter writing trio of:

Kristina Blank Makansi

Born and raised in Southern Illinois, Kristina has a B.A. in Government from University of Texas at Austin and an M.A.T. from the College of New Jersey. She is co-founder and publisher of Blank Slate Press, an award-winning small press, and founder of Treehouse Author Services, an author services practice through which she provides editorial and design services for traditional and self-published authors. In addition to the Seeds Trilogy, she has published *Oracles of Delphi*, an historical mystery set in ancient Greece.

Amira K. Makansi

Amira is a historian, writer, poet, winemaker, and wanderer. After earning a bachelor's degree in History from the University of Chicago, she traveled across America and France to learn the trade of winemaking. While traveling, she found her passion for writing through her journal and her blog (The Z-Axis). She now blogs avidly about wine, food, photography, and, of course, words. When she's not writing, she can be found at Peachy Canyon winery on Calfironia's Central Coast, where she works as a laboratory technician.

Elena K. Makansi

Elena graduated from Oberlin College where she majored in Environmental Studies and concentrated on food justice and food system politics. She has won several writing and poetry awards and scholarships and was honored to attend the Iowa Young Writers' Studio and the Washington University Summer Writers Institute while in high school. She is an artist and photographer, avid walker, vegetarian and vegan cook, tennis player, and overall curious lady, Elena lives in the central coast region of California. Elena aspires to be a hobbit when she grows up. Visit her website at elenamakansi.com.

DATE DUE

CPSIA information can be obtained
at www.ICGtesting.com
Printed in the USA
LVOW11s0512290817
546788LV00001B/3/P

9 780989 867146